ABSENT

ABSENT

EMMA SALISBURY

BACKGROUND

In 2013, the National Police Chief's Council (NPCC) formerly the Association for Chief Police Officers (ACPO) introduced a change in its approach to missing persons which resulted in an additional category of 'absent' being used for some people who go missing.

The definitions used by the police are currently:

Missing – "Anyone whose whereabouts cannot be established and where the circumstances are out of character or the context suggests the person may be the subject of crime or at-risk of harm to themselves or another."

Absent – "A person not at a place where they are expected or required to be and there is no apparent risk."

"*Absent* cases should not be ignored, and must be monitored over periods of time with consideration given to escalating to *Missing* if there is a change to the circumstances that has increased the level of risk."

HMIC Missing Children: Who Cares? The police response to missing and absent children, 2016.

DAY ONE

CHAPTER ONE

He is running towards his target yelling every profanity under the sun. The sound of helicopter blades overhead wipes out his threats but his enemy gets the gist of it, can already tell what is coming.

Fear is not an option.

He is a killing machine.

His mind is his greatest weapon.

He will not be defeated.

He tightens the grip on his gun before dropping onto one knee to take aim. He shoots at them indiscriminately, enjoying the sound of metal ripping through skin, the thud as each victim hits the ground. He sits back on his heels to survey his work and smiles. He's good at this and each day he gets better. He just needs to keep up the practice. He leans forward on his haunches, takes aim once more.

'For God's sake, there you are!'

Startled, Jason smiled at the young woman standing in the doorway balancing a packing box on her hips. 'I've only just picked up the controls, honest!' he said, dropping them as he got to his feet hastily, like a teenager caught watching porn. He still had his headset on, which meant he'd been playing long enough to check in with his on-line pals.

'We've still got boxes to unpack, Jase,' she sighed, 'masses of them, if you haven't noticed; can't the X-box wait a while?'

'Just taking a bit of downtime, Ali,' he grinned in the way that stopped her getting angry with him. Or at least it had until now.

'That only makes sense if you've actually done something this morning, hun,' Ali pouted, her eyes giving lie to the scowl on her lips. Fair enough he'd driven them across town that morning and lugged the heaviest boxes up the steep flight of stairs, but since then he'd avoided actually opening any of them.

'I want this place to look good by the time Mum and Dad get here,' she reminded him. Frown lines creased his brow as he shook his head.

'They're coming to help us move in, Ali, what's the point of getting everything unpacked before they get here? I thought the general idea of people coming to help was that they actually pitched in.' The look on Ali's face told him his opinion was superfluous. He spoke into the mouthpiece of his headset: 'Talk to you later buddy,' he said to his online team mate before taking it off, dropping it onto the bean bag he'd been slouched against before following her out of the room.

'Grab one of those boxes and bring it through to the bedroom,' Ali instructed, pointing to a stack of cardboard boxes in the narrow hallway. Nudging the door open with her hip she placed the box she was carrying on top of an unmade double bed. 'Christ, this room stinks!' She moved over to the sash window and opened it wide, wafting the stale air out with her hand.

'What's up now?' he sighed as he carried two boxes into the room, one balanced on top of the other preventing him from seeing where he was going.

She moved towards him, taking the top box from him and placing it on the bed beside the one she'd just put down. 'There's glass in this one, be careful!' she scolded, before opening a large built-in wardrobe and nodding to the box he held in his hands. 'Your clothes are in that one, still on the hangers, thought I'd make life easy for you.'

'Nice one!' he beamed, opening the box and lifting out several creased shirts before placing them straight onto the wardrobe rails. The creases would drop out in time, if he left them long enough.

Ali pointed to a large sports bag in the bottom of the cupboard, her nose wrinkling at the smell coming from it. 'Don't tell me you've got your rugby kit in there! You could at least have washed it before you moved out, or got your mum to do it.' His mother was a soft touch when it came to her son, ran round after him all day long; if he'd asked her she would have held onto it, brought it over once his kit had been washed and ironed. Not for the first time Ali slid a worrying look at Jason, if he thought she was going to provide the same level of devoted service as his mother he was going to be woefully disappointed.

'It's not mine,' he shrugged.

'Well it's not mine either,' she retorted. 'Don't tell me we've inherited junk from the previous tenant, the landlord promised he'd shift all their stuff when I paid him the deposit. I'm going to ring him now…' She headed towards the bedroom door, pulling her mobile phone from the pocket of her skinny jeans.

'Just chuck it out, Ali, what's the point of stressing yourself over a dirty sports kit? It's not ours, the flat's been empty for a while, whoever it belongs to doesn't want it. I say let's throw it out and get on with the rest of

11

the day.'

Ali was already shaking her head. 'There's a couple of things I wanted to tell him though,' she insisted, 'he promised he'd refresh all the paintwork and he hasn't, and there are marks on the settee in the lounge that I don't want us getting the blame for.' Their combined budget had got them something not much bigger than a garage as it was.

'So take a photo and email it to him,' Jason cajoled. Moving towards her he slipped his arms around her waist. 'I can think of far better ways to spend the morning…'

Ali's mouth curled into a smile. 'Fine,' she conceded, as he pulled her closer, 'but we'll need to be quick, Mum and Dad will be here at 12…' The grin on his face got wider as he homed in for a kiss.

'Not so fast buster,' she persisted, her nose wrinkling as she pushed him away, 'you need to shift that stinking kit first. While you're doing that I'll go take photos of the repairs he needs to do on my phone and send them across.'

Eager to please now his luck was in, Jason laughed as he reached for the sports bag to hoist it over his shoulder. Then he stopped in his tracks. The bag was heavier than expected, though that wasn't what worried him.

It was the greasy liquid seeping through the canvas base into the carpet below that made his stomach heave.

The slow drip of something viscous and foul.

CHAPTER TWO

She'd stepped out in front of him from nowhere. Slam! Some daft mare wearing earphones plugged into a smartphone. He'd seen her on the pavement's edge, hadn't expected her to step out. He thought that she'd seen him; his brain hadn't computed the oblivion she was in. Music blaring, head full of last night's date, she'd turned her face in his direction, locking eyes with him as he gripped onto the steering wheel, a look of surprise on her face, her mouth forming an O shape. He jammed his foot down on the brake. Hard. The car's tyres squealing as it came to a sudden halt. He swore; the smell of burning rubber enveloped him as he jumped out of the car.

'I – I'm OK!' the young woman stuttered, rubbing her hip, the only part that had made contact with his vehicle. Walking wounded. Nothing more than a cold compress and a stiff drink needed to fix her. Thank Christ he hadn't been breaking the speed limit. 'I'm sorry,' she added, 'for stepping in front of you like that. Got a lot on my mind.' He stared at her then. Words forming in his head he didn't want to say out loud. His glare said it all, spoke volumes in fact. Her sheepish smile froze; instead of telling her it was OK, that he was partly to blame so let's call it quits, he kept on staring. The woman backed away, wondering if the solemn figure was one of those road rage nutters who carried a baseball bat round in the foot well of his car, ready to explode any minute.

'You OK love?' someone called out. A crowd had formed, do-gooders and nosey bastards, hard to tell one from the other where he was standing. She moved towards them nodding her head, grateful for the 'oohs' and 'ahhs', while looking sideways at him all the time. Already someone was ushering her into a café, patting her on the back like an obedient dog. Another tosser had their phone out, taking photos of his registration number. The blare of a car horn reminded him he was holding up the traffic. He turned to the vehicle behind him, raised his middle finger in the driver's direction, staring until the other fella looked away. He climbed back into his car, put on his hazard lights to let the impatient twat behind him know he wasn't going anywhere as he reached into his pocket for a cigarette. He lit it, sucked on it greedily, stared into the distance for what seemed like an age before slamming his fist down hard onto the centre of the steering wheel.

Again. And again. And again.

*

Detective Sergeant Kevin Coupland examined the toasted teacake left on his desk with suspicion. There didn't seem to be anything wrong with it, the smell certainly had his taste buds tingling, though the butter had been spread using the same wax on wax off technique used by his wife. He looked from the toasted offering presented on a chipped plate to the slim woman with close cropped hair approaching him. 'From you, I take it?' he asked, trying to muster a smile.

'Who else, round here?' she grinned, coming to a halt beside him.

'I thought I was the one supposed to get you something, you know, to mark your return from maternity leave.'

Alex Moreton's eyes lit up. 'Oh my God, you got me a prezzie, so where is it then?' she asked, the corners of her mouth turned up in mischief. She closed her eyes and held both hands out.

Coupland had to think on his feet. 'That would be telling,' he muttered as he made his way over to a small kitchen area with his teacake, ignoring a sign sellotaped to the front of the fridge saying 'If you didn't put it in, don't take it out.' He lifted out a carton of Lurpak before smothering the teacake with butter like a plasterer with a trowel.

'I thought you were supposed to be watching what you ate?' Alex accused, appearing in the doorway making him jump.

'Don't need to, Lynn manages that all by her-bloody-self.'

'So what the eye can't see…'

Coupland shrugged. 'Something like that.'

'So go on then,' Alex persisted, 'what have you got me?'

'Later,' Coupland volleyed, trying to work out where he could slip out to at lunchtime and pick something up, wondering not for the first time why women took everything so literally.

Alex smiled as she took in her old mucker; whatever diet his wife had him on was working, he was leaner, the belly that had been starting to hang over the waistband of his trousers long gone. He always said the body of a warrior lay beneath all that flab, perhaps he'd been telling the truth all along. Alex's smile froze. 'What's happened to your hand?' she asked, staring at his swollen bloody knuckles, checking out his face for signs of other damage.

'Nothing.' He inspected his cracked knuckles as though seeing them for the first time, spreading his hands out like a starfish to prove they still worked. His heart began to race and he remembered too late that he'd forgotten to take his blood pressure tablets before he left home that morning. A weight bore down on his shoulders as he wished taking his medication on time was the only thing he needed to worry about. He tried to throw Alex off scent. 'No problems with the childminder then?'

Alex's worried frown deepened. 'Don't,' she sighed, 'I've been kidding myself Todd's with his granny for the day, it seems harder this time round than it was with Ben.' She'd been inconsolable for a week when she'd returned to work from her first maternity leave, but she'd needed the money and besides, she loved her job. Well, most of the time. Like most cops she couldn't picture herself doing anything else. She was in for the long haul now, whether she liked it or not. She'd been promoted to sergeant since Ben had been born and she didn't want to come across as a weepy mum. At least she wasn't still breast-feeding Todd; she'd never live it down if her milk came in during a briefing.

'My old childminder retired but the new one came recommended, so that's something I suppose.' She said it aloud, though it was more to console herself than anything else.

Coupland smiled. Melted butter had made his chin greasy; all that was left on the plate was a smattering of crumbs. 'He'll be fine, he'll have his big brother with him after school every day, he won't be giving you a moment's thought…You know what I mean,' he added hastily as Alex's face fell. 'Anyway,' he grinned as he diverted the conversation back to safe territory, 'what's the boss given you to ease you back in?'

Alex wrinkled her nose. 'I wouldn't use the word 'ease', necessarily,' she said as she rattled off a string of cases in varying stages of investigation. 'I've been partly seconded to the MISPER team while I review Michael Roberts' case.'

Coupland frowned, 'Missing persons? I vaguely remember the name though,' he said, 'I think I was away when his body was found.'

Alex nodded. '16-year-old victim of a fatal stabbing. He'd been missing from home for nine weeks. His killer's on remand now, he admitted his guilt from the start.'

'Yeah, like he'd actually achieved something with his life.' Coupland raised an eyebrow. 'I thought the case was closed?'

'Not quite,' Alex shook her head, her close-cropped hair not moving an inch out of place. 'Turns out the victim attended college the day he died; only nobody bothered informing us. So the team dealing with it still had him down as a MISPER. Still isn't clear where he'd been staying. One of Michael's tutors informed Children and Family Services that the boy had confided in him that he was having problems with his stepfather. Despite this, nobody went to the college or investigated his allegation so there were no confirmed arrangements in place for his care.'

Coupland ran a hand over his chin. 'But the altercation

between Michael and his killer would have still happened, unless you're telling me he was murdered at midnight when he should have been tucked up in his bed, if his step dad hadn't already given him a pasting by then.'

'Promise me you'll never work for the Samaritans,' Alex grumbled. 'The point is we'll never know how things could've panned out, will we? That's why a serious case review has been called. The DCI's been invited to attend so he's asked me to go through the file notes, be a fresh pair of eyes, make sure that any mudslinging doesn't end up with something brown and sticky coming over our wall.'

Coupland rolled his eyes, 'Rather you than me,' he sympathised.

'Funny, that's the impression I got from the boss, too.' Alex said with a gleam in her eye, her gaze dropping once more to his hands.

Coupland's mobile grumbled to life. He grunted into the mouthpiece, his eyes locking onto Alex as he listened to the control room. 'Remains have been found in an apartment block in Pendlebury. Get your coat,' he said, 'I want you on this one with me.'

Alex baulked momentarily. She'd returned to work a sergeant, the same rank as Coupland; it wasn't for him to tell her what to do anymore. She swallowed down her irritation, reminding herself of the adrenaline that kicked in when you took a call like that, and the ticking clock hanging over your head from the moment of discovery meant it was easy to tread on toes. Besides, she was probably being sensitive, what with being away for so long. 'What about my other case?' she asked.

'Prioritise,' he barked. She narrowed her eyes as she

reached for her bag. He really did need to work on his manner.

*

The entrance to Ashdown Court was through wrought iron gates. A police cordon had already been placed around the building, a mock Tudor apartment block converted from an old schoolhouse some twenty years before. The property was well kept, the vehicles occupying the car park in front of the building no more than a couple of years old. Today they were outnumbered by blue and yellow police vans parked on the kerb leading to the entrance. Alex and Coupland climbed out of his car in one swift movement, their bickering forgotten, like a married couple agreeing on a ceasefire before going out. Coupland opened the car's boot and lifted out a pair of blue shoe protectors which he slipped onto his feet. He passed a pair to Alex. 'Here goes,' he said, his shoulders set as they moved towards the apartment block.

The uniformed officer stationed at the front of the building nodded as they approached. He was older than Coupland, more salt than pepper in his thinning hair. On the home straight for retirement, a future perched behind the reception desk in one of the city's office blocks beckoned. It didn't appeal to Coupland but it was a living, he supposed. A way to make the pension stretch further. The officer pulled his mouth into a frown and dug his hands into the gap between his Kevlar vest and his uniform top. 'Not pretty by all accounts,' he greeted them. Coupland bit back a retort. He'd never seen a pretty corpse, but he knew what the officer meant. Some were less palatable than others.

'Control said the body was found in a sports bag.'

The officer nodded. 'A small one.'

Coupland stole a glance at Alex. They both knew what that meant. 'Any idea who it is?'

The officer shook his head. 'Guessing it'll be some time before we know the answer to that,' he said with a shudder. 'From what I've heard it's been there a while.'

Although the exterior of the building had kept its original features, inside was a different matter. The interior was modern, light, pale coloured walls with a carpeted stairway. A large print of a vase of flowers had been placed on a wall above a table with a post tray on it. 'Better get it over with.' Alex said, leading the way to the first floor flat. She widened her eyes as Coupland overtook her on the stairwell, 'Christ, didn't realise how unfit I was,' she muttered under her breath.

'Or maybe my healthy eating plan's paying off,' Coupland countered, smiling in spite of himself. He'd missed this, working with someone who knew him inside out, someone he didn't need to pussy foot around, well, most of the time anyway.

CSI personnel milled about on the landing, their suits rustling as they moved. Coupland's smile turned into a grimace as something foul smelling seeped into the air. He reached into his jacket pocket, retrieved a small battered jar. He stuck in a finger and smeared something clear and sticky under his nose. The overwhelming reek of Vicks VapoRub made his eyes water. He passed the jar to Alex who took a smaller swipe.

'What?' she said defensively when she caught his look, 'I don't want to walk round looking like I've got a heavy cold,' she smirked, pointing at his top lip. 'You might want to wipe some away,' she grinned, 'it's not a good look.' Coupland grunted but didn't do as she suggested, he'd rather the funny looks than suffer the awful smell that would soon be clinging to his clothes, permeating his skin so that even Lynn would wrinkle her nose when he got home and she worked in a hospital.

The entrance to Flat 2a had been cordoned off. Turnbull, a docile, long serving DC stood in the doorway recording the names of personnel as they entered or left the flat into his logbook. He'd purloined a facemask from one of the CSIs, unlooping one side from over his ear so he could speak as Coupland approached him. 'Photographer's on his way, Sarge,' he said, gaze dropping to the snot-like substance under Coupland's nose, 'though I doubt there's much he can capture, to be truthful.'

Coupland's shoulders sagged. 'Have we got a name?'

Turnbull placed the mask over his mouth as he sucked in a breath. 'Haven't even got a gender,' he responded, showing Coupland the entry on his clipboard marked 'Unidentified minor.'

'I'll phone control to see if there've been any reports of a missing kid,' Alex offered.

Coupland nodded, he didn't blame her for being in no rush to see a dead child. With two little kiddies of her own it was hard on cases like this to separate one image from another. He followed the direction of traffic into the flat. The interior was small, made to look even smaller due to the number of people milling round, stepping on upturned metal plates as they moved in and out of the only bedroom. The room was sparsely furnished save for a double bed and a dressing table. There were no sheets on the bed or curtains at the window, the occupants had been moving in by the look of things, there were packing boxes left here and there, some opened, some closed but the contents had been written on the side of them. 'DVDs and x-box games,' 'Work clothes and yoga mat.' Coupland pitied the poor buggers who'd found the body, doubted they'd be unpacking anything else any time soon. The duty doctor heaved out a sigh as Coupland approached. He was standing beside a sports bag that had been left in the middle of the room, a groundsheet placed beneath it. A tide mark indicated it contained something moist. 'Has death been declared?' Coupland asked.

The doc pointed to the tidemark around the bag's perimeter. 'Death occurred some time ago, going by the state of the…remains,' he paused, as though thinking how to phrase what he was going to say next. 'The body…ruptured…when the bag was lifted, that's why the smell's so…pungent.' The smell was overpowering, like rancid meat. Coupland glanced at the window which was open on its widest setting. With a nod to the doc he held his breath and peered inside the bag. He knew it would be grim, had readied himself for the horror of it, yet what he saw still managed to suck all the air from him, making his head throb and his throat constrict.

CHAPTER THREE

What was left of the body was curled or bent into a ball. The skin seemed to have come away at the seams leaving a slimy substance oozing into the bag's fabric. Coupland caught a glimpse of dark hair and shivered. 'Let me know if you need anything else,' the doctor said, backing away.

Coupland didn't blame him making his escape. Who in their right mind would hang around if they didn't need to? A long sigh hissed out behind him. He turned in time to see the shock register on Alex's face; she'd glimpsed the little mite too. 'How did you get on?' he asked her, moving away from the bag.

Her face was drawn, but she mustered a businesslike voice. 'No recent reports of a missing child,' she replied, shaking her head.

Coupland's shoulders dipped, 'Shit.' He craved a cigarette, needed nicotine to cleanse his lungs of the stench of rotting flesh. 'We're going to have to go further back then, pull all missing child reports for the last year,' he groaned.

'I know,' said Alex, 'I've already put in a request.'

Coupland nodded his thanks, but right now a smile was beyond him. 'Bollocks,' was all he could manage. Going through old MISPER files meant re-opening wounds, asking parents of missing children for DNA samples to help with identification. He hoped to Christ they could get a sensible ball park for when death occurred, so that a few poor buggers could be spared. He nodded at a slim built man in his thirties carrying a black case. He could never remember the photographer's name. The man waited until he'd unpacked his equipment before looking over at Coupland, awaiting instruction. 'Here,' Coupland barked, indicating the bag with an incline of his head.

The photographer nodded, tried out the camera from different angles until he was happy with the view from his lens. He took several shots of the bag where it lay before pointing the lens through the gap at the top of it, capturing the greasy sludge for posterity. 'Welcome back Sergeant Moreton,' he said shyly as Alex walked by.

'Hello Johnson…Some welcome,' she grimaced, indicating the bag's contents, 'Got your skipper's licence yet?'

'Working on it,' he beamed, putting the lens cap back on his camera, 'thanks for asking.' Coupland ignored the triumphant look Alex sent in his direction.

Just then a curly haired man with an air of entitlement entered the room carrying a medical bag. Pathologist Harry Benson scanned the personnel moving around the room before his gaze settled upon Coupland. 'Who's the SIO?' he barked.

'I am,' Coupland answered, turning to him. 'DCI Mallender's on a communication course.'

Benson raised an eyebrow but said nothing. Instead he turned his attention to Alex, 'I believe congratulations are in order, albeit belated,' he smiled.

'The baby or the promotion?' Alex grinned, 'Todd's at the childminder's for the first time today, and I'm still getting used to being called Detective Sergeant.'

Coupland stifled a yawn. 'Well this is all very touching

I'm sure but if we could turn our attention to the body in the bag I'd be much obliged.' He'd forgotten they'd gone out together once, while Alex and her partner had been on a break. Alex swore it had never been serious, which Coupland translated into woman speak for they'd never had sex, but even so the surly pathologist always seemed less of a twat when she was about.

Benson turned away from them and placed his medical bag on the groundsheet beside the sports bag. He snapped on a pair of latex gloves before squatting down and peering inside it. A sigh erupted from him that seemed to come from the bottom of his soul. Seconds later he stood up and pulled off his gloves, not bothering to unpack his instruments. 'I'm not even going to attempt an examination,' he said to Alex. 'The best thing we can do is transport it in situ.' He addressed his next comment to Coupland, 'And no, I won't be able to tell you anything until I've been able to take a proper look so don't bother asking.'

It was normal for Coupland's hackles to rise whenever he was in close proximity to Benson but on this occasion the pathologist had a point, Coupland conceded, though he baulked at Benson's reference to 'it'. The child had a family, parents who were missing him or her, who right now must be climbing the walls. Or so he hoped. 'How soon *can* you do the post-mortem?' he ventured.

Benson pursed his lips as he made to leave. 'I'll get back to you,' was all he'd commit to.

'Any chance of this afternoon?' Coupland called after him, pushing his luck.

Benson paused in the doorway and snorted. 'You're not serious? We're a technician down, I'm due to give evidence at a fatal accident inquiry later today and council workers found the body of a drug addict behind the bins in Ordsall Lane last night.'

Coupland had read through the night shift's notes first thing; no foul play was suspected, just another sad statistic. 'Yeah, but not a priority, I'd have thought.'

Benson was having none of it. 'His family are just as entitled to know what happened to their loved one leading up to his death as the family of this child.' His voice softened as he shifted his glance to Alex. 'Look, I suppose I could fit it in over my lunch break if I send out for a sandwich,' he relented, then, addressing Coupland once more, 'Now I really must go.'

Coupland shoved his hands into his trouser pockets for fear of placing them round Benson's neck and squeezing hard. 'We really appreciate it, Harry,' he simpered, 'how can we ever repay you?' swerving the elbow Alex aimed at his ribs. They stood back as several CSIs came forward to lift the seeping sports holdall carefully into a body bag. The irony wasn't lost on Coupland, for there was not much of a body to speak of. Only remains. All that was left after nature had taken its toll. Nature and an evil bastard, stripping the body of everything that made it unique, no longer recognisable in the eyes of a loved one, reducing it to nothing. Coupland didn't know what angered him more. That someone could do this to a child. Or that no one as yet had noticed they'd gone.

Turnbull was recording the items in a packing box before a uniformed officer carted it away. 'Where are the couple who reported it?' Coupland asked him.

Turnbull nodded at the apartment door opposite. 'Robinson took them to the neighbour across the landing.'

Coupland had raised his hand in readiness to knock on the neighbour's door when it was opened by a chubby man in his early thirties, a round face partly concealed by an Amish-style beard. He wore a checked shirt rolled up at the sleeves, tucked into dark jeans. The shirt fell open at the collar revealing a gold chain. Fat links which Coupland suspected were one of Ratners' finest. 'Come though,' the man began without any preamble, turning and leading the way into his flat, both detectives in his wake. Coupland hadn't even had time to flash his warrant card although Alex wore hers around her neck so jiggled the lanyard at the man's back anyway. They passed a couple of rooms with the doors to them wide open. Coupland glanced in each one to get the measure of Mr Amish, for signs of a partner for a start, but found none. The rooms were functional, nothing unnecessary had been added. No cushions, no candles, not a single diffuser. Mr Amish definitely lived alone.

At the kitchen door the man stopped, as though remembering something. 'Listen, I'm sorry,' he began, turning to the detectives while keeping his voice low, 'it's just that I'm going to be late for work.' He looked down at his wristwatch as though making a point. 'Is there anywhere else they can go?'

Coupland reared his head back; he'd hoped he and this guy were going to bond just fine. 'You mean like their own home?' he chimed. 'Oh, hang on a minute; they've got forensics crawling all over their place, what with it being a crime scene right now.' He turned on his best death-stare full beam. 'You do realise they're probably in shock, don't you? But please, we wouldn't want to put you out.'

'All I meant was could they not go somewhere else?'

'Any bright ideas where, Gunga Din?'

Alex coughed as she nudged Coupland to one side. 'What my colleague's trying to say is we're extremely grateful for the kindness you've shown to your new neighbours, Mr…'

'Rawlings…Jimmy Rawlings,' Mr Amish filled in for her.

'Thank you, Jimmy, hopefully, we'll all be out of your hair soon.' Coupland smirked as she said this, letting his gaze travel to the top of the man's thinning crown. Ignoring him, Alex continued, 'If you could just take us through to…'

'Fine,' said Rawlings, eyeing Coupland suspiciously while patting down lonely follicles on his scalp. He led them into a small kitchen where a young man and woman sat at a breakfast bar. The girl was mid-twenties, one side of a short blonde bob tucked behind her left ear. Pale skin visible beneath smudged makeup, eyes shiny and bloodshot. Her hands cradled a mug of something dark. 'Out of milk…' admitted Rawlings.

The woman's boyfriend placed an arm around her shoulders as the detectives introduced themselves. He was a similar age to the girl, dark wavy hair framing a boyish face. 'Has it gone yet?' the young man asked, and Coupland had to remind himself that the body turning up like that would be an inconvenience to them, a blot on their otherwise perfect horizon.

'Yes,' Alex answered quickly, as though she didn't trust Coupland to play nice, 'we still have a forensic team collecting evidence from the property but should be out of-' she looked over at Rawlings' stripy head, 'we should be gone by evening, tomorrow at the latest, although I would recommend you stay with friends or family for a couple of nights.' The truth was the smell would linger for several days, even if they used industrial strength cleaning fluid to clean the stain on the carpet.

'I'm not going back there!' the young woman hiccupped. 'Oh, God,' she groaned, scraping back her stool as she made a gagging noise. She turned to Rawlings who pointed back out into the hall.

'First door on your right!' he said in alarm, while sneaking another peek at his watch. Her boyfriend looked on as she stumbled out of the kitchen and lurched in the direction of the bathroom, moments later the sound of retching could be heard.

'We were moving in today. Setting up home together.' The young man addressed no one in particular. 'Ali's parents are coming round in a bit to give us a hand, her Dad's taking us all out for a meal afterwards, wanted to mark the occasion, you know?' Coupland doubted they'd forget this day in a hurry.

Rawlings squirmed. 'Look,' he began, shoving hairy hands into the pockets of his jeans. 'Should I phone in work? Let them know I'm going to be late? Only I've not been there that long, don't think the boss has quite made his mind up about me...'

No surprise there, Coupland thought, keeping his face in check. 'What is it you do, Jimmy?' he asked, trying to muster as much interest as he could.

'I work for a car valeting place, just down the road from here, not the most exciting job but it pays the bills.'

'Could do with giving mine a clear out,' Coupland told him, 'the wife says a family of ferrets could move in and

I wouldn't notice, the state of it...don't suppose you've got a card, have you?'

'I can do better than that,' Jimmy beamed, walking over to a leather jacket hung up in the hall. He reached into a side pocket and pulled out a couple of leaflets and a pen, wrote his name and mobile number on the back of them before handing one to each detective. *Shiny Happy Motors* was emblazoned across the top of the flyer above a stock image of a fleet of new cars. 'Call me and I can book you in, bring this on your first visit and you get a fiver off at the till. Let 'em know I sent you and I get commission too.'

'Everyone's a winner, eh?' Coupland nodded, folding the flyer before putting it into his jacket pocket. 'Look, we'll try and be as quick as we can, but you might want to call that boss of yours anyway, tell him you've been busy, drumming up business...' He waited while Jimmy pulled his mobile phone from his shirt pocket, tapped a couple of times on his smartphone screen as he stepped back into the hall. 'So,' he said, turning his attention to the young man, 'I take it you're renting?'

Jason nodded. 'No one my age can get a mortgage,' he shrugged, 'don't know that I'd want to be saddled with that kind of commitment even if I could...'

The young woman returned from the bathroom in time to catch the gist of what he'd said. 'I-I didn't mean it like that, Ali!' he stuttered as she made saucer eyes at him. Her complexion was paler than when she'd fled the room. Her fringe was damp where she'd splashed cold water on her face. She gave him a stony look.

'I just mean it'd cripple us that's all, the car, the holiday we've just been on, that'd all have to go if we had to save to buy somewhere. Where's the fun in that?' Ali lowered her eyes but said nothing. The young man took this as a good sign and exhaled, smiling up at Coupland as if to say close call. He'd learn soon enough that it was only a temporary reprieve, that she was merely waiting for them to be alone so she could rake over the conversation and put him straight. Biding her time.

Coupland returned his smile; it was a path he was still learning to tread. 'I'll need the contact details for your landlord,' he continued, pulling his notebook from his jacket pocket. The young man nodded, waiting as Ali retrieved her phone from a large shoulder bag on the breakfast bar, scrolling down her contacts list.

'Here,' she said, handing the phone to Coupland so he could jot it down.

Alex beamed at Rawlings as he returned to the kitchen. 'How long have you lived here, Jimmy?' Rawlings' mouth turned down at the edges as he pondered this. 'Four years, mebbe…'

'And how many people live in the apartment block?'

'Oh Christ, let me see…' he blew out his cheeks as he counted them off on sausage like fingers. 'There's the couple on the top floor, he drives a Merc, she's got one of those in your face four by fours. Grant, I think their name is. Took a parcel in for them once. Not sure what they do but they go out suited and booted every morning. Then there's Jilly, on the second floor. Divorced. Drives a soft top. Not bad condition considering the age.' Coupland wondered whether Rawlings was referring to the divorcee or the car; Alex's warning look told him to keep his thoughts to himself. 'In the flat opposite Jilly there's a young girl, not the brightest bulb on the landing but I don't suppose she needs brains for her line of work…'

'And what's that then?' Coupland enquired.

Rawlings smirked. 'Not entirely sure,' he said in a way that implied he knew full well. 'The couple downstairs are retired, don't know what they're called, just nod to them if I see them in the car park. Theirs is the people carrier.'

'Do you get on OK with them all?'

Rawlings shrugged. 'I work long hours, don't really have the time to socialise, let alone bother with my neighbours.'

Coupland clocked Alex raising her eyebrows but the guy had a point. Idle chit chat on a stair or over the wall was a thing of the past thanks to Facebook, people simply couldn't be bothered making new friends, apart from virtual ones. 'Anyone moved out recently?'

Jimmy shrugged once more. 'I suppose… I mean obviously there was someone in *their* flat,' he nodded towards Jason and Ali, 'but she was one of those stuck up city types. I've seen a few tenants come and go I suppose but it's not like I keep tabs on anyone…' Coupland and Alex exchanged looks; he wasn't doing too bad for someone who didn't give a toss.

Coupland turned his attention to the girl. 'Did you meet the previous tenant when you came to view the property?'

Ali dabbed at her nose with a tissue as she shook her head. 'It was empty, that's why we could move in so quickly…' she told him. Her phone trilled, making her jump; she looked at Coupland for permission to answer it. He nodded, waited while she listened to the person on the other end of the line, said 'yes' a couple of times before ending the call. She looked from Jason to the detectives, 'Mum and Dad are downstairs…' her voice pleading for a reprieve.

'That's fine,' Alex said, 'just give me a note of where you'll be staying.'

*

As they stepped out into the cool air Coupland shivered and rammed a cigarette into his mouth. He was about to light up when a PC leaning against the car park wall caught his attention. He was stooped forward, wiping his mouth with the back of his hand. Coupland turned to the officer they'd spoken to earlier on door duty. 'What's up with the lad?'
The older man blew out his cheeks. 'Poor bastard was the first officer on the scene. Made the mistake of peeping in the holdall to make sure it wasn't an animal.'

'He didn't bloody touch anything?' Coupland's tone was sharp; the pathologist would have a field day if the scene was contaminated, would take great pleasure in reporting it to DCI Mallender.

The PC looked stung. 'He's shaken, not stupid,' his voice taking on a sullen tone, 'did well to hold it in this long, truth be told.'

Coupland nodded, patting the man on his arm. 'Give us a minute,' he said over his shoulder to Alex as he made his way towards the stooped figure. He didn't know the officer well, there was a good ten-year age gap between them, Coupland on the wrong side of that gap, but the guy had spent the same again number of years in the force. Hailed from Ireland originally, if he remembered it rightly, moved here when his wife got a job in Salford's Media City. He liked to take care of himself, ran styling gel through his hair before every shift like it mattered, earned him the nickname Ronan, which Coupland suspected he enjoyed. 'You OK?' he asked as he drew near.

Ronan tried to form his mouth into a grin but it looked all wrong. His chin trembled as bloodshot eyes regarded Coupland. 'I've had better days, Sarge,' he responded, huffing out a laugh that was so hollow it came out as a sigh. That was the problem with the job; it made you feel as though you had to put on a brave face. Bottle it in. Refuse to acknowledge horrors that were unimaginable to those on the outside. It was easier to act as though you'd seen it all. Been there, done that, bought the bloody t-shirt. Coupland wasn't any different, he'd not only bought the t-shirt it was so old he used it as an oily rag for his clapped-out car. Street-wise. That's what they were all pretending to be. But a child in a sports bag would knock the most embittered cop off their axis.

'Do you smoke?' Coupland asked, holding out the cigarette he'd hauled into his mouth moments earlier.

Ronan shook his head.

'See, that's where you're going wrong,' he patted his jacket pockets for his pack to pull out another. The vape stick Lynn bought him on holiday was now relegated to when he was off duty. He lifted out a pack of Silk Cut and opened it. 'Here,' he said, 'take one, just for Christ's sake make sure you're well out of sight.' He saw the look that flitted across the officer's face. 'Make sure you inhale as far as you can. Trust me,' he was like a drug dealer offering a schoolboy his first toke of weed. Ronan looked uncertain. Coupland moved back a little to study him. He was average height, slim beneath his Kevlar vest, probably worked out in a gym on his days off. 'Still happily married?' Coupland asked him.

Ronan nodded.

'Want to stay that way?'

Another nod.

'Then you need a coping mechanism, son. A way to blow off steam when you get days like this.' Coupland raised his hands like a preacher. 'I know, I know, you can probably give Mo Farah a run for his money on the treadmill but you're not due to knock off shift for a couple more hours and the chances of finishing up on time today are nigh on impossible, so any hope you had of working off the tension pumping iron before you get home is bordering on non-existent. You start taking this kind of tension home with you and your missus'll be wondering who the imposter is that's taken the place of the fun-loving guy she married.' The shadow that fell across Ronan's face told Coupland he'd hit a nerve. 'We all need a release, son. For some it's a leg over, others gamble, and better guys than me have pissed their money away at the end of a shift, better in their view to go home legless than with images like that kiddie upstairs seared into their brain. Either way, they all lead to ruin.' Coupland lifted a fag from the pack and slipped it into the front pocket of Ronan's stab-proof vest. Ronan nodded at last before backing away.

'Nothing restores harmony like a lungful of tar,' Coupland said as Ronan ducked beneath the crime scene tape and quick-stepped behind a CSI van. 'They should put that on my epitaph,' he grinned as Alex came over to join him.

'They probably will,' she huffed, mouth down in disapproval. Days like today she envied Coupland's habit. He gripped a cigarette like a Catholic fingered Rosary beads. A comfort when all around was dark. She racked her brain to think of her own coping mechanism. Her days at the gym were getting less frequent with two young children at home. She rarely had time for after work drinks. Before she'd gone on maternity leave Carl used to joke that living with her was like opening a bag of Revels, he never knew which one he was going to get.

Coupland caught her staring at the plume of smoke coming from behind the CSI van. 'Can I tempt you?' he smirked, holding out the packet.

Alex shot him a look. 'Not a sodding chance,' she scolded him, 'not a sodding chance.'

*

The incident room was already bustling. The MISPER Unit had provided a list of children reported missing in the local area over the last twelve months. The murder team were working through the files to collate a range of actions that they could pursue once the post-mortem had been carried out. In the meantime the children were divided into gender and the age they were when they went missing. Anyone over the age of six was being discounted purely on the size of the sports bag.

Uniformed and plain clothed officers alike tapped away at desktop computers or made outbound calls. In the middle of it all a black man with an athletic build and hair shaved within an inch of its life sat on the edge of a desk, peering over a WPC's shoulder as she scribbled down notes with a phone clamped between her shoulder and ear. Coupland made a bee line for him. 'Ashcroft, can you get onto the landlord?' He pulled out his notebook and copied a name down as well as the address of the apartment block where the child had been found onto a post-it note block on the desk. 'Get the names and contact details of all past and present tenants in this building.' He ripped off the top sheet and gave it to the DC. 'Find out who else had access to the property, regular or otherwise.'

Ashcroft nodded as he took the slip of paper from him. 'Will do, Sarge.'

'Listen up everyone,' Coupland called out as he perched a buttock on the edge of a desk.

A young DC moved towards him carrying a tray of coffee mugs. Hair stuck out at angles, he was finally outgrowing the spots that had made him look permanently red cheeked. The suit jacket he had on was way too big for him; he looked like he was playing dress-up in his dad's clothes. He placed the tray down beside his computer before opening a desk drawer and lifting out a box of doughnuts. 'Ya snooze, ya lose,' he said, helping himself to one before placing the box beside the tray.

Coupland nodded appreciatively, especially since he was closest to the box and was able to bag a doughnut with sticky chocolate icing. 'Anyone would think it was coming up to appraisal time, Krispy,' he grinned, taking a mouthful before swigging it down with coffee. 'A proper brew as well, you're spoiling me.'

Krispy blushed, filling the space between his acne scars a deep shade of scarlet. 'Vending machine's not working, Sarge,' he confessed.

'Thank Christ for small mercies,' Coupland mumbled, wiping sticky icing off his chin with the back of his hand. He waited while Krispy demolished a doughnut that looked like it had been dipped in a Cholera victim's stool sample. 'How did you get on with Children and Families?'

DC Timmins, christened Krispy because of his penchant for the famous chain's sugar-coated doughnuts, had been tasked with contacting the social work team at Salford Council. He was a dab hand on the computer, could manipulate spreadsheets and interrogate data faster than Coupland could pull the cellophane off a packet of cigarettes and light up, and that was saying something. Quiet by nature, his skills on the computer earned him the respect of the whole team. 'They're emailing a list of all the children on the at-risk register in Salford matching the approximate age of our victim.' He glanced at his screen just as an icon appeared in the corner alerting him to new mail. 'It's just come in,' he added, pressing a button before moving over to the printer.

'Jesus you should see the press vans that have started circling, and I'm sure the guy from Granada Reports is on work experience,' DC Robinson, a sour-faced Geordie, bleated as he returned from Ashdown Court. Rubbing nicotine stained hands together, he headed straight for the kitchen area. 'A full morning's graft on nothing but fresh air, didn't even have time for my teacake.'

Coupland glanced sharply at Alex but she avoided his eye. Seems she'd picked up more of his habits than she cared to admit to. He took the print-out Krispy offered and scanned down it before walking over to the incident board where a photograph of the sports holdall and its grisly contents had been placed centre stage. He stabbed his finger at the photo. 'This morning at 10.15am, Jason Vevers and Alison Fraser dialled 999 to report the discovery of something foul smelling coming from a sports holdall in the flat they were moving into. They thought it was a dead animal but had the presence of mind not to check it out for themselves. Inside that bag were the remains of a small child, gender as yet unknown.' The room filled with expressions of disgust, so much so that Coupland had to raise his voice to be heard. 'If the killer was experienced it's unlikely he would have cocked up so royally when it came to disposing the body,' he observed.

'So it's likely that this is his first time,' Alex finished for him.

Coupland nodded. 'A child, missing long enough for its body to become so badly decomposed, yet no one bothers to report it. How does that work?'

'Either the parents did it, Sarge,' Ashcroft offered, 'or this is a missing child that's been held captive for some time before the kidnapper decided to kill them.'

'Why leave them in a bag though?' Alex interjected. 'It was obvious the body would be discovered sooner or later.'

'Maybe they were trying to dispose of the body when they were interrupted,' Ashcroft reasoned, 'ended up dumping it in the hope they could come back and retrieve it at a later date.'

'Only love's young dream move in and bugger up their plans,' said Coupland. 'I want to know who this child is. Maybe a family member is to blame but if not, someone out there is waiting for news: a mother, father, brother or sister; at least we can put them out of their misery.' What he said wasn't quite true, for the parents of a dead child were jettisoned into a new level of despair, but at least it was a despair based on fact, rather than misplaced hope. Coupland delegated tasks, referring to his actions list he read out who was going to go door-to-door, who was going to stay behind on the phones and who was going to do some actual detective work. He held up the print-out Krispy had given him and beckoned Robinson over. 'Can you go to these addresses and eyeball each kid on this list, and by eyeball I don't mean being fobbed off with they're having a kip or they're out with granny. Keep going back till you see them, or better still wait.'

Robinson's shoulders sagged as he took the print-out. 'Any chance I can get something to eat first, Sarge? Stomach thinks my throat's been cut.'

'Take one of these with you,' Coupland said benevolently, holding out the doughnut box. All that was left was a plain one, didn't look as though it had so much as jam in it, but beggars couldn't be choosers.

'Sarge,' Robinson mumbled before grabbing it and heading for the door.

'Oh, and Robinson?' Coupland called after him, 'I'll need any statements you take typing up before the end of shift.' There was a reply, he was sure of it, but it was masked by a DC nearby as he answered his phone. He suppressed a smirk as he guessed the gist of it. 'And all data comes back via Krispy,' he called out, 'he's keeping a list of each child being checked so make sure you let him know when someone's been accounted for. That goes for all of you.'

Coupland looked out through the CID room's internal window into the corridor. 'Anyone seen the boss yet?' Several detectives looked in his direction before shaking their heads. 'Thank Christ for small mercies, eh?' he muttered, shoulders relaxing. He had a chance to dredge up a bit more information before reporting up the chain, at the moment all they had was a child in a bag. Until they had the child's ID they were treading water. But Coupland was satisfied the team was doing all it could to narrow down the possible options. It was down to Harry Benson, esteemed pathologist, to get them started in the right direction.

CHAPTER FOUR

The mortuary was quiet. The only sound to be heard was the hum of the overhead air conditioning unit. Coupland breathed in and out slowly, just to reassure himself he could. He and Alex had arrived while the technicians were on a break. Coffee and biscuits then back to wheeling out the dead. Alex had gone straight to the viewing gallery upstairs, preferring not to linger anywhere near the human fridges. Coupland wasn't so reticent; heading towards a door marked 'Authorised personnel only' he pushed it open. The tiled room behind consisted of a wall of stainless steel refrigerated drawers. He made his way along them, reading the name cards on each door until he found what he was looking for: 'Unknown child.' He placed a hand on the cool metal handle, tried not to picture the mass of tissue and hair lying inside, cold and dead and alone. Coupland lowered his head. 'I'll find out who you are,' he said in a solemn voice, 'and then I'll find the bas–'

The door banged behind him and he straightened up to see Harry Benson deep in conversation with his assistant. Tea break was over then. Benson paused his conversation and regarded Coupland as he might an irritating med student. 'You'll need a strong stomach for this one, DS Coupland, you sure you want to be here?'

Coupland lifted his chin. 'Ready when you are.' His manner was brisk, he was in no hurry to see a child turned inside out but the sooner the examination was done the sooner he'd know what they were dealing with. Benson rewarded him with a curt nod, disappearing through a door at the far side of the room.

Coupland returned to where he had come from, heading through a set of double doors, taking the stairs two at a time to enter the viewing gallery.

'Thought you'd changed your mind,' Alex commented, checking her watch before slipping her phone out of her bag and swiping the screen to check for messages and hoping like hell there was nothing from the childminder. The last thing she wanted was to think of her kids once Benson got to work. What a great return from maternity leave this was turning out to be. So much for easing her in. 'Don't know how you can lurk around downstairs,' she shuddered when Coupland joined her.

'Doesn't bother me,' he shrugged, though his eyes told a different story. They sat in silence, staring ahead. They were about to watch the unwatchable. It was nigh on impossible to think of anything to say to lighten the mood. Through the glass window of the viewing gallery the technician wheeled in something covered with a plastic sheet on a trolley. The body had been left in the sports bag as it would likely burst when it was lifted out. The technician had the task of removing it and it wouldn't be pretty. Coupland looked over at Alex who was rummaging about in her bag.

'Got some mints in here somewhere,' she said when she caught him studying her. 'Want one?'

Coupland didn't but nodded anyway; it would give them something to focus on while the deed was done. He waited while she handed him a dog-eared tube of mints, took his time tearing the wrapper to retrieve a fluff-covered Polo. By the time he returned his gaze to the examination table, the technician was photographing what appeared to be a pile of rags. Once he returned the camera to a counter running along the back wall, he approached the body with a pair of shears which he used to cut through the clothing. Coupland exchanged a glance with Alex. 'You don't have to be here if you don't want to.'

'Yes I do.'

It was the set of her jaw that told him she felt the same way as he did. Attending the post mortem was like a trade off with the victim. A way of making amends. They hadn't been able to stop this from happening; the least they could do was be there for the little mite now.

The pathologist stepped forward, peered closely at the body before lifting a scalpel. 'It's a girl,' he said, leaning into the microphone above the table. The technician hadn't even finished removing the child's clothes.

'Christ, you don't mess about,' Coupland called down in admiration.

The pathologist's smile wasn't altogether unkind, but it was the kind of smile a school bully gave before punching you in the gonads. 'This was in her hair,' he said, holding up a pink hairclip. Coupland stared at the bits of putrid scalp stuck to it and his stomach lurched. Benson turned to his assistant who was busy scraping bits of tissue into little glass tubes. He handed him the hairclip. 'Make sure that gets sent off for DNA analysis.'

The technician cut away the remainder of the child's clothes, placing each item into a separate plastic bag. Before bagging one item he showed it to Benson, his words out of range for the detectives to pick up. Benson peered at the item, nodding his permission. The technician moved towards the microphone mounted above the examination table. He held up a grey piece of cloth, reshaping it with his hands until it resembled a little vest. He reached for the back of the garment and pointed to the label. He cleared his throat several times. 'All the clothing is aged for a four to five year old,' he stated before stepping away. Benson paced around the table, prodding the greasy flesh with a gloved finger, making detailed notes into a dictaphone. All the while he maintained his detached, emotionless narrative. It was no wonder the guy came across as a cold fish, Coupland reasoned, he doubted anyone could be the life and soul of the party when they'd spent the best part of a day slicing into a child.

Coupland found a spot on the top of Benson's head and studied it, his eyes not wavering despite the sounds, like meat being slapped onto a butcher's counter. He shook his head from side to side, glancing down at his hands in his lap. 'Every day a new bastard walks the earth,' he muttered, his fingers twitching as he thought what he'd like to do to the scum that had done this. He looked up in time to see Benson wrist deep in the child's torso, found a new spot on the pompous man's head and kept on staring.

The pathologist's voice broke into his thoughts. He hadn't realised he'd tuned out for so long, that he'd bypassed the slicing and sawing and rummaging. Something resembling a string of chipolata sausages lay in a metal bowl. 'A significant area of the stomach and bowel is empty,' he informed them, 'which indicates she'd gone without a meal for a considerable amount of time before death.' He paused while he ran his finger along something offal-like. 'There's an abscess on the lung which indicates pneumonia.'

'Poor little mite... Is that what killed her, then?' Alex's tone was hopeful, as though stuffing the poor beggar in a bag was OK as long as there'd been no foul play beforehand. The detail was important though. It could mean the difference between a charge of murder or perverting the course of justice.

'She'd have had a cough, quite an irritating one I would imagine, but no, I'm willing to stake my pension that we can rule it out as the cause of death.'

'Not like you to be so decisive, Harry, you're normally quite reticent when it comes to confirming details,' Coupland chipped in.

'Only when I need to be, DS Coupland, but on this occasion I can be confident the pneumonia didn't kill her.'

Coupland couldn't help rising to the bait. 'Why's that then?'

Benson poked his finger through a gap in the child's skull and wiggled it. 'There's a hole here where it shouldn't be, sergeant. If I was a betting man, I'd put my money on *that.*'

Coupland wasn't a breakfast man. A coffee and a cigarette was his staple diet first thing. Lynn had tried to introduce him to muesli but it had given him wind. Cereal went through him like a dose of salts, too. 'Toast, then,' she'd coax but the bread she'd started buying had grains in and he was convinced he'd lose a filling. This morning he'd stuck to his guns, his eyes glinting as she'd tutted round the kitchen, muttering that he was old enough and ugly enough to make his own choices. He should be grateful for small mercies, he supposed now, at least there was nothing other than his teacake to churn around inside him. 'When did she die, Doc?' he barked.

Benson stood back from the table so the technician could lift and weigh the tangled mass of organs. He considered the detective's question before returning to the body and looking down at a blackened hand. The child's nails had fallen off. 'Her internal organs had begun to liquefy, DS Coupland. I'd estimate death occurred approximately four weeks ago.'

Alex regarded Coupland sharply. 'There haven't been any reports of a missing child that fits that timescale.' Coupland's shoulders sank.

'I'll need to run some lab tests to check her blood for antibiotics,' Benson announced. 'I'll get back to you as soon as I can.'

Coupland furrowed his brow. 'How does that help?'

'For the pneumonia. If antibiotics are present, she must have been treated by a doctor.' A lead at last.

'And what about the bag?' Coupland asked. 'Anything left behind in any of the pockets?' Benson nodded at the technician who peered inside the now empty large compartment; he scooped out the matter at the bottom of it into a stainless steel dish. He fished gloved fingers around in it before shaking his head. He checked an external zipped pocket that ran the length of the bag. It was possible the bag's owner could have left some ID in there, a wallet, a sport club membership card, but it was unlikely. That only happened in the police dramas Lynn watched on TV. Coupland would sit beside her and snigger, in the same way she'd smirk when hospital dramas brought unlikely casualties back from the dead.

There was a logo down the side of the bag. Coupland had hoped the photographer at the scene had got a clear shot of it but only part of the word had been visible. He still couldn't make out what it said from his perch in the gallery.

'Regenerate,' the technician informed him, 'only spelled with the number eight at the end.' Coupland took out his pad and wrote the name down. Regener8. 'It's in Walkden,' the technician added, 'opened up about six months ago.'

'Never heard of them,' Coupland shrugged.

'Why doesn't that surprise me,' Benson drawled.

Coupland regarded Benson's angular build. Back when he was in school there were names for a physique like that, Tin Ribs, or Joe 90 if the poor kid wore glasses. He resisted the urge to lob a new name at the professor. 'I'll have you know this is pure muscle,' he said instead.

'As opposed to thick skinned,' Alex muttered.

Coupland's smile belied his need to get out of there, but there was something he needed to know. 'Had she been interfered with, Harry?'

A pause, then something resembling relief flickered across the pathologist's face. 'No, there are no wounds indicative of sexual assault either peri or post mortem. For that, I suppose we should be grateful.'

Coupland had heard enough. Since when was a dead child not being sexually abused a bonus? She was still dead; whoever did this still needed locking up. He pushed himself to his feet. He didn't need to hang around to see the organs returned to the body cavity in a leak-proof bag. He wondered whether he'd ever get the smell out of his nostrils. 'Let's get out of here,' he said to Alex, already reaching for his cigarettes.

'The bloodwork will be ready this afternoon,' Benson called after him but the only reply was the sound of double doors swinging closed.

'Thanks Harry.' Alex gathered up her belongings and followed Coupland out.

*

No sooner had Coupland slammed the car door shut than he lifted out his cigarettes, tapping one out before lighting it hungrily. He puffed on it like a condemned man, as though he wouldn't be happy until he was wreathed in smoke. He lowered the driver's window as Alex approached. 'Hurry up then,' he called out, making beckoning gestures with his free hand.

'Not bloody likely.' Alex stood her ground. 'The amount you smoke it's like working in a crematorium.'

Coupland heaved out a sigh. 'C'mon Alex, give me a break.'

But she shook her head. 'Don't think I haven't worked out why you don't like taking pool cars out. You think that if you take your own out you can do what you like in it.'

Coupland pursed his lips. She'd sussed him then. 'Fine! I'll keep the windows lowered all the way back to the station, is that a deal?'

Alex climbed in the passenger side of the car in silence, wafting her hands around to make a point.

'You'd make a great Health and Safety rep, d'you know that?' he sniped.

Alex narrowed her eyes. 'Just shut it and drive,' she sniped back.

'I see we're taking the scenic route,' Alex muttered as the tower blocks of Tattersall slid by. Thrown up in the sixties, it was Salford Housing Department's very own segregation wing. If you needed a home and weren't easily intimidated, this was where you were sent. The estate had a fierce reputation, generations of problem families happy to knock seven shades of the proverbial out of each other.

'So this kiddie could have been missing for a while, since we don't have any new MISPERS reported...' Coupland said, drumming his hands on the steering wheel when they stopped at a red light. His voice trailed off but Alex knew what he didn't want to say out loud. The child might have been killed four weeks ago; that didn't mean she hadn't been taken by her captor long before then, just as Ashcroft had suggested. God knows what she'd been subjected to in the intervening period. They both shuddered at the prospect.

*

'Sarge?' Ashcroft was seated on one of the hot desk chairs in the incident room, phone cradled in the crook of his neck. 'Sure you gave me the right number for the landlord? Only it keeps ringing out.'

'I gave you the number I was given by the woman moving into the flat, she got it straight from her phone. Try giving this fella a ring, Jimmy Rawlings, he's one of the residents, lives across the landing from the crime scene.' Coupland patted his jacket pockets until he found the flyer Rawlings had given him earlier. 'He should be at work now, call him and see if he's got another number.' He added Rawlings' number into his own phone before passing it to Ashcroft.

'I've already run a check on the landlord,' Ashcroft added, 'no previous.'

'Doesn't mean he's clean as a whistle.'

'I know, Sarge, if there's any dirt to dig up on him, I'll find it.'

Alex swivelled her chair round so that she was facing Coupland. She had a sheet of paper in her hand. 'Blood-work has come back on the child, Kevin,' she said, handing the paper to him. 'I've printed it out for you. Benson copied me in, probably knew there was more chance of me opening it.'

Coupland studied her face for clues. 'Any use?' he could always live in hope.

Alex cracked her first smile since they'd left the mortuary at lunchtime. 'Makes interesting reading.'

He took the report from her and skimmed through it. The report confirmed traces of antibiotics had been found. He looked over at Alex. Finally, something concrete.

'The pneumonia was probably caused by inhaling food, drink, or vomit into her lungs, more likely happens as a gagging reflex following excessive use of drugs.'

Coupland thought he'd misheard. 'Drugs?'

'Carry on reading...' Alex prompted.

Coupland turned back to the report, his eyes scanning to the bottom of the page, 'She was pumped full of Diazepam.'

'Just enough to keep her drowsy,' Alex replied.

'Why the hell would anyone do that?' Coupland's eyes narrowed as he re-read the last line of the report. *Excessive use of drugs*. The penny dropped. 'So this wasn't the first time she'd been given Diazepam. She'd been pumped full of it before, which is how she got the abscess on her lung?'

Alex nodded. 'More than likely.'

Coupland jotted something down in his note pad. 'Krispy, pull up a list of all the doctors' surgeries close to where the body was found,' he called over the desks.

'Will do, Sarge.' Krispy responded, tapping onto his keyboard while demolishing a slice of pizza. He really needed to speak to him about his diet. 'Nine surgeries have come up in the immediate area, Sarge. Do you want me to widen the search?'

'Not yet. Give each practice manager a call; get them to send over details of all girls aged four to five year olds treated for pneumonia approximately six weeks ago. It can be serious in a child, might have resulted in them being admitted to hospital, in fact get onto the kids' hospital too.' Krispy's hand raced across the pad on his desk as he took notes. 'Don't let any of them give you the run-around, you hear me?'

'I'm on it, Sarge.'

Coupland glared at the incident board, at the photo of the sports bag and its putrid contents. Beneath the heading 'Ashdown Court' were the names of the apartment block's landlord and residents. Another column which read 'Previous tenants' had yet to be filled in. Coupland's desk phone buzzed. He barked his name into the mouthpiece then listened to what the caller had to say. He returned the phone to its cradle, pushing himself to his feet. Alex looked at him quizzically. 'Boss is back. Time to let him know what's going on. Let him know we've got the best part of bugger all on the kiddie's ID.'

DCI Mallender was dressed in casual attire. A stickler for suits, today he wore a pale blue open necked shirt with dark blue chinos. His shock of blond hair was worn softer now, the military style buzz cut giving way to a short back and sides. His Harris Tweed man-bag lay open on his desk, a plastic folder and notepad just visible. 'Good course, Sir?' Coupland asked.

Mallender eyed him suspiciously, 'I can never be sure whether you're taking the proverbial, Kevin.'

'What, moi?' Coupland volleyed. 'I was just showing a bit of interest, boss. The wife says it's something I need to work on. Well, I think that's what she said; only I wasn't paying attention.' Mallender raised a weary eyebrow as Coupland made himself comfortable in the chair opposite and ploughed on, 'So, anything you plan to impose - I mean implement - on the team?' he smiled.

'Not unless I'm feeling really aggrieved,' Mallender warned as he pulled the plastic folder and pad from his bag and tossed them into the bottom drawer of a filing cabinet beside his desk. 'You know, the moment you get to inspector it's like you have to learn a completely different language,' he sighed.

'Parlez-vous bullshit?'

'Something like that. I thought I was pretty fluent, to be honest. I mean, I can wax lyrical on maximising stake-holder engagement with the best of them...' Coupland was lost already. 'But this entire seminar was delivered using acronyms.' Coupland raised an eyebrow, waiting for the DCI to enlighten him. 'We've been working on a quality tool which is being rolled out throughout the division, its full title is *How Good is our Service?* But for the entire conference it was referred to as HEGIOS.'

'Sounds Greek to me,' Coupland observed.

'That was bad enough, but the course leader, a woman from generation OMG, thought it was perfectly acceptable to add LOL to the end of everything she said.'

Coupland nodded in sympathy, 'I blame the Americans,' he said, 'it all went downhill after Elvis. Anyway, talking of quality tools, have you spoken to the Super yet?'

Mallender's mouth formed a grim line. 'I have, and he's insisting on an ID for this child ASAP, only there wasn't so much as an LOL at the end of *that* request,' he stated, getting no pleasure at all from the grimace that formed across his sergeant's face.

*

'How did it go with the boss?'

Coupland shrugged over at Alex as he made his way back to his desk. 'Fine, he gets that we've nothing to go on as yet, said the Super would be taking a different view if we didn't get the girl's ID soon.' Alex sighed. 'Krispy's been busy, popped over a couple of times to leave something on your desk.'

'Unless its round and covered in icing I'm not interested,' Coupland grumbled, but he shuffled the papers in his in-tray until he found what he was looking for. Rather than a doughnut he found a print out of a spreadsheet with a post-it note attached to it written in Krispy's schoolboy handwriting. The note stated he'd phoned every doctors' surgery in the vicinity of where the body was found asking them for details of all four to five year old girls treated for pneumonia in the last six weeks. He'd already spoken to a senior manager at the children's hospital; a list of acute admissions was to be emailed through later that day. The surgeries had started responding to his request for information and the attached list of possible names so far was small, but Coupland was hopeful it would get bigger as the day wore on. A second spreadsheet left by Krispy contained a list of girls five and under who'd been treated for pneumonia within Salford Health Authority which he was cross checking against information that came in from the doctors' surgeries to see if there were any discrepancies. Coupland ran his finger down the list of names; most had already been checked and scored out by Krispy. The remaining names would need following up, one name in particular, Coupland reckoned, since it was a name he recognised for all the wrong reasons. The note beside it in Krispy's handwriting made interesting reading. He called out to Alex, 'Fancy doing a tour of the local medical centres? Couple of names here worth following up.'

Alex nodded, picking up a set of car keys left on DC Turnbull's desk, 'Fine, but we're going in a pool car and I'm driving.'

'No skin off my nose,' Coupland said grumpily, deciding a quick fag between the station rear exit and the pool car park was more than doable, his fingers giving his jacket pocket a comforting pat. He hoped to Christ this trip out was the start of something positive, that they'd know the identity of the little girl by the end of the day.

*

The medical centre on Langworthy Road was a converted Victorian schoolhouse set between leafy 1950s style semi-detached houses on one side and new build town houses on the other. Alex parked the pool car on the forecourt of the petrol station behind the medical centre, flashing her warrant card at the guy in the kiosk. 'So who are we checking up on?' she asked as she beeped the car locked and they crossed the side road behind the medical centre, up along the access ramp leading into the building's arched entrance.

'Lexi Cooper, turned four last November.'

There were two women sat behind the reception desk, one wore a badge with 'Practice Manager' on it, and she tapped into a keyboard without making eye contact with anyone joining the small queue that had formed. The woman beside her wore a badge stating she was the receptionist, her gaze darting to the people standing in line then back down at the desk pad in front of her as she typed. She was dealing with a phone call that wasn't as straight forward as hoped by the look of it, her fingers increasing tempo in line with her frustration. 'I'm afraid we can't give out test results over the phone...' she repeated for the third time, making apologetic faces to an old lady at the front of the queue leaning onto a zimmer frame. Coupland moved to the other glass window, tapped onto the desk top when the practice manager refused to look up. 'There's an appointment check-in machine just by the door,' she said without stopping what she was doing, her attention fixed on the desktop screen in front of her. 'You'd all be processed much quicker if you used it. User instructions are sellotaped to the wall above it.'

'I'm glad to hear it,' Coupland replied, 'but I don't have an appointment.'

'Then you'll need to call us tomorrow at 8.30am and

we'll allocate an appointment to you then.'

'Oh, I think what I've got needs quicker attention than that,' he informed her as he held up his warrant card, placing it over her PC so she had no choice but to read it. She regarded him sharply, a scowl appearing as she realised she had to play ball.

'I'll see who's available,' she said, her voice sour.

'No need love, I'll speak to Dr Howard if he's in.'

The practice manager studied him. 'Well he *is* in, but… are you a patient of his?' She eyed him suspiciously, as though it was unheard of for policemen and doctors to move in the same circles.

'Christ, I wouldn't let him go anywhere near me… no offence like,' he said to the queue behind him.

'Very well,' she muttered, lifting the receiver of her desk phone and jabbing at a couple of buttons. 'Hello? Dr Howard, there's someone at reception insisting on seeing you… a detective sergeant… yes, that's it, oh… right away then.' She ended the call, trying hard to mask her disappointment. 'He'll see you now.' Coupland kept his smile in check but his eyes danced as she showed them the way to the doctor's room.

'Mate o' yours is he?' Alex whispered as they walked behind the practice manager.

'He worked on the same ward as Lynn before he went into general practice. Used to be a big drinker before he got married, mind you, didn't we all?' he answered, eyebrows raised.

'Percy!' Coupland beamed as a heavy-set man in a tweed suit greeted them at his consulting room door, 'long time no see.'

Percy rolled his eyes. 'That's because I never get out

from behind this desk, unless house calls count.' He shot a look at the practice manager. 'Any chance of some coffee, Ruthie? I've never known this fella turn down a Hob Nob either so biscuits wouldn't go amiss.' He turned to greet Alex.

'Detective Sergeant Moreton.' She offered her hand which he clasped between both of his own.

'Coffee for you as well, sergeant?'

Alex slid a look at Coupland who was already making himself comfy on one of the two chairs placed on the patients' side of the desk. 'Go on then,' she said gamely; there was no point sitting watching His Nibs slurp his way through a cuppa, and her stomach was rumbling, to tell the truth.

Ruthie pursed her lips. 'Of course Dr Howard, I'll see to it myself.'

'Splendid!' Percy rubbed his hands together, as though warming them before carrying out an intimate examination. 'Please, don't stand on ceremony,' he said, offering Alex the seat beside Coupland. 'Besides, I want to find out from this man how my favourite nurse is doing. I was sorry to hear she'd been through a rough time.'

Coupland made a show of shrugging his shoulders, 'She's made of strong stuff, my missus, returned to work part time already.' There was pride there, no doubting it, but his hands gripped onto the seat of his chair while he spoke.

'I wouldn't expect anything else.' Percy smiled. 'Who's her consultant?'

'Ray Brown,' Coupland replied, remembering the first time he'd met the specialist who'd treated Lynn; he'd thought they'd been having an affair and had been about to knock his head off. How could he have known that what the medic had to tell him would still feel like a punch to his guts?

Percy nodded his approval. 'He's a good man, someone I'd want in my corner if I was ever up against it.' Ruthie came in with fresh coffee in a cafetiere and china mugs on a wooden tray, a plate of assorted biscuits beside them. 'You are an absolute star,' Percy told her as he made space on the top of his desk. Ruthie's face lit up at the compliment; she was about to begin pouring when he reached for the coffee pot himself. 'I wouldn't dream of taking up any more of your precious time, my dear, please, go back to your spreadsheet, I will look after our visitors.' If Ruthie was disappointed at being dismissed so quickly she didn't let it show. She made her way over to the door, stealing a quick glance at the detectives, the tiniest of smiles on her lips.

'She's not so bad,' Percy told them, reading Coupland's mind. 'Her bark's worse than her bite and with a bit of praise she's putty in your hands.'

Coupland remembered now why Percy was so popular on the ward; he treated the nursing staff with respect and stood up for them against the faceless bureaucrats threatening to dismantle the NHS at every turn. He was also first in the canteen to buy them breakfast when their shift finished, which always helped. While Coupland told him the purpose of their visit, Percy alternated between sipping coffee and chewing on a biscuit as he listened. 'Poor child,' he sympathised when Coupland had finished. 'How can I help?'

'Alexis Cooper, known as Lexi, your records show she had pneumonia last November.'

'Go on.'

'Thing is, she's not returned to her reception class at St Bede's Primary, that's four weeks she's been unaccounted for. I'm hoping you can tell me she's been eyeballed by someone here in that time or I'll be sending my officers round to Big Jim's place for a welfare check and as you know…'

'…that will be challenging,' Percy finished for him. Big Jim owned the King's Arms on the Tattersall Estate, providing work for three barmaids and a dozen drug dealers who worked his patch stretching from Tattersall itself to Salford's Media City. The pub was a front for money laundering but in thirty years he'd only been sent down once; he had friends in very high places, and deep pockets to boot. It wasn't for the want of trying, the National Crime Agency was trying to reel him in. For all Coupland knew, there could be surveillance on him twenty-four-seven, just a shame the big boys didn't play ball when it came to sharing information. 'Worried you'll start a riot if you turn up unannounced?' Percy asked. Coupland grimaced; the truth was he wasn't sure which side would throw the biggest tantrum.

'I can check our records to see if one of my colleagues has had to treat her recently,' Percy pulled the desk top keyboard towards him, keying in Lexi's name and address, hitting the 'enter' button once he'd finished. 'You're not suggesting he'd harm his own daughter?'

Alex shook her head. 'Not at all, but she could have been kidnapped by a rival gang. Big Jim's hardly going to come to us for help if she had been.'

Percy conceded her point, squinting at the screen as Lexi's medical records appeared on his desktop. If someone had taken a gang leader's child it wouldn't be reported to the police, it would be dealt with below the radar and the results would be swift and devastating. 'She was admitted to the children's hospital for one night, discharged the next morning with a week's course of Amoxicillin. She was booked to come in here for a follow up appointment with one of my junior colleagues, but didn't turn up for the appointment.' Percy looked up at Coupland. 'If we chased up every patient who didn't show up when they were supposed to…'

Coupland waved his explanation away. 'I get it Doc, there's only so much any of us can do.'

'That makes it four weeks she's been unaccounted for.' Alex added, exchanging a look with Coupland.

'There'd be an all-out Armageddon if someone harmed a hair on that little girl's head,' Percy stated with authority. He had spent several years in Accident and Emergency, had stitched up enough casualties of rival turf wars to know the extent people would go to when one of their own had been threatened.

'Which is why we need to tread carefully.' Coupland's voice was solemn.

CHAPTER FIVE

'Shouldn't we wait for backup?' Alex asked, eyeing her side mirror before pulling into the flow of traffic.

'In theory, I suppose,' Coupland muttered. At least they didn't need to key The King's Arms into the Satnav; the two-storey red brick pub on Tattersall was notorious for trouble. Most cops had barged over the threshold at some point in their career. 'But then he'll see us coming...' The moment squad cars entered the neighbourhood smart phones up and down the estate would go into overdrive as Big Jim's gang warned him and his henchmen that dibble were on their way. If that wasn't bad enough, any police car venturing onto the estate was a target for vandals, so the standard police protocol was to send in armoured vans, which was probably not the best way to get Jim Cooper to engage with them on this occasion. 'Look, we're in an unmarked car, all we need to do is go in and eyeball little Lexi, come back out again, job done.'

'If you thought it was that straight forward how come you didn't assign it to anyone else?'

She had him there. Coupland never asked his team to do anything he wasn't prepared to do himself. Which in this case meant getting his face pulverised if his hunch was wrong. He threw Alex a sidelong glance. 'A little less analysing and a bit more action, eh?'

Alex tutted. 'Stop moaning, I'm going as fast as I can

without drawing attention to ourselves. Just because she's not in school doesn't mean she's our victim, I thought there was a code of conduct relating to non-combatants.' She was referring to the unspoken rule of engagement amongst the many gangs trading cheek by jowl around Salford that whatever their dispute, children, females and elderly relatives were a no-go area in terms of settling scores. But then back in the day so was violence against the police. Times changed, Coupland supposed, and not always for the better.

'You did watch TV while you were on maternity leave, didn't you?' he checked. 'And I don't mean Teletubbies or whatever the kids are watching these days. You did keep up with what's been going on?'

Alex bristled, 'You mean the teenage girl who was shot? Kenny Osbourne's daughter? Yeah, I saw.' Danielle Osbourne had been on her way to a girl-guide meeting when she was shot by a youth on a motor bike as a warning when Kenny had opened a night club in a rival's territory. A photo of her bandaged body on a hospital bed had been front page news. She'd survived the attack, and Osbourne's nightclub had shut down one week later. Truth was Alex had watched very little news during her time away from work. Ben was old enough now to take in what was happening on the screen and how could anyone explain the damage one person inflicted upon another? For the last few months she'd lived in a Disney cocoon, punctuated only by the Evening News that dropped through her letterbox every day. She would read it exhausted, once the boys were asleep. Though she'd rather cut off her right arm than confess that to Coupland.

'Sure you want to do this though?' She nodded towards the road ahead, the CCTV towers that had been cut down with angle grinders leaving ominous concrete stumps. What happened in Tattersall stayed in Tattersall.

'Stay in the car if you'd rather.' Coupland's tone was measured but he might as well have clucked like a chicken. Alex swallowed hard. Her time off with her boys had softened her, made her all too aware of the frailty of life, of how their world would shatter if she failed to come home one night. Get a grip, she told herself, you're a Salford cop, if you can't take the pace get a transfer to Norfolk, chaperone the royals when they're staying at Sandringham, chase sheep rustlers and hunt for missing tractors. Shit or get off the pot.

'Carl said you'd do this,' she grumbled.

'Do what?'

'Throw me in at the deep end just to test my mettle.'

'And I always thought so highly of him.'

Alex shot him a sidelong glance. 'Hmmm…' she muttered as she unfastened her seat belt, 'you coming or what?'

The management reserve the right to refuse admittance to anyone entering the premises. Coupland smirked at the sign above The Kings Arms entrance. Who was Big Jim trying to kid? He sold his gear to anyone. Squaring his shoulders, he pushed open the battered front door. Today's clientele was a motley bunch, a red eyed man with no teeth sat hunched over a pint at the bar. Beside him a guy too old to be wearing the tracksuit he had on played darts with a youth who kept both hands down the front of his joggers, removing them only when it was his turn to throw. A couple of junkies swayed beside a fruit machine, their pallid faces blending into the cheap wallpaper behind them. The barmaid was a hefty girl, looked like she could handle herself, biceps bulging beneath tight t-shirt sleeves, *I luv Dick*, tattooed on the back of her right hand. 'Boyfriend or hobby?' Coupland enquired, but her answer was drowned out by the threatening growl coming from the far side of the bar.

'There'd better be a good reason you've come into my pub, dibble.' A man close to fifty with a face made from stone moved towards him. Coupland regarded Big Jim and held his ground. 'There is.' He rolled his shoulders as he said this, despite Alex's warning look. 'Question is, are you prepared to listen to it?' Men like Jim Cooper didn't get their confident swagger from being able to handle themselves; thousands of men could do that. It was the muscle that accompanied them, the round the clock protection they could afford that other hard men could not. It wasn't just the money though, for there was always competition, some young pretender snapping at their heels offering better perks, more autonomy; it was the gravitas that clinched it, the elevated status bullies enjoyed because they went about with men with fierce reputations.

'Fuck you.'

'I'd heard prison had broadened your horizons, Jim, but I really didn't think I'd be your type.'

Big Jim's men circled him now, jaws tightened, muscles flexing. 'I could take you out right now and not one person in this pub would have seen a thing,' Jim drawled.

'I don't doubt it.'

Both men stared each other down. Alex glanced at Coupland's knuckles and wondered once more what was bugging him, why he was making foolhardy choices. 'That's the pleasantries out of the way, then,' she piped up, 'shall we get down to why we're here?'

Jim's right ear was missing a chunk, courtesy of an old rival whose body was fished out of the Ship Canal six months later, minus his nose. There'd been rumours of course, but nothing Greater Manchester Police could act on. 'I wouldn't be here if it wasn't important, Jim,' Coupland cajoled. 'Five minutes of your time and I'll be on my way.' He made no sudden movements as he said this, no raising of hands or arms reaching out. Not such a death wish then. Big Jim regarded him before lifting his shoulders in a shrug.

'Five minutes,' he said, motioning through to the back.

The back room of The King's Arms was nothing like the bar area would have had you believe. Rumour had it that Big Jim's missus was a classy piece of work. An ex-model twenty years his junior; he was punching well above his weight. The décor in this room proved it. 'Wouldn't look out of place on the cover of Country Life,' Alex commented, noticing that while she and Coupland had been allowed to enter the hallowed ground, the track-suits had not, keeping their place on the other side of the bar.

'Alanna got an interior designer in,' Jim bragged, 'cost me an arm and a leg but it's only money.' An ornate fireplace with pine cones in the grate. A bookcase, albeit filled with crime fiction and romance. Lamps on occasional tables created a cosy ambiance.

'Where's your daughter?'

Jim narrowed his eyes as he turned to face Coupland full on. 'Lexi? Why?'

Coupland shook his head. 'I'd need ten minutes to explain and you've only granted me five.'

Jim ran a hand over his shaven scalp, 'Jesus, you never did mess about, Coupland, did you? I suppose I always respected that about you.'

Coupland made a sound like a tyre being let down. 'Quit with the bullshit and answer the question. Where is your daughter right now?'

Jim's shoulders slumped, 'I suppose the bloody school contacted you?'

Alex spoke up, 'We contacted them as a matter of fact, as part of an on-going enquiry—'

'No one needs their arse kicking for our visit, Jim,' Coupland warned. 'We asked the school office when they last saw your daughter and they told us.'

Jim was silent as he processed this, causing Coupland to make a mental note to get patrol cars to drive by the school later today, and for the rest of the week, for that matter, just to be on the safe side.

Alex tried a different approach. 'I believe she's been ill?'

Big Jim locked his gaze onto her. 'What is this? Why the interest in Lexi all of a sudden?' He was starting to get arsey and the tracksuit army was only one raised voice away.

Coupland shook his head. 'No, no, that's not how it works; we ask the questions Jim, not you.'

Jim glared at Coupland, trying to work out whether to play ball or not. Decided it was no big deal. 'Yeah, she had a bad cough, ended up in hospital, right as rain now, though.'

'So why isn't she back in school?'

Big Jim's eyes had turned into mean little slits. 'Isn't this below your pay grade, Coupland, checking up on absent kids?'

Coupland wouldn't budge. 'Is she here, yes or no?' he hissed. It was the tone that said he wasn't in the mood for being dicked around, that his patience was wearing very bloody thin.

Big Jim puffed up his chest, like a toad warding off a predator. 'Alanna took her to Spain, we've got a place over there, thought the weather would do her good.' He caught a look that passed between them. 'I drove 'em to the airport my bloody self! Easyjet to Malaga.'

'So why not tell the school? Why make out she was still ill?'

'You get a fine if you take them out during term time, even in reception class.'

Coupland snorted. 'Like you give a toss about rules! And it's not like you need to worry about money. What's the real reason? Alanna finally buggered off and left you for a dentist in Alderley Edge? Got tired of her bit of rough?'

Jim lunged towards Coupland. He was quick on his feet for a big man, but Coupland blocked his fist before it made contact with his face, pushing him against the antique mirror, fingers clamped around his neck.

'Kevin!' Alex's urgent voice broke into the mist that had descended. He dropped his hand, brushing imaginary dust off Jim's shoulders instead. 'I don't give a toss about your domestic arrangements; I just want to confirm your little girl is OK.'

'She might be high maintenance but Alanna's a good mum—'

'For God's sake Mr Cooper,' Alex berated him, 'cut us some slack, we're trying to find the identity of a dead little girl, all we know is she had pneumonia the same time as Lexi.'

Big Jim studied Alex for a moment before blowing out a long breath, 'Why didn't you just say? Look, it's not Lexi, I'll show you…' he reached into the pocket of his jeans for his phone. 'I'll Facetime them. And for the record,' he glared at Coupland, 'Alanna's just taking time out to recharge her batteries.'

*

'Recharge her batteries?' Coupland bitched when they'd returned to their car. 'Looked to me like her tennis instructor was inserting new ones…' Alex smiled, 'It's fair to say neither of them were expecting Lexi to answer her mother's phone and run out onto the patio so she could Facetime with Daddy.'

'Giving Big Jim full view of Pedro rubbing factor fifteen into parts that normally don't see the sun.' Coupland grinned as he recalled the image, he didn't know which was more entertaining, Alanna's face when she saw Big Jim's ugly mug staring down at her or the various shades of purple Jim turned before he began shouting.

'What do you reckon will happen?'

'Oh, my guess is Alanna's already booked on the next flight home; let's just hope lover boy isn't being fitted for concrete boots as we speak.'

Alex placed an evidence bag containing Lexi's hairbrush onto the back seat of the car. They'd managed to persuade Jim to get it for them once he'd finishing yelling at Alanna. The lab would need to run a DNA test to confirm the body in the mortuary wasn't Lexi Cooper; they couldn't discount her on the basis of a Facetime call. At the end of the day the little girl they'd just seen on camera could have been anyone.

Alex couldn't shrug off her concern any longer. 'You were a bit gung ho back there, weren't you?'

'What're you talking about?'

'Needling away at Big Jim till you got a reaction.'

'It's called police work. How else are we supposed to get him to play ball when he hates the bloody sight of us?'

'Yeah, but given his reputation, and the fact his henchmen were standing three feet away from us, it could have turned nasty pretty quickly.'

'But it didn't, did it?'

Alex chose her words carefully, 'No… but maybe that was because I was doing my best to de-escalate the situation.'

Coupland shot her a look, 'De-escalate?' he made the word sound fetid, his lip curling as he exaggerated the syllables. 'In case it escaped your attention I managed just fine while you were up to your elbows in nappies. Didn't get my head taken off by some hairy arsed gob shite once.'

Alex bristled. 'Sorry I spoke, I'm sure.'

Coupland, never one to bear a grudge, shot her a sidelong glance. 'De-escalate my backside… Keep using four-syllable words like that and you'll make Inspector yet.'

Alex tutted. 'And to think there were days when I really missed this.'

Coupland's eyes crinkled in the corners. 'What, working with me?' He bowed his head at the compliment.

'Yeah, but only as you say, when I was elbow deep in nappies, shitty ones at that.'

*

The next medical centre was a seventies construct with its own car park at the rear. Limp pot plants sat on a cheap formica coffee table, a row of uncomfy chairs were placed around the perimeter of the room. A toy box sat in one corner. A broken abacus and a three-wheeled car had been thrown in haphazardly, a doll with a missing eye peered over the top of the box as though pleading for clemency. The receptionist didn't fare much better, a bright red nose, bloodshot eyes and a permanent sniff completed the image. 'Not exactly a poster girl for the NHS,' Coupland sniped under his breath. 'If you want to stay well, for Christ's sake don't come here.'

Alex shot him a look, stepping in front of him as they approached the reception desk. 'Just so we start off on the right foot,' she muttered.

'Ruthie would have grown to love me in time,' he threw back.

Alex drew her lips into a thin line. 'Yeah, you might want to think about that.'

A young woman wearing earphones seated in the waiting area stared at Coupland before turning to say something to the middle-aged man sat beside her. Alex spotted her pointing Coupland out. 'Friend of Amy's?' she asked.

Coupland frowned, 'A bit older than Amy…' though she did seem vaguely familiar.

'You sure it's him?' the man's voice carried over to them, causing Alex to raise her eyebrows in a 'What now?' gesture.

'No way would I forget him, Dad, he was so nasty...'

Coupland's mouth turned down at the corners as he shrugged at Alex but something gnawed away at him... he just couldn't remember where he'd seen her before. The girl's father sprang out of his chair and marched up to Coupland, leaning in so close their chests were touching. 'You nearly killed my daughter this morning, pal, and you didn't have the decency to say you were sorry or make sure she was alright.'

The woman who'd stepped off the pavement in front of him first thing. Coupland shoved his hands into his pockets and started counting backwards from ten in his head. Let the fella get it out of his system. Least said, soonest mended. Mr angry ploughed on. 'She was bawling her head off when she came home, told me some knobhead had driven into her.' Five. Four. Three. Buoyed by Coupland's silence the man pushed his face up close until they were nose to nose. 'That's why we're here,' he added. Everyone in the waiting room stared at Coupland, their loathing palpable.

Coupland had heard enough, 'What,' he growled, 'so she can get those earplugs surgically removed?'

Alex groaned. The girl was out of her seat, pulling at her father's arm. 'Dad, I'm OK, honest, just had a fright, that's all.'

'Would have helped if you'd taught her to cross the road properly or were you too busy "working away" to teach her the Green Cross Code?' Coupland made his fingers into quote marks as he said this. He was referring to the home-made tattoo inked onto the back of the man's knuckles, 'SW1' wasn't a desirable postcode, but the nickname given to HMP Manchester, previously known as Strangeways.

'You got a problem with me?' the fella asked, his chest bumping Coupland's.

Two. One. Coupland was all out of numbers and had no intention of getting into minus figures. 'Only that you're in my face,' he replied, squaring his shoulders in readiness. He opened his mouth to say something more, aware that what he wanted to say would be considered rude, aggressive even, to some. He shut it again.

'If you don't stop this I'm going to have to call the police!' The receptionist called out from behind her desk.

'We are the police,' Alex sighed.

CHAPTER SIX

Back in the pool car Alex gave Coupland the beady eye. 'That went well.'

'At least it's another kiddie we can scrub off the list,' Coupland agreed. 'Granted there was no tea and biscuits this time, but—'

'—Is there any surprise?' Alex cut in. 'I'm just relieved the receptionist let me talk her round, and that the girl's father didn't want to make a complaint. Or the girl, come to think of it, once she realised you were a cop.'

Coupland stared through the car windscreen. Something was bugging him about the doctor they'd just spoken to. A niggle he couldn't put his finger on. She'd been friendly enough, but still… Alex pecking his head didn't help his concentration. Through clenched teeth he uttered one word that sounded like 'Sorry.'

Alex turned to look at him, exasperated, 'Is that all you've got to say?' She paused; this was what she said to Ben when he was playing up, before banning cartoons and putting him on the naughty step. If only Coupland would respond to time out.

'Why did you let him get to you?'

'Who? Balloon head there? Just letting off steam…'

Alex wouldn't let it go. 'Care to tell me what this is all about, Kevin? Apart from you running into a pedestrian on your way into work.'

Coupland hissed out a breath, 'Not really, no.'

'Did you report it?'

Coupland stared at her goggle eyed, 'Did I report it? Christ Alex, you saw her, it was nothing. A scratch. Not even that. Maybe I could have handled it better, granted...'

Alex reared her head back. 'You don't say!' She chose her words carefully. 'Look, don't take this the wrong way but you seem out of sorts.' She made a point of looking at his grazed knuckles. 'You've been moody all day, I've tried to ignore it but it's not going away and now this...'

'And now what?' Coupland exploded. 'Some eejit has a go and I'm supposed to stand there and take it?'

'Well yeah, we are police officers...'

'*We are police officers*,' Coupland mimicked her, 'have you heard yourself?' His sigh when it came sounded like a tyre deflating.

Alex pursed her lips as she switched on the engine and indicated to pull out into the traffic. They drove in silence, Alex concentrating on the road ahead. Coupland was raging about something, she was sure of that; she'd just have to trust that he'd tell her when he was ready. She focussed instead on the Ford Transit in front of her, company logo emblazoned down one side, trailing a cloud of dust behind it. 'Tail light's not working,' she muttered, indicating to overtake.

'Want me to call Traffic?' Coupland volunteered in a voice that said ruining someone else's day might make him feel better.

'Nah, leave it,' she said, fiddling with the car's heating system. 'Is it me or is it bloody cold?' She checked the rear view mirror before pulling into the outside lane, eyeballing the transit's driver as she passed him.

Manoeuvre completed, Alex glanced at Coupland and sighed. Something told her the car's drop in temperature was for an entirely different reason.

*

Ashcroft was shrugging into his jacket when the phone on his desk rang. '*A gentleman in reception asking to see someone dealing with the body found in Ashdown Court this morning. Says he's had a few missed calls.*'

'What's his name?'

'*Donald Riding.*' The landlord he'd been trying to contact all afternoon.

'Tell him I'll be right down.'

Donald Riding was in his early fifties, a boxer's build with a nose to match. As he turned in Ashcroft's direction a pair of jug ears jutted out either side of his head, although the DC doubted many people had taken the mickey out of them. He glowered as Ashcroft went over to him, not bothering to return his smile. 'Can you tell me what the hell's going on?'

Ashcroft led him through to one of the bigger interview rooms; the smaller ones tended to smell of sweat and other secretions. 'I did leave you a couple of messages,' he told him once introductions were out of the way and the men were seated.

'I've only just got them,' Donald said. 'My phone had run out of battery and I've been out all day.'

'Doing anything nice?'

Donald's brow creased. 'I don't get you.'

'Well you weren't near the radio or watching TV or you'd have heard about the body on the news. Wouldn't take a genius to work out the location.'

Donald conceded his point. 'I was with my grandkids if you must know, two hours in a ball pit followed by chicken nuggets. My son split up with their mother last year, he's training security forces in Afghanistan. This is my way of keeping the home fires burning, if you like. Easy for them to forget who he is, if there's no one there to remind them, especially at that age.'

'So how did you find out?'

'I put my phone on charge the moment I got home. Picked up a raft of messages from you, the tenants who were moving in today and a couple of mates who had driven past and seen the police cordon. I went straight over to the flats but the cop on the door wouldn't let me in, said I had to speak to you lot first.' Ashcroft nodded. 'Thing is, none of it makes sense,' Donald added, 'I was only there last week, showing the lass around.'

'And there was nothing out of the ordinary?'

Donald pulled a face, 'There were no dead bodies lying around, if that's what you mean.' He studied Ashcroft. 'Is it true it's a kid? That's what my mate told me it'd said on the radio.'

Ashcroft nodded. 'I can't give you any more details than that I'm afraid,' though it wasn't as if there was much more to tell.

'Christ,' muttered Donald, 'I can't believe it.'

Ashcroft pulled out his notebook and biro. The end was chewed meaning he'd lent it to DS Coupland at some point. What was it with smokers and pens? 'Who was the flat previously let out to?' he asked.

'Dawn Tylor, but she left weeks ago. It's been lying empty.'

Ashcroft noted down her name, 'How come she left?'

'She'd got a promotion. Only a young thing too. Meant she had to move without giving proper notice but the pay rise she was getting meant she wasn't bothered about losing her deposit. I can get you her contact details if you like?'

Ashcroft nodded before leaning back in his chair while he waited.

'I don't mean now,' Donald said. 'I have them all in a file at home. I know I should go electronic, my son keeps taking the mickey out of me for still using a filing cabinet but it's the way I like it. I'll need to fax the details through to you when I get home.'

Ashcroft smiled. 'You can take a photo of the details with your phone, send them to me in a text.' Donald's brow knotted in confusion. 'Or maybe I can come by later and get them myself,' Ashcroft offered. Donald nodded, relieved.

'I'll need a list of all your residents, past and present, save me keep coming back.'

It wasn't the first time Donald had been in an interview room, Ashcroft guessed, given the lack of interest he showed in his surroundings. Usually first timers had a reaction, even if it was just blatant curiosity. 'So do you own any other properties in the area?'

'A few, here and there.'

'Nice,' Ashcroft commented, 'so what was your line of work then, before…'

'You mean how can someone who looks handy with their fists afford a property portfolio?'

'Something like that.'

'I've always worked with my hands, started out as a labourer. I'd missed out on college so ended up humping and carrying for the tradesmen. The pay was fine but it's a young man's game. I'd not been doing it for long when one of the other labourers approached me, said I looked like I could handle myself, told me there was money to be made in bare knuckle fighting. Turns out he was right. After a while I gave up labouring, well, for other people anyway. Started buying up old properties with my winnings, doing them up over time, sold a couple for profit then realised the real money was in rentals. After a while I didn't need to fight any more, had my own regular income coming in.'

'Didn't want your son to follow in your footsteps, though, considering bare knuckle fighting set you up,' Ashcroft asked, though it was more an observation.

Donald shuddered. 'You should see some of the faces that have taken over the fight scene now. If you don't throw a fight the way they want it they come after you, and they won't stop until they find you.' Donald looked onto the distance. 'Rather he was up against the Taliban.'

*

Coupland was keying in the access code to enter the staff-only area of the station when he caught the eye of a man waiting at the reception desk. The man looked familiar, although it took a few seconds to realise he was younger than he first appeared; his shoulders had a stoop to them that hadn't been present when they'd first met. His name was Peter Coombes, a 37-year-old truck driver from Swinton, father to Hannah, five, who'd gone missing 18 months earlier while out playing with her older sister. 'Want me to speak to him?' Alex offered but Coupland shook his head.

'I'll do it,' he said, doubling back the way he'd come, calling out to the desk sergeant that he'd got this.

'Peter,' he said as he drew level with Coombes, 'Let me buy you a coffee.' He nodded towards the main entrance but Peter was already shaking his head.

'I don't need a coffee DS Coupland, I just need our Hannah back.'

Coupland sighed. 'I know, Peter. Come on, I can't be dragged into a meeting if the powers that be can't find me. If we go sit somewhere out of sight I'm all yours.'

'Fine,' Peter said, although Coupland could tell he was anything but.

They went to the café closest to the station. It had been bought out not so long back, the owners trying to drag the place into the twenty-first century while not frightening off its regulars. The brass ornaments had been replaced by carefully positioned pieces of driftwood, the magnolia walls painted a nautical blue. A coffee machine stood pride of place behind the counter rendering the milk pan that had been permanently kept on the boil under the previous owner redundant. After giving their order to the guy behind the counter Coupland studied his companion. Peter Coombes been heavy set when his daughter had gone missing, by his own admission too many all-day breakfasts in roadside greasy spoons. One of the pitfalls of his job as a trucker, he'd claimed, was too much time on the road thinking about his next meal. Now the weight had dropped off him, leaving behind a husk of a man.

'It's been a while since I've seen you,' Coupland said, taking a seat beside him. 'How've you been?'

Peter blew out a sigh. 'How do you think?' He turned his head to study passers-by through the steamed-up window, 'Going through the motions…' He paused while their cappuccinos were placed in front of them, his hands automatically reaching for the sachets of sugar in the centre of the table, tearing at the paper while Coupland popped two sweeteners into his. 'Thing is you don't realise how much your world revolves around 'em, do you?' He turned to look at Coupland. 'Always said I'd never let being a dad get in the way of watching the match on a Saturday or playing five-a-side with the lads.' He made a sound then, a laugh with the joy sucked out. 'One look at those girls of mine and everything went out the window. I was smitten. Hook, line and bloody sinker.' Coupland nodded. 'Each one was like a stealth missile heading straight in my direction. I didn't stand a chance. Ballet, tap, I can't tell you the number of dance shows I've sat through, cheering them on and all the while Karen's digging me in the ribs, reminding me it's not a cup final.' He swiped at his face then, rough hands raking over pallid skin. He spent his days off work driving through the city, searching for a little girl in a Frozen sweatshirt and leggings. 'Poppy's given up her dancing, said it's not the same without her little sister. The only time she goes out is when I take her to her counselling sessions. Her school arranged it; we're hoping it helps with the guilt.'

Coupland stirred his drink for want of something to do. 'And Karen?' he asked. Peter shook his head, 'Karen's not coping, she says she is but she never went back to work. They were good to her, signed her off for six months but she couldn't go back… so now she sits at home and mopes. We can't afford the mortgage on my wages alone but she refuses to move in case Hannah finds her way back to us.'

Coupland pinched the bridge of his nose. It was unlikely Hannah Coombes would ever find her way home. She went missing the same time as two other little girls in Greater Manchester. The other girls had been abducted in two separate incidents, one while out shopping with her aunt, the other playing in her own front garden. Their killer, James Bullivant, was now behind bars, but although the date Hannah went missing tied in with these girls' murders, and evidence confirmed Bullivant was in the same location the day of her disappearance, he never admitted to abducting her, leaving her parents in a mental No Man's Land.

'We heard about that kiddie's body being found on the news DS Coupland. I promised Karen I wouldn't go home until I got an answer.'

'Once the DNA results come through we will check it against Hannah's, Peter, I promise. But you need to know that nothing I've seen so far leads me to think it is her.'

'You can't be sure though, 100 per cent sure I mean, can you, until her DNA is compared?'

'Not 100 per cent sure, no, but as I said before—'

'—If the bastard that had killed those other girls had taken her he'd have admitted it, wouldn't he? I mean, what has he got to lose?'

It was logical thinking, Coupland supposed, but that was where right-minded folk went wrong, trying to put logical thought into the actions of someone hell bent on causing pain.

'You know it's perverse in a way. Hannah was such a quiet little girl you wouldn't know she was there, even when she was right under your nose. Now that she's gone… her face is everywhere, even when I close my eyes… in a way she's more here than she ever was.'

Coupland swallowed, a vein in his neck pulsated with the rhythm in his chest.

'You promised Karen you'd find her, DS Coupland.' Peter's tone was harsher now, though his face still looked defeated.

'I know Peter, and Hannah's case is still open…' That bit was true, but with the certainty her killer was behind bars, the search for her body had been scaled down within months. The DCI's request for continued resourcing had been rejected. Coupland got to his feet. 'Look,' he said, 'I'm going to have to go, but I promise to call you the moment the DNA results come in, are you still on the same number?'

'No need, DS Coupland, like I said before, I told Karen I wouldn't go back home without news.' He waved at the waiter to bring another cappuccino over. 'When you've got something to tell me I'll still be here, I'm going bloody nowhere.'

CHAPTER SEVEN

Ashcroft could see Donald Riding hovering behind a curtain in a downstairs window as he parked his car outside the landlord's home in Clifton. The property was modest but well kept. A dormer-bungalow built in the seventies, new windows and a new front door gave the place a modern look. Neighbouring properties hadn't been so well cared for, the original features making them look dated. Donald's property benefitted from a single garage; an old jag was parked in front of it. He opened the front door as Ashcroft made his way up the garden path. The front lawn was gravelled; two large pots either side of a wooden bench. 'Not that I have time to sit on it,' Donald informed Ashcroft when he saw him glance at it.

'You've got the information for me, as agreed?' Ashcroft got straight to the point.

'Yeah, through here.' Donald showed him through a dark hallway into a large study. A desk sat centre stage in the room with a telephone and computer on top of it. The faux leather swivel chair behind it was well worn. There wasn't another chair in the room so Ashcroft leaned against a filing cabinet standing in one corner. 'These places are deceptive, bigger inside than you think,' he nodded.

'This used to be the dining room,' Donald informed him. 'I'm strictly a TV dinners kind of guy, now 'specially since the missus buggered off.'

He moved towards a shelving unit on the far wall and lifted off a box file, the label on the front of it read Ashdown Court. He placed the file on the desk before opening it. Inside there was a clear plastic pocket containing keys, each one labelled for flats one through to six. Behind it were several more plastic wallets, each one stuffed with yellowing record cards. On the front of each wallet a handwritten label stated which flat the record cards related to. Some wallets were thicker than others, Ashcroft noted, dismayed.

'Some flats appeal to short term renters,' Donald explained. 'They're less bothered about layout when it's all they can afford.' He cleared his throat. 'The new couple's details still need to be added, I only fill out the record cards once they've moved in, saves unnecessary paperwork if they change their mind.'

Ashcroft doubted the young couple would continue with their move into flat 2a, but said nothing. 'Let's start with the flat's previous tenants,' he prompted, 'see where we go from there?' He had a feeling they'd be there all night as it was.

Donald nodded, pulling out all the relevant cards and organising them into date order, giving Ashcroft a running commentary as particular names caught his eye. 'They were no trouble,' he said of one couple. 'Pair of idiots,' he said of another. 'Would have ended up with an ASBO if they hadn't gone back-packing.' One of the cards fell on the floor; he stooped to retrieve it, his lip curling when he saw the name on it. 'A right complainer that one, never paid on time either.' He stood them up on the desk, tapping them to straighten their edge like a croupier in a casino.

'Do you keep in touch with any of them?' Ashcroft enquired as he photographed each record card with his phone.

Donald gave him a funny look. 'Why would I?' he shrugged. 'I don't know where half of them have got to, care even less. I keep hold of their deposits until I'm satisfied everything is in order with the property. Some don't get any of their deposits back, but those that do, well it's all done by bank transfer, I don't need to get a forwarding address.'

'What about their mail?'

A shrug. 'What about it? If they haven't arranged a redirection it goes in the bin, what am I, the Post Office?'

Ashcroft kept his thoughts in check. He'd had countless landlords like Donald in his time, quick to pocket your rent, slow to carry out any repairs. Speaking of which… 'What about other people who have access to the property, tradesmen maybe?'

'I use the same firm for all my properties. Ryland's Maintenance Ltd. They bill me at the end of the month, much easier that way. I've got their contact details on my phone, would you like them?'

Ashcroft nodded, waiting for Donald to locate the firm in his contacts folder before copying them across to his smartphone. 'When did they last do any work there?'

Donald's mouth turned down at the corners. 'Coupla weeks ago, a radiator needed replacing in the top floor flat.'

'You don't try and do any of the repairs yourself?'

Donald gave him a strange look. 'Why have a dog and bark yourself? Besides,' he added grudgingly, 'I'm not as agile as I used to be…'

'You give them a key?'

'Yes, how else are they going to get in? Tenants don't like sitting around these days; if they don't have heating I'm abusing their human rights, so I'm told.'

Donald wasn't as attentive as he liked to make out. How else would a child's body lie undiscovered in one of his flats, bag or no bag? 'You obviously didn't do an inventory after the previous tenant left. Was there a reason for that?'

Donald looked cagey. 'She'd paid me to the end of the month, why should I care what she left in there?' He clocked the scowl forming on Ashcroft's dark features. 'I don't mean like that, obviously, I just mean the flat was hers to do what she wanted with until the expiry of the lease.'

'End of the month?' Ashcroft cocked an eyebrow. 'But it's only the 20th, and you had new tenants moving in already, no doubt after paying their deposit in cash and a month's rent up front.'

Donald was keen to defend himself. 'The girl, Ali, wanted to move in pronto, she kept texting me asking if they could get their hands on the keys any earlier, I think once she'd got her fella to commit she wanted to seal the deal and batten him in, so to speak. I said I'd check with the previous tenant, I couldn't reach her on the number she'd given me so I thought…'

'Here was a chance for you to make a quick buck collecting two rents on the same flat and HMRC need never know about it.'

Donald's face soured. 'I wouldn't quite put it like that,' he sulked.

'I'm sure you wouldn't.' Ashcroft tapped his finger

on the pile of record cards now the most recent tenant had been placed in front. 'So what can you tell me about this woman?' He leaned forward to read the name clearly. 'Dawn Tylor, you told me back at the station she was the last tenant to occupy the flat.'

Donald nodded. 'Well she was a peach.' His eyes gleamed as he folded thick arms across his chest. 'Very easy on the eye if you know what I mean… but business-like. A bit brisk some would say but she never caused me any trouble. Shame she moved out in a way, tenants like that are like gold dust. For all her good looks and fancy job, I never saw her with a fella, though I'm pretty sure there must have been one.'

'Why?'

'Well,' a gleam came into Donald's eye as some memory flashed before him, 'there was this one time…'

*

Alex found Coupland standing on the top step outside the station's fire exit, flicking through his notebook as he smoked a cigarette. 'Thought you'd be here, why can't you use the smoking shelter like everyone else?'

'Force of habit,' he shrugged, his cigarette bobbing up and down between his lips as he spoke.

She stood a couple of steps down from him, out of the trajectory the coil of smoke was taking. 'How did you get on with Peter Coombes?'

Coupland glanced up from his notebook. 'Said I'd let him know results of the DNA test the moment they come in.'

'Do you think it could be Hannah?'

Coupland folded the corner of the page he was looking

at down, returning his notebook to his breast pocket. 'No chance.' He shook his head. 'Apart from anything, they were dark curls inside that sports bag. Hannah Coombes had ginger hair.'

'Had,' Alex repeated. 'You think she's dead, then?'

'Course she's dead and James Bullivant killed her. Come on, Alex, that bastard was a pathological liar. You could catch him pissing in your pocket and he'd say it wasn't him. He took her and he killed her, we just haven't found her yet.'

Alex let out a long breath, 'I know you're right, it's just that I've seen Peter driving around so often looking for her, I've started to hope no news is good news. His optimism rubs off, that's all.'

'Misplaced hope, more like,' Coupland muttered, stubbing his cigarette out on the wall and placing the butt in his pocket. He was about to step inside when Alex spoke up.

'What else is bugging you Kevin?' Further attempts at coaxing him into a conversation during their drive back to the station had fallen flat. He'd always been prickly but he was different somehow. He'd changed while she'd been away, or maybe she'd just forgotten how to connect with him. She wondered what Ashcroft would do, he'd partnered Coupland during her maternity leave, had borne the brunt of it when Coupland's daughter had been abducted. Maybe he could give her a crash course in handling her old buddy. She made a mental note to have a word, but not before she had one last try. Steeling herself, she took a deep breath. 'Come on, are you going to tell me what's bugging you or are you hell bent on letting your blood pressure rocket till you keel over?'

Coupland stopped in his tracks, swivelling round so they were face to face once more. 'Charmin', and statements like that are meant to do me the power of good I suppose?'

Alex let out a sigh. 'I'm serious, Kevin, one day back and I'm starting to really worry about you.'

Coupland's face darkened. 'Don't bother. Not like there's anything you can do…' His blue eyes flashed with a rage so intense she wondered how the hell he was controlling it. Then she remembered the state of his knuckles. 'Kevin?' She waited as he wrestled with whatever demon was troubling him. He was so lost for words she reckoned she'd have to drag every last one out of him.

From his vantage point on the steps he could see the entrance to the shopping centre below. Truants making their way towards the bus stop, puffing away on cigarettes he'd only aspired to at that age. How come each generation felt an entitlement to better things? And who the hell determined they were better? When he left school all he'd wanted was a secure job, a home of his own and one day, if he was lucky, a family. Young men these days wanted to be club DJs, or in a boy band, driving round in sports cars hooking up with girls who took selfies of themselves pouting. Then again, maybe he hadn't got it so right after all, the way things were panning out.

'Kevin?' Alex's voice brought him back to the present. She sounded cautious. Coupland swiped a hand over his face. His throat had shut tight, strangling the words.

'Amy told me last night that she's pregnant,' he managed. He closed his eyes and let out a breath.

'Ah…' Alex reached out and touched his battered fist

with her hand. It was clenched so tight she could feel the pulse beating beneath his skin. Coupland was protective of his daughter. Resented the fact she was all grown up. Alex wasn't aware she even had a boyfriend; she certainly hadn't said anything when Alex had called in to see them while still on leave. Everyone had been so raw after the incident with… It took a moment for the penny to drop.

'Oh my God, no,' she groaned, 'not Lee Dawson?'

Coupland didn't need to answer. The stoop of his shoulders confirmed she was right. Christ. 'I don't know what to say, Kevin,' she confessed.

'And that's the bloody problem!' Coupland raged. 'My first grandchild should be something I want to shout from the rooftops, but I can't.' His phone started ringing in his pocket but he ignored it. His seventeen-year-old daughter. Pregnant. He could barely think the words let alone say them out loud. But it was worse than that. This wasn't any old pregnancy; a bun in the oven by some young buck he'd have to give a talking to before he marched them up the aisle. This was the mother of all fates conspiring against him. Lee Dawson was the serial killer who had stalked the streets of Salford avenging his father's imprisonment twenty-five years before. He'd tracked down Coupland's daughter, began dating her to teach him a lesson.

'All this because I arrested him for assault just before his dad died.'

'Nobody could've foreseen that. You didn't even know who he was.'

Dawson refused to accept that and had been hell bent on killing Amy, would've succeeded if Coupland had taken one minute longer to find them. He felt sick to his stomach at the memory of it.

'Dawson's been dead—' Alex did the sums.

'—four months,' Coupland spat. 'Amy's six months gone. She tried hiding it for as long as she could. She'd stopped eating at one point, and it was only when Lynn threatened to take her to the doctors that she confided in her, made her promise not to say anything to me until she'd made her mind up about what she wanted to do. Lynn tried keeping it to herself of course, but she's a lousy liar, I could see she was hiding something from me. I thought her cancer had come back…' His voice cracked as he said this. He glared at the sky above, as though he'd claw the clouds from it if he could, 'I wondered for weeks if I was going to lose her, thought she was trying to spare me.' A grudging laugh escaped from him, leaving a bitter taste behind.

Alex studied the set of his jaw, wondered what the hell she could say to make any of it better. 'So isn't this a good thing then,' she tried, 'after the cancer I mean, isn't a new life a blessing?'

Coupland's head reared back, his eyes blazing into hers. 'Don't you bloody well start!' he warned. 'There's no happy ending here, alright?'

Alex didn't flinch. She'd worked alongside him for too long to be chastened by a few sharp words. He might be able to hold his own in some dark alley but right now he needed someone in his corner, whether he realised it or not. 'This baby's coming with or without your blessing, Kevin. OK, I get that you've not been given much time to get your head around it but it's not your life that's going to change, it's Amy's.' That wasn't true and they both knew it. Amy was a teenager, soon to become a single mum. Coupland and his wife were doting parents, they'd want to shoulder the strain, make preparations for the baby, help Amy as much as possible. Of course their life would change. 'You're just going to have to suck it up.'

Coupland stared at her in astonishment. With his bulk came the privilege of few people talking back to him. Alex had never needed to before, they were usually on the same wavelength, and Lynn, well Lynn could do what she bloody well wanted, he loved the bones of her. He stayed silent as Alex continued, 'What you have to decide now is how you're going to deal with it.'

That was easy. 'If Dawson wasn't dead already I'd kill him,' Coupland said, but there was no humour in it.

CHAPTER EIGHT

Krispy looked up as Coupland and Alex returned to the incident room. 'Anything you want to feed back following your visits to the doctors' surgeries? I'm just updating my spreadsheet.'

Coupland avoided Alex's eye as he responded, confirming the surgery visits had been completed. Krispy clicked onto his spreadsheet and updated the form, oblivious to Coupland's discomfort. 'All good, both kiddies accounted for,' Coupland answered gruffly, 'although there was something about the GP at the last surgery…' That may have been because she walked into a brawl in the waiting room, though Coupland wasn't about to own up to that. 'Might need to go back and see her. Clear up a few things.'

'So I'll leave that action open, Sarge?'

Coupland nodded, clocking Alex's worried look but ignoring it.

Ashcroft was typing up a list of Ashdown Court's past and present tenants. 'I'll contact all the recent leavers by phone first thing, but first I want to see Flat 2a's previous tenant, the landlord thinks she had some mystery fella on the go.'

'You need to go out and see them all,' Coupland cut in.

'Why?' Ashcroft furrowed his brow.

'Because one of them could have kept a key.'

'The landlord was pretty meticulous about that—'

'—Had spare ones cut then,' Coupland said irritably, 'and because I said so. Anything's possible at this stage, you should know that.' Ashcroft shot a look at Alex who shook her head in reply as though warning him not to push it. It seemed he was no better at handling Coupland after all. But then, with Amy's pregnancy hanging over him…

'Come on. It's been a long shift,' she cajoled, 'I think we could all do with some decent shut eye. Let's call it a day, eh?' She looked over at Coupland who nodded reluctantly.

The desk sergeant looked up as they walked through the reception area. 'DCI Mallender's been looking for you, said you hadn't been answering your phone.'

Coupland let out a sigh. 'You haven't seen me, OK?'

'But I have,' said a familiar voice behind him.

Coupland pursed his lips, 'You go on,' he said to Alex and Ashcroft, 'I'll see you tomorrow.' He turned to greet the DCI, 'Sorry, boss,' he said, throwing his hands up in mitigation, 'been a long day.'

'And it's about to get longer,' said Mallender with no preamble. 'Just had the head of Salford's Children and Families Division on the phone to complain about the officer riding roughshod over the city's most vulnerable families.'

'Well I know DC Robinson can get a bit excitable, but I've every confidence—'

'—It wasn't his demeanour she was complaining about,' Mallender cut in, 'rather that he was there at all.'

'I told him to check the kids on the at-risk register are all present and correct. How else can we be sure they are OK?'

'By going through the proper channels – and by that she means her – and asking for a social worker to accompany him on emergency welfare checks, to avoid any unnecessary unpleasantness.'

Coupland rocked back on his heels. 'Oh well, pardon me for causing offence to some hairy-arsed bruiser or scummy mummy.'

'I don't need the wisecracks, Coupland, and I'm sure you don't want the complaint escalating to Superintendent Curtis.'

Coupland's shoulders sagged. 'How did she find out?'

'Two of the families Robinson called on complained direct to their social worker when he left. Said they felt their privacy had been violated. The third wouldn't let him in, made him wait on the doorstep while they made a call to check he was who he said he was. Only they didn't ring the number on the card he gave them, they rang the duty social worker who reported it up the chain to her boss who rang me. Robinson was refusing to leave apparently, said he'd been told to wait until he'd eyeballed each child on his list.'

'He was following my order,' Coupland admitted. 'Robinson was guilty of nothing other than doing as he was told.'

'I called Robinson myself, seeing as you weren't answering your phone, told him to stand down and to hot foot it to the council offices, apologise for setting off half-cocked and throw himself on his sword. With any luck a social work chaperone will be sorted out for him first thing tomorrow, although the head honcho wasn't promising anything.'

'I'm sure she bloody wasn't,' Coupland sighed.

Why would she, the way the day was turning out?

Coupland's phone pinged as he threw his jacket onto the back seat of his car. The sound it made signalled a new email had landed in his inbox. Normally he'd ignore it, anything urgent would come via control. Besides, anyone who knew him would call or send him a text, at least give him a heads up to check his mail. He paused, remembering Peter Coombes was sitting in a café waiting to find out if the dead little girl in the bag was his daughter or not. Coupland retrieved his phone from his jacket pocket and clicked on the message. It was from the lab. The test results comparing DNA taken from the victim with saved DNA from girls matching the victim's age on the list MISPER had provided had come back negative. It wasn't Hannah Coombes lying in the mortuary. It was what he expected. She was still dead; he had no doubt in his mind about that. She was murdered at the same time as those other two girls; her remains just hadn't been discovered. The result was no more than a temporary reprieve from the inevitable. For the life of him Coupland didn't know if the information he was about to impart to Hannah's father was good or bad news. He promised Peter he'd update him the moment he had anything to tell. He'd also promised he'd find his daughter. He could at least make good on one of them. He slammed his car door shut, bleeping it locked. Shoulders squared, Coupland turned and headed in the direction of the café.

*

Lynn was working day shift, wouldn't finish till seven. So when Coupland stepped into the Victorian semi they shared, instead of cooking smells he was greeted with the thump, thump, thump of music blaring from Amy's room. Justin something or other, he knew that much, whether Bieber or Timberlake he couldn't be sure. He threw his jacket over the bannister, hovering at the bottom of the stairs. He could go up and speak to Amy, take advantage of Lynn being out. If it ended in a shouting match she'd never need to know. He stepped onto the bottom step then hesitated. How come he could stare down ten balloon-heads at closing time but one wrong look from his daughter turned his insides to jelly? It had been that way from the moment he'd clapped eyes on her, that first time in the delivery room when she'd opened her eyes and stared at him, as though wondering at the hand she'd been dealt being saddled with him as a father.

And now she was having a child of her own. That part she was clear on. She was keeping it. She was staying here too, Lynn was adamant about that. Amy hadn't been back to the midden she'd shared with Lee Dawson since the day he'd tried to kill her. It was Coupland who'd packed up her things once forensics had given the all clear. Seemed he was good enough for something, then. Truth was, he didn't want a row. All he wanted was to scoop his daughter up and tell her it was going to be OK. Only he wasn't sure it could be.

There were a couple of beers left in the fridge so he helped himself to one. He scanned the mail that had been left on the kitchen table. Take away fliers, leaflets introducing candidates for the local elections; he cast a cynical eye over their word limited manifestos. 'How about "I won't let you down, fiddle my expenses or fool around with my PA." that'd get my vote.' He tossed the junk mail into the bin and reached for the TV remote control. Avoiding anything that resembled news he skipped through the channels: couples buying homes abroad, others building dream homes from scratch, a team of builders converting an ex-serviceman's terraced house while he was away. He settled on a detective drama; Christ knows he needed a laugh. He'd seen an earlier episode in the series; the female lead had chased a thug down a tower block stairwell in platform shoes. Alex would have something to say about that. On shows like these lab results came back in a matter of minutes, and overtime was never in question. The biggest lie of all though, the one guaranteed to get his goat, was that they always got their man. In this episode someone was bumping off sex workers. The drama would conclude tomorrow night. Coupland whistled. A two-hour clear-up rate; Superintendent Curtis would wet himself.

He sipped his beer while thinking about getting a meal ready for when Lynn got back. He'd have ordered a takeaway but she would purse her lips; the deal during the week was they behaved themselves; treats like take-aways and booze were reserved solely for the weekend. He looked down at his beer guiltily; decided his best bet was to destroy the evidence. He gulped it down, slipping out to the side of the house to throw the can into the dustbin. Lynn was on at them to recycle, so far he'd managed to head her off. The only people that stood to gain were bin manufacturers, he said often enough, and so their collection of multi-coloured tubs stood empty by the back door, like badly behaved children outside the head teacher's room. Coupland padded back into the kitchen. There was nothing edible in the fridge, unless you counted fish and salad. A smile flickered on his lips.

He returned to the foot of the stairs. 'Fancy home-made chips?' he shouted.

Amy's head appeared Meerkat-like around the door. 'What's Mum going to say?'

'Your Mam'll love it because she can blame me. As long as she's got an excuse when she goes to Weight-watchers she's OK.'

Amy grinned. 'I'll be down in a few minutes, then.'

*

Lynn was more amenable than he expected, reaching for a bottle of red despite his half-hearted protest that it wasn't Friday. 'Been a hell of a day, Kev,' she said, which meant they'd lost one. They didn't go into detail about their work when they were home, unless it was good news; for Lynn that was when a pre-term baby started feeding independently. For him it was each time a nasty bastard was locked in a cell. On good days she would be full of talk about miracle babies discharged early because they were thriving. On bad days their conversations were full of euphemisms, especially when Amy was around, a way of shielding her from the fickle hand of Fate. 'Caught the news on the way home,' Lynn said, pouring them both a glass, 'reckon you'll be glad of this too.'

Coupland took the glass appreciatively. Another beer would be better but he didn't want to rock the boat. He swirled the contents of the glass around, not because he wanted to check its quality, but it was a way of making the drink last longer, something to do with the glass other than gulp at it. He took a sip, sighed contentedly, 'Just the job, that.' He peered at the deep fat fryer, the chips were browning nicely. He lifted the frying pan from a cupboard beside the cooker. Poured in some oil.

'Fancy an egg?'

Lynn's eyes crinkled in the corners. 'You know how to show a girl a good time,' she smiled, laying out place mats and cutlery. They moved about the kitchen in companionable silence.

'Makes you think, doesn't it?' she observed.

Coupland, who'd been thinking of nothing more than salty chips between two slices of thick buttered bread, furrowed his brow. Had he not been listening again? Tuning out all around him bar his own simple thoughts. No dead child tonight. No plastic evidence bag containing a crusty hair clip. He'd showered before Lynn got back but he knew it would be a long time before the smell of the post mortem receded. Happy thoughts. That's what he craved. A simple life. Chips and bread and fried eggs on the side. He cocked his head as he turned to face her. 'I don't get you,' he said with caution. But they both knew that he did.

'Every child is a blessing, Kevin,' she faltered, 'it won't be long before the baby's born, we need to start making plans.'

Coupland's shoulders dipped. 'Do we have to?' He caught the look that flitted across her face, causing him to hurry on, 'I'm sorry love but it's hard to get excited about choosing a bloody pram when you've spent the day contemplating the mind-set of a sick bastard.'

Lynn flinched when he swore; she'd tried over the years to get him to stop but on this he wouldn't be moved. He'd never been a scholar; his vocabulary mirrored the circles in which he moved: the shocking and those in shock. 'Bloody' and 'fuck' seemed to sum his days up pretty well.

'I mean longer term plans, Kev,' she clarified.

Coupland's smile faded. 'Looks like all the plans have been made without me,' he said, 'I'm just the poor shmuck that has to pay for it all.'

Lynn huffed out a breath, 'And me, Kev, I work hard too.'

Coupland hung his head, 'I know that… but what I don't know is what you want from me…'

Lynn moved closer, her voice lowering as she nodded at the ceiling above them. 'She wants you to accept what's happened, Kev, so she can start to look forward to this baby. So we all can. All she feels at the moment is that she's let you down.'

'She could never let me down!' Coupland growled. 'It's not her fault she got involved with an evil—'

'—no, but it's her decision to keep his baby. That's what you're blaming her for.'

Coupland didn't answer. He turned the heat off under the eggs and switched off the deep fat fryer. The food was ready but he feared the conversation still had some way to go. He lifted three plates out of an overhead cupboard; turning his back on Lynn he placed them one by one on the counter top.

'She says you look at her differently now.'

'Jesus wept!' he sighed, lifting the chips from the fryer and giving them a shake before distributing a mountain onto each plate. 'I've only just found out!' He thought some more. 'Can you blame me though? Keeping schtum all this time while lumbering about with Damien up her jumper.'

'Kev!' Lynn's warning was too late.

Coupland spun round in time to see Amy standing

in the middle of the kitchen, staring at him. Eyes that normally made him melt now cut him dead. 'Amy!' he said urgently as she turned on her heel. He stared at Lynn, shame crawling across his face, 'Tell me she didn't hear that,' he pleaded, but he already knew the truth of it. Lynn glared back at him, not saying a word. She didn't need to. He already felt like a prize idiot, a lumbering bull in a fragile china shop. He charged out of the room after his daughter, swallowing hard as though in some way he could take back what he'd said. 'I didn't mean it love!' he called after her but it was too late. Amy had reached her bedroom but instead of slamming the door in his face she stood in the doorway, waiting while he climbed the stairs, regarding him the same way the owner of a new pair of shoes might regard vomit on the pavement.

'The trouble is we both know you did,' she said before closing the door.

The temperature in the kitchen had plummeted several degrees. 'You hypocrite,' Lynn accused him in a steely voice. She stood facing him; her hands gripping onto the work surface either side of her. Already her knuckles were white.

Coupland shut his eyes; he was in no mood for a lecture. 'What?' he asked through gritted teeth before opening them again.

'You heard me! You swan about at work, pulling out all the stops for a murdered child but won't acknowledge your own flesh and blood. What kind of a man are you?' Coupland looked away; he'd been trying to work out the answer to that for years.

'How can I love it after what its father did?' he shouted. There, he'd said it. There was no taking *that* back.

'I loved you, didn't I?' she stormed.

'That was different; my Dad wasn't a bloody serial killer!'

'No, but your old man was a bully! He soured you, made you wary, a real dark cloud at a picnic but I saw beyond that. Yes, he shaped you, but into someone who knew how *not* to behave towards the people they care about. He was your warning, Kevin, and you listened to it then, why are you not heeding it now?'

Because Amy's life was ruined and there was nothing he could do about it. The baby's father was a killer. Truth be told the baby's grandad was a killer too, given Coupland had let Lee Dawson plummet from the car park roof, hadn't lifted a finger to try to save him.

'With him of all people, though, love?' he pleaded, 'Why did she choose *him*?'

Lynn blew out a long sigh, 'She didn't know what he was going to do when she fell for him, did she? None of us do. It's not her fault.' Knowing that didn't make it any easier. Coupland's shoulders sagged. All he felt was shame. Shame that he hadn't been able to keep his family safe. Evil had penetrated - literally - its very core. And that was the crux of it. Everyone would know he had failed.

As a cop.

As a father.

As a man.

And this child would remind him of that failure day, after day, after day.

'I pictured a wedding, Lynn, nothing fancy, granted, but a church at least, me walking her up the aisle grumbling over the cost, you in a daft hat and shoes you can't walk in. Instead we're picking out a buggy to wheel Beelzebub round in.'

Lynn slammed her hand down hard on the kitchen counter, her eyes black like coal, 'Every child matters, Kevin.'

'Even one with horns?'

Lynn looked away then, and he knew in that instant he'd overstepped the mark, raked up insecurities she'd long since buried. That they'd both shied away from. 'I think I'll sleep in the spare room tonight,' she said, voice quiet as the grave. She turned then, walked quietly out of the room. He looked down at his hands, serving up a dinner no one would bother to eat. Useless hands. He turned them over staring at his grazed knuckles. He thought he'd saved Amy from that maniac that night; truth was he was already too late.

He retrieved his wine glass from the kitchen table, was about to take a swig from it then changed his mind, hurling it against the back wall. It exploded, raining shards of glass onto the tiled floor. Red wine sprayed across the wall like an arterial bleed.

DAY TWO

CHAPTER NINE

Morning briefing.

Coupland was in early. He was wearing last night's clothes but the look on his face warned anyone who noticed his casual attire to keep any wisecracks to themselves. His sweatshirt was creased to buggery, a fitful night spent diagonal across his bed, hoping that Lynn would change her mind and creep into their room in the middle of the night. He'd wanted her to disturb him, so he could say how sorry he was, that he hadn't meant what he'd said. He was a prize idiot and he knew it. Only she didn't come in, so at daft o'clock he'd gone into the bathroom, splashed water on his face and slipped out of the house, too shamefaced to go into the kitchen to see the damage he'd caused. And to think Lynn said he was nothing like his father. Who was she trying to kid?

He cast his gaze over the detectives assembled before him. Some seated, some standing, clutching paper coffee cups they'd bought at the coffee shop around the corner, not yet ready to unleash the vending machine gloop onto their innards until it was absolutely necessary. He wouldn't quite say bright eyed and bushy tailed – they had chosen the wrong career for that – but all looked as though they'd had a better night than he had. Alex sat beside him, just beyond his line of vision, but he didn't need to look at her to know she was studying him. Three cups of coffee had made him antsy. He paced as his team filled him in on progress. A full-blown search had been carried out on the immediate vicinity, all debris bagged and tagged for the CSIs to comb through. Door-to-door enquiries had produced the best part of bugger all. He jabbed his finger on the photo of the sport bag on the incident board. 'This little mite had gone without food. She'd been drugged. Someone wanted a docile child, yet she wasn't sexually assaulted.' *Yet*, every bone in his body screamed.

Each time his eye caught a member of the team they looked away. Par for the course when no one had made a breakthrough. Ashcroft sat back in his chair, arm stretched over the one beside it. 'Maybe they were building up to it, Sarge,' he offered, reading his thoughts.

'Maybe,' Coupland conceded, 'but let's not get ahead of ourselves, let's deal with the evidence as it is. She wasn't sexually assaulted. So why else would someone drug a child?'

'To keep them quiet, to make them amenable with strangers,' suggested Ashcroft.

'So, she was held by someone she didn't know...'

'Which suggests family members are in the clear—' Which took him back to the number one question eating away at him, '—so why the hell haven't they reported her missing?' Ashcroft shook his head. Robinson, beside him, took sly bites out of a teacake.

'I heard you had your gonads handed to you on a plate yesterday.'

Robinson swallowed quickly and sat up straighter in his chair. 'A complete neutering, Sarge,' he nodded. '"Protocol's there for a reason," yada, yada, "but on this occasion," yada yada...Anyway, top and bottom of it is, the head of Children and Families is willing to overlook our lack of joined-up working and has arranged for me to meet with a senior member of her team this morning.'

Coupland bit back a response. His rank made him a role model even though he seldom felt like one; if he bitched and moaned about every jobsworth that made his job that little bit harder he'd create a bunch of anarchists. Instead he smiled over at Alex. 'That case review you're working on? Make sure you're just as thorough about the protocol social work followed before Michael Roberts wound up dead.'

'With bells on,' she nodded.

Coupland turned back to Robinson. 'I want two of you assigned to this, just so's there's no *he said, she said* discrepancies later.' The seat beside Robinson was empty. 'Where is Turnbull anyway?'

Just then DC Turnbull hurried into the room, head down, avoiding eye contact, clipboard clutched under his arm. Coupland's mouth hung open. 'W-what?' Turnbull stammered. A blush swept across hamster-like cheeks as everyone took in his electric blue suit. 'Thought it was time to update my wardrobe, that's all.'

'Is that so?' Coupland shot back. 'Where did you get it?'

'You know that clothes shop on Pendlebury Road? They've started doing menswear.'

Coupland sniggered, 'That's it. You and me'll go round there this morning and I'll knock seven bells out of 'em for breaking trading standards.'

Turnbull pouted. 'It's all the rage in Milan, Sarge.'

'For good reason. The blokes over there are trim and tanned, can carry off that colour no problem. You on the other hand, my friend, are wiry and wan.'

Krispy stifled a giggle.

'Ah, nice of you to volunteer getting me another brew,' Coupland boomed, giving the young DC the benefit of his full beam smile. Blushing, Krispy headed in the direction of the vending machine, patting his pockets for loose change. As the door of the CID room closed behind him Coupland turned his attention back to Turnbull, any hint of good humour forgotten. 'Grown-ups shouldn't row in front of the kids,' his voice was low, menacing, 'but you show up late to my briefing again and you'll have a bruise up your backside that matches that faux Italian get-up perfectly.' Turnbull blanched. Coupland returned to the photograph on the board. 'Let's spend a minute thinking about why the hell we're here: someone starved, drugged and hit a little girl so hard the side of her head caved in.' He paused, letting his words hit home. 'Come on, people, give me something.'

'The landlord reckons the previous tenant had a secret lover on the go,' Ashcroft piped up, before adding, 'said he was on her landing when she opened the door to her flat wearing nothing but a smile.'

'What was he doing creeping about on the landing?' Coupland asked.

'Someone on the floor below had complained of a leak, he was checking out the flat directly above,' Ashcroft consulted his notes, 'the flat he was checking on is rented by a Jimmy Rawlings.'

'I've had the pleasure,' drawled Coupland.

'She moved out in a hurry too, didn't seem bothered about losing her deposit.'

'Maybe you were right yesterday, make Dawn Tylor

your priority. Why was she in such a hurry to leave? And who was the fella she was expecting to see that night?' Coupland paused as he looked around the room, acknowledging Krispy's return with his coffee with a nod. 'Ok, we've got a lot of bloody work to do. I want names on this board,' he stabbed a finger in the centre of the whiteboard, with the sports bag and its grisly contents on show, 'tenants, visitors and anyone else we need to trace, investigate and eliminate.' He nodded at Alex. 'I'm off to see the boss, can you allocate actions to anyone who doesn't have enough to do,' his gaze rested on Turnbull as he said this, 'and for Christ's sake people let today be the day we find out this little girl's name.'

*

DCI Mallender was back in his usual attire, smart suit with a fresh pressed crease down the front of his trousers. He regarded Coupland as he entered his office, his gaze travelling over the sergeant's dishevelled clothing. Coupland had shaved before the briefing, but had done so hunched over his desk as he'd re-read the post mortem report, so there were patches he'd missed that he was oblivious to. 'Problem?' Mallender asked, 'only you look like you've been up all night.'

'Me?' Coupland scoffed. 'Slept like a baby.' The DCI raised an eyebrow but didn't comment. Coupland perched on the empty chair opposite Mallender's desk, in readiness to make a run for it if the questions got more challenging. He brought him up to speed. 'DC Ashcroft is working through a list of previous tenants and anyone else who had access to Ashdown Court. Robinson and Turnbull are carrying out welfare checks on children on the at-risk register with a social worker provided by your new best friend at Children and Families, and I'm going back to the apartment block with Alex to interview the current tenants.'

Mallender nodded his approval, 'How many are there?'

'Six flats including the one the young couple were moving into who found the body. They're staying with her family for now, though I doubt they'll be in any hurry to move in.'

Mallender grunted his agreement, handing Coupland a stack of paper files from his desk. 'These are from the door-to-door carried out yesterday, I know nothing significant was thrown up but check through them anyway and see if there's anything we can follow up.' Coupland tucked them under one arm as he got to his feet.

'Hang on, Kevin,' said Mallender, tapping on his computer keypad as he consulted the screen. He wrote something onto a pad beside it. 'Have you remembered that appraisals are due in this week?'

Coupland didn't blink. 'Contrary to belief I do read my emails you know.'

Mallender raised an eyebrow. 'And have you done anything about them?'

'Most of 'em done already.'

'Most?'

'See, that surprised you, didn't it? Nothing to it if you follow the template that was attached.'

'That was just an example, Kevin, to show you what a typical appraisal should look like.'

'And that's what you'll be getting from me, boss, a typical appraisal for each member of the team.'

The DCI's shoulders dipped as he regarded his

sergeant. 'They're all going to look the same, aren't they?'

Coupland baulked. 'I wouldn't go as far as to say that, boss, but there will be some similarities between them, I'm sure.'

Mallender sighed. 'Just make sure you spend some time with DC Timmins. If you cut and paste a rookie's appraisal, human resources will be onto you like a shot.'

Coupland kept his face straight as he turned to go. 'Krispy will get five-star motivational treatment, boss, on that you have my word.'

He almost made it to the door when Mallender called after him. 'Oh, before I forget, I need to carry out a return to work meeting with Alex this week, how's she settling back in?'

Coupland thought carefully as he considered this. One day under her belt and she'd already read him the riot act, talked their way out of a tense situation with a notorious crime boss, and stopped him from flattening a toe rag whose daughter he'd nearly run over. 'Like she's never been away, boss,' he concluded, his Cheshire cat grin splitting his face in two, 'like she's never been away.'

*

The social worker was a harassed-looking black woman with corn rowed hair gathered into a bun at the base of her head. Almond shaped eyes and an angular nose. Full painted lips that smiled despite the task ahead. Turnbull and Robinson had arranged to meet her outside the council's Children's Services building and they'd arrived early to find her waiting on the pavement clutching a file, looking very apprehensive. She wore a multi coloured coat, collar turned up against the cold. 'Shola Dube,' she said, arm outstretched to shake the hand Turnbull offered as he stepped out of the pool car, nodding as Robinson introduced them both, reiterating what her boss had told him yesterday during his castration. 'You need to understand this isn't a finite exercise, detectives, these children move up and down a spectrum of neglect or abuse hour by hour, it's impossible to be certain who are genuinely at-risk.' Her accent was clipped, precise, as though she'd learned English from British Pathé news reels, or old documentaries on the royal family.

Turnbull smiled at her jovially. It was what he did best, sometimes gave the impression he didn't have much upstairs but he prided himself on playing the long game. He was still smarting after his dressing down from DS Coupland. The bollocking had been over the top in his view, couldn't think when he'd been late in before. 'No, I get it,' he said amiably, 'I take my hat off to you lot – social workers, I mean,' he added hastily, smarting as Shola's gaze swept over him as though assessing the provenance of his suit. He tugged self-consciously at his sleeves which were a touch shorter than he was comfortable with.

Robinson walked round to the rear passenger door, held it open. 'Sooner we get started the better, eh?' he said, glancing at his watch.

Shola Dube wouldn't budge. 'What I'm saying is that placing any child on a child protection plan is very much a last resort and is only done when there are serious concerns about the child's welfare.'

Robinson swallowed down a sigh, 'I get that...'

'A child protection plan allows the council to work more intensively with the family to deal with whatever issues are of concern.'

Robinson stole a glance at Turnbull whose shrug seemed to say 'I haven't a bloody clue, mate.' His smiled faltered. 'Am I missing something here?' He'd endured the lecture from the head of Children and Families Division yesterday precisely so they could crack on today, he didn't need another one.

A pained look flashed across Shola's face. 'Just remember we can't tell you accurately how many children are experiencing abuse. We work with the children who have been identified as needing support or protection. It's likely there are others out there we don't know about yet.' Sombre facts.

'I get what you're saying, Ms Dube, this list isn't exhaustive. We know that, but we've got to start somewhere.'

'Don't you mean 'suffering abuse?' Turnbull asked. He was a man of few words, preferring most of the time to sit on Robinson's coat tails, let him do the talking for both of them, though it didn't prevent him from taking everything in.

Shola regarded him sharply, 'Sorry?'

'You refer to these children as experiencing abuse, like some people might experience joy, but isn't abuse, or neglect for that matter, something you suffer?'

'You say potato, I say shut the fuck up,' Robinson muttered under his breath as he ushered Shola into the car. It was going to be a long day if the partners riding shotgun with him were at loggerheads. He regarded the social worker in his rearview mirror. 'We understand your position, Ms Dube,' he began, trying to smooth ruffled feathers, 'but we have an unidentified little girl in the mortuary and we have to start somewhere. And our boss wants visual confirmation on each kid on this list or he'll come and do the visits himself. And trust me, you wouldn't want that.'

Shola Dube sighed. 'There are seventeen little girls that meet your criteria, detectives. All I ask is that you prepare yourselves for the day ahead, and try not to get involved emotionally.' Turnbull shared a look with his partner. Easier said than done when the photo that loomed from the incident board was a little girl's husk crammed into a bag and your sergeant's plea for a result ringing in your ears.

*

'So what's with the crumpled clothes, then?'

Coupland had only been in the pool car two minutes, not yet long enough for the heating system to kick in. Condensation had made the car windows steam up, obscuring the outside world through a mist. It suited Coupland's mood, preferable to seeing life in miserable sharp focus. He sighed, his large bulk deflating. 'Not again…' He'd managed to deflect Alex's question before morning briefing, ignoring the raised eyebrow in response to him playing deaf and dumb. What was it with women and their endless need to get to the bottom of things, poke their noses into problems better left alone? A bloke would have clocked his creased clothes and said nothing, talked about the football when something lame played on the radio, not feel the need to fill in those moments by dissecting everything. Come back Ashcroft, he thought, sneaking a look in Alex's direction, all was forgiven. 'Look,' he tried when her mouth turned down in disapproval, 'Let's just say it's not exactly The Waltons at home right now.'

'No family's like that, Kevin, which is why we all used to watch it growing up, a bit of wishful thinking, that's all…never going to happen though.'

'I don't know,' he shrugged, 'we've had our moments over the years.' In between the curve balls life had thrown at them he and Lynn had a synchronicity that took his breath away, that, and a shared sense of humour. Lynn laughed at jokes other wives would be appalled at; she of all people understood the need to find release when the job got too grim. Amy had been the icing on the cake. 'It's not rocket science,' he sighed, 'everything was fine till I opened my big gob and ruined it.'

'Nothing you can't fix,' Alex sympathised.

Coupland tutted. 'Nothing a tin of Magnolia emulsion can't fix,' he corrected.

Alex regarded him wide-eyed. 'Ah…'

They'd driven past the junction where the road widened out into Bridgewater Road with its grand houses. Then right onto Memorial Street. The properties were more modest here. Time served tradesmen and blue collar workers. Fewer garages, the vehicles parked in front of each house were work vans, plumbers, mobile beauticians, pet grooming. 'What a racket,' scowled Coupland, 'You see all these pooch parlour vans on the road but do you know anyone who uses them?'

Alex considered this, 'No, but then I don't know anyone who owns a dog.'

'Fair point. Amy asked for one a few years back but we got her a hamster instead.'

'How did that go down?'

'Like a lead balloon. Lynn ended up cleaning up after

it, which didn't go down so well either. Six bloody years that thing lived.'

Past the play park the houses got a lot smaller, estates thrown up by the council in response to Salford's housing crisis. Pebble-dashed maisonettes with postage stamp gardens and satellite dishes. Further on and the properties became mixed tenure, older properties in need of repair rented out to those unable to get a mortgage but willing to pay an inflated rent to avoid an address on a council estate.

Ashdown Court was decent enough in comparison to its neighbours, access to a communal garden and car parking for each flat made it ideal for those working in Manchester's city centre prepared to live further out and not shell out all their wages on rent. 'Like flies round the proverbial…' Coupland muttered as Alex manoeuvred the car past press vans gathered outside the entrance to the apartment block's car park which had been closed to all except residents and police personnel. Two uniformed officers formed a human barrier across the car park's entrance, moving only to allow the pool car through. An unshaven reporter from the Evening News tapped on the passenger window. 'Can you tell me anything about the body found here yesterday?' he shouted through the glass.

'No, but I can tell you about the one that'll be found here tomorrow…' Coupland scowled through the window, sizing the reported up and down. 'I can give a full-blown description if pushed…'

'Careful,' Alex warned, 'that so and so can lip read.' Coupland harrumphed, staring as an immaculate female presenter hurried out of a BBC van, rearranging her face into a worried frown as she said her piece to the camera.

She turned to smile at them through the car park's wrought iron gates. Coupland glared back.

*

Ashdown Court was built over four floors: two apartments on the middle two floors, the top and ground floor apartments spread the full length of the building. Alex consulted a clipboard containing a print out of the names of each resident which Ashcroft had typed up the previous day. She had phoned ahead to tell each resident they were coming and only one couple had baulked at having to wait in. 'Mr and Mrs Grant have a meeting to go to, asked if we could see them first, and no, I'm not going to keep them till last just to make a point…'

'Oh, ye have little faith…'Coupland muttered. 'I don't want to wind the public up any more than you do, in fact I'll make a point of saying to them how sorry we are having to inconvenience them at all, if only the little girl could have been dumped somewhere else after she was murdered by some sicko. In fact sod it, let's tell 'em they can bugger off to their bloody meeting, the investigation can wait…'

'Kevin…' Alex warned.

Coupland glanced at the list of names, saw the Grants were on the fourth floor. 'Ignore me. There's no harm in starting at the top, I suppose,' he conceded. Why not? The day was only going to go downhill from there anyway.

Mrs Grant opened the door before Coupland had a chance to knock. The uniformed officer on the main door had let them into the apartment block; the flat where the body was found still being processed as a crime scene. 'We saw you pull into the car park,'

Mrs Grant said pleasantly, and for a fleeting moment Coupland wished he'd made them wait after all. Never did any harm to let folk stew a little. The sideways look Alex gave him said that she knew what he was thinking. Mrs Grant was wiry rather than slim. A protruding collar bone and gaunt cheeks made her look anorexic, her hair blown forward around her face to make it look fuller. When she leaned forward to shake hands with them a bony wrist stuck out from the sleeve of her jacket. She wore a matching mid-calf length dress over suede boots. Even so, her legs looked incredibly thin. 'Please, call me Judy,' she told them. They followed Judy into a large open plan living space, two leather sofas either side of a glass coffee table, a matching glass dining table in the corner of the room adjacent to a wall of kitchen units with a small island doubling as a hob and breakfast bar. Several cards stood on the top of it, beside an unopened bottle of champagne. 'Today's my birthday,' Judy explained when she saw Coupland looking. 'Never as good when it's on a work day is it? Though we'll be going out at the weekend to celebrate.'

Mr Grant had been making himself a Nespresso when they walked in, Judy beckoned him over with a bony hand. The room fell silent while he stirred in two sugars, the only sound coming from a wall mounted TV. The news channel was on, two arrested after 'men with guns' were seen wandering around Cheetham Hill. The presenter was old school BBC, pronouncing the area phonetically; it had been 'Cheeta Mill' for as long as Coupland could remember. 'Turn it down, Alistair,' Judy scolded. 'Now, can I get you both a drink?'

Coupland nodded, enjoying the look of irritation that

flitted across Hubby's face.

'So how can we help?' Mr Grant asked as he took a seat at the glass topped dining table, inclining his head for the detectives to do the same.

Alex took her notebook from her bag, waited while Judy brought Coupland's coffee over, waving away her offer of tea, juice, water. 'How long have you lived here?' she began, starting off with safe questions to put them at ease.

'Ooh, about five years, give or take.' Judy had placed two sachets of sugar and a spoon beside Coupland's coffee cup and he tore open a sachet before remembering his sweeteners.

May as well, he thought, tipping the contents in before stirring. 'What are the other residents like?' he asked.

Alistair Grant regarded him as though he was being obtuse. 'How the hell would I know? Just because we live here doesn't mean we socialise with them.'

'There's an annual barbeque,' Judy piped up. 'I think the people on the ground floor organise it but we're always busy, busy, busy. Maybe next year…'

'Maybe not,' added hubby.

'Problem?' prodded Coupland.

'Not really, just that I spend all day being nice to people, quite frankly I can't be bothered when I get home.' Judy looked away as he said this; as though it wasn't just the other residents he didn't make an effort with.

'What's your line of business?' asked Alex.

'We're estate agents, we own Thompson and Grant on Chapel Street. Thompson was my maiden name,' Judy explained.

'So what's the big meeting you've got this morning

that you're in such a hurry about?' Coupland enquired.

'We've got a couple of viewings, things have been quiet recently, we didn't want to put any potential buyers off.'

Coupland took a gulp of his coffee before turning to Alistair. 'Sounds like a buyer's market at the moment then. My wife keeps saying we should get something bigger, I'm not so sure, on a policeman's salary and all…'

'Here', Alistair replied, reaching into his suit pocket and retrieving a business card, 'have a look at our properties on-line, I'm sure there'd be something in your price range.' He smiled then, the kind of smile that showed all his teeth.

Coupland didn't trust him one little bit. He pocketed the business card. 'It's not the price range I'm worried about,' he grumbled, 'it's my wife's aspiration. She's started buying products because Kate Middleton uses them. We've got the soap she uses in our downstairs loo. Like she does her own shopping… I just go along with it, anything for an easy life. What is it they say? The hand that rocks the cradle rules the home… well, it's true in our house. You two got kids?'

'We decided when we got married that we'd concentrate on the business,' Judy explained, 'that's been our baby in many ways.' Alistair nodded his agreement.

Coupland smiled, he'd played nice long enough. 'Did you know Flat 2a's previous tenant?'

'We told you earlier we don't socialise with the residents.' Alistair's tone was sharp. He shot a look at Judy as though this statement was as much for her benefit.

Coupland wouldn't be budged. 'I'm not talking dinner parties or grilling sausages together, I mean just in passing, you know, a conversation on the stairs, the odd hello here and there.'

'Well, I suppose…' Alistair looked at his wife, who had nothing to say, '…we'd pass the time of day occasionally.'

'Did she have children?'

'God no!' said Alistair, then he seemed to remember who he was with, trying to regain his distant composure, 'I'm sure we'd have noticed… you're not thinking Dawn had anything to do with what's happened surely?'

Coupland's gaze was steady. 'So you were on first name terms, then, more than just a nod on the stairs.' It was a statement more than a question, his interest piqued at Alistair's obvious discomfort.

'Have you ever been inside her flat?' Alex pushed.

'I already told you we didn't socialise, don't you people listen?'

Coupland widened his eyes. 'You could have taken in a parcel—'

'We're the top floor flat; besides, we're never in.'

'Point taken,' said Coupland, exchanging a glance with Alex before draining his mug and standing. 'I think we're done here.' He cast a glance in Alistair's direction before turning to Judy. 'Thanks for your time.'

*

Jilly Clarke on the floor below was a straight-talking blonde, pushing fifty but carried it off well. The lines around her eyes implied she laughed a lot, the glint in them said she was nobody's fool. 'Came here after my divorce, keep meaning to buy a place of my own, you know, keep a foothold on the property ladder and all that but to tell you the truth my heart's not in it. After twenty years cooped up in the same house with my ex I like the idea of being a free spirit, moving on whenever I want to.' She'd asked if she could make them a drink when she'd answered the door; both had declined. They followed Jilly through to a light and airy living room, modern oak furniture against a backdrop of pale coloured walls. Coupland walked over to one of the two large windows which looked out to the rear of the property directly onto a building site. 'Retirement village,' Jilly informed them, 'personally I can't think of anything worse.' Both windows were open, despite it being nippy outside. Jilly produced a pack of cigarettes from a fruit bowl on the sideboard, pulling one out of the ugly packaging before offering the pack around. Both detectives turned down her offer, though with regret on Coupland's part. White smoke escaped into the room as she sat on a corner sofa tucking slim legs beneath her. Coupland leaned in to take a passive smoking hit. 'Don't stand there on ceremony, take the weight off your feet,' she chided them. Coupland sat beside her on the settee, Alex choosing to sit further away, reducing her in breaths as much as she was able.

'You should speak to your neighbours upstairs,' Coupland suggested, 'It's a buyers' market, apparently.'

Jilly gave a wry smile. 'I'll have to take your word for it.'

'You don't speak to them much, then?'

Her mouth turned down at the corners as she pondered this. 'He's friendly enough I suppose, always stops to talk when he sees you. I get the impression she keeps him on a tight rein, though.'

'What makes you think that?'

Jilly chuckled. 'He's one of those excitable men, you

know, an attractive woman talks to them and they get all giddy with it.' Both women regarded Coupland then, the way women do when there's more than one of them in male company and they're denigrating the species. Coupland rode the moment out, took out his note book to avoid making any comment. Who wouldn't be thrilled when someone attractive talked to them, he reasoned, even if it was just to ask directions? He'd never been at ease with the fairer sex, always felt slightly out of his depth. Brought up by a brutish father he was a man's man, a joker, had had neither the looks nor patter to get Lynn into bed, had to rely on making her laugh; luckily the laughing subsided once he'd got her there. So, Alistair Grant wasn't as confident as he seemed, perhaps his reticence earlier was shyness rather than ego. Coupland took out his pen and noted something in his pad to check out later. He noticed the corner of a page was turned down, remembered something he meant to check out.

'What about Alistair's missus, then?' he asked.

'Not a happy woman if you ask me,' Jilly shrugged, 'doesn't have much to say for herself, always seems pre-occupied. You can tell these things, can't you?' Alex nodded in agreement. 'She wasn't always so thin, either,' Jilly added. 'I don't want to sound bitchy but she was quite big when I first moved in here, then a few months back the weight just dropped off her. I thought she was ill, you know…'

'Cancer?' Coupland still had difficulty saying the word but no one seemed to notice.

'Yeah… I took some flowers round one day, asked how she was. Turned out she'd just been dieting, though she's taken it to the extreme if you ask me.'

'So you've been in their flat then?'

Jilly nodded. 'Just briefly, you know, we didn't become BFFs or anything.'

Alex turned to Coupland, 'That's best friends forev—'

'I know what it means,' he grunted, 'I've a daughter who watches more TV than is good for her. I blame her mother.' Coupland checked himself, in the grand scheme of things watching trashy TV was hardly a crime, not like what he was guilty of, exposing their daughter to a serial killer.

'Did you know Dawn Tylor?' Alex asked when Coupland fell silent. 'I believe she was the last tenant in flat 2a?'

Jilly nodded. 'Yeah, got to know her quite well really, given she was a lot younger than me. I mean, she was friendly enough from the start, busy though, you know the sort, thirty-something career woman, doing well for herself, worked hard, played hard...'

'Late nights, you mean?'

Jilly tilted her head to one side as she considered this. 'Partly... she liked to wind down over a bottle of wine and occasionally would invite me over to join her. Two single women in a block full of couples, well, another girl has since moved in across the landing but before her it was a gay couple...'

'And Jimmy Rawlings on the floor below?'

'What?' Jilly screwed up her eyes. 'Oh, I'd forgotten about him... Anyway, all I'm saying is that Dawn wasn't short of pals, or at least that was the impression I got. Maybe she just didn't like the idea of drinking alone. Having me there to share a bottle didn't make her feel quite so desperate. We've all been there though, haven't we?' Neither Alex nor Coupland commented.

'Any reason she liked to drink?'

'God, what reason do you need? Men? Work? Doesn't it always boil down to sex and money?' Jilly took one long last drag on her cigarette before stubbing it out in the ashtray placed on the arm of the sofa. 'She was seeing someone but it wasn't all plain sailing. She didn't say what exactly, and I didn't want to pry, though I did advise her to cut her losses, there's plenty more fish in the sea and all that. Next minute she's upping sticks and moving away, I suppose she wanted to make a clean beak.'

Coupland had a faraway look on his face, whatever he was thinking about, it wasn't in relation to the people in this room. 'DS Coupland?' Alex prompted, trying to bring him back.

'She didn't have kids?' he asked.

'No, she was a career woman, though she hinted that was something she'd like in the future.'

'And this guy she was seeing, did you meet him?'

'No, I think that's why she liked talking to me, I knew so little about her life I could be objective.'

'You got kids, Jilly?'

'Daughter at uni, bit of a daddy's girl so she stays with her father between terms, blamed me for the break up, you see. We meet up for coffee every once in a while though, lets me take her shopping, we're on good terms now.'

'What was the cause of your split?'

Jilly laughed, though it didn't make it to her eyes. 'He couldn't keep it in his pants, thought if he kept saying how sorry he was every time his flings ended everything would be OK.' Already her hands were restless on her lap, fingers itching for the comfort of another nicotine stick.

'How do you get on with the other residents?'

'We all get on fine, take in each other's post, wait in for the maintenance man if someone needs to go to work, there's an annual barbie each summer as well, we all take along a bit of food, cremate it and get pissed, it's a good night.'

'Does everyone go to it?'

Jilly thought about this. 'The couple upstairs don't anymore, they used to come but I think they're the type that judge everything by whether it's a business opportunity or not and I guess as far as they were concerned we weren't much of a prospect.'

'So what about your new neighbour, do you know her any better now?'

Jilly's mouth turned down. 'To my shame I haven't really made the effort. I mean, we nod when we bump into each other on the landing, but that's about it.'

'You don't take in parcels for each other then?'

'Not really, she's in a lot of the time as it is, doesn't need anyone to help out like that.'

'She must be good to have around then? Someone on hand to wait in for any maintenance work that needs doing…' Jilly's failure to respond piqued Alex's interest. 'What aren't you saying?' she prompted.

'Look, I don't mean to be a gossipy neighbour, after all I could be barking up the wrong tree and it's not like she causes any trouble.'

'What?'

'Well… she does have a lot of male visitors over. Only not the kind that bother saying hello on the stairs…'

'I don't get it,' Turnbull persisted when as they walked along the fifth floor landing of a tower block on the Tattersall estate ten minutes later, 'The kids on this list are on the at-risk register and haven't been seen at school or nursery in the last four weeks, yet I get the impression this is the first welfare check to be carried out in that time.'

Shola regarded him as she marched along the tower block landing. 'I cannot comment on individual cases, DC Turnbull, nor on the way my colleagues prioritise their own caseloads. Please remember that although I have been assigned to facilitate you today, several of these families are not known to me.'

Robinson pushed his tongue firmly into his cheek as he spoke up. 'But isn't there a protocol to follow?' he asked, using the vocabulary Shola's line manager had rammed down his throat when he'd set off half-cocked the day before. 'Without standardised procedures won't these youngsters fall through the net?'

Shola shivered involuntarily, pulling the scarf around her neck a little tighter. 'Children in this city who go absent from school or nursery and are at-risk of abuse, neglect or exploitation benefit from a coordinated multi-agency response to assess risk and need.' She caught the look that passed between the detectives and sighed. 'Although all concerns about these children are followed up, I suppose the quality of that follow up may be inconsistent. Some of my colleagues may telephone the family in the first instance, some may visit the child's home but it is not unusual for the family not to be in.'

'S'funny that…' Turnbull muttered.

Shola ignored him. 'Some colleagues report that they feel intimidated… that they do not feel safe going into certain homes so do not persist if they are not invited in when they go round.'

'What? So they glimpse little Johnny or Jemima through a letterbox and that's supposed to count?'

'No, it isn't… their notes should contain sufficient detail so we can identify any patterns of behaviour… record their concerns so that a further attempt to visit can be made, though the reality is that often no one else is available to accompany them on their visit, our resources are very stretched…'

'Until it gets so far down the line you need to call us in…'

Shola didn't even blink.

'So what's the point of making thorough notes when it's the same person going to follow the problem up anyway?'

'C'mon,' interrupted Robinson, 'that's the same as us in a lot of ways. Remember CYA.' CYA meant Cover Your Arse. All words and deeds had to be recorded or witnessed in case something was claimed to be true or untrue later down the line.

'You of all people must know there are no such things as cut and dried decisions, detective, when in reality every action has a consequence.'

Turnbull considered this. 'True, though I get the feeling you wouldn't be so inconsistent with your case notes, Ms Dube. You strike me as someone who is very thorough in her work, sticks to the rules no matter what.' Shola hesitated, her hand fluttering to her scarf once more.

Her reply when it came was so quiet the detectives

didn't hear it.

'I used to be,' she answered simply.

*

Their first welfare check was on the daughter of recovering addicts. The parents were biddable enough once Shola's persistent knocking got them out of bed to answer the door. Lives punctuated by visits from lanyard-wearing strangers, they showed no surprise at the visit, nor at the request to see their little girl. They listened to Shola slack-faced as she introduced Turnbull and Robinson, the mother rewarding them with a slow motion smile when she realised they weren't in trouble. Her partner ushered them in, junkie style, feet shuffling along the hallway as he scratched a rash that peeped over the neck of his manky t-shirt. Cheap carpet stuck to the detectives' shoes as they were shown into a cramped front room. The place needed not so much as a wipe down as a hose down. The room was a tip; discarded food wrappers littered every surface, the place reeked of stale kebab and onion rings. Ancient wallpaper peeled from grubby walls. Camouflaged by an oversized pile of dirty washing on the threadbare settee, a little girl sat watching cartoons, a packet of salt and vinegar crisps on her lap. Tonia Myerscough. On the at-risk register since birth due to her parents' drug addiction. The girl was pale, as though she hadn't stepped outdoors in weeks, unwashed hair hung about her head like rats' tails. The clothes she had on were a good size too small for her, the Disney princess transfer on the front of her sweatshirt had started to peel, making the young royal look as though she suffered from psoriasis. Shola turned to the girl's hapless parents. 'Why isn't she in school?'

'We thought it was the holidays,' said the father, 'is it not the holidays, then?'

'The school has been phoning you…'

'Don't answer the phone if I don't recognise the number.'

Shola sighed. 'She needs to be in school. Today. If you don't start taking her you will end up in court.'

The junkies hung their heads. 'Don't have the bus fare.'

'You can walk there in twenty minutes,' Shola persisted. Turnbull tried calculating how long a shuffle would take. 'You need to have a routine in place. You could take it in turns walking her every day.' Mummy junkie widened her eyes in alarm. 'Or you can both take her,' Shola reasoned, 'if that makes you feel better.' Tonia's parents looked at each other. Tonia, unfazed by the conversation going on around her, continued to stare at the TV, a small finger dabbing at the crisp remnants at the bottom of the packet to gather them up, the other hand expertly manoeuvring across the remote control to find the next programme.

Turnbull had seen enough. 'Look, if you're quick about it, we could take you in the car.'

'Are you out of your mind?' hissed Robinson, but Turnbull merely shrugged.

'Look, it'll take five minutes, at least the poor bugger's got the chance of a decent lunch if we get her there today.' Turnbull didn't have children; his wife had swanned off before they'd had a chance to start a family. It wasn't something he dwelt on, he'd long ago accepted he lacked the gene to love someone unconditionally, yet however useless he thought he'd be, he wouldn't be like this. He addressed the girl's mother. 'Go and get her uniform on before I change my bloody mind.'

*

Jilly Clarke's neighbour took several minutes to open the door. 'Holly Bagshawe?' Alex asked, waiting while the woman nodded before holding her lanyard up and making introductions. 'I was in the shower,' Holly told them when she let them in although her long auburn hair was bone dry. She'd secured it in a ponytail, in a band so tight it pulled the skin around her temples taut. Her skin was pale, make-up free, dark shadows beneath her eyes but nothing a bit of concealer couldn't fix. She wore a close fitting long sleeve jersey with skinny jeans that had more holes than cloth, imitation sheepskin slippers. She led them through to an interior that was the mirror image of Jilly Clarke's except the décor was shabby. A faded settee and two armchairs dominated the lounge area, a TV and set top box sat on a chipped Formica stand. A bottle of cheap vodka had been left on the coffee table in the centre of the room, a wooden fruit bowl beside it contained condom packets and lubricant.

'Can we sit down, love?' Coupland prompted when no offer was forthcoming.

'Yeah,' Holly shrugged, plonking herself onto an armchair when the detectives chose the settee. A can of red bull lay on its side beneath the coffee table, remnants from the can had pooled onto the carpet.

'You want to watch that,' warned Coupland, reaching down and placing it onto the coffee table, 'you'll not get your deposit back.' Holly didn't blink. So, she wasn't the one paying the rent on this place, then. A boyfriend, or pimp perhaps?

'You live here alone, Holly?' Alex prompted, clearly on the same wavelength.

Holly nodded. 'I don't know anything about the kid you've found,' she said. 'I don't know anyone who would hurt a kid.' Her voice was childlike, albeit a sullen child.

'Have you seen anyone coming in and out of the building who you didn't know, Holly?'

Holly's mouth twitched, 'Apart from the men who come here, you mean? Is that what you're asking? Have the others been telling you I'm a bit of a slag?'

Coupland shook his head. 'I'm not bothered whether you give it away or take contactless payments when they get here, this is a murder investigation, nothing you tell us will incriminate you, we won't be passing any information on unless you want us to.'

'I'm not a prozzie,' her tone was defiant, 'my fella brings his mates round here sometimes, that's all. He likes to party, though I try and keep the noise down. I get funny looks from the other residents as it is.'

Alex tried not to stare at the fruit bowl's contents. 'Did you know the previous tenant in Flat 2a?'

'Who, that stuck up cow? You must be joking. Looked down her nose at me, she did. All hoity-toity in her designer clothes, thought she was better than all of us.'

'So you never had reason to go into her flat?'

'What? To help her hide a dead kid, you mean? I told you, she didn't bother with me and I didn't bother with her, got it? Fancy though,' Holly added, folding her arms, 'be a turn up for the books if it turned out she did do it, what with her going about like she was a cut above the rest of us.'

'It would be unwise to draw any conclusions as this stage,' Alex cautioned. 'We are speaking to everyone as a matter of course.'

'Yeah, right, you lot have got to say that, haven't you?'

*

Crime scene personnel were removing their equipment from Flat 2a by the time Coupland and Alex reached the first-floor landing. Coupland nodded to a couple of familiar faces as he entered. 'Christ, have they not put you out to pasture yet?' he said to one man carrying an armful of metal footplates out of the bedroom. The cloying smell had lessened, revealing another altogether different aroma. 'Can you smell paint?' Coupland asked, checking out the walls which were scuffed in places, marks where photos had been removed. He tapped his finger against the bedroom door. 'Woodwork's been painted,' he said, though more to himself as Alex was deep in conversation with the officer counting down to retirement. He moved over to the window. The flat shared the same view as Jilly Clarke, the retirement village in construction. A large sign had been erected against the perimeter wall, *Borthwick Enterprises, bringing structure to your dreams*, 'I thought retired folk liked to garden,' he muttered, noting the postage stamp balconies with room for little more than a couple of pots. 'There's more landscaping here,' he added, looking onto a rockery below and a gravel path that snaked towards a seating area. Coupland turned to survey the room. It had been emptied, save for the bed, the contents taken for forensic testing. Jason and Ali had been certain the built-in wardrobe where the sports bag had been found hadn't had anything else in it that they didn't recognise but to be sure everything they'd put in it had been removed to be gone through in the forensic science lab. It was possible a weapon could have been concealed there; Coupland could only live in hope.

'Kevin?' Alex was standing by the doorway, her head tilted as she regarded him. 'They're all but finished here.' She nodded over to the officer she'd been talking to as he made his way down the stairs. 'You done here?'

Coupland's gaze fell on the dark stain in the centre of the room, where the essence of a little girl had seeped into a threadbare carpet. 'I'm done,' he replied, his tone sombre.

*

'Do you think Jason and Ali will still move in?' Alex asked while they waited for Jimmy Rawlings in the flat opposite to answer the door.

Coupland pulled a face. 'Would you?' Before Alex had time to answer,

Rawlings opened the door, making a point of looking at his watch before stepping back to let them into his flat. 'My boss docked my pay yesterday, said if I'm not in by lunchtime today he'll do the same.'

'We'll make it quick then,' Coupland promised, prompting Alex to look at him to check if he was being arsey, 'and I'll let him know you've been helping us with our enquiries.'

Rawlings looked alarmed. 'That's the last thing I need, you lot turning up out of the blue. He wasn't too impressed when I told him I'd given you some flyers.'

'What's *his* problem, then?'

Rawlings looked shifty. 'I don't think his recruitment process is that vigorous, if you know what I mean. Put it one way I'm the only one speaks enough English there to answer the phone.'

Alex and Coupland shared a look. This firm wouldn't be the only business that looked the other way when it came to hiring cheap labour; their primary focus right now was the little girl. 'We'll leave off contacting your boss,' Coupland placated him, 'as long as you continue to play ball.'

Rawlings breathed out a sigh. 'Sorry, it's just that it took me a while to get this job, I can't afford to be out of work again.'

'What did you do before?' asked Coupland. They'd been shown through to the kitchen once more. It was smaller than he remembered; Alex perched on a stool so as not to take up too much space. Coupland, not liking the look of the stools, chose to lean against the breakfast bar. Jimmy remained standing too, although Coupland doubted there was much choice in it given the man's bulk. 'I was a taxi driver,' Jimmy told them, 'did it for ten years, was good at it too. Always knew the best shortcuts, never spoke out of turn, the passengers used to ask for me specifically when they rang the switchboard. It was all going well, until I made the mistake of setting up on my own. I thought it'd be easy, the firm I worked for was always turning work down, all I was going to do was pick up the slack.'

Coupland raised a brow, 'How did that go down?'

Jimmy's shoulder's dipped, 'Not as well as I'd hoped. It was never about poaching their clients but…' his hands slid into his pockets, his voice fell as he recalled something, '…it started with bogus bookings, I'd turn up for a fare only to find they'd never made the call, didn't even know who I was, then it was rumours that I'd been inside – I haven't – but little old ladies were hardly going to book me to pick them up from the supermarket after hearing that, were they? I called it a day when my tyres got slashed, I couldn't afford to get them replaced, besides, the local garage was suddenly very busy…'

'I don't suppose you reported it?' asked Alex.

Jimmy regarded her as though she had two heads. 'Behave, do you think I'm on a death wish or something? It was simply a business disagreement, the moment I ceased trading all the intimidation stopped. Can't say fairer than that, I suppose.' What he said was true. A number of businesses throughout the city, even those without links to organised crime, were protective of their territory, relied on their supply chain to discourage unwanted incomers. Some towns operated on a one garage, one barber, one corner shop basis, leaving others that didn't to pick up the slack. There were six hair salons on the high street where Alex had her hair done; none of them were busy.

Coupland inclined his head in the direction of the flat across the landing. 'Did you get on with the previous tenant?'

'I told you yesterday I don't bother with anyone.'

'True, but you still knew who was who, you were able to name them all, apart from Holly Bagshawe, although you made reference to her lifestyle.'

Rawlings smirked. 'Lifestyle! Is that what we're calling it now?'

'What would you call it then?'

'She's a tart, pure and simple. Takes money for sex, might as well call it as it is.'

'And how would you know she does that?' Coupland asked. That wiped the sneer from Rawlings' face.

'So, what about your ex-neighbour?' Alex persisted.

'Dawn Tylor, what was she like?'

Jimmy pulled a face. 'Stuck up if you asked me,' he replied, folding fat arms across a flabby chest.

'You mean she knocked you back, Jimmy.' Coupland's tone was matter of fact. 'Might as well call it as it is.'

*

'Terrible business,' Bruce Fairweather said when he opened the door to let Coupland and Alex into the ground floor flat he shared with his wife. 'Jean's really shaken by it, I can tell you.' He'd put his reading glasses on to study their warrant cards. 'You can't be too careful these days,' he'd muttered, folding them before returning them to the breast pocket on his shirt, 'not that I know what I'm looking for.' Satisfied, he led them through to a dated living room, oversized furniture that looked as though it had once filled a sprawling family home now crammed into a much smaller living space. 'That's the problem with downsizing,' Bruce explained when Coupland's gaze fell onto a piano standing cheek by jowl beside a fish tank, 'when it comes down to it you don't want to part with anything.'

A woman with white cropped hair and dangly earrings came out of the kitchen carrying a tray. Although narrow on top, her hips looked as though they'd been inflated, making her lower half resemble a bouncy castle. 'I've made sandwiches,' she smiled, placing the tray on the coffee table before lifting out a large plate stacked high with finger rolls and four small plates. 'Bruce, can you bring the tea things through? I figured you'd be too polite too say yes if I offered to make you something to eat but now it's done you might be tempted.'

'It'd be rude not to,' Coupland eyed the selection and helped himself to a stack of butties as he plonked himself down on the end of the sofa closest to the coffee table. He hadn't realised how hungry he was. Jean settled herself into the armchair opposite, a small plate with a single roll balanced on her lap. Alex, trying to shift the remainder of her baby weight nibbled on the end of a plain ham salad. 'So, who's the piano player then?' Coupland asked between mouthfuls.

'I am,' Jean beamed, 'do you play too?'

Coupland ignored Alex's smirk. 'No, though I'm flattered you thought I might. I'm tone deaf, love, always have been, but I used to love going to the concerts at my daughter's school.'

'So she's musical then?'

'Only got as far as playing the recorder, 'fraid she inherited the same musical gene as me.'

Jean chuckled. 'Bruce and I used to teach, we're retired now, of course,' she said, patting her hair. 'I taught music at the high school.'

'She teaches piano now after school, sergeant,' Bruce cut in, 'it's never too late.'

Coupland held out his chunky fingers for inspection, remembering too late the graze across his knuckles. 'Think I was cut out for other things,' he said, before reaching for another sandwich.

'So what did you teach?' Alex smiled at Bruce. 'I take it you were at the high school too?'

Bruce shook his head. 'I was a primary school teacher, worked at St Andrew's in Boothstown, Jean and I were both union reps, in fact that's how we met, isn't it love, at a conference?'

Jean nodded.

'How long have you lived here then?' asked Alex.

'Oh,' Bruce blew out his cheeks, 'just coming up for a year.'

'It's nice enough here,' Jean cut in, 'but this isn't our forever home. We're thought it prudent to rent for a while until we make up our mind what to do.'

'I'd like us to move out to the Algarve.' Bruce added, 'but I'm worried we won't see enough of the grandchildren.'

'Every cloud…' Coupland quipped, ignoring the look Alex gave him.

'So we're staying put while we make up our mind.' Nice problem to have.

'Do you see much of the other residents?'

'Quite a bit, yes,' Jean answered, 'we've taken parcels in for most of them, what with us being on the ground floor. We don't mind, it's nice to pass the time of day.'

'What about the woman who lived in 2a. Dawn Tylor, did you speak much?'

'Not a great deal, she was up with the larks, often not back till late, but she was pleasant enough when our paths did cross.'

'You don't think she had anything to do with what's happened, do you?' asked Bruce.

Coupland ignored him. 'What about visitors, you must see a fair share of people traipsing up to the entry door?'

'I suppose, but we don't buzz just anyone in, if that's what you're asking.'

'I'm interested in anyone who's been here a lot recently, regardless of the purpose to their visit.'

'The maintenance company used by the landlord,

they're here more often than not.'

'What are they called?'

'Ryland's, I think?' Jean looked at Bruce for confirmation.

He nodded. 'Yes, Ryland's, they do everything here, from fixing leaky taps to keeping the borders tidy, although I like to keep my hand in.'

'He misses his garden,' Jean added.

'Though not the bloody mowing,' Bruce qualified, '*that* I'm quite happy to leave to the professionals. I'll do any tidying needed, although I don't know why I bother since my efforts go unnoticed by the other residents.

'It was Bruce who put the rockery in,' Jean told them with pride.

'Not that anyone offered to make a contribution to the cost of it,' Bruce huffed. 'Or even acknowledge it for that matter. Like it doesn't bloody exist. Even when I tidied it the other month, planted alpines where gaps had started to appear between the stones, no one noticed.'

'I'm sure they did, dear,' Jean said, rolling her eyes at the detectives.

Coupland had let the conversation roam while he emptied his plate. It was time to bring it back on track. 'Does this firm go in and out of the properties unsupervised?'

Jean considered this. 'Well, we're in more often than not so they've only ever done work here when one of us has been around. Can't speak for the other residents though, I mean one of the benefits of renting somewhere is the landlord or letting agent takes care of the maintenance, so I guess some residents will leave them to come and go as they please while they're out at work.'

'Could it be one of them that has done this, DS Coupland? Is that what you're thinking?'

Coupland made a point of avoiding Alex's eye. Truth was there was so precious little to go on, he wasn't thinking anything at all.

CHAPTER TEN

Coupland spent the afternoon back at Salford Precinct station reading through the door-to-door statements DCI Mallender had given him that morning. Properties visited included two rows of houses either side of Ashdown Court, several homes on the neighbouring estate that looked onto the apartment block and builders working on the retirement village behind it. The door-to-door enquiry had been carried out thoroughly, with uniforms going back to some addresses several times to make sure every member of the household had been interviewed. They had spoken to the retirement village site manager who had provided a list of tradesmen who had worked on site over the last six weeks. All of the names had a tick against them to show they'd been interviewed. It didn't help that there'd been no photograph of the little girl to show anyone. All that officers had been given to distribute was a photo of the sports bag she'd been found in together with a discreet photo of her hair clip, once the remnants of scalp had been removed.

Coupland pulled out his phone and scrolled through his contacts until he found Ashcroft's number. When the DC failed to pick up he left a voicemail asking him to fast track interviewing the owner of Ryland's, the maintenance company servicing Ashdown Court, and to make sure to ask them when flat 2a had last been painted, which going by the smell there couldn't have been more than a couple of days ago. Someone working for the firm had the opportunity to dump a bag containing a body; whether they had reason to was another matter.

*

Ashcroft listened to DS Coupland's voicemail with one eyebrow raised. 'Problem?' the man seated opposite him asked. He was sitting in a curry house off the East Lancs Road, nursing a coffee as he watched his companion devour the remains of a prawn biryani. Trevor Ryland, proprietor of T. Ryland and Son Maintenance Ltd, had made it clear he was a busy man and if Ashcroft wanted to ask him about the work he did at Ashdown Court he'd have to do it while he filled his bloody face.

'Nah,' Ashcroft replied, 'just someone telling me how to suck eggs.'

Trevor laughed, sending his double chin wobbling. 'That's why I set up on my own, no one watching over you checking your every move.'

'Can't quite see myself as a private investigator,' Ashcroft commented. 'Spying on cheating spouses isn't really my thing.' Trevor nodded his understanding while at the same time signalling to the waiter for a diet coke.

'So,' Ashcroft said, his stomach rumbling at the spicy aroma, 'like I said earlier on the phone…'

'You need me to prove I had nothing to do with that body turning up in those flats, otherwise you'll be carting me off to the cop-shop, am I right?'

Ashcroft smiled. 'Not quite, I'm more interested in how many people have access to the master key you look after.'

'That's easy,' Trevor said, smothering the remains of

a poppadum with red onions and mango chutney before breaking it in half, 'the keys to all the properties we look after are hung up in the office, my missus works in there four days a week and the three lads that work for me go in for their pay and to drop off invoices, so that makes five of us.' Ashcroft pulled out his notebook ready to jot down their names. 'I did a criminal record check on all the lads working for me before I hired them,' Trevor added quickly, 'what with us going into people's homes and that, it's in my own interest to find out if someone can't keep their hands to themselves.'

'So they all checked out?'

Trevor nodded. 'Apart from my own lad, mind, but then I didn't need a piece of paper to tell me his problem.'

'Which is?'

Trevor took a swig of his coke, 'Let's just say with a mouth like his he won't get a job anywhere else and they say charity begins at home… Breach of the Peace,' he added, before Ashcroft had time to ask, 'was a bit of a gob shite in his youth but that's behind him now, touch wood.' Trevor tapped one hand against his head, while shovelling the second half of the overloaded poppadum in his mouth with the other.

'I'll need everyone's details anyway,' Ashcroft patted his pocket for his pen, 'just to be sure.'

Trevor gave him the names, together with how long each tradesman had worked for him. 'Don't you want to know where we all were the day before last?' Trevor asked. Using a torn off piece of naan bread as a cleaning cloth, he expertly wiped it across his plate, reminding Ashcroft of DS Coupland when he wasn't on one of his wife's health kicks.

'Not really, I'd be more interested in what jobs you were doing between four and six weeks ago.'

'Christ, so the body's been there a while then.'

'That's what we're trying to work out.' Ashcroft chose his words carefully.

Trevor's eyes narrowed as he cast his mind back to the previous month. 'We did a touch-up job in there about a month ago, literally painting over scuffs on the woodwork, not even a full coat of paint. Donald has deep pockets and short arms when it comes to shelling out on repairs.'

'So, let me get this right, you've not been in flat 2a since then?'

Trevor Ryland shook his head, yet DS Coupland's voicemail said he could smell fresh paint. It was possible the landlord had decided to carry out work himself, especially if he was tight fisted, so why hadn't he mentioned anything? Ashcroft sighed. Dawn Tylor had returned his call two hours ago and he'd arranged to meet her straight after he'd finished with Ryland. He'd have to push their meeting back as he needed to find out whether the landlord had painted the woodwork himself. If he hadn't then the only other person to have motive to touch up the paintwork would be the killer. He pushed back from the table, thanking Trevor Ryland for his time.

*

Donald Riding looked quizzical when he opened his front door. 'I thought we were done?' he accused, failing to hide his irritation. There was no invitation to enter his home this time, but that suited Ashcroft just fine.

'You didn't tell me you painted flat 2a the night before

the body was found.'

Donald stepped back in alarm, 'Because of how it would look!' he spluttered, his hands rising, palm outwards, showing he meant no harm.

'It looks a lot worse now,' Ashcroft stated, taking advantage of Donald's retreat to step into the hallway. 'I reckon you and me need to carry on this conversation down at the station, don't you?'

*

Shola Dube sighed as she turned to face both detectives. 'You made a comment earlier, DC Turnbull, about me being very thorough with my case load. I didn't want to tell you this at the start of our rounds as I didn't want to be on the defensive, with you looking for trouble that wasn't there. But in many ways you are correct. My position is one of great trust, you have seen that now, and something I take very seriously.' She paused, her gaze shifting so intently to something behind them both men turned to look but no one was there. 'A few years ago, when I was still a rookie – I think that is the term you would use?' She waited for both men to nod before continuing, 'My team leader asked me to follow up a call that had come in about a little boy. There had been an allegation of abuse at the hands of his mother's boyfriend. The child's grand-mother had reported it, fearing for her daughter too, but her daughter was in denial, refusing to go to the police whenever he assaulted her. She made excuses about her son's injuries but the boy's grandmother was not so easily taken in. The boy had become withdrawn and had recently started wetting the bed. He was seven years old.' Her hand flew to her throat as she spoke, fingering the silky material around her neck. 'I had not been in the job long. Looking back I was very naïve, I thought my actions alone could change the world.' She shook her head. 'I really wanted to help this little boy. One day I turned up at the address the grandmother had given and found her standing outside the flat, sobbing. She'd called round to see her daughter but the boyfriend would not let her in. She could hear her grandson crying behind the door. I know now that I should have waited, called the police myself, at least telephoned my team leader for guidance, but that would have taken time, you know... agreeing the correct protocol. The little boy was standing in the hallway; I could see him when I looked through the letterbox.'

'So what did you do?'

'I made the biggest mistake of my life, DS Robinson. I asked him to let me in. All I remember is seeing the boy's mother lying on the kitchen floor, blood pooling around her. At least the boy's grandmother had the presence of mind to call the emergency services. I'm afraid I froze. Next thing I remember is this large man looming towards me, a knife in his hand. I screamed at the boy and his grandmother to run, I bought them some time by standing in the boyfriend's way, blocking his exit. He was so mad he started slashing at me with his knife; so many times I lost count. I didn't even have the sense to play dead, instead I clung onto him, and all the time he kept slashing and slicing.' In silence the detectives watched as Shola unwound the scarf around her neck. From her collarbone to below her jaw was a frenzy of keloid scars, criss-crossing over her skin. Part of her neck was discoloured. 'Where the surgeon tried a skin graft, but nothing really improved the appearance.'

'What happened to the moron who did this?' Turnbull asked, stunned.

'He went on the run overnight, then handed himself in. He wasn't a career criminal, just a bully.'

'A bully I hope is serving serious time.'

Shola nodded, 'Yes…but then the little boy is serving his own sentence, having to grow up without his mother.'

'If you hadn't intervened when you had he could have been killed as well. At least he had his grandmother.'

Shola hesitated, 'Initially yes, but she died a couple of years ago. He is in care now.' All three fell silent. Not the ending they were hoping for.

'So can you see now, detectives, why my colleagues may prefer not to rock the boat? My example may be extreme but there have been so many incidents where we come under threat, sometimes it's easier to do nothing.'

Turnbull ran his hand over his chin. He was thinking about DC Oldman, the rookie detective who'd joined the murder squad last year. He'd gone after a local drug dealer and ended up dead within his first week on the job. It had made Turnbull reflect on the way he worked; some chided him for being slow and steady, he knew that, he'd no more follow a scrote into a blind alley than fly to the moon, but at least he was alive. He had no intention of becoming a name on the division's roll of honour, thanks very much. He was on the home straight for his pension, a townhouse in Tenerife and hopefully someone to watch the sunset with. He understood not wanting to rock the boat. And yet here was a woman who had done the polar opposite. He regarded Shola with something resembling admiration; doing what she felt was right had put her in grave danger, yet she'd managed to come out alive, though he hoped she'd got being a hero out of her system. He found himself wondering how her partner coped with the worry, or even if she had a partner. 'How about we stop for some lunch?' he said, 'My shout.'

*

Donald Riding sat ramrod straight on the interview room chair, outrage pouring off him in waves. 'So I'm a cheapskate! That's not against the law, last time I looked.'

'Then why not mention that you'd done some work in the flat when I asked you?' Ashcroft demanded. Beside him sat a PC with gelled hair. He'd been first on the scene when the kiddie had been found and had asked if he could sit in on the interview when he heard a suspect had been brought in. He'd been warned to sit still and say nothing, and kept his part of the bargain, not counting deathly glares across the table.

'Because I didn't want to end up here!' Donald spluttered.

'Well that worked out really well, didn't it?' Ashcroft countered. 'You sure you don't want a solicitor?'

'I don't need one, I've done nothing wrong.'

'You answer my questions honestly this time, or it'll be a jury who'll be making their mind up about that.'

*

The incident room was buzzing. Krispy, phone pinned between his ear and shoulder as he tapped onto his computer keyboard looked up in time to see Coupland striding back to his desk. 'DC Ashcroft's brought the landlord in for questioning,' he chirped, pointing to the incident board where Donald Riding's name took centre stage with a question mark beside it.

Coupland's spirits lifted. Progress of sorts, then. He moved closer to get a better look, scanned the other names around it, saw that the owner and staff from T. Ryland and Son Maintenance Ltd had a line through their names to show no one from there was considered a suspect. 'Has Robinson kept you up to date with progress re the kids on the at-risk register?' he called over.

Krispy gave him a thumbs up sign. Covering his mouthpiece he replied, 'This is him now, Sarge.' Coupland nodded, deciding on a quick visit to the interview suite before reporting in to DCI Mallender.

*

Ashcroft had put Donald Riding in the smaller of the interview rooms, one where the only natural light came from a narrow window just below the ceiling. Strip lighting was required to supplement it in all but the sunniest days. The arse end of the year was fast approaching; the sun had picked up its bat and ball and stomped home, leaving the room cloaked in a gloomy shade. Coupland nodded his approval. 'No solicitor?' he observed as he entered the room, causing Riding to sigh.

'How many times, I don't bloody need one!' he chimed, 'I've done nothing wrong!' A look of irritation flitted across Ashcroft's face, Coupland assumed Riding was playing up and took Ashcroft's expression as an invitation to sit down.

'Off you go, Ronan,' he said to the PC seated at the table. The officer nodded as he jumped to his feet, though not before sending another glare in Riding's direction.

'Not that nifty with a paint brush then,' Coupland said, nodding at the white gloss embedded into the cuticles around Riding's thumb nails. Ashcroft chided himself for not noticing. 'I'm a dab hand at DIY, me,' Coupland said pleasantly, 'have to be on my salary, can turn my hand to most things, if you don't look at 'em too closely afterwards. Though it's the clearing up after that I'm rubbish at, returning things to their original place, sweeping up, cleaning brushes, that sort of thing, so what I don't get is when you have someone on retainer to do all that for you – presumably because you can afford it – you still go and do it yourself.'

'I was trying to save money!' Riding explained. 'I had a young couple moving in the next day and I could already tell the girl was the sort that liked things just so. If I call Trevor Ryland out at short notice it costs me more.'

'But Trevor had already done the work last month,' Ashcroft said, catching Coupland's eye at the significance of it.

'So why did it need redoing, Donald?' Coupland asked. 'Not as though someone had been in during that time and made a mess of the place – or had they?' They both stared at Riding, waiting him out.

'Of course no one had been in, but…' he paused, running his hands back and forward through his hair.

Coupland shook his head as he pushed himself to his feet. Placing his fists square on the table top to take his weight he leaned towards Riding but it was Ashcroft he addressed: 'We can do him for perverting the course of justice and obstruction for starters.'

'And tax evasion,' Ashcroft added.

Riding paled. 'There were scuff marks, OK? Someone

had touched the paintwork while it had still been wet, or rather their clothing had. Trevor's taken on a couple of young lads recently; they're not as thorough as he is. I was going to have a word with him about it, get him to deduct the job off my bill. It looked a mess, OK? I just wanted to freshen it up before my new tenants moved in and complained.'

Coupland's pulse quickened, he glanced over at Ashcroft to see if he'd picked up on it too. Ashcroft was already reaching for his phone. 'When did Ryland's Maintenance do the original work for you?' demanded Coupland.

Riding closed his eyes as he mulled it over. 'Sometime last month,' he said. 'I'd need to look in my folder at home to be sure.'

'Don't bother,' Ashcroft interrupted. 'I'm calling Trevor Ryland now. His job sheets are in the office, he'll be able to tell us when the work was done.'

Coupland stared at Ashcroft while he spoke into the phone. They were finally going to get a break. Something had happened in the bedroom of flat 2a the day the woodwork had originally been painted, leaving marks on the paintwork. Any minute now they were about to find out the little girl's date of death.

CHAPTER ELEVEN

DCI Mallender leaned back in his chair, studying Coupland as he spoke. 'It takes about six hours for the stuff Rylands uses to dry so we can be pretty sure we're on the right track datewise. We're looking at November 2nd for when death occurred. It ties in with Harry Benson's ball park estimate so I'm happy to work with it.'

'I agree,' Mallender said, 'we need to call forensics back in to take samples from the paintwork in case there are trace fibres trapped beneath it.'

'They're already on their way. It doesn't help that Idiot Features painted over them but he wasn't to know the significance.'

'Does he check out?'

Coupland nodded. 'He's not got any previous, was a bit of a lad back in the day but then weren't we all? Present company excepted of course.' The DCI gave the impression he was as straight as they came, although Coupland suspected there was a past that the boss preferred to keep buried. Mallender's poker face gave nothing away.

'Is Riding in custody?'

Coupland shook his head. 'He came here voluntarily, though he's still in the interview room, thought I'd let him sweat for a bit.'

Mallender blew out his cheeks, 'Let him go, you've proved your point, though if the CSIs find any fibres under that layer of paint that match his clothing you have my blessing to drag him back in.'

*

Turnbull and Robinson were standing in the middle of the CID room regaling Alex with anecdotes of their day riding shotgun with Shola Dube. 'Turnbull was ready to kidnap one kid,' Robinson explained, turning to include Coupland as he made his way over. 'Her mum kept saying she was always walking into things. Said she had problems with her coordination. Funny, given she didn't stumble once when we were there, though the little mite was totally bloody mystified by the attention she was getting.'

'Isn't bloody normal,' Turnbull grumbled, 'little kid like that should be prancing around pretending she's on X-Factor, not sticking to the shadows in case she gets unwanted attention.'

'So what did you do?'

'I persuaded the social worker to instigate an Emergency Protection Order, told her if she didn't I was going to deck the stepdad.'

Coupland's mouth turned down at the edges. The situation must have been grim if Turnbull was riled. He waited while the duo went to make themselves coffee before they gave him a full debrief, nodding when Robinson asked if he wanted a cuppa. 'A proper builder's one, mind,' he answered. 'But no sugar,' he added, dropping his voice.

Once they were seated round the desks closest to Coupland's, Robinson ran through the names of the little girls they'd carried out welfare checks on. Some of the situations they'd found themselves in had been dire, back-stories reading like tabloid headlines. The fact the girls were all alive and on social services' radar was something, he hoped. 'Anyone unaccounted for?' Coupland prompted, keen to batten down this line of enquiry one way or another.

'Just two, Sarge.' Robinson informed him, 'Kirsty Walcott and Janine Davy. Janine's mum told us she'd sent her to live with her Dad in Ipswich.'

'Why hadn't she bothered telling her social worker?' Alex asked.

'She said there was a case review coming up, she was going to mention it then.'

'That's good of her. Why the change of heart anyway?'

'Apparently it's mum's new boyfriend that's the problem, he's on the sex offenders' register, though he's adamant the girl he was involved with gave her consent.'

'Charmin'…' Alex muttered.

'Seems there's no problem with the dad's set up, and Janine's mum decided she was fed up of being supervised.' Turnbull picked up the story. 'We contacted the local police there who sent an officer round to the father's address. The officer texted me this at lunchtime.' Turnbull held up a mobile phone image of a little girl on a scooter. The date and time on the bottom of the screen confirmed she was very much alive and well.

'That leaves us with Kirsty Walcott. Mum and Dad split up last year, they've four kids together but Mum moved out only taking the daughter, by all accounts, left him with three boys.'

'Where did she go?'

'Moved to Hattersley, only there was no one answering the door when Hyde Division called round. Neighbour told them she was in Benidorm, got a month-long gig as a singer in one of the bars on the main strip. She guessed the little girl had gone with her.'

Krispy, who'd been taking notes and cross checking against the entries on his database tutted before piping up: 'You were supposed to let me have this information in real time so I can keep this spreadsheet up-to-date. According to my records Janine Davy is still unaccounted for.'

Turnbull shot him a glance. They'd barely had time to visit all the girls on their list as it was, never mind scheduling calls into the incident room to keep Krispy up to date. They'd checked in as much as they could, but the text containing Janine's photo had come in whilst conducting another visit, he'd meant to forward it on but the day had run away with itself. He hoped to Christ Coupland would understand the pressure of juggling priorities; he could do without getting his backside kicked twice in one day. 'Yeah, yeah, I know how it works,' he shrugged.

'Well if you did you'd pass on the information as you got it.'

Coupland's steely look stopped the discussion in its tracks. 'So, where are we with Kirsty Walcott?' he asked.

'The neighbour wasn't sure when Cheryl Keegan, the girl's mother, left for Spain, but airport division are going through passenger manifests over the last four weeks looking for her and Kirsty.'

'Can't the local school help?'

'By the time we started the check on Kirsty the school had closed for the day. I'm going to go call them first thing in the morning.'

Coupland turned to the photo of the sports bag and its putrid contents. 'Given the extent of decomposition, they only need to have clapped eyes on her three weeks ago and we'll know she's not our girl.'

Turnbull nodded.

Coupland caught sight of the wall clock at the back of the room. Their shift had ended two hours ago yet no one was in any hurry to go home. He leaned forward in his chair. 'Right, let's bugger off out of here; remind ourselves what a normal life looks like.' He blinked away the fact that his daughter was pregnant with a serial killer's baby. Normal had taken on a whole new spectrum.

*

Unlike the others who were throwing jackets around shoulders and gathering car keys, Turnbull returned to his desk and began tapping on his computer. 'Thought I'd given you a pass home for the night?' Coupland chided, 'shouldn't you be updating your profile on Match.com or whatever it is you get up to in the evening, while your new get up's still clean?'

Turnbull didn't budge. 'You said this morning you wanted a full report on these girls on your desk close of play, Sarge.'

'Yeah but you've already given me your summary, you know what your actions are for first thing, I'm not going to read any report you write now until tomorrow anyway.'

'That's your choice, Sarge, but I promised to have it done for you and it will be.'

'If this is about earlier—'

'—It isn't,' but they both knew it was.

Coupland regarded his stubborn DC in his garish blue suit. 'S'pose that colour doesn't look too bad in artificial light,' he conceded before heading out of the door.

'Cheers, Sarge,' Turnbull called after him, a smile tugging at the corner of his mouth.

∗

The radio blaring from the back of the house told Coupland Lynn was in the garden. They'd installed outdoor lighting at the back end of summer, meant she could still get outside during the darkest days. Fresh air was supposed to be good for you, he knew that, but he'd spent too long stooped over shallow graves to share her passion. He dropped his keys onto the kitchen table, ignoring the mail propped up against the salt and pepper pots. Justin Beiberlake was playing, a Latin track that made Lynn shake her hips as she raked up fallen leaves. 'Reminds me of happy times, Kev,' she said when she turned and caught him looking at her, and he'd laughed, grateful for her good memory.

'How was your day?' he ventured, trying to gauge how the land lay between them. The hip shaking was a good sign, but he could take no credit for that.

'Two pre-terms went home today,' she said, lifting the leaves into an empty compost bag. 'One of the dads bought me a bottle of prosecco.'

He stared at Lynn's profile, thinking of all the things he'd planned to say to make it right between them. To fix what fell apart the day Lee Dawson came into their lives and ripped their world in two. He thought back to that night on the roof of the multi storey car park and something cold slithered inside him. He could have saved Dawson, he was sure of it. But the bastard was holding the person he and Lynn loved most in the world, threatening to extinguish her like he had his other victims and a mist had swept over him. In the blink of an eye he had morphed from cop to desperate father and once he'd pulled Amy to safety, well… there'd been a satisfaction in watching the bastard fall that he'd never dared admit to. But now his daughter was having Dawson's baby. His grandchild would grow up without a father. Coupland thought of his own and knew it wasn't always a great loss but still, the gap that was left, the hole that was his now to fill. If he wanted. Lynn was torn between supporting both of them, he could see that, and her pain ate away at him like acid. He wanted to reach out to her, wanted to tell her it would all be OK, that he'd find a way to make it better again. Wasn't that a husband's role? To fix things. If not, then what was the point of him? Instead he said, 'Might be making headway on this case, too.'

'A good day all round, then.'

'Can I give you a hand?' he asked, safe in the knowledge that she'd refuse.

'What and have you tramp over my bulbs? You must be joking. Go and do something useful like tidy up that mess you made last night.' The kitchen wall where his wine glass had shattered had been wiped down leaving a faint bloodstained hue. He felt his cheeks flush with shame. He glanced back at Lynn but she had the grace not to watch him squirm. The last thing he felt like was a walk round B&Q but if that's what it took to keep the peace it was a no brainer, as Amy would say. 'Be back soon,' he called out, reaching for his car keys.

*

Coupland had no idea what colour the walls were and knew whatever he chose would be wrong, so he'd hedged his bets and bought all three tins he'd shortlisted. He let himself in, humming what sounded like *Despacito*. Lynn stepped into the hall to meet him, her face drawn. 'We've got a visitor, Kevin.' The use of his full name put him on alert. He cocked an eyebrow at her as he dumped the paint tins on the hall table. Lynn widened her eyes, nodding in the direction of the front room. He followed behind, thinking if it was someone conducting a survey they could do one, he didn't want anything to detract from their reconciliation. The woman waiting in their living room was medium height, auburn hair framing an over made up face. A hand fiddling with a locket around her neck belied her nerves. She looked vaguely familiar, only in his line of work that brought no reassurance at all. 'It's Karen Underwood, Kev,' Lynn added, waiting as the cogs turned in his head.

The woman smiled at him nervously, 'Hello Kevin, I'm—'

'—the woman who adopted Lee Dawson,' Coupland finished for her. He looked at Lynn sharply to see if she knew what the hell was going on but her brow was knotted as she offered the woman a seat. Seems she was none the wiser as to what was going on. Coupland felt as though he was outside his own body, ready to observe his reaction, after all he knew what was coming. 'I saw you at the inquest,' was all he said. He had no intention of offering his condolences, as one parent to another. The words would choke him.

Lynn, who didn't have a nasty bone in her body, was wrestling with her conscience. 'It must have been very hard for you,' she said. It took all Coupland's strength to contain himself. He clamped his mouth shut for fear of what he might say, staring at Lynn as though she was speaking in a foreign language.

Karen, taking his silence as acquiescence, sat beside him on the sofa, her hands moving to flatten the creases in her trousers. 'It's been terrible, to tell you the truth,' she agreed. 'I was shocked when I finally learned... how he died.' Her eyes slid in Coupland's direction before returning to Lynn who'd settled herself on the two-seater opposite. Karen's right hand began to finger her locket, 'but I was horrified to learn what he'd done.'

Coupland's head swivelled like a scene from the Exorcist. 'You mean the murders he'd committed?' he corrected. 'Yeah, shame about them.'

'*Kevin.*' The warning contained in his name gave lie to the smile on Lynn's face.

'We can't change the past,' Karen soothed, her words slow, practised, 'but we can try to make the future a better place.'

Christ, she'd be breaking out in song, next. Coupland ignored Lynn's glare as he tutted. 'Why did you come here? It's not like we'd ever met... not properly.'

'I also saw Amy at the inquest.' Karen faltered. Coupland's shoulders dipped. *Here we go*, he seethed, waiting her out.

'She's pregnant, isn't she?'

Lynn tried not to look like she'd been caught with her fingers in the till but she was as honest as the day was long. She looked at Coupland, waiting to follow his lead. There was a first time for everything, he supposed. 'It's not his,' he said, his poker face giving nothing away, 'so you may as well sling your hook.' Karen looked startled, but made no attempt to move.

'Kevin!' Lynn gasped, ignoring his warning look. 'How can you say that?'

'Very bloody easily if it stops this farce in its tracks.'

'So it *is* his baby?' Karen clarified, checking Lynn's reaction and for the first time she smiled, her fingers clamped around her locket. 'It's like he's coming back to me.' Coupland rolled his eyes towards the ceiling. 'I'm going to be a grandma,' she whispered, 'a new beginning.'

'Give me strength,' Coupland muttered, pushing himself up from the sofa and onto his feet.

'There's no need to get ahead of ourselves,' Lynn warned but Karen held her ground.

'I came to offer my help once the baby was here, when's it due?'

Coupland had heard enough. 'Are you for real?' he exploded, turning to give her benefit of his full beam glare, 'Jesus wept…have the last few months not registered in your world?' He paced around the room, patting his jacket pocket, the feel of his fag packet giving him the encouragement he needed. 'Let me try and explain this to you in words of one syllable: your boy tried to kill my girl. Am I happy she's up the stick by him? No bloody way! So why you think I'd want his dysfunctional family latching on after what she's been through beggars belief.'

'The child will be my flesh and blood though.'

'No, it won't, that honour belongs to the alcoholic granny who gave him away when he was a toddler. Christ Almighty, is *she* going to crawl out from under her stone and lay claim to this baby as well? Let's face it, if either of you had kept a closer eye on him we wouldn't be in this bloody mess. Way to go, grandma!'

'Kevin!' Lynn's tone was sharp. 'I'm sorry, he didn't

mean that,' she added, turning to Karen.

'Don't apologise for me,' Coupland snapped, 'of course I bloody meant it.'

Lynn got to her feet. 'I'll make us all a drink, see if we can't sort something out.'

'Yeah 'cos that'll make everything better!' he sniped in her wake.

'Look,' Karen said, rising from the sofa. She paused as she drew level with Coupland. 'We all make mistakes. I get that, so isn't it better we try to get it right this time around?'

Coupland sighed. Her composure was grating on him. He wanted anger, sparks, swearing and accusations, not tea and meditation. He checked to make sure Lynn was out of earshot before he spoke next. 'Your son was a serial killer. Bad enough I've got to stomach Amy spawning his child but as far as I'm concerned,' he cocked his ear, made sure Lynn was still occupied in the kitchen, 'his train wreck of a family can jog on.'

Coupland was staring out of the front room window, hands shoved deep into his pockets when Lynn returned. She looked around the tidy room as though it was possible Lee Dawson's mother was hiding behind the heavy curtains. 'What did you say to her?' she sighed as she placed a tray with a teapot and three mugs onto the coffee table.

Coupland considered his words. 'Nothing she didn't already know,' he said in truth. Lynn looked at him then, before lifting the tray and leaving the room, though the look she sent in his direction he didn't like one little bit.

DAY THREE

CHAPTER TWELVE

Daylight threatened between the gaping bedroom curtains. Some daft song warbled from the alarm clock radio. Coupland grunted before punching the snooze button. Had a good scratch while staring at the ceiling. He moved his hand tentatively to the other side of the bed. Stone cold. He took advantage of being on his own, passing wind for longer than he would've dared normally, before glaring back at the clock. 5am. A whole three hours' sleep.

To say they'd had words the previous night would have been an understatement. He'd followed Lynn into the kitchen as she'd stomped through with the tea things, all the while his brain whirring as he tried to fathom how to make it right. He was emotionally paralysed apparently. Unwilling to move forward, preferring to occupy silos of pity and resentment. Even as Lynn raged, her insults were accurate. There was nothing to contradict, so he'd done what any right-thinking man would do during her tirade and stared back in defiance, waiting it out. 'You need to start thinking about Amy!' she'd hurled, as though he thought about anything else. 'She'll need family round her; the little mite will need more than just us.' He didn't see how, but had the sense to keep that thought to himself. 'FOR PITY'S SAKE, KEVIN,' she'd yelled, 'how come you've nothing to say for yourself NOW?' He'd stared across at her and something inside him pulsated. He'd been under her spell for twenty years. From the moment he'd clapped eyes on her in A&E while she'd held her own with some drunk. He'd turned up with a colleague who'd come off worst in a scuffle and had been sitting in the waiting room when he spotted her. He'd waded in there and then, only to be given short shrift. *I can look after myself, thank you very much.* And from then on he'd been smitten.

Lynn had scowled at his silence, informing him she was off to bed and if he had any sense he'd go in the spare room tonight, she didn't see why she should be the one to put herself out. He'd stared after her as she left the room. Wondered what the hell he could do to fix things. The paint tins stacked in the hall mocked him. He sighed, had a quick smoke in the garden before rolling up his sleeves and setting about the kitchen wall. By the time he'd finished it was daft o'clock. He'd tiptoed into bed, careful not to disturb her; last thing he wanted was her storming into the other room on point of principle. It must have been his snoring that gave him away, alerted her to the fact he couldn't follow even basic instructions. When he woke up she was gone.

The quiet outside his window was broken by birds twittering, like being awake at this time was a good thing. Despite the temptation to burrow deep inside it he threw back the duvet, convincing himself an early start would do no harm.

*

He headed towards the staff entrance at the rear of Salford Precinct station like a man with concrete in his boots. He could have called in sick, said Lynn was sick for that matter, but he didn't want to tempt fate, wasn't it having a laugh at him already? The CID room was empty save for the night shift sergeant, summarising the night's actions on the computer's intranet ready for handover. 'Bloody hell,' he said, eyeing Coupland, 'that missus of yours finally chucked you out?'

Coupland didn't even crack a smile, the way he normally did when someone quoted one of his sayings back at him. 'Everything's peachy,' he growled, his body language barring any further comment, 'all quiet on the Western Front?'

'Surprisingly so. Five domestics, two assaults, three units in pursuit of a stolen vehicle as we speak, oh, and two old fellas are in the custody suite for knocking seven bells out of one another. One's been filling the other's wheelie bin, so the poor old sod's been having to drive to the tip with his rubbish. Decided to stay up and see who was responsible.'

'How come uniform didn't deal with it?'

'They live on a sheltered housing block. The noise they were making woke some of the residents. Several calls came into control reporting a firearm. Turns out one of the old boys uses a walking stick.'

Coupland tutted, moving over to his own desk. The report Turnbull had promised to type up was printed out and waiting in his in-tray. He glanced at his watch. The canteen would be opening up now. They wouldn't be serving food yet, but the coffee was better than the machine stuff in the corridor and if one of the old dears took pity on him she'd slip him a slice of toast. He signalled to the sergeant to see if he wanted a coffee bringing back. The sergeant shook his head.

Tucking Turnbull's report under his arm Coupland selected a table at the farthest end of the canteen, so far from the entrance no one generally bothered with it, unless they were looking for a bit of shut eye. As if by magic two slices of toast appeared by his latte. Thick sliced, melted butter forming pools where it dipped. Coupland winked at the woman who'd brought it over, then set about reading the report.

*

Morning briefing was brisk. Lack of sleep made Coupland tetchy. Word soon spread to keep out of his way or make sure no one did or said anything to set him off. Today was not a good day to screw up. Turnbull's report hadn't thrown up anything he hadn't covered in his summary the night before, other than the desperation some kids were expected to exist in. The DC had been keen to leave sharp this morning, wanted to be on the doorstep as soon as Kirsty Walcott's school opened. This was no longer about discovering the identity of the girl in the bag, this was about something more. 'You can't become their personal protector,' Coupland had cautioned when the briefing was over. He'd followed Turnbull out to the car park, wanted to have a quiet word without flapping ears assuming he was giving him another bollocking.

'I know, Sarge. I didn't realise how hard it would be. Thought all I'd need to do was check they were present and correct. But the truth is there's nothing correct about them being on that list in the first place.'

Coupland blew out his cheeks. More of his role was about supporting his team, a responsibility he found diffi-cult at the best of times. He found saying nothing while they worked it out for themselves was the option that worked best. He lit a cigarette and sucked on it greedily. It was easier saying nothing when his hands and mouth were occupied.

'I know I could have just called the head teacher rather than go in and see them, but you get a feel for things face-to-face that you just don't get over the phone.' Turnbull was preaching to the converted on that. 'And I promise I won't go off half cocked, anything I don't like the sound of I'll get straight onto Children and Families. Shola Dube's on my speed dial now.' He didn't add he'd swapped numbers with the social worker at the end of their shift together yesterday because he hoped she'd be amenable to a drink. Last thing he wanted was to jinx things. 'Kirsty Walcott's the last little girl on my list, and I'll feel better knowing that she is safe and sound on my watch.' Coupland nodded as he stubbed his cigarette out on the station wall before throwing it into a nearby bin. 'Carry on like this and you'll be wearing a cape over that new suit,' he said, before heading back into the station.

The reception area was swarming with schoolkids. They were from the local high school, going by the uniform they were wearing. 'What's going on?' Coupland asked the desk sergeant.

'DCI Mallender invited them, part of a strategy to improve communication between young people and the police service.' His words came out as though reading from an auto cue. Coupland guessed he hadn't been the first person to enquire about them. 'Didn't you read your email?' The officer kept his face straight as he asked this. 'It went to the whole station.'

Coupland pulled a face as he entered the code into

the keypad to gain access to the staff only area, smiling in sympathy at a harassed-looking teacher. That was the problem with going on courses these days. Time was you could treat it as a jolly, a day off the street with a nice lunch to boot. Afterwards, a swift pint then home to your nearest and dearest. Now you were expected to take part in a debrief, discuss with your superior what you'd got out of it and then share it with your peers. Mallender was doing his bit to keep the superintendent happy. They'd had school kids in the station before in an attempt to build bridges, the thought behind it being that youngsters were less likely to commit crime once they'd been round the inside of a station first. Coupland snorted. Most of the lags carted through the main doors at Salford Precinct had been coming here long before they hit high school, and those that needed to improve their relationship with the police were likely playing truant anyway. That wasn't the point though and he knew it. The police service was all about marketing and PR now, like law and order was an option.

Alex approached him from the direction of the custody suite, a group of teens in tow carrying clipboards. 'I see you've been roped in,' Coupland observed, nodding at the motley crew.

'You don't know the half of it,' she hissed. 'The Super wants me to give them a talk on equal ops – how it's possible to join the service and still be a wife and mother.'

'Aw, Jesus, if he's ticking boxes he'll be after Ashcroft then.'

'He hot footed it out the moment he read the email.'

Coupland's mouth twitched. 'Don't blame him; he must have a sixth sense for all that stuff now.' The thought of the little girl in the bag took the edge off his mood. He felt guilty laughing when they were no nearer finding the child's identity. 'Catch you later,' he sighed before heading in the direction of the incident room.

∗

Duketown Primary was a new-build school on the edge of Little Bolton, an overflow housing estate that had doubled in size since Salford's redevelopment had displaced local families. The new school had been promised two elections back, with the council making good on that promise three years ago when construction began, the school finally opening its doors last year. At first glance the two storey concrete building clad in corrugated steel wouldn't look out of place on an industrial estate as a head office for a vending machine sales or travel company. The structure was utilitarian, functional, not the sort of place you'd decorate in bunting on sports day.

Turnbull pressed the entry button by the entrance door, holding his lanyard up to the camera mounted on the wall, waited for the buzzer to signal right of entry. The reception area was spacious and light, it smelled of fresh paint, the plant on the coffee table in the seated area still had a price tag on it. The glass fronted office area had several workstations but they were empty, save for the woman who had buzzed him in, who was in the process of unpacking milk and teabags from a recyclable supermarket bag. A printer nearby spewed out several pages which she placed into a large shoulder bag as she looked up at him. 'I rang earlier,' Turnbull informed her, 'I'm here to speak to the head teacher.'

'You're speaking to her,' the woman smiled, slipping the

bag over her shoulder. She held up the tea and milk with one hand and pointed to a staff only entry door with the other. 'Two ticks and I'll let you through, I just want to put the kettle on first, I'm parched.' Turnbull moved towards a door that said 'Authorised personnel only', moments later the door opened and he was ushered in. 'Emily Bathurst,' she said, pumping his hand, 'I'm always the first to arrive in the morning. I'm the last to leave in the evening as well if truth be told but then it goes with the territory, I suppose.'

'Still, it beats proper work,' Turnbull said, as he was shown into a large staff room with stuffed chairs that wouldn't look out of place in a show home, with a kitchen area to one side and a cloakroom to the other.

'Sorry?' Emily asked, but the look she gave him told him her hearing was just fine.

'No, I'm sorry,' Turnbull back-pedalled, 'schools bring out the worst in me.'

'Not a happy time for you then?' she enquired, an eyebrow raised as though she was asking him where his homework was.

'I – I wouldn't say that exactly,' he stammered, 'though it's fair to say the teachers were probably glad to see the back of me.'

'I loved school, hated the thought of leaving so much I decided to go into teaching.'

Turnbull studied Emily as she poured boiling water into two cups, hovering the milk carton over his cup until he said yes or no. 'Just a splash,' he nodded. Late thirties with shoulder length hair and a kind smile, she didn't look anywhere near as fearsome as the teachers in his day, though he supposed being the same height as her helped.

'Take a seat,' she offered, handing him a mug before folding herself into a chair clustered round a central table. Turnbull took the one beside her. 'We won't be disturbed for another twenty minutes or so,' she added, 'and the chairs here are so much more comfortable than my office.'

'Thought you'd have had the pick of the bunch.'

'Oh I did,' she laughed, 'but I don't want people to be comfortable when they come to see me. No, I prefer it when folk get straight to the point; they come to me for solutions, not shooting the breeze.'

Turnbull followed her lead. 'About Kirsty Walcott,' he began, 'I need to know when she was last in school.'

Emily nodded, swivelled round in her chair so she could reach her shoulder bag. 'As you can imagine I can't keep tabs on every child in the school, even those where issues have been raised. I know her mother took her out during term time to go on holiday, but I can't tell you more than that till I look at her attendance record. I printed it out while I was waiting for you, this should have everything you need to know.'

'Why was she on social services' radar?'

Emily looked confused. 'Didn't they tell you?'

'I want to hear it from you.'

'Well, part of the problem is her attendance. To be honest, I don't think her mother can be bothered bringing her in.'

'And how do you deal with that?'

'If a child doesn't attend school it is considered a safeguarding matter. This is why we need information as to the cause of each absence. Kirsty's mum was fairly efficient when she first moved her here, sending texts to explain why she was keeping her off. Then the texts

179

stopped coming.'

'What, and that's it?'

'We're supposed to telephone the home if we haven't heard from the parents but many homes don't have landlines now and if the parents' mobiles run out of battery…' she trailed off but he got the gist.

Something occurred to him that he needed to clarify. 'How did the little girl seem on the days she did come in?'

Emily thought about this. 'Subdued at first. She hated missing school. Young children are dependent on their parents or carers for their attendance and punctuality. You know from your own experience how vital it is that children enjoy coming to school, and whilst being encouraged to attend and be on time, we will not make them carry blame or be made to feel unhappy if their parents are not supportive or effective in these areas.' She sounded like a talking handbook, as though she was on Mastermind and her specialist subject was dysfunctional families. That or she was in the middle of a job interview.

'I'm interested in Kirsty, not your policies and procedures,' he reminded her.

Emily blinked. 'I'm sorry,' she countered. 'I am responsible for all the children here, and so many have a similar story to Kirsty.' She paused for a moment. 'I think that she was beginning to understand that she was missing out socially, the other children were making friends, choosing who they played with at break time, inviting each other to birthday parties. She was missing out on that, to the point where staying at home became the preferable option.' Turnbull waited. 'Look,' she added defensively, 'I sent a teaching assistant round to her home once or twice, but if no one answers the door what can you do? After a while,

180

when I saw a pattern emerging, I referred her to Children and Families. Nothing we did made any difference so I thought an alternative approach would help. Here…' she showed him the attendance printout she'd taken from her bag and pointed to an entry: 'A holiday request – which was granted by me – was made four weeks ago. Oh…'

'What is it?'

'She was due back at school 10 days ago but never returned.'

Turnbull didn't blink. 'You have a legal duty to report the absence of any pupil absent without an explanation for 10 consecutive days.'

'You don't have to quote the rule book at me, detective. As it happens, Kirsty's mum is very adept at playing the system. Just as her daughter's absences were about to trigger her being reported to the local authority she'd bring her back in, full of apologies, promising she'd not keep her off again.'

'But that hasn't happened this time.'

Emily hesitated, 'A supply teacher has been covering her class… The secretary that collates the data is away on jury duty. Under normal circumstances…'

Turnbull sighed. He pulled out his mobile but before he dialled DS Coupland he wanted to check something. 'What about Kirsty's appearance?'

'Oh, she wasn't covered in bruises if that's what you mean.'

Turnbull's brow creased, 'So what was the other reason she was on the at-risk register? You said that her attendance was only part of the reason.'

'For being obese. Her weight was a great cause for concern, brought about by poor diet and lack of any exercise. The poor girl just doesn't get out, when she's kept off school she sits in front of the television all day eating the junk food her mother buys her.' She turned to one of several class photos on the wall behind her desk. Lifting one down, she pointed to a fat little girl in the front row. Turnbull couldn't see in a million years how a child that size that would fit into a sport bag but right now she was unaccounted for, and her absence was a growing cause for concern. He hit the speed dial on his phone. DS Coupland needed to be updated right away.

*

Salford Precinct Station

Coupland was reading through a note that had been left on his desk: Airport division confirmed Cheryl Keegan had boarded a plane to Alicante four weeks ago. She'd been travelling alone. They'd tried contacting her on her mobile but it was switched off. She was listed to return on a flight due to land at Manchester at 2.30pm this afternoon.

The phone charging on his desk started to ring. Turnbull's name appeared across the screen. The DC didn't wait for Coupland's terse greeting. '*The girl's not in school, Sarge. Hasn't been seen for the last four weeks. Thing is, I've seen a photo of her, and she's quite a big little girl, if you get my drift, on the at-risk register for neglect and poor diet as well as low attendance. I was wondering though, since she's so big for her age, how she would have fitted into that bag.*'

'The post mortem confirmed that our girl hadn't eaten for a while. It's too early to cross her off our list yet. We've tracked down mummy dearest who, by the way, is travelling alone; we're just waiting for her plane to land.'

This was their best lead yet. 'Good work,' he added, before ending the call.

'Kirsty Walcott's still unaccounted for,' he said aloud as he wrote her name on the incident board. 'Her mother's flight's due in this afternoon. Krispy,' he called out to the young DC, 'get onto Airport division, I want her arrested the moment the plane lands. That'll take the wind out of her lilo.'

*

Cheryl Keegan's arresting officer greeted Coupland and Alex Moreton on arrival at Manchester Airport police station. 'Happy bunny?' Coupland enquired as they were shown through to the custody suite.

'You'll see for yourself soon enough,' the PC replied, his dead pan face giving nothing away. The shouting could be heard in the corridor. Righteous indignation interspersed with a rapid-fire round of four letter words that would make a docker blush.

Coupland took his time, wanted the errant mother to stew a bit longer. Did no harm to keep her waiting. He turned to Alex. 'Want to lead on this one?'

'Don't mind if I do. After a morning trying to enter-tain a group of sullen teenagers this'll be a walk in the park. Do you think it's possible that she's harmed Kirsty? She wouldn't be the first mother to turn on her own child, even so…'

'There's only one way to find out,' Coupland said, pushing open the interview room door.

'About bleedin' time! Are you the one in charge here? I've been waiting ages.'

Alex cocked her head as she took a seat. 'Problem?'

183

she asked.

The woman stabbed a finger in the direction of the officer who'd escorted them into the interview room and his colleague, a WPC standing against the far wall. 'I've been dragged in here by these tossers, only no one's telling me anything!' The woman shouting the odds was older than Coupland expected, the wrong side of forty or spent too much time frowning. He hadn't realised spray tan came in so many shades of creosote. White leggings stretched across ample thighs, a day-glo pink vest peeped out beneath a zip up hoodie. She was make-up free apart from black eyeliner, her hair scraped back and coiled into a doughnut. 'I haven't smuggled any drugs, if that's what you're thinking! If you don't believe me have a look up my—'

'That won't be necessary,' Alex cut in, her tone business-like. After making the introductions she sat in one of the chairs vacated by the officer who'd detained Ms Keegan. Coupland took the seat beside her. The two uniforms remained in the room, taking up position either side of the only exit.

'I'm going to make this quick, Cheryl,' Alex began, 'we need to know the whereabouts of your daughter.'

Cheryl looked confused. 'Kirsty? Why?'

'Because we're investigating the murder of a little girl and at the moment your daughter is unaccounted for.'

'What?' The woman's voice came out like a squeak. 'You think it's our Kirsty?'

'We don't know anything to sure, only that your daughter's been absent from school for the last four weeks and yet you've not taken her away with you.'

Cheryl had the grace to look sheepish, 'I was staying

with my mate, there was no room!' She regarded Alex, eyes narrowing, 'Do the social know she's not been in school?'

'Never mind that, where is she?'

'I didn't leave her home alone if that's what you're thinking! I sent her to stay with my ex's dozy sister. She was supposed to take her to school though, even if it was just for a couple of days, get the old bat off my back. Here—' she leaned down to reach something from her bag, giving Coupland an unwanted view of a creped cleavage. 'I'll FaceTime her on my phone.'

'That won't be necessary,' Coupland cut in, 'give us her address and we'll send someone round there, pronto.'

*

It took less than an hour to establish that Kirsty Walcott was alive and well. Turnbull found her curled up on the sofa watching Judge Judy with her auntie in Swinton. 'I thought Cheryl had cleared it with her teacher,' she'd said lamely when asked why Kirsty hadn't attended school.

This time Turnbull didn't feel quite so despondent. 'The social worker who came out with us yesterday has taken over their file, she's instigating a case conference regarding Kirsty's welfare,' he informed Coupland when he returned to the station, 'she's on the ball that one,' he added.

Coupland sighed as he rubbed Kirsty Walcott's name from the incident board. 'Sometimes I don't know why I don't pack it all in, find a job where it's no big deal if I don't get a result. Sell double glazing or something,'

'You'd get sacked if you didn't hit your target,' Alex informed him.

'Fine then, something where the hours are regular and the money is good.'

'Now you're talking,' Turnbull agreed.

'Like what?'

'How would I know?' Coupland shrugged. 'I could retrain.'

'Ya think?' Alex laughed, lowering her voice as she stood beside him. 'Doesn't retrain imply that you've got the capacity to embrace change?'

Coupland scowled. 'You saying I'm too old?'

Alex shook her head, 'But you are stuck in your ways, Kevin. Creature of habit, that's what you are.'

Coupland returned to his desk to find a black plastic bag on top of it. The top of the bag was open so he peered inside. Piles of baby clothes had been folded into neat little squares. He pulled out a romper suit and held it up for inspection like a pathologist might hold a small bowel. 'Just a few things the boys have grown out of,' Alex smiled, moving towards him, 'thought they'd come in handy for Amy.'

The look he gave her made her stop in her tracks, her smile frozen in place. 'This is a joke, right?' Coupland dropped the baby clothes back into the bag as though they were contaminated. A laugh escaped from him, like a car backfiring. 'I mean, have you not been listening to a word I've said?' He stomped towards her with his hand outstretched in mock greeting. 'Hi, my name's Angry from Salford and my daughter's pregnant by Jack the bloody Ripper.' He lurched back to his desk, sweeping his arm across it knocking the bin bag onto the floor, spilling its contents. A bib with 'Daddy's little super star,' lay at his feet. 'Which bit of this car crash makes you think fluffy grow bags are the answer?' The detectives within earshot shuffled papers and feet, checked watches and lowered their heads, they'd seen him before when he went off on one but in the past it was work-related and in the grand scheme of things didn't matter, but this was a whole lot worse. Some had heard on the grapevine that Coupland's daughter was pregnant but no one knew who the father was. Until now. No wonder he wasn't handing out cigars.

'*Babygrows*,' Alex corrected him, holding her ground. 'They're not grow bags, they're babygrows, and if that's how you feel before it's even been born your poor grand-child needs every bit of help it can get.' She swept past him, scooping up the clothes, ramming them back inside the bag with a lot less care than when she'd originally put them in. Finished, she hugged the bag close to her chest. 'I'll bring them round to your house tonight, Kevin, and I suggest if it's too much sodding effort for you to be pleasant you might want to be out when I call.'

'Problem?' DCI Mallender was standing in the doorway. It was hard to tell by his demeanour how much he'd seen, but his question was directed at Alex. She shook her head. 'Can I see you in my office a moment?' he asked her, casting a quizzical glance in Coupland's direction before leaving the room. Alex placed the bag of clothes beside her own desk, aware that her hands were shaking. She could feel sympathetic glances cast in her direction, but the last thing she wanted was people taking sides. A tension headache was starting behind her ears, she reached for her handbag, took out two paracetamol, swigging them down with the coffee dregs in her cup. Picking imaginary fluff from her jumper, she headed out into the corridor and Mallender's office.

Coupland stood by his desk, seething. He was desperate for a fag, chocolate, caffeine, anything to counteract the adrenaline coursing through him. 'Get us a coffee, would you, Krispy?' he barked without looking up, his eyes fixed on his desktop screen as though reading emails was what he lived for.

'Yes, Sarge.' Krispy sprang to his feet, exchanging a look with Turnbull.

Once Krispy had gone, and the other DCs had returned to their tasks, Turnbull pushed back his chair and made his way over to Coupland's desk. 'I…I…I'm really sorry, Sarge,' he began, reflecting on Coupland's earlier remark that there were easier ways to earn a living, 'it must be a—'

Coupland's head reared back as he fixed Turnbull with a stare. 'What just happened here, DC Turnbull?' he growled.

A confused look flitted across Turnbull's face. 'I don't know,' he answered, hedging his bets.

'Then let me help you out. Sweet Fanny Adams, that's what happened. Are we clear?'

Turnbull nodded as he backed away. 'Loud and clear, Sarge,' he mumbled, 'loud and clear.'

When Alex returned to the CID room Coupland was nowhere to be seen. 'Where's he gone?' Turnbull raised his hand to his mouth, mimicked puffing on a cigarette. Alex thought about going out to join him then thought better of it. With luck and a prevailing wind a smoke would calm him, give him the chance to pause and reflect. She hoped so anyway, because what she had to tell him wouldn't go down very well at all.

It was a contrite Coupland that made a beeline in her

direction ten minutes later. 'Look,' he began, 'I'm sorry for kicking off, I was just gobsmacked you—'

'You don't need to explain.' Her tone was brisk. 'Look, it's better you hear it from me first but I've been taken off the case.'

'What?' Coupland narrowed his eyes suspiciously, 'Taken off or you've seen your backside and asked to be moved?' Funny how this had happened within minutes of him throwing his toys out of the pram, or throwing the baby clothes out of the bin bag, to be more accurate.

Alex shook her head in frustration. 'Oh, for God's sake, Kevin, have you heard yourself? It isn't all about you, you know. Superintendent Curtis has been leaning on the boss. He wants a draft of the case review I'm working on as soon as possible. To help facilitate that,' she held her fingers in quotation marks, 'he asked the boss to clear my workload so I could give it my full attention.'

'Fine,' Coupland grunted, 'managed perfectly well while you weren't here anyway.' He trudged over to his desk for his car keys before heading back out the way he came.

'Whatever,' Alex spat back.

CHAPTER THIRTEEN

Coupland gave the doctors' receptionist his best smile. 'Sorry about the other day,' he began, 'it's the long hours, plays havoc with my glucose levels.'

'Is that why you're here then?' the woman asked. 'Only you should really phone for an appointment.' She looked sideways at her colleague for backup.

'No,' he said, keeping his smile in check, 'I need to speak to the doc I saw, Helen Baxter.' His hand hovered over his warrant card in case he needed to show it once more but it wasn't necessary. The impression he'd made during his previous visit had lingered, the narky cop who'd made a show of himself was back. Coupland crossed his fingers that the girl he'd almost run over and her have-a-go father weren't also back by some unhappy coincidence.

A young woman with dyed red hair cut into layers appeared from behind the wall of patient files behind the reception desk. The hairdo was probably expensive but to Coupland it looked like it had been cut with a knife and fork. She was carrying a mug of fruit tea by the colour of it, while reading something on her phone. She glanced up at the sound of her name. 'Ah, DS Coupland, back so soon.'

The receptionist swivelled round in her chair so that Coupland could only see her back. 'He's wondering if he can speak to you again doctor.' Coupland could imagine the face that she was pulling but nodded anyway.

Helen Baxter raised an eyebrow. 'Just as well I'm on my break then,' she said, stepping into the main waiting area and gesturing with a sweep of her arm he should follow her to her consulting room for a second time that week.

He was led into the same airy room, the walls adorned with large canvas prints of a little girl. Some were formal, the type taken in a photographer's studio, the child's clothes clean on and freshly ironed, her smile shy for the camera. Others were enlarged photos of pictures taken on holiday, t-shirts grubby with melted ice-cream, a face brimming with mischief. Dr Baxter followed his gaze and smiled. 'My daughter,' she beamed, 'turned five last month. Always swore I wouldn't be one of those parents with a desk cluttered with photo frames and yet here I am…' she held up a mouse mat which had a picture of the little girl dressed like a princess. There was a photo at home with Amy dressed in a get up like that, he was sure of it. His shoulders dipped at the thought.

'Your colleague's not with you today then?' Helen smiled.

Coupland shook his head. 'No, she's tied up with admin.'

'God, she has my sympathies then,' she shuddered, 'paperwork drives me nuts.'

Coupland was only half listening, his attention was still on the wall behind her head, a blown up beach photo of a girl in a swimming costume sitting beside a wonky sandcastle. 'Where was that taken?' he asked.

Helen shrugged. 'Can't remember.'

Coupland continued to look around the room. 'So

you're camera shy, then,' he observed, pointing to a collage of photos on the side of a filing cabinet. In each one the little girl was solo, or with a group of pals the same age, school friends perhaps, a birthday trip out. In some there was an adult beside her, but the picture had been cropped so that only an arm or shoulder remained, and what remained was male.

'What?' she turned in her seat to see what it was that had caught his attention.

'You're not in any of the photos.'

'Oh…' She frowned then, as though trying to work out if he was being serious.

'I love having my picture taken,' he told her, 'it's a reminder, isn't it… of better times, I mean? Something to look back on when things get tough.'

The doctor's desktop computer pinged, not dis-similar to the sound Coupland's phone made when it told him he had an email. 'Is there another patient you wanted to enquire about, DS Coupland? Only my next appointment is waiting.'

Coupland ignored her. 'Been with your little girl's father long, have you?' he asked, his eyes resting on her bare ring finger.

'What? Oh, we *were* married,' she wrinkled her nose as she said this, 'but divorced long ago.' She blew out a breath. 'You couldn't have got a more miss-matched couple if you'd tried, but that's the problem with sex I suppose. Distorts your view for a while. All thoughts of compatibility went out of the window. Didn't stay there long, mind, not once I was a house doctor pulling an 80 hour week and he was trying to discover his muse. Shame really, there'd been an orthopod throw his cap at me back

192

in the day, he's a consultant now, married – successfully – three kids and a barn conversion in Wilmslow. Seems my mother was right all along… Our daughter lives with her dad, DS Coupland. He was her main carer anyway, made sense he'd want to carry on. Must admit I was relieved to tell you the truth, don't have the patience he has. Besides, she'd be stuck in some nursery or with a resentful au pair if I had her and I'm not so stubborn I can't see that wouldn't have been fair.'

Coupland had sensed there was something of the theatrical about her photo gallery the first time he had visited, but had been on the back foot following his altercation in the reception area so hadn't trusted his judgement. The size and sheer number of photos had given him the impression Helen Baxter was compensating for something, he just hadn't known what. 'Couldn't you have mentioned this, when we came around the first time?'

'I suppose I could… but I thought you were visiting me in a professional capacity. It's a force of habit I suppose. Doctors are so used to being asked for opinions on other people it didn't occur to me you might want to know about my personal set up too… I'm sorry, I hope I haven't wasted your time…'

'Not any more, no,' Coupland got to his feet. 'I'll need your ex-husband's contact details, and one of these photographs.'

Helen stared at him. 'Are you serious? You're wasting your time, my daughter's alive and well I can assure you, I speak to her every week, she isn't the little girl you are trying to ID.'

'I'm sure she isn't. But in my experience we can't ignore something on someone else's say-so, regardless of what they do for a living.'

'Of course, I understand your need to be thorough.'

Coupland got to his feet, 'Then you'll understand my need to be crack on, love, so if you wouldn't mind.'

The doctor scribbled her ex's details down on a sheet of paper before reaching for a photo in a frame on the far side of her desk. She removed the back of it then gently lifted it out, turning it over to study it before handing it to him. 'That's the most recent one. Taken at her birthday party.'

'You weren't there?'

For a second the smile fell, Helen looked away as she replied, 'My ex remarried. So Cara has a step mum now. We felt it was easier if I stayed in the background.'

Easier for the little girl, or the acrimonious parents, Coupland wondered.

*

A cab parked on double yellow lines close to the entrance to Salford Shopping City waited while a group of hens staggered towards it. Dressed in identical tee shirts the women's cackle carried along the road, not even tea time and they were tanked up. A couple of nights away beckoned, given the bags they were dragging behind them. 'Happy days,' Coupland muttered, ignoring their cat calls as he headed towards Costa Coffee.

A girl no older than Amy sat on a blanket on the pavement, knees drawn up to her chin, mottled arms wrapped around scrawny shins. Against his better nature Coupland went across to her. A cardboard cup lay at her feet, the change inside barely covering the bottom of it. 'Quiet day?' The girl looked up in alarm, unused to being the focus of attention. 'Let me buy you a coffee, you need one by the look of it.'

The girl shook her head. 'No, give me money.'

Coupland detected an accent, the girl's use of English making her sound more direct than he suspected she meant to be. 'I'll get you a sandwich,' he said, 'I've a daughter not much older than you.'

The girl shook her head once more. 'I need money,' she insisted, her eyes darting to something behind Coupland.

He turned in time to see a car drive off, the driver making a point of looking the other way. He turned back to the girl. 'Is he the reason you need cash love?' he asked. 'Only what he's doing is illegal, you know that?'

The girl screwed up her eyes. 'I don't understand,' she answered, but the way she said it told Coupland she did.

*

By the time he pulled into the car park at Salford Precinct Station his coffee had gone from scalding the roof of his mouth hot to tepid. He removed the lid, gulping at it as he made his way through reception. DCI Mallender was walking in the opposite direction. Coupland slowed as they drew level.

'I was only letting off a bit of steam, boss,' he told him, 'earlier, I mean.'

Mallender said nothing.

'Sometimes Alex goes on a bit, pushing all the wrong buttons because she thinks she's Kofi Annan, or Ban Ki-moon or whoever it is these days trying to make countries that can't stand each other not pee in the sand pit. If I offended her I didn't mean it, I've already said I'm sorry. I didn't think she'd ask to come off the case though. Apart from that particular gobfull I'd given her I thought we were getting on just fine.'

Mallender peered at him closely, as though checking his pupils for size. 'I have absolutely no idea what you're talking about. DS Moreton didn't ask to be taken off the case. As a matter of fact she asked if she could stay on it if she worked in her own time but I put my foot down on that; after all, she's only just returned to work; don't want her overstretched in her first week back. Now, you'll have to excuse me, I've a meeting at HQ and top brass doesn't like to be kept waiting.'

Coupland's shoulder's dipped. Alex had been straight with him all along but he'd been too stubborn to see it. He headed towards the CID room, half hoping that she would be on her way out somewhere so that he could take her to one side without anyone seeing, say how sorry he was he'd got it wrong without an audience enjoying every minute. He headed over to Krispy's desk, held out the piece of paper Helen Baxter had written her husband's details down on. 'The GP I saw this morning has a daughter, doesn't live with her though, same age as our victim so can you do the honours?' Krispy took the paper from him, nodding. He normally gave Coupland a running commentary of his actions for the day, like an eager pup trying to please but today he was quiet, as though wary of speaking out of turn. He'd been present when Coupland had chewed Alex out, and would have heard about him lambasting Turnbull. He probably didn't fancy his chances of staying on his right side. The boy learned fast, he'd give him that.

'DS Moreton around?' he asked, his voice neutral, Krispy looked over at her desk as though she might be hiding behind it. He turned back to Coupland before shaking his head.

'I can see she's not at her desk,' Coupland began, his patience wearing thin. 'Oh, do you know what? Forget it…'

A pile of statements had been left in his in-tray: taken from the house-to-house enquiries from the neighbouring streets. Ashcroft's interview with Ashdown Court's landlord and the owner of the maintenance firm lay on top of them, along with a statement from Dawn Tylor, Flat 2a's previous tenant. Coupland worked his way through them, pausing only to cross reference them against each other and the timeline that was beginning to emerge leading up to the victim being found. Flat 2a had been unoccupied for several weeks due to Dawn taking up a new job. The landlord had kept her deposit and rent paid for the following month to compensate – his words – for the lack of notice given. During that time he'd put a request in to Ryland's maintenance firm that the paintwork was to be freshened up before the new tenants moved in. The landlord didn't bother checking that the work had been carried out – although Ryland's job sheet confirmed it had – until the night before the new tenants – Ali and Jason – were due to move in. He spotted scuff marks on the paintwork which he decided to deal with himself. There was nothing untoward about the flat that evening, he claimed, he had no reason to suspect anyone else had gained entry that shouldn't have. Certainly no one who would hide a child's body in a bag in the bedroom cupboard.

Dawn's statement suggested she hadn't been as relaxed as the landlord implied about losing her deposit and month's rent; she accepted she'd broken the terms of her lease but described Donald Riding as creepy; stating she'd caught him lurking outside her flat one evening for no apparent reason. She'd been glad to move out of there, nothing on earth would make her stay a day longer than she had to, though she had got on well with Jilly Clarke in the flat above. DC Ashcroft had updated the statement following a subsequent phone call with Dawn where she seemed cagey about her reason for moving out, insisting it was work related, and no, she couldn't remember who'd been visiting her the night the night she'd caught Riding snooping about on the landing.

The neighbours from the properties adjacent to Ashdown Court didn't have much to say. The apartment block came with its own self-contained car park so there was little opportunity for anyone in the neighbouring houses to get to know its residents, not that anyone showed any inclination; what with work and family commitments they had enough on their plate.

The statements he and Alex had taken from Ashdown Court's residents were just as unhelpful. There were no nosy neighbours there. Just a group of people who shared a building, who on the whole preferred to keep to themselves. Someone was lying. Someone out there knew who the little girl was. Someone had killed her, stuffed her in a sports bag like an old rag. The problem was, who?

Two hours slid by before Coupland even raised his head. A quick call to Jimmy Rawlings confirmed that he'd reported a leak to the landlord which tied in with Dawn Tylor seeing Donald Riding outside her flat. He'd made a handful of notes, underlined throwaway comments that were worth raking over. It wasn't so much what people said, than what they omitted to say, that intrigued him. Some needed coaxing, failing that threatening with obstruction, but either way sometimes you needed to scratch the surface a little harder to see what lurked underneath. Was that what he should have done at home, he wondered? Looked to see what was really going on before opening his mouth. He had a habit of going off at a tangent once an idea took hold, which was great if he was on the right track, but when he got it wrong… his shoulders sank as a thought occurred to him. How could he have been so blind? He almost collided with Krispy in the corridor, the young DC automatically apologising for getting in his way. Coupland didn't hear him, so lost in his own thoughts he wasn't aware of anyone or anything around him.

When Alex returned to her desk ten minutes later she saw that although Coupland wasn't at his desk he was around somewhere, his bin was full to the brim with paper coffee cups and the top of his desk was scattered with chewed pen lids. 'The Sarge was looking for you… Sarge,' Krispy told her, 'but he left in a hurry just before you got back.'

'Well he can't have got far,' she said, eyeing the car keys on his desk. 'I'll go see if I can find him.'

After grabbing herself a decaffeinated tea from the canteen Alex headed outside to the smoking area. There, like a wildebeest drinking from a watering hole, Coupland could be seen in profile, sucking on a Marlborough Light. The tremor in his hand wiped away any sniping remark she'd been about to make. He turned as he heard someone approach, his blue eyes piercing into hers as he gave her a nod. 'Finally decided to give it a go?' he said, holding up his smoking hand.

Alex shook her head, 'Just wanted to check you're OK… There's something eating you up, buddy, and I don't know how to help.'

A breath hissed out. 'You can't.'

'You'll get round to the idea of this baby soon enough,' she continued. 'I know what you're like, you just need to see beyond its father.'

Coupland pulled his lips into a thin line, the closest he could muster to a smile in the present circumstances. 'Lynn was pregnant when I met her.'

Alex widened her eyes, 'Are you saying Amy isn't—'

'I'm not saying anything because you're not giving me a bloody chance,' he spat, his eyes narrowing.

She raised her hands, 'OK, OK… Look, I promise to keep it zipped.' She pressed her lips together with her fingers to make her point.

'The father was some toss pot who had let her down, they hadn't been together long when she found out and he buggered off pretty much the moment the blue line appeared on the stick.'

'And you knew from the beginning…'

Coupland glared at her. 'Of course I bloody knew! She told me from the offing; that was Lynn all over, straight as a die. I'd asked her out and she'd stared at me and said, 'You might want to change your mind when you hear this…' Anyway, I was already keen on her, told her it didn't matter. By the time the baby was due I knew I could love it like my own. We got wed in a registry office, her dad wouldn't stump up for a church do in the circumstances…' he tailed off then, as though weighing up whether he wanted to say out loud what was burdening him. 'Only she lost the baby.' He said the words quickly, as though that would hurt less in some way. 'Eclampsia.'

Alex gasped, 'I'm so sorr—'

'Don't,' Coupland cut in, 'I know you mean well but… it doesn't help. It never did…'

Alex nodded.

'Anyway,' Coupland hauled in a breath as he continued, 'we carried on, picked up the pieces, Lynn retrained as a paediatric nurse, found it healing, she said… then a couple of years later Amy came along.' Coupland turned away. 'Thing is, I think Lynn's reading things into my problem with Amy's baby that aren't there.'

'What do you mean?'

'I was gutted when Lynn lost the baby, couldn't have felt any worse if it had been my own, and yet here I am resenting this child because of its father. She's adding two and two and making five, thinking that maybe I was relieved all those years ago that she lost the baby after all.'

'Then you need to set her straight.'

'How can I, when we're barely even talking? We got a visit from the granny-to-be from hell last night.'

Alex frowned.

'Lee Dawson's adoptive mum, which was hardly conducive to a cosy heart to heart.'

'And then I come along today with my size ten feet…'

'It was a nice gesture.'

'Just lousy timing.'

Coupland nodded. He'd finished his cigarette, stubbing it out on the bin provided. He didn't bother reaching for another. Something was niggling at the back of his skull, a comment he'd read earlier in the pile of statements that wouldn't go away. He checked his watch. As long as he got a move on he'd be fine. 'About what I said earlier…' he began, backing away, 'I know you didn't ask to be taken off this case, and I know I've been acting like a knob. Can we rewind today and start again?'

Alex flashed him a lop-sided smile. 'No bloody chance, mate! I quite like the idea of throwing it in your face whenever the mood takes me… Hang on, where are you off to now?'

Coupland grinned. 'Need to see a man about a desirable residence.'

Alex shrugged. 'Fine, but for Christ's sake talk to Lynn, otherwise the only property you'll be looking for will be a bedsit for one.'

Coupland returned to the CID room to pick up his car keys, moving the pile of statements he'd read through earlier onto Krispy's desk. 'I want you to run background checks on this lot, find out if any of these names have priors for anything, doesn't matter what, parking violations, anything, I need to know.' Krispy nodded, but the look on his face suggested something was on his mind. 'Spit it out, lad,' Coupland barked.

'Sarge,' Krispy began, 'you asked yesterday for reasons why our victim's parents wouldn't have reported her missing. Well maybe they don't know she's missing.'

'What do you mean?'

'Well maybe she doesn't live with them—'

'We're already working with Children and Families department to check on all kids in residential and foster care, son.'

'No, I don't mean a situation where the child officially lives away from their parents, I mean where the parents may be working away, and they've left their child with

202

someone they trust.' Coupland let out a snort of derision at Krispy's use of the word. 'You know what I mean,' Krispy added hastily, 'the person responsible for the child wouldn't necessarily be on social services radar, and they may not want to admit that she's gone.'

Coupland considered this. 'You could be onto something there.' He marched over to the incident board, wrote the word 'Invisible' over the photo of the sports bag.

'Who's invisible?' Turnbull asked, returning from the canteen.

'This little girl,' Coupland answered, jabbing his index finger against the photo, 'we need to turn the way we've been trying to find her identity on its head.' He stared at the detectives gathering around him. 'What if she's been invisible her whole life? Like she never even existed? I mean let's face it, the only reason anyone's giving a damn now is because her body turned up where it shouldn't.'

'Are you saying she's here illegally?'

'That's exactly what I'm saying. Turnbull, I want you to go back to that social worker, find out what contact she has with refugee charities – or direct with illegal immigrants for that matter – it's no time for her to be coy.' Turnbull scratched the stubble on his chin, 'It'll be like looking for a needle when we don't even know where the haystack is.'

'Then the sooner we get our backsides in gear, the better.'

*

Coupland parked his car in front of Thompson and Grant Property and Estate Agents, a double fronted building at the smart end of Chapel Street heading into Manchester's city centre. Two large windows displayed photographs of spotless homes. He scrolled through the inbox on his phone while finishing his cigarette, checking for messages: Krispy had got hold of Dr Baxter's husband, attached to his email was a photo of a little girl wearing the reception class sweatshirt of Ellenbrook Primary. Coupland didn't need to pull out the photograph Helen Baxter had given him to see they were one and the same but he did anyway. Didn't pay to be sloppy, to rely on memory alone. It was why most witnesses, even well-meaning ones, were unreliable.

If Alistair Grant recognised Coupland when he walked into his place of work he didn't let on. He approached him with a smile, nodding at the property schedules in the window. 'Anything in particular take your fancy?' he asked, his brow furrowing as he drew close, his gaze moving up and down Coupland as he tried to work out if he'd been in before.

Coupland cocked an eyebrow, 'All of 'em, but unless I'm promoted to chief constable any time soon I'll be staying where I am.'

The smile faded on Alistair's lips. 'You're the detective…'

'The very same,' Coupland said brightly.

'Ah, DS Coupland…' He turned to see Judy Grant leaning against an internal door that led through to a back office. 'Has Alistair showed you the new development in Clifton we're handling? I can picture you in an executive townhouse, and they're competitively priced too.'

'I bet they are,' he smiled, then, 'mebbe I will take a brochure, show the missus I do listen when she tells me we've got itchy feet. Though I've always fancied a time-share personally, Tenerife maybe.' That'd likely be out of the question now, he surmised, what with a baby on its way. Alistair's ears pricked up: 'I have a friend who specialises in—'

Coupland waved his suggestion away. 'Have to go on the back burner I reckon, at least for a while.'

'I'll get you the brochure on the Clifton development,' Judy said, heading into the back office. Coupland sidled up to Alistair until he was alongside him, speaking in a low undertone. 'Why didn't you tell me about your affair with Dawn Tylor?' Alistair glanced at him sharply, his eyebrows disappearing into his hairline. 'Yeah, you're right to look alarmed, doesn't put you in the best of lights, does it?'

'Keep your voice down!' Alistair hissed, his eyes darting to the rear office door. 'It finished ages ago. I can't believe she told you.'

'She didn't,' Coupland said, 'you just did. You're going to have to come down to the station,' he handed him a card, 'and this time I want the full version of events.'

'But what does this have to do with your investigation?'

'The point is you lied to me. And it sets me off wondering what else you've lied about.'

'Nothing I swear,' Alistair said hurriedly. 'Now please, I've put my mistakes behind me, I'm trying to build a future with my wife.'

'Good luck with that,' Coupland said, moving towards the shop door.

'What shall I say to Judy about why you've left? She's gone to get you a brochure on that development.'

Coupland regarded him coolly. 'Tell her anything you like, you seem to be good at plucking stories from thin air.'

Broadgate Place was a new development of starter homes on the edge of Kersal, box-like and crammed together so they could boast being detached. Coupland counted the front doors until he found the one he was looking for; parked his car in front of number eight.

The woman who answered the door was different from Jilly Clarke's description. Make-up free, her hair tied back in a ponytail, she wore a long sleeved baggy jersey over leggings. A far cry from the image of a go-getting career woman. 'You've caught me on a day off,' Dawn Tylor told him when he showed her his warrant card. 'I'm still in the throes of unpacking,' she added when he eyed the boxes standing in the narrow hallway, 'I hadn't realised how much stuff I'd accumulated until the removal men came.' She showed him through to a small living room, inviting him to sit on one end of the corner sofa, while she sat at an angle to him. The room was decorated in neutral tones, a rectangle rug at its centre. A mug of coffee sat on a side table, untouched. 'Can I make you a drink?' Dawn asked when she saw him glance at it, 'I've got a machine in the kitchen, won't take me a second. Though to be honest I think I prefer tea.'

Coupland shook his head at her offer, 'Too much of a good thing…' he observed.

'Sorry?'

'Too much of a good thing… can leave a bad taste in the mouth.'

Dawn narrowed her eyes, 'So, how can I help? I've already spoken to your colleague, I'm not sure there's anything I can add.'

'You can start with your relationship with Alistair

Grant,' Coupland said. 'And why you saw fit to conceal it.'

Dawn sighed, 'For God's sake, is this his way of getting back at me? Blabbing to you when as far as I'm concerned it's history.'

'I wouldn't know,' Coupland placated, 'but why don't you tell me your version of events, see if they match up?'

Dawn tutted. 'Times like this I wish I'd never met him…'

'Go on…'

Dawn tucked one leg under the other as she leaned back into the sofa. 'The problem with being a business analyst is you end up analysing everything.'

Coupland's smile was kind. 'I wouldn't be so sure, love, my missus does that and she's been in nursing all her life.'

'Fair enough,' Dawn conceded, 'truth is Alistair wasn't up to much, not really. Friendly enough but nothing to send your pulse racing. I suppose I'd describe him as an efficient lover, he did the bare minimum but no more.' Coupland winced at the brutality, wondered fleetingly what Lynn's view would be on the subject. Competent? Could try harder? Or maybe after the tantrum he'd thrown the other night he was no longer fit for purpose. He pushed *that* thought out of his mind. 'But then I wasn't looking for a relationship,' Dawn added, 'I was doing well in my job; the long hours didn't give me time for anything else. I suppose he was convenient.' Her smile as she looked at Coupland was lop-sided. 'You know fast food isn't good for you but sometimes you just need to fill a hole.' Coupland's eyebrow's shot into his hairline. 'Alistair was so pleasant when we first met.' *I bet he was*, Coupland thought, forcing his eyebrows back into their normal position. 'He made me laugh every time we bumped into each other; I supposed I was intrigued that unlike the men I worked with he could be so charming without trying to make a move.'

'And how soon after you thought that did you start sleeping with him?'

Dawn laughed, 'Yes, I know, another gullible young woman falling for the flannel of an older man, but like I said before it suited me just fine.'

'Did you give him a key to your flat?'

Dawn looked confused, 'What? No…I didn't need to, I'd text him then leave the door on the latch. He'd tell his wife he was going for a workout.'

'How long did this go on for?'

'Three very happy months,' Dawn replied, 'followed by three bloody awful ones.'

'How come?'

'He started to change, started saying how he'd fallen for me, that we had a future together. I mean, we'd never been out on a date, hadn't even eaten a meal together, whatever possessed him to think we had anything in common other than casual sex?'

'So you put him straight?'

'Yeah, I put him straight alright. The only thing was…'
'What?'

'Well as far as I was concerned it should have been all done and dusted, we go back to the way we were, get on with our lives and pretend none of it had happened. Only it didn't work out like that.'

'What do you mean, what did he do?'

'It wasn't so much what he did next,' Dawn replied, choosing her words carefully, 'it was more a case of what he'd already done.'

CHAPTER FOURTEEN

'I see you've come prepared,' Coupland quipped, eyeing the solicitor Grant had brought with him, a tired looking man coasting the last couple of years to retirement. He said nothing other than introduce himself before proceeding to pick at the skin round his nails. 'At this point you're just helping with our enquiries,' Coupland reassured Grant, 'though I daresay it makes sense to plan ahead.'

'You didn't make it sound as though I had much of a choice when you called round.'

Coupland inclined his head. 'Well, granted, if you'd baulked at my invitation I would have had to insist.'

Grant leaned back in his chair, satisfied. 'So here I am.'

'And where does your wife think you've gone this gloomy evening?'

'To the gym.'

'She's a trusting woman, that one, I'll give her that. I think my missus would be wondering why I hadn't morphed into Vin Diesel by now if I'd claimed to have spent as much time "working out" as you.'

Grant's satisfied smile fell away. 'It's not something I'm proud of, DS Coupland, and to be honest, I thought it was all behind me now that my relationship with Dawn is over.'

'Not on good terms either from what I understand.'

Grant regarded him, 'What did she say?'

'That no other fella measures up.'

A smile spread across Alistair's lips.

'Give over, man,' Coupland drawled, 'she meant for all the wrong reasons. She wonders what she saw in you, other than a convenient leg over after a tough day at work... I think they're booty calls now,' Coupland added, 'so my younger colleagues tell me, only you get my drift. I'm trying to recall the word she used... efficient, that's it. She said you were efficient in the sack, did what was expected but no more.' He paused to let that sink in, his voice taking on a serious tone, 'But putting a pin in the condoms you were using was a pretty low trick.'

Grant dropped his gaze. 'I thought she'd want to commit if there was a baby on the way.'

'But instead the opposite happened. You freaked her out so much she put in for a transfer at work, even moved to another area in the hope that you'd leave her alone.'

'Which I have done!' Grant insisted. 'When she moved out I realised I'd made a stupid mistake. Yes, I'd become infatuated with her, and I admit what I did was reprehensible, that's why I came clean!'

'She told me she caught you in the act.'

Grant raked his fingers through his hair in frustration, 'Fine! But I admitted it straight away. Look it was selfish of me but thankfully no harm was done. An error of judgement, yes, but one I could fix since my plan didn't work.'

Coupland recalled the baggy top Dawn was wearing when he'd turned up unannounced, the untouched coffee in the living room and the cardboard box in the hall with a picture of a baby's crib on its side. Alistair wasn't the only one trying to fix their mistakes. Coupland doubted Dawn's pregnancy had any connection to the dead little girl. Nor did being a cheat make someone a killer.

'We're done,' he said, getting to his feet.

*

The car park had been full when Coupland returned to the station; he'd had to make do with a parking space outside Gala Bingo across the road. His shift over, he trudged his way back to retrieve it. The sound of raised voices coming from the shopping centre nearby made him turn. Two boys carried grocery bags towards the neighbouring estate. Shoulders hunched with the weight of them the younger one, maybe eight or so, began to lag behind. The older one, wearing his high school tie as loose as he could without it coming undone stopped and turned, 'Come on, knobhead,' he moaned, sighing as the little one jutted his head forward and down, pumping his legs like a Jamaican sprinter so he could catch his brother up. Coupland recognised the older one from earlier in the day, the careers visit to the station. 'Fuck sake,' the older boy said when the straggler drew level, 'give 'em here.' He grabbed his brother's bags, the weight of the shopping making the ends of his fingers bulge. Freed from his heavy load the little one skipped beside him, every couple of steps glancing up in admiration. Coupland wondered what it would have been like to have a brother. He'd never been a reader, didn't watch many films for that matter, had no romantic notions of sibling camaraderie; but it would have been someone else to stand up to his old man, someone else to share the beatings.

The thought when it came to him was like a body

blow. He pulled his mobile from his jacket pocket, found the number he was looking for and dialled.

DAY FOUR

CHAPTER FIFTEEN

Jimmy Rawlings was waiting at the rear entrance to Shiny Happy Motors. The look on his face suggested he was far from happy to see Coupland. 'The boss doesn't bother coming in this early but I don't want to take any chances. I still don't get why you need me.'

Coupland smiled until his face ached, 'Because you told me that your boss wasn't too scrupulous about checking papers when he was hiring and we think the little girl found in your neighbour's flat was over here illegally. I need to find a way of connecting with the migrant community if I've got any hope of finding her identity.'

'What, you expect me to help when I nearly lost my job because of you earlier this week?' Rawlings scowled. 'How does that work?'

'It doesn't, but then this isn't a polite request either.' Coupland's smile was fast turning into a grimace.

Rawlings sighed. 'So who do you want to speak to?'

'Anyone working here whose work papers may be shall we say… questionable.'

It was Rawlings' turn to grimace. 'You'll need to speak to the whole bloody workforce then.'

Five minutes later two dozen men gathered in the back yard behind the car wash rollers, listening while Coupland explained why he was there. The majority of them were of Eastern European origin; Polish, Romanian, Slovakian made up the bulk of them, muttering in their own language as they kicked at the dirt floor. There were some Africans, mainly Nigerian; they stood apart from the other groups that had formed and when they spoke their English was clipped, enunciated in a way Coupland could only aspire to. Even though the victim was Caucasian, it was worthwhile including them, Coupland reasoned, they could be sharing the same living quarters with a family whose child was missing, or hot bedding – where several people working different shifts would use the same bed – this was common among low paid migrants, particularly those working in forced labour conditions.

The men huddled in groups, speaking in their native tongue as they smoked roll-ups, eyeing Coupland with suspicion. The air was thick with hostility and fear. 'They think you're going to round 'em up and send 'em back where they came from,' Rawlings chipped in.

Coupland ignored him, turning to a group standing nearby. 'Does anyone speak English?' he asked. After some debate a middle-aged man raised his hand. He was thin, gaunt features framed by dark brown hair. He was dressed like many of the older men standing around him, a cotton shirt beneath a crew neck jumper with jeans. The younger men wore jogging bottoms with football tops. Slovan Bratislava, Maribor, Legia Warsaw were the teams Coupland recognised. He turned to Rawlings' grubby sweatshirt bearing the Shiny Happy Motors company logo. 'How come no one else is wearing uniform?'

'The boss likes to order them in specially, made to measure, like. They can take a couple of weeks for delivery.'

Coupland stared at the cheap polyester straining over Rawlings' paunch. 'Try again, sunshine, this is me you're talking to,' he drawled. Rawlings sighed. 'If immigration comes knocking the boss can say he's only just hired them, hasn't got round to checking their papers. It's less plausible if they're wearing the company uniform.'

There was logic in that, Coupland supposed. He nodded to the man who'd raised his hand, beckoning him over. 'What's your name?'

'Jakub Borak,' he answered.

'Can you translate for me?'

Jakub nodded. 'I will do my best. I am from Poland originally, but I speak several languages including Russian and Romanian, most of the workers know a little of both of these languages so I should be understood.'

Coupland thanked him, turning to the assembled crowd.

'I'm not from immigration,' he said aloud, waiting while Jakub relayed his words. 'I am with the police, but,' he added hurriedly, arms out like Canute holding back the tide, 'I am here because I am investigating the murder of a child, nothing else. I don't want to know anything about you, and I have no intention of passing any information about you on to the authorities, but I do need to know if a little girl from your community is missing.' He was met with silence. He waited while Jakub cascaded his plea to the groups that had formed. As the crowd heard his words translated their body language changed, they broke away from their huddled cliques, turning to study the people around them, exchanging comments followed by shrugs or nods. Coupland felt that tingle of anticipation when something started going to plan. He had their attention, possibly their trust; he sure as hell didn't want to lose it. 'The little girl was five years old,' he added, 'she'd suffered a head injury before being concealed in a bag.' He waited once more for the translator to speak. Borak stumbled over some of the words, had to ask someone standing close by to help him with others. Coupland guessed descriptions like head injury and concealed in a bag weren't standard phrases you'd pick up over time. One of the men looked incredulous, he'd been standing with a group of Romanians and he turned to them barking two syllable words Coupland guessed were expletives.

'He thinks you suspect one of them,' Rawlings said from the wings.

'Cheers Sherlock,' Coupland sniped, 'I'd worked that one out for myself.' He flapped his hands once more until he had their attention. 'If I thought any of you were responsible I'd have come here mob handed, taken you all on a one-way trip down the cop shop for questioning. Instead I'm here on my own, asking for your help. I want to do right by the little girl and her family, nothing more. So I'm asking you, do you know anyone whose daughter, niece, sister or cousin went missing about a month ago, maybe longer? You may have been told she was taken back home or sent to live with relatives. Maybe at the time the explanation you were given made sense, but now...' Coupland waited, his gut clenching, he'd felt certain he was onto something, that his earlier hunch had been right. Seeing those two boys carrying heavy shopping the night before had made him question the family dynamic he'd been focussing on. The little girl didn't have to be living with an older couple; she could be staying with a sibling, a cousin even. The groups closest to Coupland fell silent. Some shook their heads at him to let him know they couldn't help. Others looked at him expectantly. He turned to the translator.

'They are waiting for your permission to return to work,' Jakub told him.

Coupland's shoulders dipped. He'd been so sure… 'Fine,' he barked, moving to where Jimmy Rawlings leaned against the wooden fence that separated the workshop from the road. 'Are you sure that's everyone?' he asked. 'Has anyone not turned in today?'

'You don't turn up, you don't have a job,' Rawlings told him.

Coupland shoved his hands in his pockets and sighed, watching while the men filed past. Several younger men hung back. They were in their late twenties, well built, tight t-shirts revealing tattooed arms. They were in a heated debate but fell silent when Coupland looked over. One of the men made to move towards him but his friend grabbed his arm. He barked a rebuke before shrugging out of his grip and continued across the yard. Coupland was already moving towards him, ready to block his path if he changed his mind and tried pass him. The man came to a halt in front of Coupland. 'GABRIEL!' one of the others called out his name. He ignored them, standing his ground in front of Coupland.

'I know who she is,' he said.

CHAPTER SIXTEEN

Gabriel pointed to his friends who were now gathered around him. 'We are from a small village in Albania. There are not so many Albanians here, so we look out for each other, you know?'

Coupland wasn't sure he even knew where Albania was, 'Go on,' he urged.

'In my country there are no, how do you say it… prospects, for our generation, we don't want to live like our fathers did. We do not want that kind of life. One day some men came to our village. They spoke to my friends about the life it was possible to have in England. When my friends told me, I asked if I could meet these men, I wanted to hear about this for myself. I am not a stupid man, I'd heard stories of people coming to my country and taking advantage of gullible people. They'd ask for money up front and then not bother to come back for them. These men had heard these stories also. They said they would only take a small payment up front. The rest of our costs they would cover. They were investing in us, they said. We would only need to start repaying them once we were working so it was in their interest to help find accommodation for us, help us get work, and before long we would be earning enough to send money home to help our families.'

The others in Gabriel's group remained silent. 'Their English is like mine,' he told Coupland, 'but they are unwilling to speak up. They feel shame that we have been gullible after all. The men that came to our village made it sound so easy. In my country there is no work for unskilled men like us, but they told us in England we would have money, our lives would be so much better. All we had to do was pay them travel costs plus expenses for administration.' Coupland wasn't sure what administration was required for herding folk into the backs of lorries but he said nothing. 'They wanted £1000 up front, the rest we could pay off once we started work.' One of the other men spoke in Albanian; his words came out rapid fire, angry, his arms raised in frustration. Gabriel laid a hand on his friend's shoulder, nodding. 'He says that we should have listened to our families and walked away, that we were stupid after all, but at the time it seemed,' he paused as he tried to think of the right words, 'how do you say it, when you think someone is speaking the truth, but they are not?'

'Plausible,' offered Coupland.

The man nodded, satisfied, 'Plausible,' he repeated, as though trying it out for size. 'So we paid them their money, not complaining when we spent days hiding under blankets with no food. There were two girls travelling with us, they were young, one just a small child. The older girl told me her mother was dead and her father drank too much. She wanted to make a better life for her sister as far away as possible from their past.' He looked away then, as though picturing something foul.

'What happened when you got here?' Coupland probed.

'They forced us into manual labour, we had no say in the jobs they made us do, they take so much of our earnings there is nothing left over to feed and clothe yourself properly. Because the authorities don't know we are here we do not have the freedom to find other work; we have no papers, we cannot even seek medical attention when we are sick.'

'Where are you living?'

Gabriel nodded towards a small window above the kiosk where punters waited while their cars were valeted. 'There are six of us living in one room, others are brought in by car or van then picked up again at the end of their shift. But it is worse for the women. They are forced into domestic work and prostitution. I've heard of some that are sold as house maids, forced to work seven days a week for no money, they are fed scraps and locked in their rooms at night so they can't escape.'

'And the girls you met?' Coupland prompted. 'What happened to them?'

'They were sent out begging. Every day they are driven to the same place and made to stay there until evening, any money they have collected during the day is taken from them by these men. We used to pass them both sometimes, on the street, when we were labouring on a nearby building site. We rarely spoke, what is there to talk about other than compare notes on the hell we are living? But recently I saw the older girl on her own, and I asked after her sister. She told me she was ill, that she had been sent away to get better. Again, this seemed…plausible… we are invisible here, we have no rights, no access to doctors without questions being asked, none of us want to end up in a detention centre, so if the little girl had gone to stay somewhere where she could get better…' his words trailed off.

'Do you know where these people are keeping her older sister?'

The young man shook his head, 'No, but I can tell you where you will find her. Every morning they take her to a shopping centre where she begs all day, sitting on the pavement in front of Costa Coffee.'

Coupland's pulse quickened.

It was the girl he had spoken to yesterday.

*

The girl was sitting in the same place he'd seen her the day before. She had on the same clothes, denim leggings and a dark hoodie. She'd drawn a smiley face on a torn piece of cardboard and wedged it in front of the paper cup at her feet. There was more change in there today, several pound coins and a couple of fifty pence pieces. The smiley face seemed to be working its magic. 'Aren't you worried someone'll nick that?' Coupland asked, nodding at the cup and its contents, 'You've got enough in there to get something to eat, why don't you come inside and I'll get you a drink as well?' The girl looked him over as she considered his words, wondering why he looked familiar while at the same time slipping the money into the pocket of her hoodie in case he was tempted to run off with her takings himself. 'How about you keep your money and I get you something to eat anyway?' he offered.

The girl narrowed her eyes. 'I need cash,' she said this slowly, as though he hadn't grasped the concept of begging. This time when she spoke Coupland detected an accent similar to Gabriel and his friends.

He reached into his pocket and pulled out his warrant card, stooping so that he held it within her line of vision.

'I'm a police officer, love, and I need to speak to you urgently. Now I know that boss of yours will be swinging by here soon to check on you, so why don't you give me a few minutes of your time before he does, eh?' He held his hand out to help her to her feet.

'What is this about?' she asked, following him inside the café.

'Wait here,' he answered, holding out a seat in a quiet corner, close enough to the large window that they'd see if her minder came looking for her but not so close he'd see them first. She sat down without argument, concentrating on the floor by her feet. Coupland brought over a tray with two lattes and the first sandwich he saw in the display cabinet; he doubted she'd be fussy. He placed the items on the small table between them and sat down in the chair opposite. 'Where's your sister?' he asked, getting straight to the point.

The girl looked surprised. 'How do you know I have a sister?'

Coupland wafted her question away. 'I'll tell you how I know in a minute, right now I need to know where you think she is.'

The girl's face clouded, 'Think? Oh, God, has something happened to her?' Her voice had risen several octaves, two women on a neighbouring table glanced in their direction.

'I don't know yet,' Coupland cautioned. Until she gave him a DNA sample he had nothing but the anecdotal evidence of strangers to suggest this girl and the kiddie lying in the mortuary were related. 'When did you last see her?' he asked.

'Four weeks ago.'

Something jagged moved inside him. He took a sip of his latte. 'Where is she now?'

'She was ill, she had to go away to get better…'

'Do you know where she was taken?'

A pause. 'No.'

'What was wrong with her?'

The girl glanced at the grubby blanket on the pavement outside, marking her spot. 'This is no life for a child,' she told him, 'begging on the street no matter what the weather. She became ill; nothing I did could make her better.' The girl looked away, 'There is this woman, she is wife to one of the men, I think. You can buy medicine from her; she takes the money from our wages. I could not afford much…'

'Have you spoken to your sister since she left?'

The girl inspected her hands. Her nails were broken and dirty. Glances from the other diners made her drop them to her knee. She picked at a loose piece of thread on her leggings self-consciously. She shook her head as she looked up at him. 'They said that the family she is with don't have a phone.'

Coupland's mouth turned down. 'Do you believe that?'

The girl stared at him. 'I do not know what to believe anymore. When we left our home I promised my sister that she'd be safe. The men bringing us here were helping us get a better life. I trusted them… at first, anyway,' she sighed, '…and now I don't know where my sister is... the men who took her away told me if I didn't believe them I could go to the police but the police would send me back to Albania and then I'd never see her for sure.' There were dark shadows under her eyes, lines across her brow that shouldn't be possible in someone so young.

Her cheekbones were starting to jut out.

'How long have you been living like this?'

'You mean begging on the streets of your city?' She gazed out of the café window, at the passers-by. 'Six months. They sent us here the day we arrived. Told me that we had to start working straight away to pay off our debt. My sister is five years old, she couldn't understand why she wasn't allowed to go and play with other children her age. I didn't have an answer for her. She would play up sometimes… refuse to go along with it…'

'So what did they do?'

'The woman would give her something to take the fight out of her… made her willing to go up to people and ask them for money.'

'Did they make you do anything else?'

'You mean did they make me have sex with strangers?' She laughed then, but it was a desperate laugh, the sound someone made before they jumped off a bridge. A release of tension before they called it a day. 'They made me work if one of the other girls was ill, but it wasn't me they were interested in.' A stone formed in Coupland's stomach. 'They said there was a big market over here for children, if we didn't bring in enough money begging then we knew what to expect.'

Coupland let out a long, slow breath. He took out his note pad and pen. 'Time to start from the beginning. What's your name love?' She made a series of sounds that he couldn't grasp, other than the first letter. M something. 'Probably better you write it down,' he said, pushing the pad towards her and handing her his pen. Her writing was neat, block style, and he was able to make out the letters upside down. 'Mariana Gashi. Have I said it right?'

She nodded.

'Can you write down your sister's name too?' He waited until she'd finished, then slid the pad back to his side of the table and turned it the right way up. 'Zamira,' he said aloud to check he was pronouncing it correctly. Mariana nodded once more. 'Do you have a photograph of her?'

Mariana reached into the pocket of her hoodie. 'I have a small photo. We had some taken when the men who brought us here arranged our papers. She pulled out loose coins, used tissues, a hair clip and a small compact mirror. 'It was my mother's,' she explained when his gaze fell on it. 'Here,' she said, handing the passport size photograph to him.

Coupland was aware she was placing something in his hand but his mind was elsewhere, not on the handbag size mirror Mariana had mistaken him staring at, but at the pastel pink hair clip beside it. It was identical to the one they'd retrieved from the victim, except without bits of scalp stuck to it. He slipped the photograph in his notebook and got to his feet. He pulled out his phone, turning away from Mariana so she wouldn't overhear his conversation. He tapped DCI Mallender's name from his list of contacts, listened to it ring. 'Boss,' he said when the familiar voice came down the line to him, 'We've got an ID.'

*

Coupland paced up and down the smoking shelter at the back of Salford Precinct station, the tip of his cigarette glowing red before the smoke hissed from his nose. He clutched at a coffee he'd picked up from the canteen since abandoning his latte in Costa Coffee. At last, they had a name for the child, and a photograph too.

Zamira Gashi.

A motherless girl hidden beneath a dirty blanket.

A father too half cut to notice his kids had gone.

A sister trying to make their lives better.

He pictured them cold and hungry in the back of a truck. Tired but excited, a new life beckoning, their luck about to change for the better. What must they have thought when they were told they had to beg and do God knows what else for a living?

Mariana's story was corroborated by the duty doctor who after examining her had taken Coupland to one side. 'She's been given regular injections of Depo-Provera to stop her getting pregnant,' he said, adding, 'She told me all the girls who went with the men were given it.'

'Who gave it to her?'

The doc had shaken his head. 'She keeps referring to some woman. Said she came and gave them the injections then took the money to pay for them out of what they earned.'

'Along with everything else they had to pay for,'

'Making their debt go up rather than down.'

The doctor had nodded, grim faced. 'I've heard of some traffickers removing organs because of the money they can earn when they sell them on, only the conditions the victims are operated on are unhygienic. I saw the aftermath during my stint in A&E. The prognosis is never good.' The doctor's words came back to Coupland as he tried a sip of his coffee. The liquid felt like sandpaper in his throat. He tipped it away.

The entrance door behind him slammed and he turned as Alex bleeped a pool car open. 'I heard you ID'd the girl.'

Coupland grunted.

'Next of kin informed?'

'What's left of them. Poor kid's barely into her teens but the gang controlling her were pimping her out for sex, they'd got designs on the littl'un too.'

Alex nodded. That was the problem with the job; it made you nod at things that would make the public shudder. 'What's going to happen now?'

'What do you think?' Coupland tutted. 'The DCI's escalated it to Curtis who'll be on the hot line to the NCA as we speak. "Thanks very much, DS Coupland, don't let the door hit you on the way out."'

Alex pulled a face. 'You're a bit wide of the mark there, Kevin,' she scoffed.

'What do you mean?'

She looked at him as though he was simple, 'Since when do we get any thanks?'

*

Taking one last lungful of smoke before flicking his cigarette butt in the metal container provided, Coupland made his way into the reception area. The desk sergeant called out to him before he reached the internal staff door. 'Social worker's here,' he said, indicating a smartly dressed black woman seated by the main entrance door. Coupland nodded. The desk sergeant studied him for a moment, 'You alright?'

Coupland couldn't get rid of the image of someone squeezing a child into a bag, a child that now had a name. 'Coming down with a cold,' he muttered, before rearranging his mouth into a smile. He approached the woman with his hand outstretched.

She smiled as he introduced himself. 'Shola Dube,' she replied, 'I am already acquainted with detectives Turnbull and Robinson.'

Coupland's smile turned apologetic, 'Don't let that put you off, love, they mean well but…' He keyed in the entry code before standing back to let Shola pass through. 'Have you dealt with many victims of trafficking?'

Shola's mouth turned down. 'More than I'd like… although to be truthful I do not feel equipped to deal with their issues.'

Coupland huffed out a breath. 'You and me both. On a personal level I want to nick the guy who fed that girl and her sister a pack of lies and throw away the key for a long time. However, that pleasure is above my pay grade, the National Crime Agency will take over this case now.' What he wouldn't give to be there when the bastards were tracked down, in truth he wanted to knock seven bells out of every one of them, but he'd learned over the years not to be too open with staff from other agencies, no one was above quoting something said in the heat of the moment out of context if things went belly up. 'The NCA will pursue the gang responsible, assuming they can gather enough intelligence. My investigation into Zamira Gashi's murder ends here.'

The social worker studied him. 'But not here, sergeant…' Shola observed, placing her fingertips against her temple. 'If only there was an on/off switch for our conscience.'

'Hmmm…' grumbled Coupland, 'a problem most of my clients haven't been afflicted with.'

Shola smile was sympathetic. 'So this girl's sister is definitely your victim, then?'

Coupland looked thoughtful, 'Still waiting on Mariana's DNA to be processed but I'm pretty certain, yes.' He could show her the hairclip, if he needed to, after all it had cinched it for him, it was a dead ringer for the one she'd pulled out of her pocket in Costa Coffee. But he'd rather have the irrefutable proof, so as not to prolong her agony. They'd reached the interview room where Mariana was waiting for Shola.

'Now you're here as her appropriate adult we need to take her statement as soon as possible. I'll give you a few minutes with her though, she's like a rabbit in the headlights at the moment. There's a WPC in the interview room, though she hasn't spoken a word to her.' Coupland hesitated before opening the door. He turned to Shola. 'What will happen to her now?'

'I am to take her to a short term holding centre out by the airport where she will be assessed.'

Coupland's face clouded over. 'A detention centre!' he hissed. 'Assessed for what? She is the victim of a crime here.'

'She still needs to be assessed, DS Coupland. There is 24 hour medical support at the facility, and a mental health nurse. Many of these girls arrive at the centre with pregnancies they didn't know about, STIs, malnutrition. She will be cared for. At least she won't be begging for her meal tonight.' She lowered her voice. 'How much does she know about what's happened to her sister?'

Coupland winced. 'The barest details, though she's not taken them in. I think she's holding on for the DNA results, hoping there's been some mistake.' Coupland didn't blame her one little bit. The phone in his pocket vibrated. He made his apologies to Shola and glanced at the screen. DCI Mallender had sent him a text:

You are needed upstairs. Now.

'And so it begins,' he said to Shola before turning on his heel and going back the way he came.

*

Superintendent Curtis pranced around his office like a track and field athlete warming up at the start of the hundred metre sprint. He'd slung his dress jacket over his chair revealing sweat marks on an otherwise pristine shirt. He was the highest ranking officer based at Salford Precinct; head honcho, chief arse kicker supreme. DCI Mallender was seated, his head swivelling this way and that to keep up with Curtis as he paced the room. The pacing stopped as Coupland walked in. 'Ah, Kevin,' Superintendent Curtis began, 'I was just saying what an excellent result.'

Coupland looked askance. 'We haven't solved anything yet, Sir,' he reminded him, 'we still need to find Zamira's killer.'

'Who?' Curtis's brow creased.

'The little girl found in the sports bag, Sir,' Mallender responded.

Curtis gave a flick of his head. 'Off our hands now the NCA is involved.' He said this with ease, the hint of a smile tugging at the corners of his mouth. Once a case was escalated up the chain to the NCA it no longer needed to be accounted for in a station's performance data. As far as they were concerned the case was closed – with a positive outcome to boot. 'However, for the purposes of this investigation the CID room will remain the hub,' Curtis continued. 'The DCI taking over the case has asked if we can accommodate his team here, and I have told him yes.'

Coupland looked up at the ceiling, 'Give me strength,' he muttered, hovering beside Mallender as he hadn't been granted permission to take a seat.

'Sorry?' Curtis screwed his face up even more.

Coupland threw his arms open in frustration. 'These guys can't find shit in a blocked toilet, Sir, and now you're asking us to give up the scant resources we have for them to come in and pillage the intelligence we've gathered…'

Curtis positioned himself behind his desk, regarding Coupland with a death stare. 'I'm not asking you, detective sergeant,' he growled, 'I'm telling you.' He sighed then, in a way that implied he'd been having a lovely day until Coupland came along and peed in his sandpit. 'This is a tremendous opportunity for us, DS Coupland,' The Super had gone from addressing him as Kevin to DS Coupland in less than a minute; he was surpassing himself. 'The Chief Constable's office will be watching our collaboration. Our station, and the officers in it, will be under intense spotlight.' Mallender threw Coupland a warning look. *Just suck it up and bugger off*, it said. It was Curtis's way to treat everything as a career opportunity. Whatever crap landed at their door, however tedious, there was always something to be learned from it, a sound bite he could share at his next media outing. Easy enough when you weren't the one shovelling it away with a teaspoon instead of a spade because of cutbacks.

Coupland knew he was beaten but refused to go down without a fight. 'If they were any good at this surveillance lark, Sir, kids like Zamira and Mariana wouldn't be exploited right under our nose.'

'I don't think Greater Manchester Police is in any position to throw mud,' said a voice behind him, 'given its handling of the Rochdale case. Never mind failing to spot what was going on, you ignored it when it was brought to your attention.' No one had heard the familiar looking Asian man enter the room. He'd moved so silently it was as if his feet were on castors. Coupland glanced down at the man's shoes to check for wheels.

'DCI Akram.' Curtis made a beeline for him, pumping his hand like a politician at an election rally.

'Call me Amjid, please,' the DCI replied, turning to shake hands with Mallender, then Coupland. Akram was medium height with short-cropped hair; dark rimmed glasses framed a young looking face.

'Long time, no see, Sir,' said Coupland.

'Good to see you Kevin,' Amjid replied, 'pleased to see you're still in one piece.' He was referring to the last time the NCA had rolled into town when a profes-sional hitman had been targeting witnesses to a drive-by shooting. Coupland had almost been caught in the line of fire.

'You know what they say: You can't keep a good man down.' He was smarting over Amjid's previous comment but didn't want to show it. What DCI Akram said was true; gangs of men, predominantly of Pakistani origin, had preyed on vulnerable girls by offering them drink, drugs and gifts, before raping and prostituting them. A subsequent, minister-led investigation into the handling of the allegations made by the girls at the time highlighted a culture of victim blaming and an eagerness not to appear racist. 'You can't hold us to account for something that happened in Rochdale,' he said evenly, unwilling to let it drop. 'It's twenty miles and two time zones away for a start.'

'I'm not,' said Amjid, 'but *you're* trying to hold the NCA to account for everything that happens to these migrants the moment they reach our shores.' Coupland gave a slight shrug of his shoulders.

Mallender, ever the peacemaker, turned to him. 'It takes time to gather intelligence on these gangs, Kevin, hopefully Zamira's sister will be able to provide information that would take Amjid's team months to harvest themselves. Her evidence could make a real difference to this investigation.'

Did that mean Zamira's death made a difference too? Coupland wondered. He wasn't so sure. Apart from jettisoning her sister into a life riddled with grief and guilt in equal measure, he couldn't see that anything would change. The vulnerable would still be exploited. 'And what thanks will Mariana get for helping you?' he asked Amjid. 'Carted off to a detention centre and treated like an illegal immigrant. Before you know it she'll be deported—'

'Actually, that's not true…' Amjid's tone was firm, he was aware he was treading on Coupland's toes but the gobby detective would have to deal with it. 'Child trafficking is handled differently now. Children don't have to prove they were coerced or deceived into coming here the way adults do. The Palermo Protocol states any situation involving children being moved for the purposes of exploitation is to be considered trafficking, whether the child agreed to it or not.'

Coupland drew his mouth into a thin line. 'I stand corrected. Mind you, I am only paid up to here,' he held his hand out flat, palm downwards, just below his chin.

'Splendid,' observed Curtis, rubbing his hands together. With a satisfied smile he lowered himself into his seat. He pulled his reading glasses onto the bridge of his nose, shuffling the scant few papers in front of him. He regarded the detectives over the rim of his glasses, as though surprised they were still there. 'You know where I am if I can be of any further assistance.'

They'd been dismissed.

*

The CID room was crowded. Uniformed officers and detectives charged about clutching computer printouts, civilians Coupland didn't recognise had taken over the phones. The National Crime Agency had landed.

'Listen up, people.' He raised his voice above the cacophony of sound, his hands signalling for a bit of hush. 'Firstly, I want to introduce those of you who haven't met him before to DCI Amjid Akram. He and his team will be commencing an investigation into people trafficking from Albania by a gang operating in and around Salford.' He paused, there was no way he could soft soap what he had to say next. 'As Zamira and Mariana Gashi are thought to be victims of this crime, DCI Akram's team will also take over the investigation into Zamira's murder.'

A collective groan reverberated around the room, mutterings of 'You've got to be kidding,' and 'Typical', could be heard from officers, who, like Coupland if the truth be told, felt like they'd just been castrated. They'd only just written Zamira's name on the incident board and now another team was taking over. Despite this Coupland kept his tone neutral. 'As such we have to hand it over to the big boys, we don't have the resources to deal with it at local level and besides, they have experience dealing with this type of crime.' Christ, what had happened to him? He was beginning to sound like Mallender. Amenable, co-operative, he'd be giving up his desk next. 'I want you all to show DCI Akram's team how hospitable the Major Investigation Team at Salford Precinct can be. As of now you share local intelligence, which I know is going to be a challenge for you Turnbull, what with you having precious little in the first place but work with me on this. I want DCI Akram to be so impressed with the way his team have been treated he leaves a five star review on Trip Advisor. Got it?'

'Yes Sarge,' said Krispy on behalf of the team; the rest of them were too glum to respond but grunted that they'd got the message: Play nice. No hair pulling at break time.

'So who's the SIO now, Sarge?' asked Turnbull.

'I knew I could rely on you,' sighed Coupland. He turned to Amjid. 'Talking to DC Turnbull here is like shouting into a well, there's a slight delay before he receives the message.' He turned back to face his DC. 'DCI Akram is the SIO in relation to Zamira Gashi's murder and tracking down the gang responsible for bringing her here, capiche?'

Turnbull nodded, satisfied.

'Thanks, Kevin,' said Amjid. 'I thought we could start by pulling together a summary—' but Coupland wasn't listening, he was eyeing two of Amjid's team as they perched their bums on his desk, exchanging banter as they gave their tea order to a colleague who jotted it down on a sheet of paper he'd just torn from Coupland's desk pad.

The man then had the audacity to head over to where Turnbull was standing and hand the list to him. 'I like mine milky,' he said, when Turnbull looked at him confused. Turnbull said nothing, after all hadn't Coupland just told his team to play nice? With a sigh he made to go over to the kettle they'd been using while the vending machine was playing silly beggars. He seemed biddable enough, though the blush creeping up his neck told a different story.

'Stay right where you are, Turnbull,' boomed Coupland, cutting Amjid off mid-sentence. He moved over to a nearby desk, knocked on it several times until he had everyone's attention once more. He looked around the overcrowded room, at his dispirited team and the bright eyed whippersnappers who'd taken away their ball. 'Sorry to break up the party so soon but I don't think I made myself clear earlier, so you're going to have to bear with me just a little bit longer. When I asked my team to be hospitable, I meant, for those of you who aren't bright enough to understand the sub text, that they should show you the same courtesy I expect you to show them. Apart from Krispy here, who's still wearing training pants, every member of my team has more years of service than they'd care to admit to, they've seen things that never mind making your hair curl would give you a full blown bloody afro. They've a lifetime of front line policing behind them. Yeah, they get pissed on and puked on every Friday night shift and I know it's not sexy, that you lot think you're better than that, but while you're ensconced up at HQ they are at the sharp end, dealing with the aftermath of things I hope you'll never have to see.' He moved over to where Turnbull was standing. 'We're a tight unit here, a family even, and we've earned the right to take the mickey out of each other, as in any family. Just like when I'm at home I reserve the right to wind my missus up but if anyone else tried it they'd lose their teeth. DC Turnbull here is like a stick of Blackpool rock, cut him in half and you'll see GMP stamped right through him. So if you know what's good for you, sunshine,' he said, taking the drinks list from Turnbull and returning it to the officer who'd given it to him, 'you'll take this back before I shove it where it'll come out brown and sticky, never mind bloody milky.' He scanned the room to check their visitors had got his message, his eyes settling on the two men slouching on his desk. 'Oi, Ant and Dec, you two better shift yourselves before I really lose my rag.' The men swallowed as he eyeballed them, then jumped to their feet as though there was a competition to see who could stand up first. Satisfied, Coupland clapped his hands together like a pantomime genie. 'Right, show's over, folks. As you were.' He clocked the beaming faces of his team as he said this. He might not be leading the case anymore, but he'd just kicked one into the back of the net for them and they were grateful.

*

Coupland joined Amjid and his cronies as they gathered around the incident board. The passport size photo of Zamira that Mariana had given him had been enlarged before being placed at the centre of it. The blown up photo made her features grainy. Even so it was possible to make out wavy hair around a slim face dominated by large brown eyes. She looked apprehensive, as though she already knew the new life she'd been promised didn't bode well. Coupland picked up a marker and wrote a couple of numbers and a letter on the board. 'It's a partial number plate of the car used by the person watching Mariana the first time I went over to speak to her, before I knew she was connected to the case. The car drove off when I turned to see what she was looking at and no, before you ask, I didn't see the driver. It was a dark coloured four by four, that's about all I could make out.'

'There's not enough detail there for us to run a check,' said Anthony McPartlin's lookalike.

'I know that,' barked Coupland, 'but we can at least keep an eye out.'

'We?' interrupted Amjid. 'Your remit is to pass over information; from now on in we're the operational personnel on this case.'

So much for playing nice then. 'Fine.' Coupland held up his hands in mock surrender as he backed away, 'I know when I'm not wanted.' He nearly collided with Alex as she returned to the CID room carrying a manila folder.

She looked wistful. 'I see the big guns are in town. I'm only sorry I wasn't around more to help.'

Not that it would have changed anything, Coupland thought sourly, protocol was protocol. He flashed her a half-smile. 'Don't worry about it, we can rest assured the investigation's in capable hands now.'

Alex peered at him. 'You reckon? Oh, before I forget, Gerry on the desk says the social worker is ready to take Mariana to the detention centre so if you want to take her formal statement before she goes...'

Amjid's head couldn't have swivelled round any faster if he'd been possessed. 'If you don't mind, DS Coupland, I'd prefer officers specially trained in interviewing trafficking victims to take her statement.'

Coupland conceded with a tilt of his head. 'Be my guest,' he said, as Amjid conferred with Ant and Dec before sending them to interview her. Coupland eyeballed them as they passed him, in case they were daft enough to gloat.

Alex tried to diffuse the tension. 'At least you rescued her sister, Kevin.'

At least.

Coupland hated what those two small words implied. The mitigation of loss, the reduction of blame.

At least the little mite's at rest now.

At least she won't suffer any more.

At least you found out her name.

It didn't make him feel better one little bit.

'How's the case review going?' he asked to change the subject.

'I thought these things were cut and dried.' Alex harrumphed. 'Seems to have taken on a life of its own. It's never just one mistake that causes the proverbial to hit the fan, is it? It's a whole series of events that make the outcome inevitable.'

'How so?'

'Michael Roberts' tutor informed Children and Family Services he had cause for concern about his stepfather more than once but no one followed up his referral.'

'But his stepfather didn't kill him.'

'No, the killer was someone he'd started hanging round with, maybe someone he wouldn't have bothered with if his home life had been stable.'

Coupland shot Alex a look. If they were to apply that magical way of thinking to everything then Coupland really was to blame for his daughter being pregnant with a serial killer's child. After all, the scumbag wouldn't have gone anywhere near her if he hadn't been hell bent on getting one over the cop who'd put him away. 'I don't see what the problem is,' he said, frowning.

Alex shrugged. 'Fine, but why didn't his tutor tell anyone he'd seen him when he turned up for class on the day he died?'

Coupland rubbed his hand over the back of his neck, moving his head this way and that. 'Misplaced loyalty?' But even as he said it his antennae was twitching. 'Maybe there was more to their relationship…have you asked him?'

'There's the thing, he was only on a temporary contract at the college, and since then HR have had a new IT system installed which has had a few teething troubles…'

'Which includes losing personnel records,' Coupland summarised for her.

Alex raised an eyebrow. 'Something like that.'

'Have you tried contacting Children and Families to see if they kept a record of the tutor's contact details when he made the referral?'

'The best they could do was pass me on to the duty manager who promised to look into it as soon as she could.'

'And given there's no longer a life at risk that could be sometime never.'

'Precisely.'

'What about getting a list of the other students in his class? Maybe one of them remembers this tutor?'

'The Student Records Manager cited data protection.'

'You could go back and threaten them with obstruction.'

Alex raised her other brow until they were both symmetrical. 'I'm trying to do this collaboratively,' she reminded him.

'And there was me thinking it was squeaky bum time,' Coupland smirked. 'Who knew arse covering could get so complicated?' He threw his hands up to fend off her retort. 'All the boss wants to know is we didn't drop the ball and by the sounds of it we didn't.'

The set of Alex's jaw told him that wasn't enough. 'Look, I can't re-write Michael Roberts' history but I can sure as hell find out who is accountable for any shortfall in the way he was treated. In the eyes of the law justice may already have been served but that's only a part of it.'

She had a point, he supposed. 'Look, if there's anything I can do…'

Just then one half of the Ant and Dec duo stomped back into the incident room, a sour look on his face as he made his way over to his DCI. 'This'll be interesting,' Coupland muttered, positioning himself so that he could try to lip read the conversation. The swear words were easy enough, and there were plenty of them, and he was obviously the topic of the conversation as the DC tried hard not to look in his direction but failed.

Amjid's shoulder's dipped and with a shake of his head he turned, his eyes settling on Coupland with a look of defeat. 'Mariana is refusing to speak to anyone other than you,' he said.

'Be gracious,' Alex whispered, as she returned to her desk, 'no one likes a gloater.'

Coupland raised an eyebrow, managing to keep his face straight as he followed Ant into the corridor. 'Three's a crowd,' he said as they reached the interview room door, 'so unless you're planning on turfing your pal out you can jog on.'

*

Inside the interview room Mariana was becoming agitated. 'When will the test results come back?' she demanded the moment Coupland entered. 'I need to know what happened to my sister.'

'I know,' Coupland said, 'they're being fast tracked through but it can still take time.' He moved into the spare seat beside the Declan lookalike, keeping his face in check as the detective shuffled his chair so there was a wider gap between them. 'Mariana, my colleague here,' he turned to detective beside him, 'sorry, we haven't been properly introduced…'

'DC Briars,' he answered, shifting his gaze to Mariana, 'call me Declan.'

Coupland glanced at him sharply. 'You're kidding, right?'

Declan's brow creased, 'Why?'

'Never mind,' Coupland muttered, returning his attention to Mariana. 'Do you know the address of where you've been staying?'

Declan snorted. 'These gangs don't hand out change of address cards when they traffic people, you know, the victims are usually transported in the back of vans, or taken on different routes to and from their place of work so they can't find their way on their own.'

Coupland ignored him. 'Mariana, that car that I saw drive away the first time I spoke to you, is that the car that picks you up and takes you to the spot outside Costa Coffee every day?'

Mariana's mouth turned down. 'Sometimes.'

'How long does it take to get there each morning?'

Mariana shrugged. 'About fifteen minutes, sometimes twenty.'

'You don't wear a watch,' demanded Declan, 'how can you be sure of the time?'

Mariana regarded him as though he was stupid. 'There is a clock on the front of the car, on the, how do you say it...?'

'Dashboard,' Coupland offered, 'at the front, beside the steering wheel.' He held both arms out to mime holding onto a steering wheel, causing the other detective to snigger. DCI Akram would be watching the interview via a video link to the incident room but this was no time to be coy.

'Yes,' Mariana nodded, 'the clock is on the dashboard. Sometimes, the journey takes longer though, when we are stuck at the roadworks.'

'Do you mean traffic lights, like the ones just a short way up from the coffee shop?'

Mariana shook her head. 'No. The driver says "bloody roadworks," whenever we stop there.' Mariana's voice grew louder as she mimicked the driver's words: "'You'd think they'd have finished by now, bloody roadworks.'"

Coupland turned to Declan, 'Just about every road I use to come in every day has been butchered these last few months but cross check with the council. You're searching for roadworks within twenty minutes of the Costa Coffee on Hankinson Road. Work that's been going on for some time, by the sound of it. It'll do no harm running it by the guys in traffic, too.'

'I'm on it.' Declan got to his feet and hurried out of

the room.

With the NCA detective out of the way, Coupland tried to reassure her. 'You're doing well, Mariana. With your help we can catch the people responsible for bringing you here under false pretences.'

Mariana looked confused.

'The men who came to your village tricked you, with your help we can find them; make sure it doesn't happen to anyone else.'

'And my sister?' she prompted.

Coupland had no answer to that. 'The place where they take you back to each night, is it a large building?'

'No.'

'Do you go upstairs or is it all on one floor?'

'Upstairs. There are two floors.'

'What's on the ground floor?'

She thought about this. 'Nothing. That's where the men stay who make sure we don't leave. We are allowed to use the kitchen and their toilet.'

'Has anyone ever left?'

Mariana shook her head. 'No one is allowed to leave until they pay their debt.'

'I'm guessing no one's ever done that?'

Another shake of her head. 'They charge us for the food we eat, for the bed we sleep in, there is always a cost. Over time we owe them more and more money.'

No surprise there. 'How many of you are there?'

Mariana considered this. 'About thirty of us.'

'Any other children?'

A nod. 'Yes.'

'Anyone else there from your village?'

She shook her head. 'I don't think so.'

'I spoke to a young man who travelled over from Albania with you. He and his friends are from the same village as you.'

'Gabriel?'

It was Coupland's turn to nod. 'Did you ever stay in the same accommodation as them?'

'No, I told you, the men and women were separated, it is just women and children where I am living.'

'In the time you've been staying there, has anyone else gone missing like your sister?'

'No, they keep a close eye on us so we pay off our debt. Zamira hasn't gone missing; she was taken to stay with people until she gets better.'

'Did you hear any of the men talking, the ones who kept watch on you? Did they call each other by name?'

'No.'

'Can you tell me what they look like?'

Mariana looked at him and shrugged.

'Were they tall, short?' prompted Coupland. 'Well built or skinny?' He held his hand above his head to indicate height, then imitated a Mr Universe pose. He moved his hand to below head height.

'No, they were tall,' Mariana confirmed, 'well built. Very little hair, I think they shaved it maybe.'

Coupland's shoulder's dipped; shaven headed and stocky, that was half the men in Salford. 'Any piercings?' He pointed to his eyebrows, nose, lip. Mariana shook her head. 'Any tattoos?'

'One of them had a tattoo on his arm,' she confirmed. Great, they'd narrowed it down by a third. He decided to call it a day. The details around her journey at the start and end of every day had been their best lead. He hoped to Christ they'd get something from it. He signalled to the social worker that they were free to leave.

Three sharp taps on the interview room door and Declan's Siamese twin entered but hovered in the doorway as though an invisible force field held him back. He held up an iPad. 'The DCI said you'd want to see this straight away.' The DNA results were in. Coupland summoned him closer; taking the iPad from him he tapped on Benson's email and opened the attachment. His face was grim as he read the content.

'You might want to sit back down,' he said to Mariana.

CHAPTER SEVENTEEN

By the time Coupland returned to the incident room a street map detailing the roads around the coffee shop where Mariana was taken to beg each day had been blown up and laminated before going up on the wall beside the incident board. DCI Akram stood in front of it tracing several routes with his index finger. Coupland moved closer, studying streets where the well-off and the hard up rubbed along cheek by jowl, looking at addresses at odds with each other on the social spectrum yet occupying the same square mile. Media City had brought wealth to Salford, there was no denying that, but some parts of the city hadn't caught up with that wealth. There were blind spots dotted here and there, places where crimes were committed under everyone's nose, only people were too hard up or too busy to give a toss. Who wouldn't go to the car wash that was half the price of the one on the top road? Or buy their Christmas presents from a fella selling cheap copies from the back of a car? Sometimes it was easier to turn a blind eye.

DC Briars had contacted Salford Council for information on road closures. 'There's been resurfacing work on several roads within a fifteen minute drive of Hankinson Road, but they haven't lasted for more than a couple of days, so the traffic guy at the council told me.'

'Couple of days my backside,' Coupland huffed. 'What about Great Clowes Street? They've been renewing the gas pipes there for what seems like an eternity.'

Declan referred to his notes. 'Works been going on there five weeks.'

'Is that all?' Coupland pulled a face. 'Mariana said the roadworks have been there almost as long as she's lived here.' He used the term 'lived' loosely. He moved closer to the map. 'What else have you got?'

Declan skim read the print-out he was holding. 'Roadworks on the A576 Great Cheetham Street West.'

Coupland studied the map then nodded. 'That'd work. Some old flats are being developed along Bury New Road.' Coupland and Amjid exchanged a look. 'That's normally a fifteen minute drive from the coffee shop,' Coupland informed him, 'but it could easily become twenty minutes to half an hour when the lights are stuck on red.'

'Who are the developers?' Amjid asked.

Coupland pulled the map from the wall and placed it on Krispy's desk. 'Stop whatever else you're doing and give this priority, son.' He jabbed his finger along Bury New Road. 'I want the name and background check on the developer working on the flat conversion along this stretch of road.'

Krispy nodded. 'I'm on it.'

'Come to think of it,' Coupland added as an afterthought, 'find out who owns Shiny Happy Motors as well.'

As Coupland returned to the incident board his gaze fell onto the photo of the sports bag Zamira had been found in. 'Shitting Hell,' he muttered, pulling out his note book, flicking through the pages until he found one with the corner turned down.

'What is it?' Amjid's tone was sharp.

Coupland pointed at the photo of the sport bag, to the name of the local gym that ran down the side of it. 'I meant to go through their membership list.' He couldn't believe he'd forgotten to write it up as an action for the team. 'I could go over there now,' he offered, shamefaced, 'or get Turnbull to give them a ring.'

'What, and warn whoever's involved that we're onto them?' Amjid said, 'No, it's better that we keep well away from there, at least for the time being.'

'Sarge?' Krispy's voice offered respite from Coupland's embarrassment. He hoped to Christ his DC had found something that would make up for his own oversight. 'The company in charge of the development is Borthwick Enterprises.'

Coupland recognised the name from signs erected around the city. 'They've got a few large contracts on the go,' he observed. 'Never had any reason to cross paths with them though.'

Krispy held up his iPad. 'The company's got a website. They sell high end private apartments, converting old buildings into silly-money flats.'

'Nice work if you can get it.'

'The company is owned by Adrian Borthwick, known as Midas to his friends and associates.' Krispy started reading out Borthwick's bio.

'Skip to the relevant bits,' Coupland said impatiently.

Krispy nodded. 'He also has interests in that car valeting firm, Sarge.'

Coupland turned to Amjid. 'I was there yesterday; it's how I found out about Mariana and her sister. This is our bloody man.'

'Are there photos of him on Facebook?' Amjid asked.

Krispy tapped onto his iPad before holding up Adrian Borthwick's profile page which contained a photo he'd posted on-line in the lead up to the election. A publicity shot taken during a ministerial visit to showcase the boost to youth employment by companies like his taking on apprentices. A group of spotty youths stood either side of Borthwick and the Minister, grinning for the camera.

Coupland moved beside Amjid to get a better look. A muscle man wearing a black security uniform stood in the background. Coupland pointed him out. 'He looks like one of the fellas Mariana described that kept watch on them during the night.'

'And the type that likes to spend a lot of time at the gym, Sarge,' added Krispy.

*

Two dozen of the NCA's finest squeezed into Salford Precinct's CID room alongside senior officers from Nexus House, the headquarters of Greater Manchester Police's Major Incident Team. 'How come they don't all bugger off and have their meeting at HQ?' Turnbull groaned. 'Leave the rest of us to get on in peace.'

'The Super was adamant apparently,' Coupland replied, 'think he's frightened we'll be airbrushed out of the picture if we don't play the gracious host.' They were standing at the back of the room; chairs were for elite officers only, going by the look of it. The Tactical Aid Unit took up the most space, leaning back into their chairs with legs splayed, claiming as much territory as possible. Having no role to play, Coupland stared along the line of his own glum-faced team standing either side of him, arms folded as they listened to Operation Simba.

'Why bloody Simba?' asked Robinson.

'Akram's son is a big fan of the Lion King, apparently.'

Silence settled upon the assembled group as DCIs Akram and Mallender moved to flank Superintendent Curtis at the front of the room. A large projector screen brought over from Nexus House was positioned behind them. Ant and Dec had wired it up to Krispy's desktop and were in charge of the slideshow narrated by their boss. Krispy looked on, forlorn. An image of Adrian Borthwick, alias Midas, came up on the screen, it was the one Krispy had found earlier on Facebook but it had been blown up to get a clear view of his head and shoulders. This was followed by another, more recent photo. Midas was heavier in this shot, his hairline a little thinner.

'A surveillance team is already in situ at the development on Algernon Way,' Amjid informed them, 'cameras have been set up at the entrance to the site, we will be following his movements overnight before commencing the raid at his home and various business premises at 6am tomorrow.' A video link had already been set up in the CID room so that Akram and Mallender could monitor every stage of the raid remotely. 'We are particularly interested in this man,' Amjid continued as the body building security guard came on screen. He was shaven headed with grey stubble, wearing dark tracksuit bottoms cuffed at the ankle over Nike Air Max trainers. 'He matches the description supplied by our witness, and we are confident that over the next few hours he will lead us to where the migrants are being kept. It is likely that they are being housed in a property close to the development given our main witness's description of her journey to work every morning.' Coupland baulked at Amjid's use of the word work, since when had begging been classed as an occupation? He caught Turnbull's eye, could tell his DC was thinking the same thing. 'I want you to familiarise yourselves with these images,' Amjid continued, 'We have reason to believe these men and their associates are behind a large scale operation trafficking migrants from Albania into Salford, and may be responsible for the murder of five year old Zamira Gashi. Their identities have been confirmed by migrants transported at the same time as Zamira and her sister, currently working at the car valeting company owned by our key suspect.' Amjid paused. 'A search warrant has been granted for several sites he owns around the city; let's not put it to waste. We need hard evidence to put these men away, and that is down to you.'

Coupland raised his hand.

'What is it?' Superintendent Curtis barked.

'Mariana mentioned there was a woman who sold medicine to them when they were sick, will the wives or partners of these men be detained and questioned too?'

Curtis looked at Mallender who turned to Akram; after all, this was his gig. Akram referred to his iPad, swiping his finger expertly across the screen. He paused then looked up, either he'd found what he was looking for or couldn't be arsed swiping the screen any more. 'Yes,' he concurred, 'their partners will also be detained.'

Coupland nodded, although not entirely satisfied. At the end of the briefing he made his way over to Mallender, his face dark. 'He'd forgotten that Mariana had said a woman was involved, hadn't he?'

Mallender glanced at Akram to check he was out of earshot. Superintendent Curtis had already left the room.

'We don't know that,' he placated, 'he's had a lot to coordinate in a short space of time, I've not seen anything to make me think he's not all over it.'

'He's not all over the bloody murder,' Coupland raged, 'let's face it nothing looks better on the CV than landing a trafficking gang.'

Mallender sighed. 'Be reasonable, Kevin,'

'Purlease…' Coupland chided. 'Isn't that how Greater Manchester Police ended up with the Rochdale mess, by thinking some lives were worth less than others? What's a dead little Albanian in the grand scheme of things?'

Mallender laid a hand on Coupland's shoulder. He wasn't prone to being tactile, nor was Coupland used to the close proximity of other men, unless he was pinning someone to the floor. The DCI's gesture threw both of them out of their comfort zone; Mallender might as well have grabbed his testicles for all the reassurance it gave. 'Be very careful about the accusations you make against a senior officer,' he warned. It wasn't said as a threat, Coupland knew that. It was a reminder; that just like the affections of the girl three years above him in high school, there were some things he couldn't win.

Coupland sighed. 'Can you blame me? Just as we find out the victim's identity we're told to stand down from the investigation. Precious time is being lost while they go after the big fish.'

'I know, but what if the big fish sanctioned her murder? An independent line of enquiry into Zamira's death could jeopardise this whole operation, so if you're looking for me to give you the green light to carry on regardless of what you've been told you're wasting your time, do you understand?'

Coupland raised his hand in surrender. 'Loud and bloody clear, boss,' he found himself muttering once more, 'loud and bloody clear.'

*

Coupland held his breath as he let himself in with his key, half expecting the safety chain to be pulled across given how he'd been carrying on lately but it wasn't. He breathed out a sigh of relief; the day hadn't turned out so bad, all things considered. He'd managed to blag a place on the raid, not with the Tactical Unit, neither Mallender nor Akram trusted him anywhere near a firearm, but they'd sanctioned him to be part of the sweep team who would arrive in convoy once the property was secure. It meant a return to the station at 5am, but it was not as if there was any chance of him getting much sleep, the amount of adrenaline pumping through him.

Lynn had got in before him, had already made a start on the evening meal. Something ready-made from Marks and Spencer was humming in the microwave. A bottle of wine stood open on the table. 'Brave, considering what I did with the last one,' Coupland quipped, regretting it instantly when Lynn didn't laugh. Not even the hint of a smile.

'We need to talk, Kev.'

Coupland's shoulders dipped. Wanting to talk was never what it purported to be. It was code for having his testicles removed. A bollocking dressed up as a civilised conversation. 'Where's Amy?' This would give him some idea as to the severity of the situation.

'Gone to the cinema with a pal.'

Coupland blinked slowly as he removed his jacket,

placing it over the back of a chair. He poured himself a drink. Only dregs remained in Lynn's glass, she nodded when held the bottle up at her.

'Go on then, what've I done now?'

Lynn sighed, 'For Christ's sake, when will you stop?'

'What?'

'You've spent your whole life trying so hard not to be like your dad you've forgotten who you are.'

'I have no idea what you're talking about.'

'You're a good man, Kevin. Otherwise I'd never have married you.'

'And there was me thinking it was my startling good looks that drew you in, you know how to kick a man when he's down.'

'Stop it!'

'What?'

'Can't you be serious for once in your life?'

'This *is* me being serious! If this is about me sending the granny from Hell packing last night I've got nothing to apologise for. There's only so much I can take—'

'—and that, Kevin, is my point.' Lynn leaned against the kitchen counter triumphant.

Coupland creased his brow. 'I'm not with you.'

'We're all shell-shocked by what's happened, you know. You, me, but most of all Amy. She's the one going to have to deal with telling her child about its father. And be the one putting up with strange looks from the other mums at playgroup, or be on the defensive at parents' night if there's a problem with behaviour, or making friends or whatever it is marks out a psychopath from anyone else.'

'For a minute there I thought you were describing me,' Coupland quipped.

Lynn ignored him. 'How's she ever going to know what normal looks like with Lee Dawson's shadow hanging over them?'

'So what are you saying? That she should have had an abortion after all?'

'Since when does looking back fix anything?' she sighed. 'And besides… every life is precious.'

Coupland wasn't so sure, he wished to Christ there was a way that someone's conscience could be weighed and measured at birth, he was convinced some people were born without one. Now wasn't the time to split hairs though. He nodded his head in what he hoped would come across as agreement. 'About that…' he began.

'Kev.' Lynn wasn't listening; she was building up to something. The microwave had pinged but she made no move to take out whatever had been nuked inside it. 'Do you ever think about the baby?' She turned away then, busied herself getting plates from the cupboard but her movements were slow. She wanted to study his reaction but was scared to, in case she didn't like what she saw. Coupland moved across the kitchen, taking hold of her arms he turned her so that she was facing him. He dipped his head and stared at her until he had her full attention. 'Every day, love. It's impossible to look at Amy and not wonder…' he coughed the lump from his throat. 'It never made any difference to me; you know that, about the father, I mean, none of it mattered at the end of the day, did it?' Even as he said it he knew he was proving the point she'd been making all along, but this time it met with no resistance. 'I'll clear the air with Amy,' he said.

The evening meal was eaten in silence, albeit a companionable one, the TV on but down low, Lynn absorbed in her favourite soap, Coupland's head full of tomorrow's raid.

DAY FIVE

CHAPTER EIGHTEEN

Coupland kept pace behind the convoy of Tactical Aid Units as they snaked their way along Bury New Road. Simultaneous raids were being carried out at Adrian Borthwick's, aka Midas's home and his other business interests but Coupland wanted to see the place where Zamira and Mariana had been kept. Surveillance cameras had tracked the security guard pictured with Borthwick on Facebook going into and out of a dilapidated property behind the flat conversion at Algernon Way. They'd found their target, all they had to do now was wait.

Beyond the car windscreen the sky was dark like a bruise. There was little traffic at this time, save for articulated trucks making their way to Tesco and Aldi. Coupland slowed his car to a stop, waited while an officer from the head of the convoy jumped out of the van and cut through the security chain on the gate at the site's main entrance with bolt cutters. The officer remained beside the gate as the convoy entered the compound, securing it after the last vehicle had gone through in case anyone inside the building tried to make a run for it. Coupland moved his car forward, slower now, smooth tarmac giving way to potholes beneath his wheels. He held back, increasing the gap between him and the TAUs, until eventually coming to a halt. The driver of the surveillance unit manoeuvred it so that the camera on its roof had full view of their target - a derelict two storey block close to the apartments being redeveloped. The windows to the front of the property were boarded up, cloaking the area in darkness. No one from the road would think it was occupied. Mariana had told them the migrants were transported by car, so it wasn't as if there'd been any pedestrian activity to arouse suspicion.

The rear doors of the unit in front opened spewing out a sea of black as firearms officers took up position. A voice warbled over the radio checking with DCI Akram that the transmission was clear. It was the officer heading up the surveillance unit. Other units around the city radioed in the same message, making sure that Akram had simultaneous views of the raids as they took place. Coupland grabbed his Kevlar vest, pulling it over his hooded 'Police' sweatshirt. Behind his car officers from Immigration Enforcement bided their time. It was their job to round up any victims found on the premises and take them to a safe place. DCI Akram's voice came over the radio confirming the targeted sites were in view.

Armed police lined up at the entrance to the building in silence, directed by NCA officers wearing police issue baseball caps. At the front of the line an officer holding a battering ram pulled his helmet's visor over his face. Coupland held his breath.

Any. Minute. Now.

Akram gave his signal over the radio. The door caved in on impact. 'POLICE RAID! STAY WHERE YOU ARE!' An explosion of noise erupted from the building as tactical officers surged inside: the sound of heavy boots on stairs; screams and foreign sounding swear words; bare feet scuffling on floorboards and furniture being upended. The front of the building was flooded in light as portable beams manned by the surveillance team were trained on the entrance. Moments later a man in a dark blue tracksuit was brought out in handcuffs; another was carried out spread-eagled before being placed on the floor as officers searched him. The enforcement officers waiting behind Coupland climbed out of their vans to collect the migrants as they were led out. The children, bleary-eyed, looked on as their mothers pulled them close. No one cried. It was as if this chaos was all they'd come to expect. Another chapter in their disordered lives. The older children were wary of being rounded up yet no one made a run for it; many were malnourished, running anywhere would have been impossible. Coupland watched the scene unfold as he climbed out of his car and moved towards the floodlit area. He'd promised Mallender that he'd stay out of the way. His presence on the raid was a courtesy extended by DCI Akram. He was there to observe, nothing more. He studied the hand-cuffed man as he was led into a cage at the back of a van. He looked nothing like the security guard featured on Midas's Facebook page. Neither did the man spread-eagled on the gravel. Coupland's brow furrowed as he pushed his way through the tide of people coming out of the building. The ground floor was split into two derelict rooms, bare concrete floors with exposed brick walls. In the first room a solitary light bulb hung from the ceiling. Three camp beds lined up in the corner. Empty beer cans and crushed cigarette packets littered the floor beneath them. Coupland moved closer, his eyes narrowing. The room next door had been turned into a makeshift kitchen. A cooker had been installed against one wall. A shelf had been hammered onto another, a kettle and microwave on top of it. A washing machine stood on its own beneath an opaque window, its door open, giving off a smell of sweat and soiled clothing.

Upstairs resembled a doss house. Rows of camp beds and sleeping bags. Thin blankets stained every shade of yellow. The room stank like a urinal. Small bottles containing murky liquid stood beside some of the beds. Several beds had rows of them. Coupland stood back to let an officer help an elderly woman down the stairs. Only the stragglers were left now, those too ill or too heavily pregnant to be herded downstairs in the first tranche. Enforcement officers moved between the makeshift beds throwing the migrants' belongings into clear plastic bags. Ant and Dec stood in the centre of the room directing proceedings. As Coupland approached them Ant's eyes opened wide, he muttered something to Declan before stepping back a couple of paces to speak into his radio, all the while not breaking eye contact. His mouth formed a thin line as Coupland drew level. 'Authorised personnel only,' he said, 'and I've just checked. *You're* not authorised.'

'DCI Akram didn't give you clearance to enter the building.' Declan was trying hard to be amenable. 'Eyes on the ground, that's all.'

Coupland nodded, he'd expected nothing less. These men were career cops; they followed orders to the letter, never went above or beyond them in case there were consequences. 'Did the TAU clear all the rooms?' he asked.

Ant regarded him coolly. 'You still here?'

Coupland ignored him, turning his attention to DC Declan. 'I'm guessing the suspects in cuffs were found in the room downstairs, right? The so-called security guards?'

Declan nodded.

'You've only detained two men, yet three camp beds have been slept in.'

Ant sighed. 'Just because there are three camp beds, doesn't mean all three have been used tonight.'

'I checked them, they were all warm. The fella that's missing is the one photographed beside Midas on his Facebook profile. More like a right hand man than a gofer. We can't lose him now. For Christ's sake the surveillance team even filmed him coming in here last night, so where the hell is he?'

Ant looked up at the ceiling. 'Shit,' he mumbled.

'He can't have gone far though, we've blocked all the exits,' Declan offered.

'The exits that we know about,' Coupland cautioned. 'These fellas know the lie of the land better than we do.' He turned back to Ant, demanding: 'How many rooms were cleared?'

Ant looked at Dec as though to say he could take over now things were going pear shaped. Declan flared his nostrils but spoke into his radio anyway. The TAU leader's response was instant. *'Three rooms and the hallway were given the all-clear.'* Coupland tried to keep his irritation in check, raising his arms in a *what the fuck* pose.

'C-can you be more precise please?' Declan stammered into his radio. The TAU officer's response this time was clipped: *'Two rooms on the ground floor, one room on the first floor.'*

Coupland huffed out a sigh. 'Jesus wept, what about a toilet?' he demanded.

'There wasn't one,' came the terse reply, *'Who the hell is*

this anyway?

'*Is that DS Coupland?*' DCI Akram's voice boomed over the airwave.

'Negative.' Declan choked the word out, signalling for Coupland to stand out of earshot.

'*Is there a problem, DC Briars?*'

Declan regarded his radio with alarm. 'Sorry Sir, the reception's really bad here.' He switched his radio off and pocketed it, his face crestfallen.

'If you want to redeem yourself you need to find this fella's hiding place,' Coupland said, glancing around the room before heading towards the stairs.

'What are you talking about?' Ant's tone was cautious, he'd cocked up and was willing to clutch onto a straw, even if it was Coupland holding the other end. As Coupland passed by a camp bed he paused, bending to retrieve a small Lucozade bottle, its contents replaced with a yellowy brown liquid. 'Now the boys might pee in these but there must be somewhere the women go,' he reasoned, returning the bottle to its place beneath the camp bed as he headed to the stairs, both DCs hurrying in his wake. 'It only needs to be a small space, a corner even.' He went back into the kitchen, to the opaque glass window above the washing machine. A clothes airer stood beside it, laden with sheets. Coupland pulled it out of the way. A bucket overflowing with dark liquid and floaters stood in the cramped corner. Beside it a shaven headed body builder doubled over like a contortionist. It was the fella seen standing beside Midas in the Facebook photo. Before Coupland had a chance to say 'Gotcha', Mr Universe uncoiled himself to his full height, shoulder slamming into Coupland sending him crashing to the ground. Ant and Dec lurched forward but not before he'd picked up the toilet bucket and held it out like a weapon. He started backing away, 'Grab him for Christ's sake, it won't kill you!' Coupland ordered, but both DCs held back. There was a window behind him which led to God knows where. The surveillance team hadn't bothered to light up the back of the building and sniffer dogs hadn't been deemed necessary for this job. If he slipped away from them now he could be out of the country by lunchtime. Coupland pushed himself to his feet and squared his shoulders, arms out wide in case he tried to push past him again. All the while the titan backed towards the window, the shit smelling bucket held out as though warding off evil. 'You picked the wrong bloke on the wrong day, pal,' Coupland said, jerking his head back before whipping it forward – crack – right into the bridge of his nose. Mr Universe dropped the bucket as his hands flew to his face; only a member of the River-dance cast could have sidestepped what tipped out of it. Undeterred, Coupland grabbed his wrists and read him his rights before marching him outside.

*

The welcoming party at Salford Precinct didn't look quite so cheery on Coupland's arrival. 'You've got to be kidding me,' the custody sergeant said when he saw one of the suspects had a broken nose.

'A&E has given him the all clear,' Coupland told him, 'the duty doc'll do the same.'

The sergeant picked up his phone and summoned him anyway. 'Just to be on the safe side,' he cautioned.

The men were processed into custody. 'Do you have

any issues with understanding what people are saying to you?' the Custody Sergeant asked. They shook their heads. 'Do you need any help with reading or writing or learning?' Coupland didn't need to know the career history of these fellas to see they were familiar with the custody process. They didn't baulk at the questions asked, nodding or shaking their heads where relevant. 'When you went to school did you go to a special school or did you need any extra help?' More shakes of the head. Coupland watched as their personal belongings were taken from them before going through to the cells. From his vantage point beside the desk he scanned down the entries in the custody book, saw that Adrian Borthwick, otherwise known as Midas, and his wife were in cells 1 and 2. 'That's us fully booked,' the custody sergeant told him when he clocked him looking. 'Swinton and Eccles are taking the overflow. Talking of which, can you smell that?' He wrinkled his nose as he peered over the counter, stared at the brown smear leading up to the desk. 'Some twat's stepped in shite and trodden it all over my bloody floor.'

*

Upstairs Coupland's welcome wasn't much warmer. 'Boss wants to speak to you, pronto,' the civilian on the desk called out, coughing as something foul reached his nostrils.

'Need to get cleaned up first,' Coupland told him, 'act like you haven't seen me.'

'I mean the big boss,' the civilian replied, eyeing Coupland with some degree of sympathy. 'Superintendent Curtis has demanded your presence. Immediately.

He told me to stress that to you the minute you walked in.'

'Thought he'd be too busy arranging a press conference to see the likes of me.' News like this was gold dust, a gang busted before the good people of Salford even knew they existed. 'Aren't those his dress shoes I can hear doing a jig on the ceiling above?'

The civilian nodded, leaning forward conspiratorially, 'He's speaking to the press later this morning, he's waiting on his wife driving a fresh shirt over.' He regarded Coupland when he didn't smile. 'I'm guessing someone's up to their gonads in something brown and sticky.'

Coupland gazed down at his shoes. 'Not *quite* up to my gonads,' he observed, 'but I might as well be.'

*

Coupland studied the vein that throbbed in Curtis's neck when he entered his office. It was a useful barometer, warned him of the extent of the Super's displeasure. Today it seemed to have taken on a life of its own. 'DCI Mallender not joining us?' he asked, glancing around for back up.

'DCI Mallender is with DCI Akram in the incident room preparing to watch the video link of our suspects being interviewed.' Coupland nodded. Virtual policing. The senior ranks spent so little time in the actual presence of criminals he doubted they'd recognise one unless they wore a black and white striped sweater and carried a swag bag. So, Mallender wouldn't be here to plead leniency. Coupland had some serious grovelling to do. 'If this is about earlier…'

The Super's eyes nearly popped out of his head. '"If

271

this is about," DS Coupland? Is that the best you can do?'
Coupland dropped his gaze to the items on top of Curtis's
desk. The crystal paperweight etched with the GMP
logo at its base. The silver framed photo of his wife and
child. Blotting paper and a pricey looking fountain pen.
Coupland wondered at the luxury of writing something
you had time to let dry. '…We're looking at insubordination at the very least,' Curtis continued, 'gross misconduct
if our suspect decides to make a complaint.' Coupland
should have realised news of his run-in with Mr Universe
would have travelled fast. 'I prevented an identified gang
member from escaping,' Coupland baulked. 'If it'd been
up to Ant and Dec there he'd be long gone by now.'

'Who?' Curtis narrowed his eyes. 'Never mind,' he said
impatiently, 'there was a cordon around the whole site, he
wasn't going anywhere.'

'No, Sir, we replaced the padlock on the gate we went
through when we entered the site. There's a difference.
We only secured one exit. Who's to say he didn't have a
key for a padlock on one of the other gates?'

'There were officers stationed at each exit—'

'—that we knew about, Sir,' Coupland interrupted. 'It
was dark and we were on an unfamiliar site. He could
have found a way out. It's not like we had the Dog Unit
as backup.'

Curtis made a choking sound. 'What the hell is that
smell?'

'You did say I had to come here pronto, Sir, I've not
had time to clean up yet.'

The Super looked as though he would explode. 'Just
get out of my sight,' he ordered. 'I'll let you know what
action will be taken in due course.'

At the back of Coupland's locker a pair of trainers lurked. An unwanted present from Lynn when she'd tried to get him to take up jogging. 'I run after toe rags every day of my working life, why would I want to do it for fun?' he'd levelled at her.

'It's not for fun, Kevin,' she conceded, 'but it'll be good for you.' The exercise bike she'd bought when that failed had been relegated to the garage. She'd kept her Zumba up, though he suspected the sly prosecco she had on the way home with her mates was incentive enough. A pair of jogging bottoms lay discarded on the locker room floor. Coupland gave them a sniff, decided they were better than what he had on and changed into them, the glare of his New Balance trainers in stark contrast to the washed-out grey.

A crowd of officers had gathered in the CID room, staring at the large screen as they waited for the trafficking gang's interviews to be streamed live. Coupland moved towards the front, to the desk DCI Akram was using as base camp. Akram wasn't there, neither was Mallender. Unless virtual food was available to download at the click of a mouse, he suspected they were in the canteen filling their faces. The laptop on Akram's desk was open. Footage of the site's dawn raid was on the screen, the image paused on Coupland as he led a bloodied suspect from the building. Coupland sighed, clicked on the minimize button and searched for the video clip of the raid on Midas's home, a detached house at the head of a cul-de-sac in Boothstown. Coupland's lip curled as he watched Adrian Borthwick comply with the arresting officers as he was led out into the road, his face poker straight while he followed instructions. He showed no resistance, placing his hands on his head when told to do so then moving them behind his back like he was playing Simple Simon. He wore trousers and a jumper that wouldn't look out of place on a golf course, his tousled hair the only clue he had dressed in a hurry. His wife wasn't quite so agreeable. Make-up free and her hair scraped back in a pony-tail, she cursed at the officers escorting her into the van, her face twisted in spite. Three small faces looked down from an upstairs window. A liaison officer remained at the property while a relative was contacted to collect the children. NCA officers entered the building carrying boxes and large plastic bags. Coupland pressed the zoom button to see what they brought out.

'What the hell do you think you are doing?'

Coupland spun round to see DCI Akram bearing down on him, a weary looking DCI Mallender in his wake. 'I just wanted to see how the other raids had gone down,' Coupland answered.

'A damn sight better than the one you attended,' Akram stated, pushing past Coupland to get to his chair.

Coupland held his ground. 'Christ Almighty it's clear he's got previous, he was never going to come quietly, what was I supposed to do?'

'What were you supposed to do, DS Coupland?' Akram exploded. 'It wasn't your call, you weren't even supposed to be in the building at that stage of the operation.'

'I could see something was wrong from the start, he hadn't been brought out with the others, I was worried he was going to evade capture, Sir.'

'Save it for the Superintendent, DS Coupland,' Mallender sighed, 'he's asked to see you right away.'

'Oh, I've already had my testicles removed boss, I came down here to see if I could do anything to stick 'em back on.'

'Help?' Akram butted in. 'You do realise you may have compromised this whole investigation?'

Coupland threw his arms out wide. 'Look, I'm sorry, I'm sure it'll blow over. You know what these wise-guys are like.' Akram was about to say something when his phone rang. He nodded into it as the officer on the other end of the line confirmed the interviews were ready to proceed.

Mallender leaned forward to speak into Coupland's ear. 'Just give us some space,' he instructed, nodding to the row of chairs at the back of the room. Coupland did as he was told.

The first to be interviewed was Midas, AKA Adrian Borthwick, the lynchpin of the trafficking gang. Amjid made notes while Ant and Dec, who were conducting the interviews, spoke into the tape stating everyone present in the interview room. Amjid wore a Bluetooth headset connected to earpieces worn by both detectives so he could direct the line of questioning. He sat stony faced through the first 'No comment' but five minutes in his patience began to wear a little thin. 'Bollocks!' he shouted at the screen, his hand slamming down on the desk in front of him. Midas's wife followed suit, even stating 'No comment' when asked how many children the couple had. The interviews with the first two security guards picked up during the site raid went much the same way. Akram was all but hyperventilating, his Bluetooth headpiece thrown into the bin beside his desk in anger. Finally the security guard apprehended by Coupland shuffled into the interview room, his bulk concealed by a set of joggers far too big for him, the grey cloth hung in loose folds like an elephant's scrotum. A tampon had been stuck in one nostril to stop the excessive bleeding, purple bruising spread out from the bridge of his nose forming shadows beneath his eyes. He didn't bother with 'No comment'. He stared into the video lens and gave his name, 'Austin Smith, my mates call me Reedsy,' his words came out in a nasal whine, 'and I want to make a complaint about police brutality.'

'That's all we fucking need!' Amjid exploded, slamming his other palm down on the desk top before arcing it wide sending everything on top of his desk flying.

Mallender swivelled round in his seat until he eyeballed Coupland. 'I think it's better if you go home, Kevin,' he said, his tone implying that this was an order, one that today of all days he didn't expect to be challenged.

*

Coupland had drawn level with the exit doors when he heard someone call out his name. He turned to see DC Declan Briars make his way towards him. He held up his hands as though warding off a blow. 'Look, I'm sorry if I've dropped you in it,' Coupland said. 'I really thought we'd lose him if I didn't stop him in his tracks.'

'You were right,' Declan informed him, slightly out of breath, 'I don't mean about him having an escape route, but I've just had word back from the search team that there were weapons hidden out the back of that building, if he'd got to them who knows what he would have done.'

'I appreciate you telling me,' Coupland responded. 'You might want to share that with the powers that be, seems I'm persona non grata at the moment.'

'I'm on my way, Sarge,' Declan nodded. 'I'm sure by tomorrow things will look different.'

'I hope you're right,' Coupland said as he headed out through the exit, clutching a plastic bag containing his shit-smelling shoes.

His mood was reflective during the drive home. Could he have handled his confrontation with this Reedsy fella any better? There was a part of him, granted, that had got a great deal of satisfaction in seeing blood pump from the sicko's nose. Why couldn't he just accept he'd been caught? He never understood why some cons felt as though they had to go down in a blaze of glory. He blinked angrily; try as he might his thoughts returned to Lee Dawson, another martyr who'd refused to accept the inevitable, and look how that had turned out.

He drummed his fingers on the steering wheel. The car radio was tuned into the local radio station, a DJ that loved the sound of his own voice asking listeners to call in and tell him about their day. A married couple phoned in who were redecorating their home; a delivery driver lost somewhere off the East Lancs Road; a group of factory workers ordering in pizza while the boss was out. And what would Coupland's contribution be, he wondered? Driving home with his windows down because he'd walked into a shit storm. He turned the volume up when the news came on; the Super's media trained voice boomed over the airwaves:

'*Our intention has always been to disrupt and dismantle organised crime in Salford. I am pleased to tell you that in collaboration with the National Crime Agency we achieved that today. Following several raids throughout the city this morning we targeted not only*

suspected criminals but also sought out potential victims of exploita-
tion and moved them to safety. Several arrests have been made for
offences including human trafficking and sexual exploitation. A
number of local companies found to be employing illegal immigrants
have been shut down. Let me make this clear – if we suspect you are
enabling this wicked industry in any way – we will come after you.'

'Spoken like someone whose footwear only ever smells of spit and polish,' Coupland muttered into the void.

DAY SIX

CHAPTER NINETEEN

The mood in the CID room was sombre. During a search on Austin 'Reedsy' Smith's phone the NCA tech guys discovered images of kiddie porn. 'Don't blame the Sarge for decking him,' Turnbull muttered out of earshot of any of DCI Akram's officers. 'Nasty stuff too by the sounds of it, filmed over several locations.'

Krispy turned to him. 'So what does that mean?'

'It means this crime syndicate is bigger than we thought,' Turnbull informed him. 'It also means we won't be getting rid of this lot for quite some time…' Coupland sat at the back of the room once more in case another sharp exit was required. His sleep had been fitful, replaying Reedsy's capture in his mind to see if there could have been a way to bring him in without breaking his nose. Despite his best efforts could he be turning into his father's son after all?

DCI Akram, standing at the front of the room, glared over at Coupland's team until there was silence once more. 'The forensic lab has found DNA linking Midas to the site where the migrants have been held although no DNA could be found to implicate his wife. We've released her without charge for the time being.' He looked over at Coupland as he said this, as though expecting him to pipe up some objection. Coupland remained tight lipped.

'Officers found more than £40,000 in cash in his home,' he continued, 'a replica gun and financial documents proving they were engaged in human trafficking.' Several grunts of satisfaction reverberated around the room. 'Our tech boys are certainly pulling out all the stops. A search of his laptop shows that he was using cash from both the building and car valeting firms as a front, using company funds to cover smuggling related expenses. This means we can pursue a conviction for trafficking… Weapons were also discovered at the building site,' he added as an afterthought, this time avoiding Coupland's eye.

'I can give you a hand putting the case together for the CPS if you like,' Coupland offered. Akram didn't bother looking at him.

'That won't be necessary.' DCI Mallender stepped in. 'This is just the tip of the iceberg, Kevin, There's every chance we can throw the book at them: Forced Labour, Slavery, Servitude, Sexual Exploitation. The good news is that in the face of these charges they've been happy to start talking, in fact it's hard shutting them up.' No surprises there, thought Coupland. Mallender cleared his throat. He had a strange look on his face and Coupland got the impression he wasn't going to like what was coming next. 'However, there is no forensic evidence linking any members of the gang to Zamira's murder.'

Coupland thought he was hearing things; one look at the faces of his team told him otherwise. 'Hang on, boss, there's bound to be trace fibres, they're rubbing shoulders with the migrants every day.'

'From the fibres found on Zamira's clothing we can link her to the building where she and her sister have been held, and we can link Midas and the security guards to the building, just not directly to the crime scene.'

'What about their cars?'

'There are fibres present, but they've admitted transporting the girls to and from their begging site outside Costa Coffee. It doesn't implicate them in a murder.'

'Do any of their cars match the partial number plate I gave you?'

Akram looked blank.

'Remember, I wrote down a partial number plate of the car on the incident board? I told you it had been lurking across the road from where Mariana was begging. The driver took off before I could get much more.'

A slow blink. 'Yes… well… I'll double check but the point is, registration or not, the trace fibres link Zamira to their cars but they've already admitted they transported her to the begging site.'

'They're bound to admit the lesser charge, anything rather than murder.'

'It's possible,' Akram conceded, 'but the stretch they're looking at for trafficking alone makes me think they're telling the truth. Besides, we've got our work cut out as it is. I'd rather go with what we have and get them off the streets than go for a murder charge that is largely circumstantial.'

And there it was.

At least we'll put them away. Like that was supposed to make everything better.

'Let me interview the security guards.'

DCI Akram looked askance. 'Are you out of your mind, DS Coupland? Austin Smith has already submitted a complaint about you. You're going nowhere near them.'

'Look, just him then, if I'm going to have the book thrown at me what harm can an interview do? Oh, I get it, apart from reflecting badly on you.'

'*That's enough.*' There was steel in Mallender's voice telling Coupland to back off. Coupland held his gaze for a fraction longer than necessary before slumping back in his seat, arms folded over his stomach. The briefing continued, but the tension in the room was palpable. Every so often members of his team glanced in his direction sending a reassuring nod.

'It's all bollocks, Sarge,' Krispy mouthed at him forcing Coupland's pursed lips into a smile. Days like this it was easy to believe your actions amounted to sod all. Zamira was still dead, and there was every chance her killer was going to get away with it. It gave Coupland comfort to know he wasn't the only one hurting.

DCI Akram began detailing the evidence found at the property on the building site at Algernon Way, 'Officers found just under two grand in cash and a notebook used as a ledger.' He held up a photograph of an evidence bag full of small brown bottles and blister packs of tablets. 'Turns out they were running a proper little pharmacy. If the migrants needed medicine they had to pay for each dose on a daily basis, the gang were charging them a pound per tablet.'

Turnbull looked at the detectives sat either side of him, 'Christ, that's a hell of a lot of chest infections.'

DCI Akram looked over at Turnbull and shook his head. 'They were mainly used by the girls to treat STIs.'

Coupland's mood deteriorated. 'Jesus, if it wasn't bad enough that these kids are forced into prostitution, any earnings they do get to keep is spent on medicine to get rid of clap.' He shook his head. 'What about the woman Mariana told us about? The one who gave Zamira drugs

284

to make her do as she was told? You sure it's not Midas's wife?'

'Her DNA doesn't match.'

'Then we need to find her! For Christ's sake, she's pivotal to this case. She doped a little girl to make her biddable, who the hell in their right mind would do that? There's every chance this woman is the link to Zamira's killer.'

'Maybe so.' Akram's words were clipped, as though any conversation he had with Coupland was an unwanted one. 'But we have the trafficking gang lynch pin and his sidekicks, the case against *them* can go ahead.'

Coupland got to his feet. He'd heard enough, if he stayed any longer he'd say something he shouldn't.

'Kevin,' Mallender's tone was sharp, 'the briefing isn't over…'

Coupland huffed out a sigh. 'I'm done, boss,' he said, heading towards the door.

'DS Coupland…' Mallender warned.

Coupland paused in the doorway and turned, nodding at the assembled group. 'Look, I get it, uncovering the trafficking gang has been a huge achievement. But I'm a simple cop and all I see is a murder we didn't solve. That little girl didn't walk out of where she was being kept of her own accord, did she? By the sounds of it she could barely stand, she was pumped so full with drugs.' He jabbed his finger in the direction of the corridor and the custody suite beyond. 'Those security guards were involved in moving kids like Zamira and her sister around the city. Even if they're not responsible for killing her they damn well know who is.' He stomped out before Mallender called his name for a third time. Out to the smoking shelter for a nicotine hit, his fingers touching the cellophane around the packet for reassurance.

Three strides into the yard and he'd lit up, his eyes narrowing as he inhaled the tar as far as it would go. He was twice as deep in the sticky stuff now. First for using greater force than was necessary for apprehending a suspect, and now for showing insubordination to a senior officer. Maybe he should do them all a favour and hand in his warrant card. He took another drag on his cigarette as he wondered how Lynn's day was panning out. Her job wasn't easy by any means. Sick babies brought tension to any relationship, mums too fearful to speak and dads too angry to let anything get done. Yet she managed to get through her shift without storming off each time someone pushed her buttons. 'I'm there for the babies,' she told him often enough, 'they need me no matter what.'

The world had moved on since Coupland joined the force. Mobile phones and social media. Cyber crime and grooming. The public were told to ring Crimestoppers rather than go to their local station, and the eyes and ears of community policing had been replaced by CCTV. He shook his head as he stumped out his cigarette. 'Sorry, but I'm not having it,' he muttered, 'no bloody way, Jose.' Nothing could replace that feeling in the gut, the one that made him lock onto a suspect and not let go. And the feeling in his gut was that Austin 'Reedsy' Smith knew more than he was letting on.

*

'You looked like you needed to let off a bit of steam,' the civilian called out as Coupland passed the reception desk. 'So I told DCI Mallender just now that I hadn't seen you.

I hope I did the right thing?' Nodding, Coupland slowed his pace. 'Only he told me to tell you when you did appear that your presence is wanted upstairs.'

Coupland squared his shoulders, 'I thought it might be.'

DCI Mallender was already in Curtis's room. So was DCI Akram. Coupland looked from one to the other, confused; it didn't take three of them to mark his card. Besides, he reported into Mallender, and as such, any bollocking was his prerogative to give, not Akram's.

'Sit down, DS Coupland,' ordered Curtis. Coupland did as he was told, joining them at the large meeting table where tea and coffee had been laid out for three people. He wouldn't be staying long, then.

'As you know Kevin, DCI Akram and his team have amassed enough evidence against Adrian Borthwick and his cohort to build a strong case for the CPS to pursue human trafficking along with a myriad of other offences.'

'So I understand, Sir,' he replied, playing ball.

'This will be a lengthy exercise, as I'm sure you can imagine,' added Curtis.

Coupland nodded. 'I don't doubt it.'

'Therefore, after some discussion, and with guidance from HQ, we feel that the NCA's resources are best deployed tracing and intercepting any and all other suspects involved in the trafficking of these migrants.' Coupland waited. 'It simply isn't viable to widen the scope of this activity to include the investigation into Zamira Gashi's murder.' Coupland bowed his head. This was the moment where he'd be asked for his warrant card. Unpaid leave while a decision was made about his future.

'We know that you've been under a considerable

amount of pressure recently, Kevin,' DCI Mallender said evenly, 'and that your outburst earlier, and conduct during yesterday's raid was completely out of character.'

Coupland stared at Mallender, grateful for the lifeline he was throwing him. 'Thanks, boss,' Coupland said, 'absolutely.' He wasn't sure whether the DCI was referring to his health scare after he'd rescued Amy from Lee Dawson, or her pregnancy. A police station was no different to any workplace he supposed, gossip spread like wildfire.

Mallender threw Coupland a look. 'Which is why DCI Akram is happy for you to resume the murder enquiry.' Coupland resisted the urge to say whoopy bloody doo by counting to ten instead. The murder investigation had lost two vital days while the NCA had pranced about. Granted, they'd got a result. A major one at that. But still.

'Well, if there's nothing else?' he asked through gritted teeth.

Mallender moved his head from side to side while eyeing his fiery sergeant. 'No,' he responded, trying, but unable to keep the relief from his voice.

Coupland marched back into the CID room, repositioning the incident board so it was centre stage. 'Listen up, you lot,' he called out to his team, 'we're back in business.'

Several cheers went up around the room. 'About bloody time,' Robinson muttered as Coupland's team gathered round while he reallocated tasks.

'The NCA will have their hands full preparing their case for the CPS so the dream team have been given the green light to carry on with the murder investigation.' Coupland beamed. 'And yes, that includes you, Turnbull, in case you were wondering.'

'Do we just continue where we left off, Sarge?' he asked.

Coupland shook his head, 'Not quite, we know Zamira's identity, and we also know she never went anywhere without those security guards transporting her, and one of them told her sister that they were taking her somewhere to recover from her chest infection. Did they know at that point she wouldn't be coming back?' Coupland studied the faces of the officers around him, 'Call me old fashioned but to my reckoning that means one of those toe rags killed her, or delivered her to the person that killed her. That's what we need to be working on now.'

'Have you had a chance to question them, Sarge?'

Coupland shook his head. 'They're being transferred to HMP Manchester tomorrow pending trial so it doesn't look likely either unless we come up with something concrete.'

'They couldn't have been working in isolation Sarge,' said Turnbull. 'How did they get access to Ashdown Court? And why dump the body there, of all places?'

Coupland beamed, 'You're talking my language, Turnbull, I knew there was a reason I let you stick around. Whoever dumped that little girl either lives in the apartment block or knows someone who lives there,' he said. 'We need to go back over the information we've already gathered. Ashcroft, can you go through the previous tenants' statements, look for any inconsistencies, anything which at the time didn't seem out of the ordinary but now with the trafficking angle there might be a whole new connotation. Krispy can you check out their financial records, flag anything up, however trivial. If someone hasn't paid a parking fine I want to know about it.'

'Do you want me to go back to the maintenance firm?' Ashcroft asked.

Coupland shook his head. 'They checked out, didn't they, first time around? And I don't think the landlord's guilty of anything more than being a creep either, so let's focus on people that have stayed there.'

'What about the current tenants?' asked Robinson.

'You and Turnbull go over the statements that Alex and I took, see if you pick up something we didn't. I'm going to go over the security guards' statements with a fine tooth comb. If I want to interview Reedsy I'm going to have to present a damn good case to DCI Akram.' The body building security guard was implicated in Zamira's murder, Coupland was sure of it, and the sooner he worked out what the hell that connection was, the better.

*

Two hours later Coupland's shoulders ached from poring over several pages of statements. He sat up straight in his chair, stretched out his spine while raising his arms above his head. Zamira's photograph took centre stage on the incident board. She looked different alive. A gap-toothed little girl with rosy cheeks, hair combed back into a bobble, a pink clip holding the wispy bits in place. Nothing like the bloated, rotting husk in her post-mortem photos. 'Who did this to you?' Coupland asked, his shoulders returning to their stoop at the sight of them. When her body was released for burial it would be in a closed casket. No way would her sister get to see inside the coffin. A dozen names featured on the incident board. Some had question marks next to them. Some were underlined. Nothing concrete linked any of them to Zamira's murder. They needed information, evidence, anything, to justify questioning them further.

Coupland called over to Krispy to check on progress. The young DC's shoulders were dipped in a similar way. 'I take it there are no developments,' he asked.

'Nothing, Sarge,' Krispy answered, his eyes not leaving the screen as he scrolled through pages of bank statements.

'Let me know if anything changes.' Coupland said this more to bolster Krispy than anything. It was easy to get demoralised when you didn't feel you were making headway. Something occurred to him. 'Krispy,' he said, getting out of his seat as he moved towards the DC's desk. 'Stop what you're doing for a minute and go onto Reedsy's Facebook page.'

Krispy nodded eagerly at the change of task. 'What am I looking for, Sarge?'

'These toe rags aren't as smart as they like to make out. Remember that gang last year who stole a load of designer watches then posted photos of themselves on Facebook wearing them?' Krispy nodded. 'That's the mentality that we're dealing with, son. Besides, if anyone can find something on-line that links him to this murder, it's you.'

Krispy's fingers were already flying across the keyboard. 'Give me five minutes, Sarge, I'm all over it.'

Coupland returned to his desk, gathered up the security guards' statements and tossed them back into the trafficking case file. The line of questioning wasn't relevant to Zamira's murder, more to how they'd moved large numbers of migrants into the country and the sites around the city where they were taken to work or beg. He needed to get in front of Austin Smith. Tell him he'd be pursued for murder if he didn't co-operate.

'Sarge.' Krispy leaned back in his chair, started manoeuvring his desk top screen so that Coupland could see the image it contained. 'You might want to see this.'

Coupland found himself staring at a Facebook post of Reedsy posing beside a bench press in bright coloured pyjama trousers. The name of the gym was visible in the background. Regener8. It was the same name as the logo on the gym bag Zamira was found in.

Reedsy's DNA had already been checked. It linked him to Zamira but not to the sports bag. So, if the bag didn't belong to him it had to belong to another member, someone who'd intended to shift the body before it was found. Someone that Reedsy may well be acquainted with.

'Gotcha.' Coupland grinned.

CHAPTER TWENTY

Regener8 was housed in a large glass and concrete building on Karndean Street with a poster in the kerbside window advertising membership deals. The reek of chlorine greeted Coupland as he pushed open its double doors. The wall separating the reception area from the gym was glass from floor to ceiling. A row of treadmills overlooked the pool beyond, each occupant scowling as they pumped their hands to keep pace. Beyond them there were exercise bikes and rowing machines, resistance machines resembling implements of torture. Flabby bodies dripped in sweat as far as the eye could see. Coupland picked up a brochure containing the price list and baulked. 'Do people really pay this much to look miserable?' he asked the receptionist who stared back at him, a blank expression on her face.

The serious end of the gym was the weights corner. Big men with shiny heads stood over doppelgangers as they lifted barbells resembling car tyres just for the sake of it. Puffed out chests and arms the size of tree trunks. Coupland rolled his shoulders. A fella in jogging bottoms and a tee shirt with the gym's logo on the front gave instructions to a man using a bench press, squatting down to eye level to make his point. Not as hefty as the other men but what he lacked in width he made up for in facial hair. A bushy lumberjack beard concealed most of his face. He caught Coupland staring in his direction and nodded, saying something to the other man he got to his feet, summoning to another member of staff to take over. He dipped his head to step through the gym door and Coupland could see he was bigger than he first looked, and realised the backdrop of gladiators would make giant men look puny.

'Are you looking to join?' he asked Coupland, looking pointedly at the receptionist as though showing her how it was done. Coupland laughed, 'Christ, no, I was wanting some information, that's all.' He flashed his warrant card under the instructor's nose. 'Thought I'd come down and get it myself.'

The prospect of a sale now gone, the instructor's demeanour changed, his false smile replaced with caution. He waited while Coupland took out his phone, tapped a couple of times until he'd pulled up Austin Smith's Facebook page. He scrolled down his posts until he found the photo he was looking for. The picture taken of him mid-workout. 'It's pretty obvious Reedsy here is a member,' Coupland said, holding the screen so the instructor could see it. I just need to know who he knocks about with.'

The instructor's eyes darted to the big men standing around the water cooler. 'Can I ask what this is about?'

'Sorry, I didn't get your name,' Coupland asked, ignoring his question.

'Purves,' he said, 'Gym manager.'

'Right, Mr Purves,' said Coupland. 'Can you give me the names of anyone he seems particularly pally with?'

Purves shrugged. 'The guys following our body building programme are a pretty tight bunch when they're here,' he said, 'but I don't think it goes beyond these sessions. I mean, with the strict diet they follow it's not like they go out drinking together afterwards.'

Coupland's head cocked to one side as he considered this. 'I'll have to take your word for that,' he said. The body builders had resumed lifting weights again causing their outlines to slope, mushroom heads jutting out from rounded shoulders, thighs so wide they moved around the gym with a swagger, reminding Coupland of Silverbacks he'd seen on a wildlife documentary.

'I'll just have a copy of the membership list, then.' He held his hand up to stop the objection Purves was about to make. 'Save it. Unless you want a lardy cop hanging around making the place look shabby, I'd do as I asked.'

Purves shrugged. 'No skin off my nose,' he muttered, moving behind the reception desk to get the details up on the screen. 'I'm leaving anyway. The real money's in personal training.'

'I'll have to take your word for that, too,' Coupland growled as he handed him a memory stick to download the information onto.

*

Coupland headed back to Salford Precinct station with the memory stick proving Austin Smith's gym membership tucked into his inside jacket pocket. Every so often he patted it like a Lottery winner checking their ticket was still safe. Bypassing the smoking shelter and the canteen he made a beeline for the CID room to lock it in his desk drawer. Krispy was still at his desk; his head popped up behind his monitor as he heard someone walk in. Coupland held up the memory stick and grinned.

'I'll get straight onto it, Sarge,' the young DC assured

him, eager to please.

Coupland was already shaking his head. 'No you won't, when was the last time you left before me in the last week, or month come to that?'

Krispy remained silent.

'You are allowed a life outside this place, you know, there are times when it may not feel like it but it's what we do outside of here that keeps us sane.'

'Sarge.'

'So stop what you're doing and bugger off, that's an order.'

Krispy nodded as he logged out of his computer. 'Yes, Sarge.' He pushed his keyboard away, his shoulders lifting at the prospect of an early dart.

'Only make sure you go through the membership list first thing, ready for morning briefing,' Coupland reminded him as he headed through the door.

The next hour Coupland spent trawling through Reedsy's Facebook page in the hope there would be something else to incriminate him but there was nothing, unless you counted his penchant for taking selfies in wine bars and videos of him and the two security guards arrested with him working their way through the menu in just about every chicken shop in Salford. So much for his body being a temple. Coupland looked at his watch, decided to call it a day.

*

The atmosphere at home matched Coupland's lifted mood as he shut his front door behind him. No cooking smells but the coffee machine was on. The smell of some fancy blend Lynn normally bought at Christmas wafted down the hallway to greet him.

'Are we expecting someone?' Coupland called out. The thought of round two with Lee Dawson's mother made his heart sink.

'No, just you and me, Dad,' Amy called back, pausing in the kitchen doorway. 'Mum's held up on the ward, said she'd pick up a takeaway on her way home.'

'Wouldn't mind a curry.' Coupland pulled his phone from his pocket then stopped. He was about to text the woman who had read him like a book for twenty years. Smiling, he put his phone away.

'Thought we could have a coffee together,' Amy said, beckoning for him to sit down. 'Well, not me of course, I'm having a smoothie, but I've made the one you like, and,' she added shyly, 'I've been baking.' Coupland stared at the misshapen sponge cake upended onto a cooling tray, covered in blotchy icing. 'I know you like it still warm,' she said, cutting him a slice. The kitchen was a tip, every bowl and utensil had been used in the creation of this masterpiece but nothing they couldn't clear up before Lynn got back. She always rang them from the takeaway reminding them to warm the plates up. Amy poured his coffee and brought it to the table, slipping into the seat beside him, her hands circling her smoothie.

Coupland placed his hand on his daughter's arm. 'I'm sorry Ames,' he whispered, hoping to Christ she didn't ask him what for. Where the hell would he begin? That their relationship had broken down? That the life she'd chosen to live wasn't the one he had hoped for? That he hadn't been able to keep her safe after all? That she was pregnant? She smiled at him then, but her eyes were shiny.

'Hey, don't cry.' He dabbed at the corner of her eye with his thumb. Amy's mobile rang, shattering the harmony between them. 'It's OK love,' Coupland urged, 'you'd better answer it.' His daughter was from the generation that didn't phone each other, after all, why speak when a few misspelled words or an emoji would do? For someone to want to speak to her it must be important.

She pushed herself up out of her chair, moved over to the kitchen counter to retrieve her phone. She glanced at the screen to see who was calling, 'It's the midwife,' she told him before answering. Coupland kept his gaze on her as she took the call. Noticed her hand snake protectively around her bump. He tried to make eye contact but she was focussing on the caller. Whatever was being said didn't require a two-way conversation. 'I see…' she said at last before returning the phone to the counter.

'Ames?'

She turned to face him, her other hand reaching out to hold onto the back of a chair for support, 'She'd been so chatty at my ante-natal check I'd opened up to her,' she began, 'told her everything, you know…'

'…About the father.'

Amy nodded.

'And my reaction…'

Amy's head bowed. 'She's told me she's put in a referral to Social Services, Dad, someone from there will be coming out to see us.'

The breath huffed out of him leaving a sour taste in its wake. He stumbled towards her, wrapping her in his arms as much as her bulk made him able to.

In his pocket, Lynn's call from the takeaway went unanswered.

DAY SEVEN

CHAPTER TWENTY ONE

Coupland's mood was solemn at morning briefing. He and Lynn had spent the previous evening trying to reassure Amy but nothing could erase what was going through their own minds. They'd worked hard all their lives, always done the right thing, brought Amy up to share their values, yet here they were, about to have strangers come into their home. Strangers with the power to make judgements about whether they were fit to bring up a child. He couldn't get his head around it.

A social worker, assigned to his family. Lee Dawson really was the gift that kept on giving. 'Where the hell were they when my Mam buggered off?' Coupland had snarled once Amy had gone to bed. 'No one gave a toss that I was left on my own with a drunk, never mind one handy with his fists.'

'They get involved sooner now, have more interventions that they can use,' Lynn had answered but her words sounded hollow.

'Sarge?' Krispy's voice broke into his thoughts and he realised the team were waiting on him. Combing through the interviews from the current residents of Ashdown Court had brought nothing new to light, nor had Ashcroft's trawl through the statements provided by the previous tenants. Krispy was the only one of them eager to speak; he'd been working through Regener8's membership list on the memory stick Coupland had brought in yesterday evening. His search had yielded a result. 'I cross-referenced the gym membership list against Ashdown Court's residents already questioned in relation to the murder,' he began.

'And?' Coupland barked.

'One name appears in both lists. A tenant by the name of Jimmy Rawlings.'

Coupland nodded as he considered this. Rawlings had been questioned briefly after Shiny Happy Motors had been raided but it was clear he was just an employee willing to look the other way when it came to his boss's recruitment policy. He'd cooperated when Coupland asked for access to the migrants working there, was that because he had something to hide after all? 'Good work,' he said eventually, deciding to throw Krispy a bone, 'and as a reward you get to bring him in.' Krispy's face beamed. 'But take a couple of uniforms with you,' Coupland cautioned, 'I don't want it turning ugly.' He turned to Ashcroft, 'You go with him, he might be all grown up but I want a steady hand on the rudder. Full forensic sweep of Rawlings' flat, DNA swab taken on arrival, the full works.' Ashcroft nodded.

Actions delegated, Coupland strode to the vending machine out in the corridor. He shoved a fist full of coins into the slot, his fingers pushing randomly at the numbers. He needed a sugar lift, didn't give a toss what form the chocolate took, Mars Bar, Minstrels, a bar of Dairy Milk. He'd once seen an alcoholic drink hand sanitizer to get that much needed hit; at least *his* options were palatable.

Alex came from the direction of the DCI's office clutching a box file to her chest. 'Problem?' she asked, surveying him.

'Apart from this machine refusing to part with its goods?' He jabbed at the refund button with his index finger but it refused to play ball. A bounty bar dangled precariously from the edge of its shelf, like a jumper having second thoughts. 'We're good, aren't we?' Coupland asked her.

Alex peered at him, wondering where this lack of confidence was coming from all of a sudden. 'What's up?'

Coupland sighed. 'Social work are sticking their beak in with Amy. Want to come and find out more about the set up at home.'

If Alex was surprised she didn't show it. She angled her head defiantly. 'Let them,' she replied, 'it's a box ticking exercise nothing more. They'll come with their questions which you'll answer *politely*,' she stared at him good and hard as she said this, 'then they'll leave and forget any of you ever existed.'

Coupland wasn't convinced. 'What if they can tell I'm…' he paused to find the right word, 'reticent.'

'Wow, someone's been swallowing a dictionary,' Alex mocked. 'Seriously though, kids don't get covered in bruises due to reticence, Kevin, just be yourself.' A thought occurred to her. 'When I say be yourself, obviously I mean a more… amenable version.' She smiled.

Coupland threw his hands in the air. 'Fine, I get it; I can do Mr Nice Guy when I need to.'

'Glad to hear it. Oh and I managed to get hold of Michael Roberts' tutor, thanks for asking, I'm on my way to meet with him now.'

Coupland swallowed down his guilt. 'How did you track him down?'

'The college HR system came good in the end. I think

calling the manager every hour and making a nuisance of myself helped.' She regarded the vending machine and the chocolate bar playing hard to get. 'Some things respond better to a swift kick.' She handed him her files; placing an arm either side of the contraption to steady it she aimed her boot just above the offending bar. It wobbled unsteadily before nose diving into the tray below. 'Sometimes softly, softly doesn't cut it,' she said as she took back her files.

'You're preaching to the converted on that one,' Coupland said in a low voice. 'Here, you have it.' He handed her the chocolate bar. 'Consider it your welcome back present.'

'You spoil me, ambassador,' Alex replied before heading out to the car park.

*

The custody sergeant narrowed his eyes as Coupland approached the booking-in desk. 'I take it you've nothing unpleasant stuck to your shoe this time, DS Coupland? Only my officers spent twenty minutes cleaning up after your mess the other day.'

'It wasn't my mess, I can assure you,' Coupland corrected him.

'So, to what do I owe this pleasure?'

'Just need a quick word with Austin Smith, if I may, clear up a few things before he's shipped off on remand.'

The desk sergeant rested his elbows on the counter top, nodding sagely. 'I'm sure you do, what with him lodging a complaint about you.'

Coupland rocked back on his heels, even managed a laugh. 'No, it's not about that, water under the bridge if you ask me. I want to speak to him in relation to Zamira Gashi's murder.'

Another nod. 'Even so, DCI Akram has made it explicitly clear.' The custody sergeant turned his computer screen to face Coupland, opened his email account to show a message had been circulated to the custody officers on each shift stating that 'Should DS Coupland try to approach Mr Smith, DCI Akram must be contacted immediately.' That was the gist of it; the words Akram used were a lot less choice. 'This chat we've had stays between you and me,' the officer told him, 'but I can't let you in to speak to Smith.'

It was Coupland's turn to nod. It had been worth a try, but his card had been well and truly marked. A prolonged bout of swearing signalled the arrival of a new guest. The desk sergeant straightened himself, returning his computer screen to face the right way. As the custody suite's door opened an angry fat man glowered in Coupland's direction. 'I should have known this would be down to you!' Jimmy Rawlings shouted, 'You know the car wash has been closed down, don't you? I've lost my job, probably going to lose my flat too and now you're trying to fit me up with murder.' Coupland said nothing. 'What's that old saying?' Rawlings sneered, 'No good turn goes unpunished. Huh, bang on the money if you ask me. Last time I go out of my way to help you lot.' Rawlings jostled against the officers restraining him but he soon ran out of steam. Beside him Krispy gave his details to the custody sergeant. Rawlings wasn't done with Coupland. 'Went out of my way to be straight with you,' he spat.

Coupland regarded him. 'You didn't tell me you were a member of Regener8.'

Rawlings shrugged. 'You didn't ask.'

'Do you know Austin Smith, known as Reedsy?'

Rawlings looked blank.

'Mr Rawlings has the right to a solicitor,' the Custody sergeant interrupted, widening his eyes at Coupland. 'The arresting officers can take it from here.'

Coupland took the hint. 'I'll be upstairs,' he called over his shoulder as he headed out the way he came, 'keep me updated.'

*

'Rawlings' answers are plausible, Sarge,' Krispy said when he and Ashcroft returned to the CID room. 'He knows Reedsy in passing, that's all. Not exactly bosom buddies.'

'To be fair he's not exactly the type most body builders would compare bench presses with,' added Ashcroft, 'besides, he's only just become a member. They had an offer on last month apparently, waived the joining fee.'

'He told me when I questioned him that he never stepped foot in Flat 2a,' said Coupland.

'And he still maintains that,' Ashcroft nodded. 'The DNA test will confirm if he's telling the truth one way or another.'

'How long before we get the results?'

'The lab has said it'll be processed as fast as it can, Sarge, wouldn't commit any further than that.'

He could hardly blame them, it wouldn't be the first time they'd come up short and he'd given them the full hairdryer treatment for their trouble. Coupland rubbed his hands together. Things were starting to move, though not fast enough for his liking. He reached for his phone. He could wait around here, breathing down the necks of his squad, or do something useful. He hesitated, he didn't want to get DCI Akram's back up more than was necessary, didn't want to get Mallender's back up either, come to think of it. The boss had supported him taking over the case again when he could have thrown him to the wolves, especially when Reedsy had submitted his complaint; it would only be a matter of time before police complaints got in touch as it was. The questioning, the paperwork, would tie him up for days. Better to act now, while he was still able. Mind made up, he dialled the number and waited.

CHAPTER TWENTY TWO

Alpine House Detention Centre wasn't signposted.
Only those in the know knew its location at
Manchester Airport's Terminal Two. A corrugated iron
structure with metal shutters, floodlights and bollards
around its perimeter gave it the appearance of an out of
town storage depot, only its contents were of the human
variety: thirty-two detainees held in eight rooms.

'It is cold here,' Mariana told him when she was
brought into the cramped reception area which doubled
as a visitors' room for their meeting. 'They give us one
blanket for our bed but it is so thin. I suppose they think
we are not used to any better. Either that or we don't
deserve it.' The interior of the building was as austere
as the exterior, with no natural light. Windows had been
boarded up and covered in metal grilles when the facility
had been turned into a detention centre. 'I feel like a
prisoner, when I arrived here they told me I would be
allowed outside in the yard with a member of staff, only
they never have enough staff.'

'You'll know some of the other people here, though,
from where you'd been held?'

Mariana nodded. 'I recognise some, but people do not
stay long. Some have already moved on. Sometimes they
are taken in the middle of the night. When you wake up
each morning, you can never be sure who will still be here.'
A new arrival was being admitted at the reception desk.

A man in his sixties, his arm in a sling. Two members of staff stepped out from an adjacent office to search him in full view of everyone present.

Coupland looked away, his gaze settling on the custody officers lining the main corridor which led to a dining room on one side and a TV room on the other. 'At least you're safe here.' The words came out before he could check them, and he found himself flinching at the cold stare he received in return.

'The worst has already happened, Mr Coupland. I do not care what they do with me now.'

For want of something to do he reached down to the plastic bag by his feet and handed it to Mariana. Its contents had already been checked at reception. Deodorant, lip balm, moisturiser, items Amy would have considered essential. He'd put some chocolate in there too, and a phone card to operate the pay phone in the corner of the room. 'In case you need to call a lawyer,' Coupland explained. He patted his pocket for his phone. 'I need to ask you something.' Over the years he'd learned it wasn't so much about asking the right question. He tapped on the phone's screen, pulling up Reedsy's Facebook profile. 'Did this guy drive you to your begging pitch?'

Mariana nodded.

'Did the other men drive you sometimes, the ones in this picture?' He showed her another photo pulled from Reedsy's Facebook account of the three security guards eating together. Another nod. Sometimes it was about asking the same question in the right way. 'Were they the only people that drove you?'

Mariana shook her head. 'No, there was a woman. I told you about her, remember? She brought us the medicine. She always used to complain about the traffic.'

Coupland nodded. He was about to put his phone away when he remembered something. A couple more taps and Jimmy Rawlings' ugly mug appeared on the screen. 'What about him?'

'No.' She opened the bar of chocolate and broke off a square. 'I have never seen this man.'

Something occurred to Coupland. 'The man who told you he was taking Zamira away to get better, was it one of the regular drivers?'

Mariana nodded. He handed her his phone to scroll through the photos once more. 'Him,' she said, holding the phone so that Coupland could see Austin 'Reedsy' Smith in all his gym-clad glory.

*

Coupland had put his phone onto mute while he'd been in the detention centre. Now, as he left Alpine House it started to vibrate. He peered at the screen to see who was calling, swiping right when he saw that it was Lynn. She started speaking before he had time to say 'Hi.'

'*A social worker's coming round this afternoon to do an assessment, Kev, can you wangle an hour off to be here?*'

Coupland paused, his other hand outstretched to beep his car unlocked. 'You sure you want me?' he asked, turning to look back at the detention centre. A building without windows, its residents as much in the dark now as when they'd hidden in locked containers at Portsmouth. He wondered what the future held for Mariana. Sometimes it was better not to wonder too much.

'*Kev?*'

'I dunno.' The thought of having to play nice made

him uneasy.

'*Come on Kev, it'll look bad if you're not there.*'

Coupland looked at his watch. It was unlikely Jimmy Rawlings' DNA result would be back for a couple of hours yet; besides, Mariana had as good as ruled him out. He took a breath, 'What time are they coming?'

*

He was greeted by the steady drone of the hoover when he let himself in. 'Take your shoes off,' Lynn ordered as he stepped into the hall. He did as he was told, nearly colliding with Amy as she backed out of the downstairs loo carrying bleach.

'Use the one upstairs, Dad,' she pleaded when he made to go in. 'Sure you wouldn't rather it if I buggered off?'

'No!' they said in unison. Lynn switched off the hoover, coiling the wire round its upright handle before returning it to the under stairs cupboard. 'Sorry love,' she whispered, greeting him with a kiss, 'just want everything to be perfect.' She caught sight of her reflection in the hall mirror, 'God, I look a right state. I'll pop up and change. Amy, are you going to put on that dress I put out for you?' Amy nodded, combing her hair with her fingers before sweeping it up onto her head in a bun.

'Bloody Hell, feel like I've walked onto the set of Stepford Wives,' Coupland grumbled but Lynn wasn't listening, she was busy tucking strands of Amy's hair behind her ears.

'Kev,' she called over her shoulder as she made her way upstairs, 'can you cut up the sandwiches I've brought back from the supermarket? Oh, and arrange them on the new tea set, the way I do when we have people over.'

Coupland stomped into the kitchen. 'Trust me, they won't be judging us on whether we leave the crusts on a pile of ham butties.' Even so, he did as Lynn asked; it was OK to voice his opinion as long as the job got done the way she wanted, easier for all concerned in the long run. He carried the plate of sandwiches into the front room. Overhead, the floorboards creaked as someone used the bathroom upstairs. It was no good. 'I need to pay a visit,' he called out, slipping into the toilet while no one was looking.

'Dad!' Amy's voice whined at him through the toilet door. The rest of her sentence was muffled, probably telling tales to Lynn, he didn't wonder.

'For Christ's sake Amy,' he grumbled as he opened the door five minutes later, 'not like it matters whether the downstairs loo has skid marks in it.' Three pairs of eyes stared back at him in silence. Lynn and Amy looked as though they wanted the ground to swallow them up. Standing between them, the social worker's wry smile told him she had heard a lot worse. Coupland stepped forward to offer his hand. 'We meet again, Shola,' he said, trying to dodge the daggers Lynn and Amy sent in his direction.

CHAPTER TWENTY THREE

Coupland was already on his way back to Salford Precinct Station when his phone's screen lit up. It was Krispy. He jabbed at the Bluetooth button on his steering wheel. '*Rawlings' DNA isn't a match, Sarge*,' he said, bracing himself.

Coupland was already on Broad Street, past the 24 hour solicitors and tattoo parlour. He blew out a sigh. 'Thought you'd say that,' he muttered before ending the call.

DCI Mallender was on the phone when Coupland entered his office. A raised hand warned him to wait. With no way of letting off steam, Coupland shuffled his feet, waited while the boss finished his call. 'I suppose it saves me having to come and look for you,' Mallender stated when he replaced the receiver. 'That was Professional Standards, they've received Austin Smith's complaint, one of their officers will be getting in touch to arrange an interview with you.'

'Interrogation more like.' Coupland's shoulders dipped, this wasn't quite the way he pictured the conversation panning out. He decided to go ahead anyway. 'I need to interview him, boss,' he blurted.

Mallender's eyebrows disappeared into his hairline. 'Did you not just hear what I said? This man is pursuing a complaint against you, how the hell can you be seen to be impartial with him in an interview room?'

'If an experienced senior officer was with me…'

'Oh, no, don't try roping me into this fiasco; I've stuck my neck out for you as it is.'

'I know and I'm very grateful, but if Smith didn't kill that little girl he damn well knows who did. Are you really happy to let this investigation grind to a halt because some tosspot took exception to me preventing him getting to a loaded gun?'

Mallender sighed, cradling his head in his hands as he leaned his elbows on his desk.

Coupland wasn't done yet: 'The gym bag Zamira was found in? He's a member there. Come on boss, kiddie porn was found on his phone. I've just come back from Alpine House; Mariana's confirmed Smith was the one who told her he was taking Zamira somewhere she could recover from her chest infection. She never saw her again after that.'

Mallender leaned back in his chair, studying Coupland before looking down at his phone as though willing it to ring. 'Just remember I'm your superior officer, not your bloody wing man,' he sighed, pushing himself to his feet.

*

Interview room 3, Salford Precinct Station.
Austin 'Reedsy' Smith was seated at a narrow table, a polystyrene cup with an inch of scummy tea in front of him. 'We have been spoiling you,' Coupland observed, signalling for the two uniformed officers to leave, 'surprised we didn't offer you one of the Super's hobnobs while we were at it.'

'I'm on a gluten free diet,' said Reedsy.

'Looking good on it too,' Coupland observed. He

waited for the officers to close the door behind them before dragging the plastic chair out from the table and sitting down. 'Your nose is coming on a treat, the bruising's all but gone now.'

'I'm still going to have you for it,' Reedsy snarled, 'pointless trying to be Mr Nice Guy now.' Coupland laughed, 'You think that's what I'm doing? If you want to nail me to the cross, sunshine, go ahead and fill your boots. I'm here for one reason and one reason only, to determine your involvement in the murder of a little girl.'

'Will anyone be joining you?' Smith's solicitor asked. A young man whose hair was already thinning, the collar on his shirt had the tell-tale line of the previous days' wear.

Coupland turned as the door opened once more and DCI Mallender stalked in. Behind him DCI Akram could be seen in the corridor spitting his dummy out. Coupland's eyes twinkled as he offered him a smile. 'For the purposes of the tape I'd like to confirm who is present,' Mallender began, before repeating the reason Smith was being questioned.

Smith was already shaking his head. 'Look, I just drove them around when I was asked to. I didn't touch anyone and I didn't fucking kill the little girl.' Coupland glanced at Smith's docile solicitor. Midas was being represented by the managing partner of the law firm he had on speed dial; Smith was having to make do with whoever had been on call at the time.

'Maybe, maybe not,' Coupland conceded, 'but whichever way you dress it up, a little girl ended up dead. A girl you've admitted you drove around.'

Smith leaned back on the hard plastic seat. 'No, not

her, I meant in general, I drive these kids around in general.'

'We've got DNA placing Zamira Gashi in your car, and we can place you in the hovel where she was being held with her sister. Which tells me you're a lying…' Coupland caught Mallender's eye, 'which tells me you you're more involved than you're letting on. Besides…' he added, his eyes locking onto Smith's. 'Her sister has identified you as the person who took Zamira away on the pretext she was going somewhere to recuperate.'

'I was employed as a driver, it was my job to drive them to work and back, no more.'

'For the purposes of the tape I'd like to clarify that for 'work' you mean sites where they would sit and beg, or worse still, where the little one would walk up to people and ask for money. Or prostitute themselves after you'd trained them to be docile.'

Smith glared at his lawyer who gave a small nod. 'Yeah,' he replied, 'though I never promised she'd get better.' Bingo. Smith had dropped himself in it and hadn't even realised. Coupland looked at Mallender to check he'd picked up on it too. A slight nod told him so far so good. Coupland got up from his chair and walked around the table until he was standing behind Reedsy. He bent down until his mouth was close to his ear. He could feel Mallender tense. 'That's an awful lot of kiddie porn on your phone,' he commented in a stage whisper, 'and you've just admitted you were the one that drove Zamira on the day she died. Come on, big man, do yourself a favour.' Coupland placed a hand on Reedsy's shoulder causing Mallender to clear his throat several times until he removed it. 'Do you think if it was the other way round, your so called mates would be keeping shtum?'

'I'm not going on remand everyone knowing I'm a grass.'

'As opposed to being a kiddie fiddler?' Coupland laughed, returning to his side of the table though he remained standing, positioning himself behind his own chair, gripping onto the back of it. He looked from Mallender to the duty solicitor to Reedsy once more. 'Do you know what they'll do to you?'

'Look, I'm not a paedo, and I'm no killer either.'

'So you drove Zamira to the person who did murder her, in which case you're aiding and abetting a child killer. You say tomato, I say ketchup – you get my drift. Whatever your involvement it won't endear you to your new neighbours. The best thing you can do is tell me what happened so we can get you straight in the segregation unit.'

A look of alarm flashed across Reedsy's face. 'OK, so I did drive her that night but she was alive when I left her!' He stared at Coupland wide-eyed, 'Look, I'd met this girl in a bar the week before, asked her out for a drink and she'd said yes, I was on my way to meet her when Midas called, he wanted me to transport the kiddie but I was in a hurry…' He clammed up.

'If you end up on the main wing and someone gets wind of what you've been doing they'll be ripping you a new arsehole quicker than you can say *buy me dinner* first.'

'DS Coupland…' Mallender cautioned.

'I'm not a killer! I just dropped her off…'

'Mind you, it's amazing what medics can do these days, I saw a documentary not so long ago about sphincters made from rubber.'

'You're intimidating my client,' Smith's solicitor piped up.

'Ya think?' Coupland sneered. 'That's nothing compared to the welcome party he'll get on his first night inside. They do things with butter that you never see on Bake Off. One fella was only there a week before he poked his own eyes out, said he couldn't stand the stress of wondering when he was going to be jumped on.'

'Oh, God.' Reedsy hunched forward in his chair, pressing the palms of his hands against his ears as though blocking out Coupland's words. Satisfied, Coupland returned to his seat.

Mallender turned to glare at him. 'I think we're done here,' he hissed. Coupland held up a hand and waited.

'I-I only take them where they're supposed to go...' Reedsy stammered, 'it's the same person I hand 'em over to every time. I've no idea what happens after that—'

'The content on your phone suggests otherwise...'

'OK maybe sometimes I stay and watch but I never do anything to them! She was alive when I left her... I swear.'

'From bully boy to kiddie pimp, your mam must be so proud. All I need is the name of the person you were taking Zamira to.'

Austin Smith let out a shudder. Wiped the snot from his nose with the back of his hand.

Then he gave him the name.

Coupland blinked. He hadn't seen that one coming.

Turned out it really did take all sorts.

CHAPTER TWENTY FOUR

Coupland halted the interview and headed straight to the CID room. Krispy, on the phone, smiled apologetically for keeping him waiting. Coupland wrote down the name he'd been given on a pad and waved it in front of him. Sensing the urgency the young DC put his hand over the mouthpiece. 'What is it, Sarge?'

'Have you finished those financial checks?'

Krispy's face fell.

'No matter, but do one on him, pronto. Go back as long as you need to, bank accounts, HMRC penalties, VAT receipts, the whole kit and kaboodle. Anything that ties him in with Midas or any of his companies.'

Krispy ended his call, cutting the speaker off mid-sentence. 'I'll get straight on it, Sarge.'

An hour later Krispy marched over to Coupland, placing a scanned copy of a bank statement on the desk in front of him. A pen had been used to highlight regular debits from Genting Casino. 'He'd racked up quite a debt with them last year but it was settled with one payment.'

'Let me guess, from Borthwick Enterprises.'

Krispy nodded, placing a printout of a screen shot next to the bank statement. 'A lump sum was paid into his bank account six months ago. With regular payments all from the same account.'

'Bloody hell,' said Coupland. He turned to Krispy appreciatively. 'I don't know how we'd manage without you kid.' He paused as he considered the truth of this, a smile spreading across his face as something occurred to him. He rummaged in his desk drawer, pulling out a sheet of paper which he waved under Krispy's nose. 'Seriously, if I had a gold star I'd pin one on you, you'll just have to make do with a pint once we've nailed the bastard, providing your mam'll let you stay up past bedtime, that is. In the meantime, I think you'll agree this appraisal has gone really well, so if you could just sign here I'll add in the comments I've just made and that'll be HR off our backs for another twelve months.'

Krispy grabbed a pen from his pocket and signed. 'Bloody red tape, eh Sarge,' he said.

Coupland couldn't have beamed more if he'd said 'papa.'

*

A police van parked round the back of the premises while Coupland waited in the doorway but it was really just a precaution. He didn't expect any trouble.

'Detective Sergeant Coupland,' said Alistair Grant rising from his chair to greet him. 'I take it you've come about that property we discussed? I'd be happy to arrange a view—'

Then he clocked the uniformed officers entering the premises. 'What the hell—'

Coupland took a step forward. 'Alistair Grant, I am arresting you for the murder of Zamira Gashi, you do not have to say anything but it may harm your defence if you do not mention, when questioned, something you later rely on in court.'

A uniformed officer moved towards Grant, placing a

hand on his arm. He shrugged him off. 'Th-This is outrageous!' he stammered, 'I don't know where you've got this ridiculous idea from. You are completely delusional.'

'Am I?' Coupland spat, 'I hope to Christ Zamira was delusional when you killed her, that she was so off her face she didn't know what was happening.'

'You're unhinged, do you hear me? I'm not going anywhere with you.' Grant stepped backwards, beyond the uniformed officer's reach, and turned towards the back office. The officer grabbed at him, pulled his wrist until he was folded forwards at ninety degrees then snapped on his cuffs.

'Why make it hard on yourself?' Coupland sighed. 'Not as if you'll be going anywhere, not for a long time.' He turned to the other officers gathered around. 'I want this place turning upside down.' He turned back to Alistair. 'Where are the keys to your flat?'

'You've no right—'

'Dear oh dear, do you really think I'd come here without a warrant? Now you can make it easy on that wife of yours by letting us walk in the front door, if not we'll just barge through it. Personally I don't care which manner we go in, either way it'll give the other residents something to gossip about.'

Grant glowered.

'It's been an absolute pleasure,' said Coupland with a smile as wide as a crocodile. 'I'm arranging complimentary accommodation as we speak, south facing and full en-suite facilities.'

*

Alistair Grant's solicitor arrived at the station within half an hour of his call. He asked to confer with his client before the interview started then looked on distracted when Coupland began his questions. Coupland had used the time Grant spent with his lawyer wisely. He'd telephoned the gym to ask if Grant had been a member, and if so why hadn't he appeared on the list they'd handed over to him? The receptionist confirmed that he had indeed been a member until the middle of the year when he cancelled his membership with no explanation. Probably about the same time he'd started on a different kind of workout with Dawn Tylor, Coupland didn't wonder.

The phone on his desk rang. 'DNA swabs have been taken, Sarge,' Turnbull confirmed down the line to him. Coupland grunted his thanks, getting to his feet as he did so. Before making his way to the interview room Grant was being held in he took a detour to the Evidence Management Unit where he signed out a transparent, tamper-proof bag, a barcode label displayed prominently on the front. He placed the bag gingerly in the inside pocket of his jacket.

Grant was in the smallest of the interview rooms. It was stuffier in here, the smell more rank. Neither Grant nor his lawyer had been given refreshments; either they'd not been offered or they'd had the sense to turn them down, Coupland couldn't be sure. He waved a transcript of Austin Smith's statement under Grant's nose before taking a seat on the opposite side of the table. 'I've a witness statement here that implicates you in the murder of Zamira Gashi.' Grant screwed up his eyes, making Coupland sigh. 'Don't play the "Who?" game with me, Alistair. Remember the little girl your new neighbours found when they moved into the flat below you? Or are there more dead little girls we don't know about? So many out there you've started to lose count?'

'Don't be ridiculous!'

'Ridiculous?' Coupland snorted. 'I have a witness states you were in Flat 2a the night Zamira died. Says he delivered her to you like Royal Mail. That this wasn't the first time you'd had little girls brought to you either.'

'I don't know what you're talking about.'

'You know, for an educated man you've made some serious errors of judgement in recent months. Don't let jerking me around be another one.' Coupland rubbed under his chin, it was a reflex action, keeping his hands occupied when what he really wanted was to haul the creep up by the scruff of his neck. He'd like to see what Professional Standards made of *that*. 'I'll make it easy on you,' he offered, 'let's start with your finances.' He waited.

Grant laughed nervously, eyeballing his lawyer before speaking once more. 'Look, I admit the business has hit a few rocky patches these last couple of years, as you can imagine…'

Coupland was already shaking his head. 'You're talking to someone with no imagination, so you're going to have to help me out.' He tilted his head to one side as he regarded Grant. 'A grammar school boy, am I right?' Grant nodded. 'Well, there you have it; I'm a secondary modern lad myself. You're going to have to explain these rocky patches to me in words of one syllable, just so I can keep up, like.'

Grant obliged. 'I blame all those online agencies. Undercutting us, I mean. It really impacted our bottom line.'

Coupland screwed up his eyes. 'So you went out and

murdered a little girl? That's a big leap, Alistair; you're going to have to join a few more dots for me.'

'I was just explaining why the business was struggling.'

'So it was nothing to do with the cash you kept withdrawing to bail you out of your gambling debt?'

Grant's face blanched. 'I-I couldn't take it from the joint account,' he stammered. 'I didn't want my wife to find out.'

'Find out what? That you had an out of control gambling habit, or were embezzling company funds?' Grant didn't reply. 'So what did you do?' Coupland prompted, leaning back in his chair. This interview was pivotal to the investigation and he didn't want to blow it by saying something on tape that would come back to bite him in court. 'Bear in mind,' Coupland cautioned, 'that I only ask questions I already know the answer to.' He pushed a photocopy of Alistair's bank statement under his nose. 'A large sum of money from Borthwick Enterprises went into your account six months ago, care to explain why?'

'I thought I was on a winning streak, OK? Kept hoping my luck would turn but it didn't. Instead I'd racked up so much debt it was out of control. I already knew Adrian Borthwick, I'd sold a couple of small developments he'd built a few years back, I'd kept in touch with him, he was a client after all, and I needed the business.'

'What with you having a bit on the side and all.'

'It wasn't like that.' He hesitated then, but one look from Coupland told him now wasn't the time to be reticent. 'Anyway, our paths crossed a few times round the blackjack table, he was one lucky son of a bitch I can tell you. Everything he touched turned to gold.' Hence the Midas nickname, Coupland reasoned. 'So I asked him for a loan. He didn't bat an eyelid, said he was happy to oblige on the basis I did something back for him.'

'And what exactly did he want you to do in return?'

'He asked to use some of the empty properties on my books as backdrops to a couple of films he was producing.' Grant looked away. 'I thought it wise not to ask what kind.'

'So what happened?'

'Nothing, that's as much as I know.'

Coupland planted his huge fists on the table, his nose twitching. 'I love the smell of bullshit in the afternoon, Alistair, and I've always loved a challenge. You know, in all the years I've carried my warrant card I've never lost a blinking contest. I'm like the Duracell bunny, me, I can keep going all night, or until you have the sense to call it a day.'

Grant straightened himself in his chair. 'These tactics might work on your normal clientele, DS Coupland, but really, you'll need to do better than this. Now I suggest if all you've got is the word of some low life...'

'Who can give me dates and times when he's delivered kids to you,' Coupland cocked an eyebrow, 'evidence that makes him reliable as far as any court will be concerned.'

'Look,' Alistair said quickly, 'you've got it all wrong.'

'That's what everyone says,' Coupland cut in, 'funny that, even when the facts prove otherwise. Even when, like in your case, it bloody well screams you're up to your eyeballs in it.' Coupland pulled the clear plastic bag from his pocket. Zamira's pink hair clip was inside it. His steady gaze ranged over Grant as he spoke next. 'Do you recognise this, you sick—' he swallowed the rest of his sentence;

right now he needed to stay objective, whether he felt it or not. Grant stared wide-eyed at the bag's contents but said nothing. 'No matter,' Coupland shrugged, placing the exhibit on the table, 'when the DNA results come back they'll connect you to Zamira and the sport bag she was found in. The very same bag you used to take out with you to con your wife into thinking you were off to the gym when instead you were having your own personal training session with Dawn Tylor.'

Grant glanced at his solicitor in alarm but apart from raising an eyebrow the man said nothing. Coupland suspected he had kids of his own, young ones at that, given the bags under his eyes and the dried vomit on his tie. 'It was a bloody accident, OK?' Grant blurted.

It was Coupland's turn to raise an eyebrow, 'What? She accidentally fell into a sport bag and zipped herself in?'

'No,' Alistair's shoulders sank. 'I don't mean that part. I did that,' he lifted his gaze to meet Coupland's, 'but she was already dead by then.'

Coupland put his game face on as he spoke carefully for the tape, 'You'd better start at the beginning.'

CHAPTER TWENTY FIVE

Alistair Grant sat forward in his chair, his forearms resting on the table top. Every so often he clasped his hands together before laying them out flat. Coupland tried not to picture them folding a child into a bag.

'Judy and I had been trying for a baby for several years. She'd got her heart set on becoming a mother from the moment we married. As time wore on and nothing happened she became depressed, she even stopped eating at one point. I had to do something to fix things. We'd tried several rounds of IVF, but it's so bloody expensive it wiped out our savings. I used to play poker before we got together, thought all I had to do was round a few pals up and pick up where I left off. Only instead of topping up our funds I was taking money from the company; when that ran out I took out a loan against the business. Financially we were dying on our feet.'

'Is that when you decided to cut your losses and head off into the sunset with another woman impregnated by a leaky condom?'

Grant hung his head. 'I wouldn't quite put it like that—'

'Which is why I'm here, sweetcheeks, to help you articulate it in words of one syllable.' Coupland changed tack. 'At what point did you start going to Genting casino?'

Grant looked at him.

'Yes, we've been through your accounts with a fine

tooth comb, you liked splashing the cash in there as well, didn't you? Splash being the operative word since you couldn't have pissed it away any faster. So had Dawn dumped you at this point?'

'Does it matter?'

'Just putting together a timeline, gives me something to cross check against if I think you're telling me porkies.'

Grant sighed, 'Yes, Dawn and I had finished by then.'

'So you had all these free evenings while the missus still thought you were going to the gym, did she never wonder with all the time you were putting in why you didn't have abs like that fella from Poldark? I mean, surely she'd have been telling you to give it up by now, get a refund and join Slimming World instead?'

'She was preoccupied with getting pregnant.'

'Not on the nights you weren't there, she wasn't.' Coupland remarked, but then she wouldn't be the first gullible wife to be blindsided by her husband, he supposed.

Grant sighed once more. 'I got talking to Adrian one night and I told him about the shit storm I was in. He agreed to help, only it came with strings attached.'

Coupland blew out his cheeks, 'Who knew eh? You take money from a gangster and surprise sur-bloody-prise they want something shady in return.' For a savvy fella Alistair Grant had been spectacularly dense. 'So what did he have you do?' Apart from killing kiddies, Coupland added in his head.

'He wanted access to the properties I had up for sale or rent, the ones where the owners had already moved out.'

'And what was he using the properties for?'

Grant's head dropped.

328

'You're going to have to say it,' Coupland persisted, nodding at the tape.

The words tumbled out. 'He arranged for kids to be brought to the properties, to have their photos taken…' he made it sound normal, like a school photographer coming to take a class photo.

'What kind of photographs?'

Grant said nothing.

'The kind you'd have been happy to have taken of your own,' Coupland persisted, 'when you eventually have one?'

A small shake of his head.

'Yet you still gave him access, knowing what was going on. Christ Almighty…' It beggared belief the blind eye some folk turned when it didn't affect them.

Grant's mouth dropped at the corners. 'I asked him what he thought he was playing at. Where the kids' parents thought they were. I couldn't understand why the police weren't looking for these children. He just laughed, told me to stop fretting; kids like these didn't belong to anyone, not any more. No one would even know they had gone.'

'Didn't you ask why… for the tape,' Coupland reminded him when he shook his head.

'No.'

Coupland needed to clarify the part Grant played in this seedy operation. 'So you turned up to each property to let Midas' henchmen in with the kiddies, did you?' A nod, followed by a barely audible 'Yes.'

'Or was there more to it than that?'

Grant considered this. 'I let them in, moved furniture about if they asked me to, cleaned up afterwards,' adding, when Coupland furrowed his brow, 'Sometimes, the little ones are sick.'

Coupland's foot began to tap against the hard floor. 'After all the drugs they've had pumped into them, you mean?'

'I suppose…' Grant caught sight of the look Coupland gave him. 'You need to know this isn't who I am,' he spluttered. 'I got mixed up in this by accident!'

Coupland had heard enough. 'I don't get you, how do you fall into sexual exploitation?'

'You're twisting my words.' Grant had the gall to sound wounded.

'He has a point,' his solicitor muttered.

Coupland threw the lawyer a look. 'Nice of you to join us,' he said evenly, 'now sharpen your pencil.' He made a point of straightening the crease in his suit trousers. 'I used to love Jackanory as a kid.' His smile was a reflex action, there was no warmth there. 'And your client has just spun a story the Brothers Grimm would be proud of. It's a big leap from 'cleaning up afterwards' to packing away a child's body.' He stared Grant down. 'I want a full account of the evening Zamira Gashi died, minus the fairy-tale.'

Grant drew in a breath. 'I got a call from Midas saying he had a special client coming into town and he wanted to shoot some promotional pictures for his arrival.' He ignored the snort of derision from Coupland. 'I didn't have much time, Judy had lined up another appointment at the IVF clinic and I couldn't let her down so I thought why not use Dawn's old flat? I'd got a key as we had it on our books to let out, and I knew it wasn't occupied anymore for obvious reasons.'

330

'You don't say,' Coupland drawled, writing something down on the sheet of paper in front of him.

'Only I get a call from the courier.'

Coupland tensed, these kids really were passed around like parcels. 'By 'courier' you mean Austin Smith?'

'Yes. He said he had to be somewhere, was going to have to drop this kid off early. I told him I had plans too so we agreed I'd leave the door to the flat unlocked for him and he'd leave her inside. The children were usually quite docile, I knew from past experience she wouldn't know what day of the week it was. He said she'd be fine on her own till I got there; after all I was only going to be an hour. He told me the photographer was coming at 9pm and promised to be back after last orders to pick her up.'

'How did he get into the apartment block?'

'I wedged the main door open, put a 'Wet Paint' sign that had been left inside the flat by the maintenance team over the handle. Told him to remove it when he left.'

'So what happened?'

A look of contrition flitted across Grant's face making him look all the more pathetic. 'I was late getting back. Judy felt unwell on the way home and I'd had to stop a couple of times. When I let myself into Dawn's old flat I must have given the child a fright. She'd been sleeping, the drugs had started to wear off but she was still groggy. She started backing away from me, crying and saying things in a foreign language. I tried to calm her but she wouldn't listen. The bedroom had just been painted and the window had been left open to dry. She ran towards it and climbed up onto the window sill. The drugs she'd been given must have made her unsteady, I don't think she intended to jump. She called out for her mother and then she just fell. I ran to the window and saw her lying on the rockery below.'

The image seared itself into Coupland's brain. A frightened little girl running from a stranger. A girl who in her short life had learned it was OK to climb into the back of lorries and hide in containers; disoriented with the drugs she wouldn't have realised she wasn't on the ground floor.

'What did you do then?'

'I ran downstairs to check on her.'

'Was she dead?' Coupland asked.

Grant nodded.

'For the bloody tape man!' Coupland demanded.

'Yes!'

Coupland scratched his chin, his hand moving down across his neck, grazing his nails against his skin. He felt something moist, drew his hand back to see blood on his fingers.

'What exactly did she call out?'

'What?'

'You said she called out for her mother. I'm asking you to repeat what she said.'

Grant screwed up his face. 'Mama. It was more drawn out than that, but that's what it sounded like.'

'*Mariana,*' Coupland muttered under his breath. He folded his arms across his chest, his hands burrowing into his armpits for fear of what they'd do if he let them loose. 'So then what?'

'I panicked. Judy had gone to bed for a lie down but even so I knew I didn't have long before she'd start wondering where I was. I ran to my car, I decided to put the child into the boot when I saw my sport bag. I thought if I put her in there… it would keep my car tidy while I decided what to do with her. I threw a couple of the large stones in the boot too, you know, from the rockery where she'd hit her head. It was dark but I thought there might be blood on them.' Coupland thought back to the statement he'd taken from the couple living in the ground floor flat, Bruce Fairweather replanting a rockery unaware it was a crime scene. He turned his attention back to Grant. 'I went back up to the flat to tidy it up. I had cleaning products in my car from the other houses I'd gone to, industrial strength. There wasn't any mess inside but I wanted to remove any trace that she – or I – had been there. I phoned Midas's lackey—'

'Reedsy, just so we're clear?'

Grant nodded. 'He came straight round. He'd managed to get hold of the guy coming to take the photos and told him not to bother. He warned me to keep my mouth shut. My luck was in according to him; no one would miss her because he'd told her sister he was taking her to stay somewhere for a while. The intention was that Midas's client would likely have kept onto her but there were other girls who could take her place easily enough.'

'Wasn't he worried the girl's sister would ask him where she was?'

'He reckoned six months from now she'd be off her face selling sex for Midas; she wouldn't even remember she had a sister.'

Coupland clenched his jaw, 'Seems like you'd thought of everything.'

'No, not really. I was in shock. When I got up the next morning I remembered I had a dead girl in the boot of my car. I spent the whole of that day wondering where I could leave her. Only you can't leave bodies lying around, can you? Not if you don't want them found. I realised I'd have to bury her, so I spent the following week looking for suitable locations.'

'Midas wouldn't bail you out of this one, then?'

'I'd sworn Reedsy to secrecy. I didn't want Midas to find out, I dreaded to think what he'd want from me in return for that kind of help.'

'So fast forward four weeks…' Coupland prompted him.

'I'd been moving the bag between the properties on my books as they became vacant but it was getting too risky. I'd decided I was going to drop her in the canal behind the apartments at Salford Quays when Judy asked if she could borrow my car. Hers was in for a service and she had a couple of viewings. I panicked, hid the sport bag in a wardrobe in Dawn's old flat thinking I'd retrieve it afterwards. Next thing I know there's a young couple moving packing boxes in…'

Coupland blew out a breath as he read over the notes that he'd written. The CPS would have a field day but there were details he wanted to shake from him first, like the name of the photographer Midas used and any information that could lead to the identity of this 'special client'. Coupland understood he would be unable to act on it; the information would have to be handed over to DCI Akram as it fell within the scope of the trafficking case but as long as it resulted in the sick bastards going away he couldn't care less who got the collar.

'I think Mr Grant here has earned himself a tea break,' Coupland said, planting his fists deep into his pockets as he left the room.

*

In the corridor outside the CID room Coupland toyed with getting a sub-standard coffee from the vending machine or a marginally better one from the canteen. Deciding he'd take his chances he stooped to put his loose change in the coin slot. Krispy, on his way back from the gents, eyeballed him as he retrieved his drink.

'Judy Grant's in reception, Sarge.'

'I bet she is. Was she there when the flat was searched?'

Krispy shook his head. 'Not going by her demeanour. All she knows is the message Grant's solicitor left on her mobile phone's voicemail – that her hubby's here and could she come as soon as possible. She thinks there's been some mistake and she's here to pick him up.'

'Is that so?' Coupland said, blowing across the surface of his drink before taking a sip. His phone rang. Ashcroft's name flashed up on the screen. 'Anything to report?' he barked.

'*We've gone through the place with a fine tooth comb. Picked up a laptop, iPad, a Pay As You Go mobile. Still going through it. His wife isn't here though, Sarge.*'

'No, she's waiting for him at the desk. A glutton for punishment if you ask me. Look, I'm about to charge him, so if that fine tooth comb drags up anything of interest...'

'*I'll keep you posted, Sarge.*'

'Oh, and can you get back onto the landlord and check if it's correct that he was using Thompson and Grant as letting agent for Flat 2a, and if so why the hell didn't he tell us?'

'Will do.'

Coupland checked his pocket for more change. Slotted in enough coins to get a sweet tea, cursing as the hot liquid scalded his hand. He carried both cups out to reception; holding the door open with his hip he nodded in Judy Grant's direction. 'Come through to one of the interview rooms,' he beckoned, 'it's quieter there.'

Judy Grant had been sitting on one of the hard plastic chairs and her smile told him she mistook the interview room to be comfortable. 'I was visiting my aunt, DS Coupland, I only picked up the message about Alistair when I returned to my car,' she told him. 'I'd have got here sooner but for the temporary lights. Bloody road-works, you'd have thought they'd have finished by now.'

Coupland stopped in his tracks. Ignoring the funny look Judy gave him and the pain as the heat from the thin plastic cups burnt into his fingers, he mustered something that resembled a smile. 'After you,' he said, pushing the door to the interview room open with his elbow. 'Take a seat,' he added, placing the cups on the table between them. He pulled out his phone, telling Judy: 'Back in a minute, there's something I need to do first.'

Out in the corridor he tapped the name of the last person that had called him. Ashcroft answered immediately, *'Sarge?'*

'Check out the browsing history on the laptop you bagged.' A pause.

'Now? Am I not better bringing it in for the tech boys?' Coupland's silence gave him the answer he needed.

'Hang on.' Ashcroft's breathing became heavy as though he was running downstairs. There was a clunking noise accompanied by a few choice swear words.

'You still there?' Coupland demanded as the line went quiet.

A sigh, *'It's password protected, Sarge.'*

Coupland thought back to when he and Alex had first questioned Judy and Alistair, pulled out his notebook to check. 'Try December07' he instructed, 'it was her birthday the day we went round to take her statement.'

The sound of fingers tapping across a keyboard travelled down the line. *'And we're in,'* Ashcroft said triumphantly. *'There's a lot of stuff on IVF,'* he said, then silence followed by more tapping. When he spoke next, his tone was subdued. *'There's been regular visits to a website selling pharmacy drugs without prescription.'*

'I suspected there might be,' Coupland grunted, 'and what about the landlord?'

'Donald says Grant offered to find him tenants off the books. It meant Grant didn't need to declare the commission he made on any deal and keep the cash for himself. Donald's as tight as the proverbial duck's backside, so it suited him fine. As it turned out Ali and Jason replied to an ad he'd already posted on Gumtree which was why he didn't think it was worth mentioning.'

'I bet he didn't,' Coupland grumbled into the receiver before ending the call.

He turned to glance at the interview room door but instead of going though it he headed towards the station's exit. He pulled out his cigarette pack, lighting one up as he flicked through his note book until he found what he was looking for. The partial registration of the car that had been parked across the road the first time he'd spoken to Mariana outside the coffee shop. He'd recalled the four wheel drive, its engine idling. He hadn't been sure of the colour but he recognised it now, wedged between a Volvo estate and a Mondeo. A black Hyundai Santa Fe, the number plate matching the partial registration he'd written down. He tossed his cigarette away before he reached the end of it, grinding it over and over into the gravel with his foot.

A round of applause greeted him in the incident room. 'Nice one, Sarge,' Turnbull called out. 'I hear he's made a full confession.'

'There's definitely a case for manslaughter and perverting the course of justice,' Coupland conceded, 'anything more than that we'll have to see, though it gets better.'

'How so?'

'His wife's the one been supplying the migrants with drugs.'

'Has she confessed too?'

'Haven't cautioned her yet, she turned up to collect her husband, only the first thing she did was moan about the traffic, using the same expression Mariana used when she described one of the people who drove her to and from her begging pitch.' He let that sink in.

'If she's been involved in that, what else could she be she involved in?' asked Turnbull. Coupland was several steps ahead of him. What if Alistair was trying to protect his wife? Bad enough that she may be the woman who injected Mariana with a contraceptive so she could be pimped out, but what if she'd been the one who administered the drug that caused Zamira to lose her balance?

'You going to interview her now?' Alex had been composing an email on her computer, she hit the 'send' button before turning to give Coupland her attention. 'That's my report on the Michael Roberts case done and dusted, I can ride pillion if you like.' Coupland nodded his thanks.

'Kevin.'

Coupland turned at the sound of Mallender's voice. He wasn't alarmed by his presence; unlike the Super he was happy to come and seek someone out face to face when he wanted to speak to them rather than have them summoned to his inner sanctum. He assumed word had reached him about Alistair Grant's arrest.

'Boss?'

Mallender's face was serious. 'A call came in from control about an hour ago. A child's remains have been found in woodland backing onto Worsley Brow. A murder team from Nexus House has been assigned.'

Something pulsated in the pit of Coupland's stomach. 'Go on,' he said, 'I can tell there's more.'

'The remains have been there for some time, Kevin. I've just got off the phone with the superintendent heading up the investigation. He got the lab to cross check DNA recovered at the scene with samples kept on file for missing children. It's a match for Hannah Coombes...' He paused, allowing the news to sink in. 'I told him you'd want to let her family know, given the relationship you'd built up with them.'

Coupland felt pressure on his arm, looked down to see Alex's hand. '*Go*,' she urged, 'you need to be the one to tell her parents. I'll take care of things here.'

He swallowed down the lump in his throat. 'Check out the IVF clinic Alistair claimed they went to the night Zamira died. I don't think for one minute they had an appointment that night, I reckon he said that to keep his wife out of it, a way of making amends for his affair.'

'I can do that, Sarge,' said Turnbull.

Coupland nodded his approval. 'Fine, you've been elevated to DS Moreton's pillion rider,' he said, 'you up to the job?'

'Be an honour, Sarge.' Turnbull's hand touched the side of his forehead in a mock salute but Coupland had already gone.

*

He'd taken his own vehicle. No need to announce his visit to the neighbours by turning up in a patrol car, they'd be alerted soon enough once the press got wind of it. He'd asked for a Family Liaison Officer to be assigned as a priority but control had called to tell him she was an hour away. Coupland pondered this, decided to go ahead anyway, the family had lived in limbo long enough.

From the outside the semi-detached bungalow looked like any other on the road. A fenced-off front garden with grass replaced by stone chips. Rectangle paving slabs leading to a UPVC front door. In the early days there'd been potted shrubs standing either side of it; now the containers lay on their side long since forgotten, the plants reduced to withered stumps. A curtain in the downstairs window twitched and Coupland paused at the gate, letting whoever it was get a good look at him.

A tired cop in a creased suit.

A woman's voice shouted something and moments later the front door flung open, Peter Coombes eyeing him as he ushered him in, a combination of hope and fear coming off him in waves. Coupland followed Peter into the front room in silence, nodding as Hannah's mother stepped away from the window to greet him.

Karen was smaller than he remembered, her eyes and mouth etched in lines that looked as though they'd been hammered in with a chisel. Her clothes were creased too, as though she'd slept in them, or didn't change them very often. The coffee table looked as though she'd set up stall for the day: magazines, a paperback, the weekly gazette. There were biscuits too, and several cups of untouched tea. Coupland's gaze travelled along the school photographs on the wall above the fireplace. Hannah in her nursery sweatshirt, her sister Poppy in her pinafore. In others both girls wore matching uniforms, their smiles changing from shy to gap toothed as the years went by. In the most recent photograph Poppy was on her own, a grim-faced child with nothing behind the eyes. She sat off centre, as though unwilling to hog the limelight. Karen saw Coupland study it. 'She wanted to keep a space for Hannah,' she explained, 'for when she comes back.'

Coupland hauled in a breath as he turned to face them. Karen stared at him but he blinked and looked away. 'I think it'd be better if you both sit down.'

'I'll stand if I want to, thank you very much.' Peter sounded as though he'd swallowed gravel and already Karen had her hand out to reach for him. Her other hand rose up in front of Coupland as though warding off evil.

'Don't you say it,' she warned, 'don't you fucking well say it.'

'I'm so sorry,' Coupland began, his voice little more than a whisper.

*

Coupland reversed into a space in Salford Precinct's car park in time to see Superintendent Curtis climb into the back of a smart car. He was in dress uniform, the buckle of his jacket belt pulled a notch tighter than it should. Coupland stayed put, pretending to check for messages on his phone in case Curtis spotted him and summoned him over to check whether he'd spoken to Professional Standards yet. He waited until the car pulled out into Broad Street before he ventured out.

'Why's the Super looking so shiny?' he called out to the sergeant on the desk.

'Meeting with an attaché from the Albanian embassy.' He caught the look that flickered across Coupland's face. 'I heard he's flying out there in a couple of weeks, hoping to garner greater collaboration.'

'They've got golf courses in Albania then?' Coupland muttered as he keyed his access code into the security pad. His first port of call was to head to the interview room where Alex and Turnbull were questioning Judy Grant. He opened the interview room door causing four heads to turn in his direction. He eyeballed Alex and she stared back at him steadily, speaking into the tape to say that she was leaving the room. He waited until she'd closed the door behind her.

'Any joy?'

Alex blew out her cheeks. 'It's all "No comment" at the moment,' she informed him with a wry smile.

'No matter,' Coupland shrugged, 'the evidence on her laptop proves she's up to her neck in it.'

'I've arranged a video line up to see if Mariana can identify her as the person who administered drugs to Zamira on the day she last saw her sister alive. The NCA want to question her separately about her involvement with the trafficking gang.'

Coupland considered this. 'I reckon Midas called in more favours than Grant's admitting to right now, but getting Judy involved as a medicine woman makes perfect sense. Even if he'd grown a conscience later down the line there was nothing he could say without implicating them both.'

Alex nodded. 'Oh, and you were right, there was no IVF session booked for that night. So why's he trying to protect her?'

Coupland shrugged. 'She wouldn't have needed to get involved if they hadn't been strapped for cash, and that was down to his gambling. Maybe he felt the IVF was compensation.'

'Wow, who's using magical thinking now?'

Alex's face grew serious when Coupland didn't rise to the bait. 'How did it go?'

Coupland's mouth turned down at the corners. 'About as grim as it gets. I stayed till the FLO got there. She called their daughter's school and arranged to go and pick her up.'

'Poor kid.'

Coupland nodded, though he couldn't be sure which of the sisters she meant. Alex turned to go back into the room. 'Don't worry, I've got this,' she told him before opening the door. 'At least Zamira's family will get justice now.'

*

Coupland didn't need to knock; DCI Mallender's door was already open, some sixth sense making him look up from the file he was reading as Coupland hovered in the doorway. 'Just the person,' he said, getting to his feet and moving to the other side of his desk where he perched a buttock, motioning for Coupland to take a seat. 'I've had the SIO heading up the Hannah Coombes' murder inquiry on the phone. She wants you to prepare a victimology report and email it across in time for this evening's briefing.' Victimology was the process of finding out what the victim and their family were like. It made sense that the murder squad sought Coupland's help; within a matter of hours he could furnish them with information that had taken him months to gather.

'I'd prefer to deliver it in person, boss,' he said, tapping his index finger against his temple. 'It's all stored away up here, I can tell it faster than I can type it.'

Mallender smiled. 'Thought you'd say that, told her to expect you as soon as you'd finished up here.'

'They're going to go after James Bullivant for this though, aren't they?'

Mallender was already nodding. 'Sounds like his hallmark's all over it,' he said, 'but they want to get it right, don't want to put the family through the wringer for some lawyer to throw it out.' Mallender cleared his throat as he got up to close the office door, when he returned to his perch his head was tilted to one side as he regarded Coupland, the way folk did when they spoke to the bereaved. 'Look Kevin, you know what the rumour mill in this place is like, I heard about the situation Amy is in and I just wanted to say if you needed to talk…'

Coupland was already shaking his head. 'Over-rated, if you ask me, boss. Talking's all very well, but it doesn't change anything, doesn't make anything better, just keeps on reminding you of the shit storm you're in.' Besides, since when did a pregnancy become a 'situation'? Maybe what he was feeling *was* a form of grief, for being robbed of the joy he'd anticipated when Amy became a mother.

Mallender let out a sigh. 'Fair enough, I just felt there's been an elephant in the room for the last few days.'

Coupland laughed, but the humour was forced. 'Only the one?' he said, getting to his feet. 'I've got more elephants than a Namibian game reserve but that's just the way I roll, boss, now will that be all?'

'You can hand this file back to DS Moreton.' Mallender reached over to his side of the desk and lifted the folder he'd been reading when Coupland had entered. 'The Super's happy enough with the report, though he's circled a couple of grammatical errors he'd like to be corrected before he signs it off.'

'And there was me thinking top brass had too much time on their hands,' Coupland said, taking the file from him and heading for the door.

*

The mood in the CID room was upbeat. Judy Grant had been charged with forced labour and sexual exploitation; however, the CPS was confident with the case already put to them that more charges would follow. Turnbull began to clear the incident board. He paused as he removed Zamira's photograph. 'Why didn't they run away?' he pondered.

'You never heard of Stockholm Syndrome then, where victims bond with their aggressor?' Alex had returned to her desk, was scrolling through her phone to check there were no messages from the childminder. No news was always good news.

Turnbull blew out his cheeks. 'Yeah, but this is

different. They spent ten hours every day begging on the streets, it seems counter intuitive they didn't ask someone for help.'

'A victim's acquiescence doesn't amount to consent. Look at the behaviour of victims of domestic violence. They're not willing participants, they just don't know how to get out of the spiral of abuse and after a period of time become helpless.'

Robinson, who'd been following the conversation, chuckled. 'Ease off him, Sarge, he's got a date, he comes out with all sorts of crap when he's nervous.'

Coupland, who'd wandered in mid-conversation, regarded his DC with admiration. 'Wonders'll never cease, Turnbull, I thought all your girlfriends were inflatable.'

Turnbull ignored the jibe and smiled good-naturedly. 'I'm taking out that social worker if you must know. 'Bout time I started living again after my divorce.'

'Not tonight, though?' Robinson asked. Arrangements were in place to decamp to the pub at the end of shift, he'd already phoned ahead and asked the landlord to cordon off the back room and throw in some food; those with families were already on the phone asking for a late pass.

Turnbull shook his head. 'No, we're going for a meal tomorrow night. I'm guessing tonight'll get messy.'

Coupland reached into his jacket and pulled out his wallet, handed a roll of notes to Robinson. 'I've got a briefing at Nexus House. Put that behind the bar, I'll be over as soon as I can.'

Alex saw the file clamped under his arm. 'Did the boss give that to you?'

Coupland nodded. 'The Super's been playing with his

crayons again, said you've to make a couple of changes before he approves it.'

Alex cursed under her breath as she took the file from him and returned to her desk. 'No time like the present,' she said; an unhappy expression on her face. Coupland moved behind her so he could scan the report over her shoulder. He zoned in on a paragraph, which he read aloud: "'A whole range of issues need to be significantly improved relating to the social work team. There were a lot of missed opportunities for intervention.'" His head jerked up when he came across a familiar name. 'Shola Dube? She carried out the welfare checks with Turnbull and Robinson. She was the one took Mariana to the detention centre,' he lowered his voice, 'and the one Turnbull's about to go on a date with.' She'd been the social worker who'd turned up at his home, too. Friendly but firm. No immediate concerns but she wanted to do a follow up visit in a month. Didn't seem the type to cut corners.

'Oh, I remember seeing her in reception,' Alex said, head down as she keyed in the Super's corrections.

'I know I said give 'em a hard time but why has she been singled out?'

'Remember I told you I was going to see Michael's college tutor?'

 Coupland grunted a yes.

'Well, he's admitted he kept something back from the original investigation.'

'You don't say,' he waited while she keyed in the last of the Super's revisions and pressed the 'save' button. 'It turns out a social worker did get in touch when he first reported his concerns about Michael's home life.'

'Shola?'

Alex nodded, 'She came to the college to speak to him and Michael together. She was concerned for his safety but Michael was adamant he didn't want to be put into care, not even stay with foster parents while social services investigated the claims about his stepfather. In the end Shola suggested he find a friend whose sofa he could sleep on for a while. That was the last his tutor saw of him until the day he turned up for class out of the blue...'

'The day of his murder...'

'The tutor said when Michael turned up that day he seemed happier, was more confident than he'd been in a long time. When he asked him where he'd been he told him he'd been staying at the social worker's place...'

Coupland glanced at Alex sharply as though he'd misheard but her face told him otherwise. 'Apparently after their meeting Shola had contacted him to see if the situation at home had got any better and he'd confided that he couldn't hack it any more... so she told him he could stay with her.'

'Christ, you're not saying...' Coupland turned to watch Turnbull as he shuffled the incident board into the corner of the room, a daft grin plastered across his face.

'No, nothing like that, he was full of praise, according to his tutor. Said she'd been kind to him. He'd made her promise not to tell the authorities where he was until he'd had time to think about this future. He reckoned that thanks to Shola he felt ready to resume his studies.'

'Only that night he has a run in with a dodgy acquaintance and the tutor decides it isn't worth wrecking someone's career telling everything he knows.'

Alex nodded, 'Pretty much.'

'Staying with Shola had nothing to do with his murder.'

'Agreed.'

'And by the sounds of it the last weeks of this kid's life were happy.'

'No doubt about it.'

'She'll likely lose her job.'

'I know.'

'Christ Almighty…' What was it Jimmy Rawlings had said to him in the custody suite when he'd been brought in for questioning? 'No good turn goes unpunished,' Coupland muttered.

'I was asked to review the case, Kevin, I can't be held responsible for the consequences.'

Which was why one day Alex would overtake him on the greasy career pole, while he, with luck and a prevailing wind, would do well to keep his sergeant's stripes. He glanced at his watch. 'I've got to go,' he said, patting his pockets for his keys, 'I'll see you in the pub.'

'I don't need to ask what you would have done,' she called after him. 'It's written all over your face.'

'My face always looks like this,' he smiled.

*

The call came as he climbed into his car. Lynn's name flashing up on the screen like a five-minute warning. With a cigarette clamped between his lips he hit the 'reply' button. 'I'm running late for a meeting, can I call you b—'

'*The baby's coming, Kev!*' Lynn sounded out of breath, as though she'd been running.

'B-but it isn't due yet,' he stammered.

'*Sometimes baby doesn't want to wait.*' She was trying to be cheerful but her voice was laced with tension. The baby wasn't due for three months. Time he thought he had to get his head around the situation.

Coupland slammed the car door shut. He glanced back at the station building as he calculated how fast one of the traffic boys could get him to the hospital, decided to chance it himself. 'You've said in the past that three months is way too soon.' His voice had gone up an octave.

'Now's not the time eh, love? Your daughter needs you.'

The contents of his stomach flipped as he started the engine. 'She said that?' A low moan in the background suddenly got louder. The line went dead.

Coupland put his foot down hard on the accelerator.

*

Hospital corridors had a way of going on forever when you were in a hurry. Coupland jogged to the labour ward, holding his warrant card in the air for everyone to see. His legs felt heavy and his chest felt like it was doing an Irish dance. His daughter needed him. The door of one of the delivery suites opened and a crowd of medics came out pushing an incubator towards a lift. Seconds later the lift doors swallowed them whole. The door to the delivery suite remained open and a familiar face stood in the doorway. Lynn was wearing scrubs. Hearing footsteps and heavy breathing she turned as he approached. 'Don't look so worried,' she smiled. 'Amy's fine.'

'I didn't know you were on shift?'

Lynn shook her head. 'I'm not, but they're letting me sit with him. The extra pair of hands will help them too.' Coupland had stopped listening at *him*. So, it was a boy then.

Slugs. Snails. Puppy dogs' tails.

A skateboard.

A fishing rod.

The TV turned up loud when the football was on.

He thought of his own childhood. A Scalextric race track set up in the front room. His mother complaining each time she tripped over it. His father hitting him for giving her lip. He blinked that image away.

'Dad?'

Coupland looked past Lynn to see Amy reclined on several pillows stacked into a 'V' shape. Someone'd put a sheet over her lower half, but the carnage of childbirth was still evident. Lank hair stuck to her temples. Her face was flushed and clammy. Her eyelids were swollen too, as though she'd been crying for a long time. He hovered in the doorway, as though an invisible force field was holding him back.

'You OK, Ames?' he managed.

'They had to take him away Dad, said he needs extra help. All I've got is a photo one of the midwives took.' She smiled then, holding her phone up for him to see. It was like stepping back in time. Waiting for him in the playground, holding up a picture she'd drawn, her little face anxious for him to like it. 'Come and have a proper look, Dad,' she said shyly.

He didn't want to because he loved her. Wasn't sure how he was going to bloody well feel. He couldn't let her down again. His phone rang then. He grabbed it, grunting into the receiver.

'*DS Coupland? Inspector David McAndrew here from Professional Standards. We've received a complaint from a Mr Austin Smith, relating to an alleged assault at the time of his arrest. I'd like you to come and see me to give your account of the incident.*'

'Later,' Coupland growled before ending the call.

He sucked in a breath and with something resembling a smile took a step towards Amy's bed.

THE END

Acknowledgements

It is said that it takes a village to raise a child. It certainly took an entire community of friends to keep the wheels on this truck during the last year. Dear friends, neighbours, I won't embarrass – or offend – anyone with individual name checks – you beauties all know who you are. In terms of organisations and professionals that kept me on the straight and narrow, I'd like to send a big shout out and 'Thank You' to:

Nicola Bourke Yoga, Barefoot Sanctuary, North Berwick

https://www.facebook.com/East-Lothian-Yoga-School-with-Nicola-Bourke-141025012658776/

Barbara Clarke Therapy

http://www.barbaraclarketherapy.com/

Fletchers Cottage Spa - the healing hands of Kirsty Steel

https://www.archerfieldhouse.com/spa/

Gordon Walker Hypnotherapy, for making me a better version of myself:

http://www.walker-hypnotherapy.co.uk/

WAY (Widowed and Young - a charity supporting those under the age of 50 when they lost their partner).

https://www.widowedandyoung.org.uk/

Audrey, Ali, Ali, Solveigh, Tina, Murray, Anne and Caroline. Keep doing what you do. You guys rock!

Thanks also to Lynn Osborne for her eagle eye and words of encouragement when I needed them most.

Reference Material

I hadn't set out to write about human trafficking when I started writing this book. All I knew was that I wanted to find out how it was possible for someone to be unaccounted for, and my research led me to the less reported consequences of this cruel trade. Because of the clandestine nature of this crime many children do not come to the attention of the authorities. This is some of what I discovered during my research:

In 2016, 3175 unaccompanied children applied for asylum in the UK.

Last year Europol, the European Police Office, warned that 10,000 children who entered Europe in 2015 had disappeared.

References: Savethechildren.org.uk; Refugeecouncil.org.uk; Manchestersafeguardingboards.co.uk

For Dave

About The Author

Emma writes full time from her home in East Lothian. When she isn't writing she can be seen walking her rescue dog Star along the beach or frequenting bars of ill repute where many a loose lip has provided the nugget of a storyline. Find out more about the author and her other books at: https://www.emmasalisbury.com

Have you tried the Davy Johnson series? Why not try the first chapter of TRUTH LIES WAITING…

CHAPTER 1

It's funny how the do-gooding public think prison is the answer, like a magic wand that wipes your criminal score-card clean. Only it isn't like that, the problems you leave behind are still waiting for you when you step back out into the daylight, except now they're much bigger, and this time you don't have as many choices. I was one of the lucky ones, moved back into my family home and into a job that paid decent money. I should send a shout out to my probation officer; she came up trumps, getting me in at Swanson's rather than pretend work on a poxy job creation scheme. OK, packing cardboard boxes is boring as Hell, but you can have a laugh with the guys on the shop floor and turn the radio up when you run out of things to say.

Even so, only one day in the job and already things started going pear-shaped. I was heading towards the bus-stop at the end of my shift when a small boy riding a BMX bike mounted the pavement, circling round me a couple of times like a playground bully eyeing his victim. Close up he was older than I'd first thought, maybe thirteen or so, with shaved blond hair and a forehead that was way too wide for the rest of his face. His eyes were sunken and further apart than was right and a mouth that hung open as though his lips were too heavy for his jaw.

'You Davy?' it came out as a statement rather than a question, but I nodded anyway.

'Gotta message f'ya.' The kid had a nasal whine, the kind that'd get on your nerves if you had to listen to it all the time. I wasn't worried by the sight of him though; a boy on a bike makes a bee-line for you and says they've got a message; it's not that big a deal round here. As far as I know, Hallmark and Interflora don't stock '*Glad you're out of chokey*' gifts and where I'm from your first stretch inside is a rite of passage. News of my release is bound to have got around.

'Mickey's givin' ye till the end o' the week to make your first payment.'

I nodded in agreement, his terms seemed reasonable; he was hardly going to write off my loan because of my spell inside.

'Said to tell ye he's adjusted the figures.'

Ah. Bike Boy's voice was beginning to grate but he had my full attention. 'Said something 'bout the credit crunch an' compound interest, or was it compound fractures?' the boy stated maliciously. 'Either way he said I wasn't tae worry if I forgot the gist, so long as I told ye how much yer payment has gone up tae.'

I had a feeling I wasn't going to like this. Bike Boy paused for effect, as though I was an X Factor contestant about to learn my fate: whether I was to stay in the competition or return to the life I'd been badmouthing every week.

'Two hundred quid,' he said firmly.

I was confused. That was the amount of my original loan. I'd been due to pay it off fifty pounds a week until Mickey got bored but now he seemed to be giving me the chance to pay off the debt in full. It'd be a stretch, after tax I'll be clearing two fifty a week but it'd be worth it.

Bike Boy smiled, not altogether unkindly but there was a glimmer of pleasure there, even so.

'Two hundred a week until further notice.' He clarified matter of factly.

'Yer havin' a laugh!' I began to object but the kid was already pedalling away, job done. I know my spell inside meant Mickey'd had to wait for his money but this was some penalty. After bus fares and board I'd be working for nothing.

And so this morning I'm trying to manage my expectations. To start my day as I mean to go on. Good things don't happen to Davy Johnson, never have done, never will. I'm your original walking talking magnet for bucket loads of shit but today I'm going to look on the bright side; the sun is shining, I have a pack of smokes in my pocket and I have a job. I take a cigarette from the pack and light it, drawing down hard, enjoying the sensation of the nicotine inflating my lungs. Is it so wrong to be drawn to something that really isn't good for you?

The sun's rays beam down steadily and I roll my overalls to my waist before lying back on the wooden bench, savouring each lungful of smoke. My upper body tingles; already the skin on my chest is beginning to turn pink. Be good to get some colour, get rid of the grey pallor that is the trademark of a stretch inside. I close my eyes, lifting my cigarette for a final drag before returning to the pallet of cartons waiting for me. All I need to top the day off is a nice cold beer and I promise myself one at the end of the shift with a couple of guys from the shop floor if they're up for it.

A cold chill across my stomach makes my eye lids snap open. There, in my eye line, blocking out the sun like a spiteful raincloud stands a familiar but unfriendly face. Police Constable MacIntyre arrested me six months ago and here he is larger than life staring down at me as though I'm a giant turd. I look past MacIntyre to the squad car parked by the factory gates and the officer in the passenger seat picking his nose while scrolling through messages on a mobile. I don't think they're supposed to use their phones on duty but I know better than to air unasked-for views. Instead, I push myself to a sitting position, pulling my overalls up over my shoulders whilst checking across the factory yard to see if my visitors can be seen from the main building. Candy Staton, the boss's PA, has her back to the canteen window while she busies herself getting drinks for the managers. Petite with long shiny hair tied back in a ponytail, she is the prettiest girl I've set eyes on in a long while. She smiled at me on my first day here even though she must have seen my personnel file. I wonder what she'll make of the new guy not yet a week in and bringing police to the door.

'Heard they'd let ye oot.' PC MacIntyre is a prize prick with eyes that tell you he likes a drink almost as much as he loves a ruck. Thick-set arms protruding from a dumpy body, his Kevlar vest provides an illusion of muscle. 'Thought I'd come see for myself.'

I say nothing. I learned long ago not to rise to the bait; that smart mouth answers got me locked up for the night. Instead, I stare at the man's forehead as though looking for his third eye. 'What's this… fancy dress?' MacIntyre smirks at my overalls and work boots while at the same time taking a step closer, all the better to intimidate. Slowly I push myself up from the bench, making us equal in height though we both knew which man has the upper hand. Over the officer's shoulder I can see Candy pause by the window, watching us.

'Look,' I reason, arms outstretched to let MacIntyre know he'll get no trouble from me, 'I need to get back, we only get ten minutes for a break.'

The officer sniggers as though this is the funniest thing he's heard in ages. '"We only get ten minutes for a break!"' he mimics, 'Who ye trying tae kid, son? Work's no' good enough fe the likes o' you,' he snipes, 'I know for a fact ye'll no' last the shift.'

Not for the first time I wonder whether there is a section in the police training manual called *Easy steps to Provoking and Needling;* only this is a skill MacIntyre really works hard at. Each meeting is like an Olympic pissing contest except there can only ever be one winner. I stay silent, yet still there's only a slim chance of me coming through unscathed.

'What they got ye doing then, sweeping the floor?' MacIntyre smiles but his eyes are cold and hard.

'Packing boxes,' I mutter, wondering if this simple answer can incriminate me in some way, although for what, I can't imagine.

MacIntyre nods as though he already knows this answer and I've merely been sitting some kind of test. 'Ye don't have to be Einstein then, eh?' he smirks. I shrug, I've been told I was thick by every teacher in school, if this insult is intended to wind me up he's way off beam; you can't be offended by a fact.

'Then again, with your pedigree…' MacIntyre taunts. Here it comes, the bit about my Dad being an alkie and handy with his fists, especially where Mum was concerned. How come his jibes always end up with my Dad? He was a wrong 'un so I'm destined to be one too, is that it?

'I mean,' MacIntyre grins as though he's second guessed my thoughts and has deliberately chosen to change tack, 'what with ye mum being on the game and all, not exactly going tae come across many great male role models are ye?'

I keep my mouth clamped shut but it's getting really hard not to rise to his bait. Digs about me or my old man I can cope with, but there's not a soul on this earth who'll get away with saying anything bad about Mum. She put food on the table every day of my childhood, made sure I had decent clothes and a roof over our heads. In fact, life improved once Dad was no longer around and Mum was grateful to have a job that meant she was there for me when I'd been small. *Ye gotta roll with the punches, Son,* was the way she explained it, *ye have to deal with the hand ye've been dealt.* It wasn't her fault I'd got in with a bad crowd. Yes, my bravado cost me a stint inside, but it was a mistake I had no intention of repeating.

'Cat got your tongue?' MacIntyre's sly little eyes follow my gaze toward the office window and Candy, a knowing look flitting across his face. 'Way out of your league, Sunshine,' he smirks, nodding in her direction. 'Especially when she hears about your pedigree.'

'Go fuck yersel'.' The words shoot out before I can stop them and in that moment I know how the rest of the day will pan out. Even at that point, there is little I can do to change the pattern of events. PC MacIntyre's eyes light up like a child on Christmas morning. 'What did ye say, ye lanky streak o' piss?'

'Ye heard me,' I say, in for a penny, in for a pound. I pull myself up to my full height, which I know will look to the copper in the car like I'm squaring up but by now I no longer give a shit. I turn towards the wedged open fire exit I'd emerged from fifteen minutes earlier. The prefab building which has been my place of work for two whole days had offered endless possibilities; even the vain hope that Candy Staton would notice my existence. I look back to the canteen window; she's noticed me now, right enough, but for all the wrong reasons.

I turn to MacIntyre. 'They're expecting me,' I say simply.

'They're expecting ye to fuck up,' he says scornfully, 'Why don't you do everyone a favour and crawl back under your stone?'

Ignoring him, I walk towards the open factory door; I figure putting some space between us might stop him feeling the need to intimidate.

'Not so fast, Pal,' he warns, putting his hand on my chest to prevent me from moving but I brush it aside, the sooner I get back indoors the better. A crowd has gathered beside Candy at the canteen window, watching as MacIntyre's bulk blocks the entrance into the building, a smile plastered across his face.

40583612R00206

Printed in Poland
by Amazon Fulfillment
Poland Sp. z o.o., Wrocław